Wolf's Choice

LAURA TAYLOR

ISBN: 1532882238
ISBN-13: 978-1532882234

Cover design by Linda Gee
https://www.facebook.com/artbymeisarn/
Cover images used under license from Shutterstock.com

ALSO BY LAURA TAYLOR

THE HOUSE OF SIRIUS

Book 1: Wolf's Blood
Book 2: Wolf's Cage

Book 4 coming soon

To Linda.
You (and Cassie) are a true inspiration. And you continue to exceed all my expectations with the gorgeous cover art. May your days be bright and your nights shine with the light of a million stars.

ACKNOWLEDGMENTS

Thank you Narinder, for making sure that I never stop learning. The English language is strange, beautiful, frustrating and unexpected, and will continue to baffle me for years to come.

Thank you Ellen, for all your help with the psychology and for taking the time to talk even when you were thousands of miles away.

Thank you Fabien, for your insights into the characters and for always making me laugh.

SHIFTERS OF THE LAKES DISTRICT DEN
EIGHT YEARS AGO

Rank	Name	Age	Years in the Den
1	Baron	30	11
2	Anna	48	27
3	Silas	38	13
4	Caleb	31	7
5	Heron	53	40
6	Raniesha	35	11
7	Simon	30	8
8	Luke	24	4
9	Caroline	27	10
10	Mark	20	3
11	Cohen	25	3
12	Alistair	27	2
13	Tank	26	2
14	Kwan	18	3
15	Aaron	17	3
16	Eric	35	0

PART ONE
EIGHT YEARS AGO

CHAPTER ONE

October 1st

Tansy Woodburn arrived at her front door and took a deep breath. She felt sick, as she always did when she came home, but she straightened her shoulders, plastered a carefully neutral expression on her face, and opened the door.

Her father was in the living room, and he glanced up from the newspaper he was reading. "Good afternoon, sweetheart. How was school?"

"It was very good," she replied politely. "How was your day?" Her father was on the local county council, an important man in the community, and Tansy had been drilled since she was a young girl on the need for impeccable manners, so as not to embarrass him in even the most insignificant of social settings.

"The usual. Meetings, calls from the media, filing a lot of reports." He took her hand and tugged her down to kiss her cheek as she passed. "There's a leg of lamb in the fridge. Go and put dinner in the oven, and then change out of your uniform. You'll have time to do your homework before they arrive."

Tansy's mother had died of breast cancer when Tansy was just five years old, and her father wasn't well – an ongoing complaint about his heart that left him breathless, along with regular attacks of arthritis – so it had become Tansy's job to do the cooking. And the laundry, and the vacuuming, along with trying to keep up with her school work. She'd become good at juggling the demands of being a full time student as well as a full time housekeeper. But for all her skills in the kitchen, it was a rare day that she got to enjoy much of her cooking. A proper young lady should be thin, her father frequently reminded her, and it wasn't unusual for him to wait until she had served herself and then swiftly remove half the food from her plate. Tansy

1

had long ago stopped protesting, seeing that her objections were an exercise in futility. If her father wanted her thin, then thin she would be. Her father always got his way in the end.

She put the lamb in a roasting tray, prepared potatoes, carrots and pumpkin to go with it, and set the gravy in a saucepan, ready to be heated up closer to the meal. Then she went to her room to get ready for their dinner guests.

Her homework was a trifling thing, a few simple maths equations, a short report to write on an article for history, and she was finished in under half an hour. Knowing she had a little time spare, she glanced longingly at her computer, the one she had bought herself by saving up her weekly allowance for as long as she could remember… but then she shook her head. If she started up with her programming now, she'd lose track of time and end up being late for dinner.

Instead, she went to the wardrobe and picked out an elegant dress in light blue. It had long sleeves, as autumn was well underway and the weather was cooling down, but a skirt that ended just below her knees. She chose black shoes, but didn't put on any tights. Made sure she was wearing clean underwear. And stood in front of the mirror, staring at herself critically. She looked beautiful, the image of the perfect, poised daughter of a respected businessman.

She wanted to throw up.

Instead, she blanked her mind, deliberately calming the shaking in her hands, and turned her attention to her hair. It was light brown, long and straight, and she'd received plenty of compliments about how pretty it was.

Once, several years ago, she'd hacked it all off with nail scissors. Her father's anger had been terrible, and his punishment severe.

And after the bruises had faded, he'd taken away all her fantasy books, so she had nothing to read, and forbidden her from using his computer – she hadn't had one of her own then – and had deleted all of her files. At that time, she'd just discovered programming, fascinated by the intricacies of the various languages and using her spare time to write a few rudimentary programs of her own, and the loss had been heartbreaking.

For all that she hated her hair, she hadn't been willing to risk her father's anger again, and so it had been left to grow. Nonetheless, she pulled it back from her face now and twisted it around, securing it with a clip. Elegant, but hidden. It would have to do. Hoping for the best, she headed for the living room.

Her father was watching the early news, his friends due to arrive in around fifteen minutes, and he looked up as she came in.

"You look very pretty," he said warmly. But then he stood up and came over to her, reached out and undid the clip from her hair, letting the long strands fall about her shoulders. "You know I like it better this way," he said, running a few silken strands through his fingers. "You wouldn't want to disappoint me, now would you?"

"No, sir," Tansy replied robotically.

"Good girl. Now go and set the table. I want everything to be perfect when they arrive."

Two hours later, Tansy was clearing the table, the meal over, her father's friends accepting his offer of a liqueur as they migrated into the living room. The meal had been uneventful, several compliments directed her way for the food, and more for how pretty she looked. The men were all in their fifties, longtime business associates of her father, as well as friends on a more personal level. Tansy had been careful as to how much she'd put on her plate. Her father wouldn't say anything tonight, not in front of their guests, but if he felt she'd eaten too much, then tomorrow he might well prevent her from eating dinner at all, not willing that she should put on any weight to mar her flawless figure. She stacked the dishwasher carefully, then obeyed her father's call to join them in the living room.

There was a spare seat on the sofa next to Robert, a man with grey hair and wrinkles, a double chin sagging beneath his jaw, and Tansy sat down next to him, a hollow smile attached to her face. Her mind was already winging its way far from here, lost in fantasies of unicorns and dragons, great shining beasts that let her ride on their broad backs, and of sharp-toothed wolves and lions who slew vicious trolls and goblins.

Robert smiled at her. "You look extremely pretty tonight," he said, a hint of huskiness in his voice, and if Tansy had been paying attention, she would have shuddered at the tone. He rested his hand on her knee, and Tansy glanced around, dimly aware of the other men looking on, eager expressions on their faces, her father watching silently from the second sofa. Robert slid his hand higher, taking the edge of her skirt with it, exposing her knee, then her thigh to his view. "The prettiest girl I know..."

Tansy felt weak, knew there was no point in resisting, knew there was no escape for her from this cold, dark reality. Then Robert's hand slid higher still, and she knew the horrors of the night were only just beginning.

CHAPTER TWO

In the shape shifters' Den in the Lakes District in northern England, the stomping of heavy, booted feet could be heard as Caroline, one of the few females on the estate, strode across the foyer.

Hurried footsteps came after her, along with muttered curses as Baron, the Den's alpha, tried to keep up. He finally caught up with her as she stalked into the library, ignoring his demands that she turn around and face him.

"What the hell is your problem?" Baron demanded, marching into the library and slamming the door behind him.

"This house is run by a misogynist, that's my problem," Caroline spat, glaring at him from across the room.

"Misogynist? What the fuck have I done now?"

"Brought yet another stray in here. More new recruits, more time and energy spent training people you've scraped out of the gutter-"

"Eric has plenty of skills that could benefit this Den," Baron interrupted, more than willing to defend the estate's newest member. "He's a plumber, he knows a few things about electrical circuits, he can repair anything from a washing machine, to a lawnmower, to a car, and he's-"

"He's a MAN!"

"What?"

"You've been alpha for three years. And you've brought in seven new recruits, and *every single one of them* has been male. We only have three women in this Den-"

"Four."

"Oh, like Anna really counts. She's in Italy more often than she's here-"

"She is your alpha female!"

"And she doesn't do anything to actually help this Den. But that's beside the point. We're desperately short of women, and you're doing

4

nothing to fix that problem."

"New recruits are difficult to find at the best of times. We have very strict rules about who we can bring in-"

"But that hasn't stopped you finding male after male who fits the bill. You haven't come up with a single fucking female who you've considered to be even halfway suitable."

Baron opened his mouth to bite out a sharp retort... but then he paused. Okay, so maybe Caroline had a point. Between finding new recruits, training them to adhere to the Den's rules and accept their new lives as wolf shape shifters, and fending off the Council, who still held serious reservations about the validity of this Den, Baron had been completely snowed under. And she was right about the gender imbalance. Four women to twelve men was leaning more than a little heavily to one side.

But maybe the solution to the problem was simpler than he had imagined, Baron realised as he regarded the woman glaring at him with her arms folded. Caroline was not a particularly high ranking wolf, sitting smack in the middle of the pecking order of the Den, and she was currently the lowest ranking female... but she was also intelligent, resourceful, and persistent to an almost ridiculous degree.

"Okay," he said slowly, weighing up the risks versus the benefits of the idea that had just occurred to him. "You want women in this Den? Then how about I give you permission to go find some?"

"What?" Caroline was looking at him like he was speaking in Russian.

"Team up with Simon. He's got access to a hundred or more databases and you can search for potential candidates in schools, hospitals, prisons, homeless shelters... anywhere you think suitable people might be lurking. Put a list together and bring it to me. And if any of the women are suitable, we'll see about recruiting them."

Caroline looked rather startled at the idea. "You want me to find our next recruit?"

"Just a list of potential candidates," Baron emphasised. "Don't contact anyone directly until I've checked them out."

He half expected her to swear at him and storm out of the room, with a flurry of accusations that he was making her do his job for him. But then again...

"Okay," Caroline said, expression resolute. "Challenge accepted. Hold onto your hat, Baron. Because this Den's about to get a whole lot more interesting."

October 4th

Caroline marched into the Den's IT office where Baron was seated at a computer and slammed a sheet of paper down in front of him. "You asked for a list. Here's a list."

Baron glanced up at her with an exasperated look. "Ever heard of knocking?"

Caroline shrugged. "No."

He rolled his eyes, but picked up the paper nonetheless. "Where did you find these?"

"It's a list of inmates soon to be released from jail. Minor crimes, no serial killers or genuine crazies. And none of them have siblings or parents who might come looking for them. Simon hacked the database for me. He's created a file with the background on each of the women." Simon was the Den's IT expert, a capable hacker, though there was still the odd system he struggled to get into, but most of the ones they needed to access were simple enough to crack.

Baron waited while Caroline reached over his shoulder and pulled up the file, and then took a seat beside him. "This one has kids," he said, dismissing the first woman on the list as he scrolled through the file. "This one is married. This one has kids."

"One kid, whom she hasn't seen since he was born. His father has sole custody."

"But there's still the risk she'll decide she wants to see him one day, and that creates ties and complications that we don't need to be dealing with. This one's a drug addict," he went on, turning back to the list. "Drug addict. Another drug addict."

"What's wrong with drug addicts?" Caroline asked, as he rejected half her list on a whim.

Baron gave her a disparaging look. "Can you imagine what would happen if a shape shifter got high? Public exposure, shifting in front of civilians, chaos, mayhem... we don't recruit drug addicts," he repeated firmly, then turned back to the list. "This one stabbed her husband to death – too violent."

"Silas killed a hundred people when he was fighting in Afghanistan."

"He was in the military. Killing people was his job," Baron corrected her. "Which is what he's doing for us now. There was nothing personal about it. People who kill for personal revenge are generally too unstable to unleash our kind of power on. Alcoholic," he went on, dismissing more women from the list. "Drug addict. This one dropped out of high school and became a prostitute. No."

"What's wrong with that? Raniesha used to be a prostitute."

"She was a prostitute with a business diploma. We need people with some measure of intelligence and education, not just bums on seats."

"Cohen was homeless when we recruited him. Not exactly a shining example of humanity's best and brightest."

"Just because he was homeless doesn't mean he's an idiot. He completed high school and did the first year of an engineering degree before we found him."

"Oh, for fuck's sake!" Caroline yelled at him, thrusting her chair back with such force that it fell over. She stalked across the room and punched the wall. "You're being deliberately difficult. You're willing to recruit all manner of pond scum so long as they're male, but one little defect in a woman, and you blacklist her. This is bullshit!"

"So keep looking," Baron said calmly. "Make me a new list."

Caroline snarled at him. But then she picked up the sheet of paper and a pen. "Okay, then could I have a little more detail on what I'm looking for? So maybe next time you won't just throw my whole list out the window."

"Someone with the ability to accept a life of fantasy and mythology," Baron stated patiently. "Someone who doesn't have – or want – children. No drugs, no crazy violence, reasonable intelligence, non-suicidal, minimal family or social connections. Don't limit yourself to ex-cons," he added, trying to be helpful. "Try terminally ill patients looking for a miracle. Homeless people. No battered wives," he added as an afterthought. "We need people who will fight back, not just stand there and take it. And yes, if you want to call me a bastard for that one, go right ahead. Antisocial teenagers are another good bet."

"Fine," Caroline said as she finished writing. "I'm going to find someone," she said, almost defiantly. But to her surprise, Baron's expression softened ever so slightly.

"I hope you do," he said seriously. "If nothing else, we're going to need more women to maintain the bloodlines."

The comment blackened Caroline's mood even more. "Oh, well at least we're good for something," she scoffed. "Because it would be too generous for you to just want some women around for the sake of it. Us being half the human population, and all. You may as well just reduce us to good breeding stock, a pretty possession to be bought and sold. You fucking sexist pig."

Baron didn't react at all to the torrent of abuse. His gaze was dark and melancholy as he looked at her. "We lose the bloodlines," he said slowly, "and we lose the Den. We have no women from the line of Harkans, and the Council is still threatening to shut us down over it. And you already know that I care too much about this place to let that happen."

Caroline was lost for words. He was right. If she'd learned nothing else in the past three years, she at least knew that Baron's interests always, *always* lay with the good of the Den. The amount of effort he'd put into holding them together after the massacre three and a half years ago was far beyond what anyone could have asked of him, and despite their tendency to butt heads at every turn, Caroline was beginning to find that she had a genuine respect for him. Even if she didn't always agree with his decisions.

"I'll find someone," she said again. But this time, rather than a threat, it was a promise.

October 5th

"Oh, you can't be serious."

Caroline paused in the doorway of the IT office, listening to Simon apparently talking to himself. He was seated in front of one of the computers, hunched over the screen and concentrating intently.

"You can't do that. There's no way you'll get in."

She wandered closer, peering over his shoulder to see if he was watching a video, perhaps... but she didn't understand anything that was on the screen.

"Who won't get in where?" she asked, as she took a seat next to him.

"Some kid hacker," Simon replied, not taking his eyes off the screen. "He claims he can hack into a county council's system and delete parking tickets for one of the guys on the hacking forum. But he's just a kid! He's only been on the forum for a couple of years, and yeah, he's a fast learner, but he's... Oh my fucking God, he's done it," Simon said, sitting back with a look of both disbelief and admiration. "The little shit actually did it. I have never seen anyone learn to hack that fast. The kid's a genius!"

Caroline snorted out a laugh. "Sounds like we could do with him working for us," she said. She'd meant it as a joke, but Simon nodded.

"I've been keeping tabs on him," he said, as he typed a short message to the boy, then logged out of the screen. "In a couple of years, depending on how things go, I might suggest to Baron that we look at recruiting him. God knows, with technology developing the way it is, I'll need some help with all this at some point in the future."

"Who is he?" Caroline asked, more curious now.

"Don't know. He goes by the name 'Skip' online, but I've no idea what his real name is. He's sixteen, lives somewhere in England, but that's all I've managed to find out. The kid's good at covering his tracks, I'll give him that. But he doesn't have a whole lot of experience yet, so I'll find a way to track him down, sooner or later. So, what have we got?" he asked, turning his attention to Caroline.

"Jack shit," she said grimly. "Baron tossed the lot of them. We don't recruit drug addicts, apparently." A trace of irritation slipped through. "I thought you'd recruited people before," she couldn't help complaining.

"Didn't they give you some guidelines about how to do it?"

Simon cringed. "Sorry. I've only ever recruited one person: Mark, when he was dying of leukaemia. All I was told was to find someone with a terminal illness who could be converted in a hurry. I'm not exactly a pro at this."

Caroline sighed. "Sorry," she apologised, reminding herself not to take this out on Simon. He was trying to help her, after all. "But it looks like ex-jailbirds aren't going to cut it. Can we try terminally ill patients instead? That's worked well enough in the past."

"No problem," Simon replied, and a few minutes later, he'd worked his way into the system of one of the main hospitals in London. "Female, terminal illness... No children," he added, muttering to himself as he glanced at the list of conditions Caroline had written down. "A lot of these patients are on regular doses of morphine for pain relief. Does that count as a drug addiction?"

"I'm guessing not," Caroline said uncertainly. "The rules of the Den only forbid recreational drug use, not medicinal. Even we use opium as a pain reliever. If it came to it, I could argue the point with Baron."

"Okay... Any particular age range you'd like to focus on?"

"No one too old. We want someone who'll be physically fit enough to learn to fight, and someone who'll hang around for a good few years. So no one over fifty. Ideally I'd go for the twenty to thirty-five age bracket."

Simon worked for a few more minutes, narrowing down the list of patients. "Two likely candidates," he said finally. "A woman with pancreatic cancer and another with leukaemia. I'll do some digging into their backgrounds. Give me a couple of days, and I'll let you know what I find."

October 7th

"What's happening?" Caroline asked Simon, as he came into the library. He'd asked her to have a meeting with him, and Caroline was a little surprised to see Baron walking in the door behind him, and then Heron as well, and she frowned at the grim look on Simon's face.

"No luck on either of the women in the hospital," he said, cutting to the chase as he sat down, a file in his hand. "One of them has a large, extended family who are sitting with her twenty-four seven, so the chances of us being able to talk to her privately are pretty much zero, and the other passed away this morning."

"Fuck," Caroline swore. Another dead end...

"But I do have some other news, that's turned out to be rather more interesting than I had expected. You remember Skip, the hacker I was telling you about the other day? Turns out he's not a boy. He's a girl."

9

Caroline sat up straighter at that. It wasn't often they came across a female hacker. The girl's age could be a problem though, and she frowned as Simon opened the file. He pulled out several copies of a report, handing one to each of them. "Tansy Woodburn. I wanted to get Baron in on this, and Heron, since Anna's still away, because if we're going to do anything, I'd like to do it sooner, rather than later." In Anna's absence, Heron was the highest ranking female in the Den, and also a source of considerable wisdom and experience.

"You originally said you'd think of recruiting her in a few years," Caroline said, glancing over the report.

"Interesting developments on that front," he replied enigmatically. "Just have a look at her stats first of all."

Caroline did. Sixteen years old. Still in high school. Mother deceased. Living with her father. Reclusive, teachers described her as a 'loner', few social contacts outside her immediate family. "How did you find all this stuff?"

Simon shrugged. "Like I said before; she's damn good with computers, but she's still young, and relatively new at all this. I got her to accept a chat with me, and then traced the connection back to her home. Once I had an address, the rest was easy. Did a bit of research, and this is what I came up with. Her father is on the county council," he went on, shuffling a few other papers in the file, "so that does make things a little more complicated. But just out of curiosity, I did a little digging into his business files, and then his home PC. And I found some rather remarkable things."

He handed each of them another sheet, and Caroline recoiled. Beside her, Heron hissed in a sharp gasp. "What the fuck?" Caroline asked.

"He's a paedophile," Simon said flatly. He nodded to the sheet of printed photographs he'd given them. "That's just a small selection of the filth on his computer. And the interesting, but not surprising part... He's got his daughter involved."

Baron swore under his breath, then took the rest of the file from Simon and looked quickly through the contents. "This is horrific," he said, stating the obvious, while Caroline just gritted her teeth and tried not to look at the images.

"So you see why I'm not inclined to wait a few more years before we do something," Simon said.

"Absolutely," Heron said, sounding shaken. "The sooner we get her out of there, the better."

"As much as I'd like to agree," Baron said, face grim, "her father's position in the community does make this a lot more high profile than I like to do things. You're right on some counts," he conceded to Simon. "She seems to be quite the computer genius, and goodness knows, we're going to need more of that around here. She's a loner, she has more than enough reason to want to leave her father, she has no other immediate relatives to complicate things… but you can't just make the daughter of a council member disappear without someone asking some hefty questions."

"What if we don't make her disappear?" Simon said, an unusual sort of determination in his voice. "What if she does it herself?"

"How do you mean?"

"She's sixteen. So she can legally leave home and the courts would almost certainly not make her go back. So she runs away, tells the cops she's staying with a friend, and no one can do anything about it. There's enough evidence on her father's computer to get him arrested without needing to involve Tansy in the court case, which immediately discredits him in the public eye, and as far as the police are concerned, it gives Tansy a very plausible reason for not wanting to go home, so they're even less likely to pursue the matter. There are no aunts or uncles waiting in the wings, so we're not going to be fending off questions from concerned relatives. So long as Tansy is amenable to the whole scheme, and willing to play her part, there's no reason why any of it should arouse suspicion."

"Okay, not a bad plan," Baron conceded. "But there's still the significant question of whether or not she would want to become a shape shifter. Or whether she would be willing to run away from her father at all. Children in these situations can have a tendency for unreasonable loyalty to their abusers. So as much as you're keen to get her out of there, don't go rushing things. I want a proper investigation into the girl. Have Silas tail her for a while. See where she hangs out, whether she has any particular friends at school, whether there are any other loose ends that we haven't picked up on. And then," he said, turning to Caroline, "if everything checks out, we can talk about how you're going to contact her directly."

CHAPTER THREE

October 23rd

Tansy deliberately dawdled as she wandered down the road. She was on her way home from school, and her father had announced this morning that he was having 'friends' over for dinner again. He'd sent her on her way this morning with a kiss and a sharp instruction not to be late, and Tansy had spent the rest of the day moping, unable to summon even the most rudimentary enthusiasm for school. Even though she had a double maths class today, and that was usually her favourite.

When she reached the park at the corner of her street, she paused. She often stopped here on the way home, taking a little time to herself before stepping into that dreaded house again, and after a moment's thought, she headed for the swings, despite the warning to be home on time.

Halfway there, she stopped in her tracks. In the shade of one of the tall trees, there was an old lady sitting on a picnic rug. Odd. There was usually no one else here. She hesitated, not sure whether she should stay or not. The woman was reading a book, and she looked like she hadn't even noticed Tansy arrive. And as Tansy stood there, wondering what to do, she noticed what else was on the rug. The woman had a small picnic spread out around her, a bag of crisps, a leftover half of a bread roll, a plastic box with a few strawberries in it.

Tansy headed for the swings, curious, but cautious. The woman had food, and hunger was gnawing at Tansy's stomach in a way that made her feel sick. But walking up to a complete stranger was a nerve-wracking prospect. Adults, she had learned from hard experience, could be dangerous. Besides which, she didn't really know how to start up a sensible conversation. She didn't have friends of her own, didn't get to talk to many people besides her teachers and her father's 'friends'. Her father never let her socialise with kids her own age in her free time, never let her go to another girl's house after school, never let her attend birthday parties or weekend events. And as a result, the kids at school had decided to shun her, not inclined to put effort into a relationship when Tansy never had the opportunity to reciprocate. She chatted with a few people online, of course, but it wasn't the same as having a real conversation, face to face. So she loitered in the park, rocking idly on the swings, casting tentative glances at the woman. She was concentrating on her book, and as Tansy watched, she picked up another strawberry and put it in her mouth.

Tansy abandoned the swings and wandered closer to the woman, her mouth watering at the sight of that leftover food. She reached the roundabout and indulged in a single turn of the circle. Then she sidled closer, up to the edge of the tree's shade. The woman looked up as she noticed her presence, gave her an unconcerned smile, and turned back to her book.

Tansy waited, not sure if she should interrupt or not... and slid a fraction closer.

The woman slipped a finger into her book to keep the page and looked up. "Hello," she said simply.

"Hello," Tansy said, glancing at the bag of crisps.

"You look like you're on your way home from school," the woman said with a smile. Then she noticed the direction of Tansy's gaze. "Would you like some?" she offered, picking up the bag and holding it out.

"Yes, please," Tansy replied in a whisper, darting forward to take the bag. She retreated a few steps and set about devouring the crisps... and then glanced down the road towards her house. Snacking before dinner was forbidden. She would get in such trouble if her father found out, and with a wave of guilt, she went to put the bag down again-

"Would you like to sit down?" the woman asked, patting the rug beside herself.

Refusing would be rude, Tansy thought to herself, suddenly caught between two of her father's rules. She wasn't supposed to be eating this food, but she must also always behave politely to adults. "Thank you," she muttered, taking a seat, telling herself she would only stay for a few minutes.

"You can have some strawberries as well, if you'd like," the woman said, placing the box within Tansy's reach. "My name's Heron."

"I'm Tansy." She glanced around. Her house wasn't visible from here, another few hundred metres down the road. There was no one around to see her breaking the rules, so she picked up a few of the strawberries and ate them quickly.

She thought about leaving, but was surprised to find that she didn't really want to. Despite her automatic caution when it came to adults, there

13

was something soothing about this woman. Something peaceful and safe... and a sudden, unexpected memory told her why she felt so comfortable in this woman's presence. Heron reminded her of her aunt. Not so much in looks – Tansy's aunt had been younger, with bright red hair – but in the way she spoke. Calm, patient, and with an odd, lilting quality that Heron somehow mimicked perfectly. Tansy had spent weekends with her aunt when she was younger, blissful miniature holidays that had been filled with fun and adventure, and none of the dark memories of life in her father's house. But then when she was eight or nine, her aunt had married a foreigner and moved to Australia, and then been killed a few years later in a tragic skiing accident. Memories of the woman still brought up a strong sense of nostalgia.

After another moment or two, Tansy's attention was drawn to the book Heron had. "What are you reading?"

"It's a fantasy story," Heron replied. "It's called 'My Mother's People'. It's about a girl who's lost her mother, but she finds out years later that her mother was part Fairy, and so the girl goes off on an adventure into the forest to find the Fairy people and live with them." Heron sighed. "Sometimes I'd like to do that. Just run away into the forest and live with the fairies."

Tansy snorted, not meaning to be rude, but finding it a funny idea anyway. "That wouldn't work," she said frankly. "Fairies are all delicate and fragile. If I ran away, I'd want to live with the lions." Fierce, angry beasts who would rip apart anyone who tried to come near her.

"Lions would be wonderful. But fairies are magic. I don't know of any magic lions roaming around."

"Yeah," Tansy agreed, seeing the flaw in her plan. "It would be hard to teach them who to eat, and who not to."

Heron broke into laughter at that. "You have someone you want them to eat, then?" Tansy couldn't quite manage to laugh back, though she knew it probably seemed an odd thing to say, and Heron's laughter faded out.

"Can fairies make you invisible?" she asked instead.

"Not in this book," Heron replied. "But I've never met a real fairy, so you never know."

The conversation continued for a while. Heron was a lot of fun to talk to. She wanted to know all sorts of things about Tansy, like what her favourite breed of cat was, or what sort of books she liked to read. They talked about the songs on the radio, and Tansy's fascination with computer programs, and then finally, Heron sighed.

"It's later than I thought it was," she said, glancing around. "I'd better get going." Tansy looked around as well, and realised it was starting to get dark. She glanced at her watch, dismayed to see it was five o'clock. She was late. Her father was going to be so mad...

"Is it time for you to go home now?" Heron asked... and in an odd moment, one that she would never be able to explain, Tansy felt something inside of her break.

She glanced down the road towards her house. "I'm not going home," she said, not sure where the sudden decision had come from. She couldn't go home. She just couldn't do it any more. Not walking into that house, and having her father pretend to be so proud of her. Not being polite to his friends. Not sitting there, still and compliant, while the men around her created living nightmares that never seemed to end.

Heron seemed confused. But there was also another expression on her face, one that Tansy couldn't quite place. "Won't your parents be worried about you?" she asked awkwardly.

"My mum's dead," Tansy said, the world seeming suddenly surreal. "But my father... I'm not going home."

"Why not?" There was that strange expression again. Tansy thought perhaps it was an odd combination of hope and fear.

She wasn't supposed to answer the question. It was against the rules. It would be such a disappointment to her father, and people would think she was a terrible daughter, not raised to be a proper young lady, and he would take her computer away, and... "My father's having friends over tonight," Tansy said, feeling dizzy. She felt like she'd come to the edge of a great cliff, and for the first time, instead of being afraid to fall, she was inclined to jump, and see if perhaps she had wings after all.

"I can't keep being nice to them," she said, feeling cold and empty inside. Completely unexpectedly, tears burst from her eyes, a sudden flood that ran down her face, heedless of her commands that they stop. "I always have to be nice to his friends, and I can't do it any more. I just can't..." The very idea of it brought a fresh wave of terror. Tansy didn't have the faintest idea where she would go. Or where she would find something to eat. She just knew she couldn't go back. She glanced up at Heron.

The look of rage on Heron's face stopped her cold. She must think Tansy was being horribly rude, saying bad things about her father's friends, and behaving not at all like the proper young woman she'd been taught to be. But an instant later the look was gone, and Heron cleared her throat. "Well... perhaps you could come home with me, instead," she said slowly.

The idea was at once tantalising and terrifying. Tansy remembered the weekends she'd spent at her aunt's house, big, tasty dinners and her own bed to sleep in and long walks through the woods... but what if there were other people who lived with Heron?

"Do you have a husband? Or children?" While Tansy didn't fancy the idea of a man in the house, living with other children would be fun. Someone she could make friends with.

"No, I don't, but I live in a very big house with some very good people.

15

Some of them are about your age. We're not truly related, but we see each other as family."

Family? Tansy shook her head. She knew all about what 'family' did to each other… "No. I don't want to live with men."

Heron seemed at a loss for words, and Tansy wrapped her arms around herself, drawing her knees up to her chest. "Sweetie… not all men are like your father's friends," Heron said gently. "No one in our house would do anything bad to you. Ever. I wouldn't let anyone hurt you."

Tansy considered that. "Okay…" she agreed reluctantly. "But what about my computer!" she remembered suddenly. "I have to go back and get it."

"We have lots of computers in our house," Heron said quickly. "Or we could buy you a new one, if you like. And clothes, and anything else you need."

"I can cook," Tansy said suddenly. "I don't have much money, so I can't pay rent, but I can cook. And do laundry. And-"

"Whoa, hold on. You don't have to do anything like that. You're still in school, so the only thing you should be worried about is doing your school work."

"But… I have to do something to help around the house. Otherwise they'll want…" Perhaps they would want some other form of payment for their kindness. Tansy shuddered at the thought.

"Well…" Heron said, seeming to think the idea over. "You've said you're very good with computers. And we always need help with computer related things. You could help to maintain our network and install new programs, and that sort of thing. How does that sound?"

"But my father isn't well," Tansy said, feeling suddenly forlorn as she realised this crazy plan could never work. "I have to stay and help him. He can't look after the house by himself, and I have to… He needs me. I can't just leave…"

"Tansy," Heron said, her voice suddenly firm, and Tansy noted a touch of anger in her tone. "You listen to me. You do not owe him anything. Parents are supposed to look after their children, not the other way around."

Tansy stopped, and looked at Heron, eyes narrowed, suddenly seeing her in a new light. "Who are you?" she asked carefully. "Why are you here? Because you seem like magic. Like in the story books. You just appear out of nowhere and take me away, and make everything better. Are you magic?"

That odd look came over Heron's face again, hope, and fear, and a strange determination that Tansy didn't understand. "We have a certain kind of magic, yes," Heron replied.

"And if I go with you, I'll never have to come back here?"

"You'll never have to come back," Heron confirmed. And that made up

Tansy's mind.

"Then yes. I'll go with you."

Heron's mind was racing as she led Tansy to her car, a small blue sedan that the Den used for 'civilian' purposes. This first meeting was supposed to be a simple get-to-know-you, a brief assessment to determine whether it was worth spending more time and energy on this young woman. Taking her home with her, all but kidnapping her, for all that Tansy was coming willingly, was a gross breach of Den protocol and an outrageous risk to security.

Baron was going to kill her.

But what other option did she have? She could hardly just leave the girl here, not when she had nowhere to go tonight. And after her admission that there was a handful of men waiting at home to do unspeakable things to her, the idea of talking her into going home in order to buy the Den more time was out of the question.

No, Heron admitted to herself, as she started the engine and pulled away from the curb. This was the best option, perhaps the only option that would allow Heron to finish the day with her conscience intact. And for all that he would object to the impromptu change in plans, Heron was sure that once she'd explained herself to Baron, he'd see that she was right.

CHAPTER FOUR

Heron pulled into the carpark at a supermarket on the way back to the estate. Tansy had been asking a thousand questions about her new home, who else Heron lived with, how big the house was, how she would go to school, and Heron had done her best to answer each one. She'd explained that she intended to home school Tansy for the rest of her education, as she had done for Kwan and Aaron, the two boys who were just a year or two older than Tansy. She'd described the estate and the manor, the huge stone house that had stood for hundreds of years, the wide lawn and thick forest, and told her a little about the people who lived there.

Now, she led Tansy into the supermarket, the flood of questions thankfully at a pause while they turned their attention to more urgent matters. Clothes were the first order of business. Underwear, socks, pyjamas, a pair of trainers, Tansy having scowled at the selection of more feminine footwear on offer, and then Heron asked her to pick out a few sets of clothes, jeans or skirts, tops, a jumper. In a day or two, Heron told her, they would go online and order a full new wardrobe for her, but for now, she would need some things to get her through the next few days.

But that was where the excursion ground to a sudden and puzzling halt. She led Tansy to the women's section, and waited... and waited... "Is anything wrong?" she asked gently, as Tansy stood and stared at the racks of clothes.

"What sort of clothes do you want me to wear?" Tansy asked, sounding both annoyed and defeated.

"This isn't about what I want. You can choose the things that *you* like."

Tansy seemed confused by that. "But I don't... I can't..." She sighed. "I'm sorry," she said, letting her hair fall forward to cover her face. "I don't want to be rude."

"You're not being rude, sweetheart," Heron said, trying to be supportive, and feeling rather out of her depth. Though she'd done a little reading on the effects of childhood abuse over the past few days, she'd expected to have a lot more time to wrap her head around Tansy's experiences than she'd had so far. "Please, tell me what the problem is, and I can help you solve it."

Tansy peered up at the racks of clothing again. "I don't like any of this," she said, and from the distress in her voice, it seemed she was genuinely upset about the clothes, rather than just being fussy.

"Okay, well... what sort of clothes do you like?" Heron asked, not sure what to suggest.

"Not dresses. Or skirts," Tansy said, turning away from the nearest racks.

"Okay, what about trousers? Jeans?"

Tansy pulled out a pair of trousers, an elegant cut in beige. "No."

Heron held up a pair of jeans. "What about these?"

"I'm not allowed to wear jeans."

Ah. One of her father's decrees, no doubt. And while Heron wanted to contradict the strict rules, she didn't want to badmouth Tansy's father, not when the girl probably still felt a strong sense of loyalty towards him. "Well... lots of people in our house wear jeans. And I think it would be perfectly okay if you wanted to try it."

Tansy didn't look entirely convinced, but she glanced at the pair Heron was holding, nonetheless. "No," she said finally. "These are boring. I want..." She wandered over to the next rack. "I don't know. Something *nice*."

Heron looked over the racks, and picked up a pair of grey trousers in a stylish cut. "These are nice."

She watched as Tansy forced a smile onto her face. It came out looking more like a grimace. "Okay."

Nope, apparently not. "You don't like them, do you?" Heron asked gently.

Tansy shrugged. Heron put the trousers back on the rack. "Um... okay, what about leggings?" she offered.

Tansy cringed. "No."

"What sort of clothes did you wear at home?"

"My father chooses all my clothes. He makes me wear dresses, in really boring colours."

"What sort of colours would you like?"

Tansy folded her arms, glaring at the clothing racks. "I don't know..."

Heron looked around, not sure what she was looking for, but the few clues Tansy had given her were a starting point, at least. She found a jumper in yellow, bright and cheerful, but not overly feminine. "How about this?"

Tansy looked the jumper over. "Not bad," she said hesitantly. "It's not as boring as the others, but it's still not…" She peered at the rack over Heron's shoulder, and a look of glee lit her face. She darted around her and snatched up a jumper, bright pink with a sparkly flower embroidered on the front. "This!" she said emphatically, holding it up in front of her. "Is this okay?" she asked suddenly, her enthusiasm fading to be replaced with a nervous uncertainty.

"That's a fine choice," Heron said firmly, and Tansy's smile returned. The jumper seemed like a good fit, so Heron was surprised when she put it back and pulled out a larger size… and then rejected that one as well, settling on one that was two sizes too large. "This one," she confirmed, clutching the jumper tightly.

"Are you sure you need it in that size?" Heron asked. "I think it's going to be too big."

Tansy shook her head solemnly. "Nope. It's perfect."

Heron opened her mouth to argue… and then thought better of it. She wasn't entirely sure what was going on in Tansy's mind, but given her background, it wasn't a surprise that she might have some issues surrounding her body image. So if she wanted clothes that were too large, Heron didn't see the need to make an issue out of it. "Okay, well, let's pick a few other things as well." Based on Tansy's first choice, she bypassed the 'ladies' section and headed for the 'girls' clothes. She picked up a pair of jeans with colourful flowers embroidered down the sides. "What about these?"

"Nice," Tansy agreed, once more swapping the clothes out for a bigger size. "And this," she added, pulling out a bright aqua t-shirt with a dolphin on it. She added it to the trolley, then stood back, a look of satisfaction on her face.

"Okay," Heron prompted her. "What's next?"

Tansy's cheerful look vanished. "Um… I don't know. We go home?"

Heron laughed. "No, sweetie, I meant what other clothes do you want."

"But I have a full set of clothes now," Tansy said, pointing to the trolley, looking nervous all over again. "I don't need more. And I have pyjamas and shoes and… It would be too much. And I don't have any money to pay for it, and…"

It wasn't the first time she'd brought up the issue of payment, and Heron shuddered to think what she might be expecting to have to give in exchange for the clothes. But for all her compassion with Tansy's situation, Heron had little experience with the kind of psychological issues she was dealing with, and didn't know how best to handle the situation.

"Um… well, how about you pick out one more outfit," she encouraged her. "Because when this one gets washed, you'll need another one to wear." That would get them through a few days, at least, and then they could order more clothes online once they all had more of a handle on what was going on.

As Tansy hesitantly picked out more clothes, Heron tried to make sense of her choice of clothing. If her father had made her wear dresses, then it was a fair call for her to want to avoid them. And if she'd been restricted to drab navies or greys, then the desire for a little colour was understandable. But Tansy's choices were all in bright, almost garish colours, and bore childish pictures of flowers or cute animals. They were the sort of clothes an eight year old with a princess fixation might choose, a far cry from the preferences of a normal, fashion-conscious sixteen-year-old.

But then she thought back to Tansy's offer to do laundry for the house, or to cook, and she had to wonder for how long she'd been forced into the role of mature adult, dressing as a woman, not a teenage girl, doing the housework, taking care of her father. Was this simple rebellion from the status quo, Heron wondered, as she smiled and nodded at Tansy's latest choice of a pink t-shirt with little unicorns embroidered into the fabric. Or was it a symptom of a deeper problem? After being forced to mature far quicker than she should have, could Tansy be trying to make up for a lost childhood, reclaiming a girlish innocence that had been stolen from her far too early?

After she'd chosen a second outfit, Tansy decided she needed to use the toilet. While Heron was waiting, she pulled out her phone and sent a brief text message to Baron. They tried to keep such things short and lacking detail, knowing that phones could be tapped and information had a way of going astray, so the message simply contained three words: Incoming. ETA 8:30pm. He would understand the message, and take appropriate precautions to prepare for their arrival.

When Tansy came back, they headed for the toiletries section, choosing a toothbrush, comb, shampoo and then Tansy glanced at the makeup section. Heron was surprised she'd be interested in that sort of thing... but then Tansy reached out and picked up a large, plastic bracelet from below the makeup display. It was gaudy, bright pink, thick as Heron's thumb; the sort of thing that would be the treasured possession of a five year old child. But Tansy loved it, so, after a nervous, hopeful glance at Heron, who responded with a bright smile and a nod, it went into the trolley, along with a necklace of bright plastic 'gems' and two more bracelets in various colours.

Heron was heading for the checkout with the trolley when she suddenly realised she'd lost Tansy. She glanced back and found the girl staring at the toy display they'd just passed.

Tentatively, Tansy reached out and picked up a toy; a polar bear, pure white, with a wide grin on its face. She glanced at Heron, and put the bear back. Chewed her lip. Stared longingly at the bear on the shelf. Then turned and followed Heron, leaving the bear where it was.

21

Fighting back a sudden urge to cry, Heron went back and picked up the bear, adding it to the trolley of purchases without a word. And then, with a lump in her throat, she led the way towards the checkout.

Baron stared at his phone, utterly flabbergasted. 'Incoming. ETA 8:30pm.' It was the 'incoming' that was the problem, the Den's universal code for when a non-shifter was coming onto the estate. The entire place went into lockdown, every secret door shut, every sensitive file hidden, and absolutely every single shifter in human form, no exceptions whatsoever. If they had enough time, they went so far as to hide the dog beds and dishes and vacuum up the fur... but half an hour wasn't nearly enough time to sanitise the manor. What the fuck was Heron thinking?

With a shake of his head, Baron raced out to the upstairs landing and hit the button marked 'Fire Alarm'. Immediately, the large clock mounted on the front of the manor began to chime, playing the 'quarter to the hour' melody, though it was already 7:53pm. If any outsider asked, they simply told them that the clock was broken and sometimes went off at the wrong time... but in reality, it was a signal to the entire Den to get in human form NOW. It could be heard in the furthest corners of the estate, and was the quickest, most reliable way to effect a lockdown, when at times, seconds mattered.

"CAROLINE!" Baron bellowed from the top of the stairs, needing swift answers as to what the fuck was going on. After having Silas tail Tansy for the past two weeks, Baron had finally given Caroline permission to arrange a face-to-face meeting with the girl, allowing her to run the operation for the most part, and the last he'd heard, Heron had gone off this afternoon to meet the girl in a park near her house. How they'd gone from a simple meet and greet to a full scale lockdown was beyond him.

Caroline came bolting out of the library, no doubt more due to the clock chiming than from Baron's yell, but she hurried up the stairs anyway, ready to kill whatever it was that was causing them trouble.

"What the hell is this?" Baron demanded, thrusting his phone at her. She took one look at the message, then the sender... and cursed like a seasoned sailor.

"You know that Heron went to see the girl?" she said. "Tansy? I'd say this means she's bringing her in."

"She can't bring her in. We can maintain lockdown for a couple of hours, but not for days. How the hell are we supposed to live here with an uninitiated newbie? Who, from the sounds of that file, is a potential basket case as it is?"

Caroline stared at the screen again, as if it could answer their questions. "She must have a good reason for it."

"A fucking good reason! Do you realise what-"

"Baron!" Caroline yelled at him, cutting off his rant mid-sentence. "You know Heron. She's solid. Sane. Reasonable. She would not be doing this without a good reason."

"Fuck... all right. Standard lockdown protocol. And I want everyone in the kitchen, right now. Game faces, people. The world just got a little more crazy than usual."

CHAPTER FIVE

Tansy helped Heron collect their bags of shopping out of the car, and then followed her apprehensively up the stairs to the manor's front door. It was a huge building, grey stone and tall chimneys lending it a distinctly old world quality. Inside, the foyer was beautiful; worn wooden floorboards that gave the place a lived-in feel, a high chandelier, gleaming banisters sweeping up a grand staircase.

Heavy footsteps sounded almost immediately, and despite Heron's assurances that they were wonderful people, Tansy felt suddenly nervous about meeting her new friend's 'family'. She worried about what they would expect from her, Heron's insistence that she had to do little more than maintain their computers sounding too good to be true, and then she felt self conscious about the school uniform she was still wearing. It was hardly appropriate clothing for such an important first meeting as this, and her father would never have allowed her to meet any of his business associates dressed the way she was.

Two people appeared out of a side door, and Tansy shrank back behind Heron. One was a woman, dressed in jeans and a black t-shirt, with short black hair and a fierce look on her face… which immediately brightened into a smile when she saw Tansy. She was a little intimidating, but not overly threatening, and Tansy tried to smile back, hoping the woman would be friendly.

But then she looked at the man beside her and her smile faded. He was huge, thick muscles, a wide neck and a short beard, with a scowl on his face that made him look like a thug. Tansy felt herself shake in fear.

"I'm so sorry I'm late," Heron apologised immediately. "But I met this charming young lady in a park, and we got talking… and long story short, she isn't terribly happy with where she's living, so I've asked her to come and stay with us. Her name's Tansy," she said with a smile, beckoning

Tansy forward. "And this is Caroline, and Baron. Baron runs the house, for the most part."

Tansy tried to smile, and politely offered her hand for them to shake. Caroline's hand was firm, but warm... but Baron's was huge, a strong grip that engulfed her hand and made her feel tiny, and Tansy felt her face heat as she completely forgot her manners. She should have said it was a pleasure to meet them, she realised afterwards, embarrassed at making such a bad first impression.

"We'd love to have you stay," Caroline said sincerely. But Baron looked far less happy about the arrangement.

"You should have called," he said to Heron, his voice deep and grim. "We were worried about you."

"I'm sorry. We stopped on the way to do a little shopping for Tansy," Heron said, holding up the bags. "I completely lost track of time. We've missed dinner, haven't we?"

"We kept some for you," Caroline said dismissively, but Tansy felt another wave of embarrassment. Being late was unacceptable, as her father had told her often enough, and she was ashamed of herself, realising that they were late because she'd taken too long to choose her new clothes.

"I'm sorry," she apologised anxiously. "I didn't mean to make us late."

Strangely, Baron's expression suddenly softened at the apology. "It's no problem," he said, his voice much less harsh than it had been a moment ago. "There's plenty of food left. Are you hungry?"

Tansy nodded, then thought perhaps she shouldn't have.

"Let's get you something to eat then, and afterwards, Heron can show you to your room."

Tansy glanced at Heron. They were going to let her eat dinner, after they were already late? But Heron gave her an encouraging nod, and Tansy fell in behind her as she led the way to the dining room.

Tansy stared at her plate, fighting back tears as unfamiliar emotions swamped her. Caroline had prepared a meal for her, twice the amount of food she was normally allowed to eat, and she'd sat beside Heron as they both ate, listening as the others discussed the day's events, a few of the names Heron had told her in the car popping up in the conversation. Tansy had finished her meal, waiting politely for Heron to finish... and then Caroline had asked if she'd like some more.

More? After she'd already eaten a full plate? Tansy fought with the urge to say yes. Proper young women were expected to be thin, and she was already feeling guilty over the amount she'd eaten. But she was still hungry... She glanced up at Heron, unsure what her response should be.

But then Heron nodded to Caroline, the decision made for her, and

Caroline had refilled the plate and set it in front of her again. Now, she tried to eat politely, blinking back the tears that threatened to fall, relieved as her hunger was assuaged for what felt like the first time in years, and yet also apprehensive about the consequences of her greed. When she had finally finished, she was struggling to stay awake, the drastic changes of the day suddenly catching up with her.

"Come on," Heron said gently. "I'll take you upstairs. You look exhausted."

Tansy managed to say goodnight to Baron and Caroline, then followed Heron up the stairs. She was shown to a room right next door to Heron's, and she stared about herself in awe. It was a large room, a double bed in the centre, beautiful photographs of wolves on the walls, a huge wardrobe and her own ensuite bathroom. "My room is right next door," Heron said, setting her bags of clothes by the wardrobe, "so if you need anything, you can just knock on the door. Or even knock on the wall, if you prefer. I'll come right over."

Tansy nodded, then glanced anxiously at the door. "Does the door have a lock?" she asked meekly, not wanting to be rude.

"Yes, of course." Heron showed her the mechanism, locking and unlocking it... but Tansy wasn't convinced. "Can you lock it from the inside, and I'll test it from the outside?" she asked, fear overcoming her natural timidness. There were men in this house, big, strong men, and the thought of one of them being able to get into her room at night was making her bold and stubborn about the lock.

But Heron simply nodded. Tansy went outside, heard the lock click shut, and jiggled the knob. Secure. She pushed her shoulder against the door, jiggled the knob more firmly. Still nothing.

Heron unlocked it from the inside. "Is that okay?" she asked gently.

But Tansy shook her head. She'd never been allowed to have a lock on her door at her old house, but she also knew she wasn't particularly strong. "Maybe someone stronger than me could break it," she suggested fearfully.

A strange look of grim determination appeared on Heron's face, and Tansy worried for a moment that she'd upset the woman. She didn't want to make a fuss in her new home... but she was going to be behind that door, taking her clothes off, getting changed, sleeping helplessly... It was too important a thing not to ask.

Heron stepped outside the door for a moment and glanced up and down the hall. "Caroline!" she called suddenly, and a moment later, Caroline appeared in the doorway.

"Tansy's worried about how strong her lock is," Heron explained. "Could you do us a favour, and try to break into the room?" She turned to Tansy. "Do you think Caroline would be strong enough to break it?"

Tansy looked the woman up and down. She'd seemed very friendly at dinner, smiling at Tansy, and not complaining about how much she ate, but as she looked at her now, she noticed that she was indeed a strong woman, biceps thicker than many men's, her stomach washboard flat, her shoulders wide. She nodded. "Yeah, that should test it out properly."

She followed Heron into the bedroom and turned the lock. Caroline jiggled the knob. Nothing. A thump sounded against the door, like she'd just thrown her shoulder against it. A scuffling sound... and then a booming thud, and Tansy imagined the woman had just kicked her booted foot against it with all her might. Another thud. More jiggling of the knob. And then a muffled curse.

"Nope," came her reply. "Can't break it. You're going to have to let me in." Tansy was startled to find herself grinning, and she glanced up at Heron mischievously. She unlocked the door, finding a very frustrated looking Caroline on the other side.

"Who the hell installed that lock?" she said gruffly, winking at Tansy. "It would take an elephant with a battering ram to break through that."

"Thank you," Heron said with a smile, and she and Caroline shared a look that Tansy didn't quite understand. "Everything okay now?" she asked Tansy, and she nodded. "Okay, then get some sleep, and I'll come and take you down to breakfast in the morning. I'll be right next door if you need me."

Tansy thanked them both, said goodnight, and closed the door. It was at once lonely and exhilarating, being in her room by herself. Heron wasn't far away, she reminded herself, feeling the quietness settle in around her. And then she looked at the bed. She got to sleep in it all by herself tonight. No one opening her door in the middle of the night. No fat, grey-haired men shoving her about. Nothing at all to fear.

She changed into her pyjamas, settled herself under the blankets, and, leaving the lamp beside the bed on, she wrapped her arms tightly around her new bear, and was soon fast asleep.

Heron waited in her bedroom after putting Tansy to bed. She was half expecting the girl to call her back, perhaps with questions, perhaps with fears that needed to be allayed, but after twenty minutes, she was more or less convinced that Tansy was settled for the night, so she headed out of her room and down the stairs.

Baron was waiting in the library, staring out the window at the darkness while Caroline paced the room, and they both looked around when Heron came in. An explanation was in order, she knew, and she wasted no time in giving it, knowing that the security of the Den had been compromised by her actions.

"I know this was not the plan," she began immediately. "But you've both read her file, and you know what was going on in that house."

"True," Baron agreed, "but that in itself isn't a reason to risk public exposure by bringing her here. Or rushing her into things she's not ready to accept. There's a big difference between wanting to escape her father, and wanting to be turned into a wolf."

"I know," Heron said contritely. "But for the record, I wasn't the one to suggest Tansy leave her home. I was talking to her in the park, and when it was time to leave, she flatly declared she wasn't going home. Bringing her here seemed like the only viable option, given the situation. But aside from that... in all honesty, even if she hadn't said she wanted to leave, I would probably have tried to talk her into it." Baron's expression turned grim at that, so Heron rushed on. "Her father was pimping her out to other men," she said flatly. "Tansy told me that he'd invited some men over for dinner tonight, and that she was expected to 'be nice' to them." Her throat tightened, the fiery rage she'd felt at the news flooding back, and she was suddenly blinking back tears. "And so help me God, I was not going to leave her there. Not to go home and be molested by a bunch of adult men."

Baron turned away, letting out a deep sigh and cursing under his breath, while Caroline looked like she wanted to break something.

"Fair enough," Baron said, and Heron imagined that he must be feeling rather conflicted at the moment. He was too compassionate to allow that kind of evil to continue to be inflicted on the girl, but at the same time, he also cared deeply about his Den, and anything that put it at risk was a cause for concern. "What's done is done," he conceded finally, "and I can't say you made a bad call, given the circumstances. But what about the rest of it? We're shape shifters. We can't keep the Den in lockdown for days at a time."

"We won't need to," Heron said firmly. "Tansy accepts a world of fantasy quite readily. Before we left, she asked me if I was magic; she seems to be under the impression I'm some kind of fairy godmother, or guardian angel. I have every hope that she'll accept the truth of this place much more easily than most people do. So tomorrow, after breakfast, we can all sit down together, and I'm going to tell her what we are."

"That's a hell of a short trip into a very strange new world," Baron pointed out darkly.

"No argument from me there," Heron agreed. "So if you have a better suggestion, I'm all ears."

It was a little past 1am when Silas headed down to the kitchen. He wasn't paying too much attention – the house was dark and quiet, and he was used to being the only one up at this time of night. Sleep never came particularly easily for him, and a midnight snack seemed in order.

He stepped into the darkness of the kitchen, fumbled around to find the light switch, and flipped it on-

"Aaaaah!!"

The scream came from the far corner, followed by a thud, then the sound of crockery breaking, and he jerked backwards, automatically reaching for his daggers, only to find they weren't at his side.

Fucking hell. Tansy stood in the corner, arms up in front of her to defend herself, a box of cornflakes lying on the floor surrounded by the pieces of a broken bowl.

"Fuck! I'm sorry. I didn't mean to scare you. I'm really sorry." After two weeks of tailing the girl, seeing her downcast face and wary behaviour, he'd come to feel a strong protectiveness towards her, and he cringed at the idea of scaring her now. She'd been through enough pain and fear in her life already.

They both stood there for a moment, frozen at opposite ends of the kitchen... and it occurred to Silas to wonder which of them was more startled.

Finally, when Tansy didn't move, Silas took a tentative step forward. "Here, I'll help you clean that up," he said, retrieving a dustpan and brush from beside the back door.

"I'm sorry," Tansy whispered, sounding like she was holding back tears, then she darted away from him, cowering in the corner as he slowly approached her.

He stopped. "Hey, it's okay. It was my fault for startling you. I didn't expect anyone to be down here."

"I shouldn't be here," Tansy said, her thin frame shaking. "I'm sorry..."

"It's okay. Let me just..." He carefully swept the shards together, then tossed the pieces in the bin and put the dustpan away. "See? No problem."

Tansy was edging away to the door. "Hey, no," he said, holding up his hand. "You're hungry, right?"

"I'm sorry," she said again. "I already had dinner, and I'm not supposed to..."

"Look, if you want some food, that's totally okay. You want cornflakes? I can leave, if you'd rather be alone..."

She glanced at the pantry longingly. Silas moved towards the door.

"No," she said softly. "You don't have to leave. This is your house. I can... I can go..."

Fuck. What was he supposed to do now? Silas had no idea how to relate to people in normal, everyday circumstances. The way he usually dealt with them was that if they were his enemy, he killed them, and if they weren't, he killed *for* them, protected them with deadly force. He was sadly inexperienced when it came to more placid forms of interaction. "We can both get some food. It's okay."

"But I broke something. I'm not allowed to break things."

"We have plenty more bowls." Shit, what had this kid been through that breaking a bowl was such a big deal? But then again, Silas knew exactly what she'd been through. He'd seen such atrocities back in Afghanistan, before he came to England.

"I'm just going to make a sandwich," Silas told her, thinking maybe if he stopped staring at her, she wouldn't feel so scared, and he headed for the fridge at the other end of the kitchen. Actually, what he really wanted was a chunk of raw meat, eaten in wolf form. Baron had told them all they could shift in their bedrooms, so long as no wolf was seen or heard out in the main house until tomorrow morning – supposedly he and Heron were going to tell this girl all about their world early the next day – but he could hardly just pick up a raw bone and walk off with it with the girl standing there. So a sandwich would have to do.

He took out bread, a side of cold roast beef, a tomato, and set about making a snack on the kitchen bench. Out of the corner of his eye, he saw Tansy still standing frozen in the corner, watching him nervously. And when it became apparent that she wasn't going to get any food for herself, Silas quickly made a second sandwich. He put it on a plate, cleaned up the bench and then set the plate on the table, taking a seat a good distance away from it with his own plate.

"There's a sandwich for you," he said calmly. "If you want it, it's yours. If not, that's okay."

He took a bite, making an effort not to watch her, and was rewarded when she very slowly edged towards the plate. Took a seat. Picked it up and took a tiny bite, watching him all the while.

"I'm Tansy," she said unexpectedly, fiddling with her food.

"I'm Silas," Silas said. Silence fell again, and he ate quickly, finding the entire situation unbearably awkward. He'd just finished his sandwich and was clearing the plate away when Tansy suddenly spoke again.

"How did you hurt your face?"

Silas self-consciously put a hand on his scar, a long, jagged line running from his left eye to his collar bone. He barely thought about it any more, so used to seeing it in the mirror every day, but it must look horrific to someone like her. "I had a fight with a very bad man. He was hurting a lot of innocent people. He tried to kill me." The memories were still raw, even after so many years. Not so much because of the fight, but because of the cause of it…

"You don't like thinking about it, do you?" Tansy said, and Silas was surprised at the unexpectedly insightful statement.

"Not really, no."

"I have things I don't like to think about, too," she confided in him.

What the fuck was he supposed to say to that? "Goodnight," he said

30

awkwardly, heading for the door, not knowing how else to end the conversation.

"Goodnight," she replied, and then added, with a politeness that was strangely out of place, "It was nice meeting you."

Silas padded out the door on silent bare feet and headed for the stairs. When he reached his room again, he let out a long sigh, not knowing what to think of the odd encounter. She was not what he had been expecting at all.

CHAPTER SIX

October 24th

Early the next morning, Tansy followed Heron into the library. They'd had breakfast – another feast in which Tansy had been allowed to eat toast, eggs, bacon and orange juice – and then Heron had told her that they needed to have a meeting with Baron and Caroline to discuss some details about the estate.

She'd met a few more people over breakfast; Kwan and Aaron, two boys who were around her own age; Mark, Alistair and Luke, three young men who smiled and laughed, but actually made Tansy horribly nervous, all three of them being fit and athletic in a way that made her feel small and weak; Raniesha, another of the women in the estate, who had dark skin and was a good friend of Caroline's. And she'd seen Silas again briefly. He ducked into the room, glanced around at the crowd, then grabbed a bread roll and an apple and hurried off again. He was an odd one. For all his tattoos and scars, he had a strange quietness about him, like a dog that had been beaten once too often. And like a dog, Tansy had the strange idea that if provoked, he could be dangerous, but if spoken to softly and shown a measure of kindness, he would prove to be the most loyal of friends. She'd been terrified last night when she'd first seen him, convinced he was going to hurt her. But then he'd reacted so strangely, seeming almost afraid of her, and it was so odd for a man to be scared of someone like her that she found herself quite curious about him.

Inside the library, Tansy sat down beside Heron, Baron and Caroline seated opposite them across the table.

"I'd like to begin," Baron said, once she was settled, "by saying that I've spoken to everyone in the house, and they're all very glad to have you here. You'll be introduced to everyone individually later, but for now, just keep in mind that you're very welcome to make this your home, and if you need anything, you only have to ask. Heron's told me she's going to help you buy some more clothes, and that you'd like a computer of your own. Is there anything else you need?"

There was, actually, but Tansy was feeling a little too overwhelmed to think of everything right now. It was only after she'd woken up this morning and the reality of what she'd done had sunk in that she'd started to remember all the things she'd left behind. "Some books," she said meekly, feeling confused and disoriented. She'd run away from home! That was just... outrageous. Her father would be furious. And his friends... they would have been so angry when she didn't show up last night. Tansy felt a thrill at the thought of disappointing them all, gleeful at the idea that for once, she'd messed up all of their plans.

"No problem," Baron said, in reply to her vague request. "Heron can help you find the ones you want online, and we can order them today. We'll show you around the estate later, as well. It's a big house, and there are some rooms that are private, but there's plenty of space for everyone to feel comfortable."

Tansy just nodded. Baron was staring at her with a serious sort of frown, and it was making her nervous. He looked fierce, not like Silas, who just wanted to be left alone, but like her father, who liked to take charge of things and tell people what to do.

"Now, the next thing," he went on, "is that we have to tell you a few things about the estate. You've probably realised by now that we're not a normal family. We have lots of different people with different backgrounds. But we all live together because there are a few, very important things that we all have in common."

He nodded to Heron, who took over the explanation. "Yesterday in the park, we were talking about magic things," she began, a strange tangent to the conversation that had Tansy frowning. "We talked about magic lions and whether fairies could make you invisible. And when we left, you asked me if I was magic."

Tansy nodded, in two minds about the whole idea. On the one hand, it was stupid. Magic wasn't real. Fairies didn't exist.

But on the other hand... Well, it was hard to explain. She'd seen enough movies, read enough stories to believe that there was *something else* in the world besides what people could see and hear and touch. Some people called it God, or angels. Others called it Fate. And still others called it magic. "You showed up just when I needed you to," Tansy explained, feeling awkward. "And you took me away from all the horrible things. So that's kind of like magic, right?" She waited for Heron to laugh at her...

"It certainly is," Heron said seriously. "So let me ask you a very important question: how would you feel if I told you that it wasn't a coincidence that I was in the park yesterday. What if I told you I had been looking for you?"

Tansy was immediately on guard. "Are you magic?" she asked again, repeating her question from last night. She had an odd sense that something important was about to happen, a strange kind of premonition that she was on the verge of a great turning point, not just in her own life, but, as ridiculous as it sounded, in the whole history of the world. She glanced at Baron, and then at Caroline. Both of them were watching her carefully.

"Do you really want me to answer that?" Heron asked, an odd note in her voice.

"Yes," Tansy said. "Are you an angel? I've heard that angels sometimes come and help people, and they look like normal people, but they're not."

Heron glanced at Baron, a look that seemed full of significance, and that odd feeling of premonition got stronger. "I'm not an angel," Heron said. "But we are different from normal people. We can do things that most people can't. And the truth is… we've been watching you for a little while. And we think you're the right sort of person to learn to do what we can do."

"What can you do?" Tansy asked, nervous, and curious, and excited and terrified all at once.

"Do you like dogs?" Heron asked, another odd turn of the conversation.

"I think so," Tansy said. "I've never really spent much time with them. But I've seen videos, and they seem nice enough."

"Okay," Heron said. "Well, I have one that I'd like you to meet. She's quite big, but she's very friendly. Is that okay?"

Tansy nodded, so Heron got up and went to the door. She opened it, and a large wolf paced into the room. It sat down on the floor a few feet from Tansy, and she stared at it in awe.

"You can talk to animals?" she whispered, trying to guess what the animal had to do with magic and angels and strange abilities. "That's a wolf, isn't it? Can you speak to animals?"

"It's a little more complicated than that," Heron said, watching the wolf, though she didn't take her seat again. "Watch carefully. And remember, you're perfectly safe here. Nothing bad is going to happen."

Tansy nodded, turning her full attention to the wolf.

It watched her, a strangely human intelligence shining in its eyes. And then its fur crackled with a strange blue light, like a thousand tiny strikes of lightning. The wolf blurred before her eyes, and when its form cleared, Tansy was shocked and amazed to see that it had become a human. Raniesha. The woman she'd met at breakfast.

All of a sudden, Tansy burst into tears. She leapt off her seat. Turned to face Heron with wide, accusing eyes, her heart thudding in her chest, her lungs gasping for air as she suddenly realised that everything she had ever been told about the world was wrong.

"It's you!" she blurted out, Raniesha forgotten on the floor. "You're the fairies. You're the magic fairies. And I've wanted you to come and get me so many times! But I didn't know where you lived, and I didn't know how to find you... but you live here! And you... You came to get me. How did you find me? How did you know where I live?"

Heron reached for her cautiously, as if not sure whether she was going to run away. "It's okay," she said, putting her hand gently on Tansy's shoulder. "You're perfectly safe. No one's going to hurt you."

Tansy darted forward, catching Heron in a fierce hug, as if by holding onto her, she could make sure this strange dream would never end. "Don't ever make me go away," she sobbed into Heron's shoulder. "Let me stay here with you. I can be a wolf! I could be a really great wolf. I want to be magic, like you. Let me stay here forever!"

Heron wrapped her arms around Tansy and held her close, and Tansy felt herself shaking with fear and relief and a hope so strong it made her dizzy. "You can stay," Heron whispered into her hair. "You can stay here forever."

Later that morning, Heron sat on the sofa in the manor's lounge, Tansy by her side with a laptop balanced on her knees, Raniesha on Tansy's other side. They were looking at an online store, the screen displaying a range of children's clothing, and Tansy was slowly working up a sizeable collection of things she wanted to buy. She was wearing her blue top with the dolphin on it, along with her childish jewellery, and with her tiny figure and long hair pulled into a ponytail, she looked like she was about twelve years old.

"What about this one?" Heron pointed to a top with a fairy on the front, but Tansy shook her head.

"No. Fairies are small and silly." She scrolled down the page, then found one she liked better, a brightly coloured unicorn on the front. "What about that one?"

"Oh, that's very pretty," Raniesha said enthusiastically. But to Heron's surprise, Tansy's face immediately lost its playful smile.

"No," she said, moving on. "I don't think I like it."

"These are pretty," Heron said, pointing to a pair of jeans with butterflies on them.

"No!" Tansy said, her tone exasperated. "Not like that."

"But you liked the t-shirt with the butterflies," Heron said, confused by her seemingly random tastes. "You said butterflies were nice."

"But I don't like those ones," Tansy said stubbornly, scrolling down the page. At first, Heron had thought it fairly easy to work out Tansy's taste in clothing. No skirts or dresses. Bright colours only. Glitter was especially good, and while she might tolerate a few items in blue or green, she preferred the pinks and yellows. She was, as Caroline would have put it, a 'girly girl', unicorns and butterflies and flowers decorating the vast majority of her choices.

But now they seemed to have hit something of a roadblock, with Tansy suddenly rejecting half a dozen items that Heron had expected her to like.

"What don't you like about it?" Raniesha asked carefully. Since her demonstration of her shape shifting abilities, Tansy had taken an immediate shine to her, inviting her to join this shopping session and seeming to take her opinions seriously.

Tansy sighed, a scowl on her face. "I'm not pretty," she said darkly.

"Oh, that's not true," Heron said, alarmed by her apparent lack of confidence in her physical appearance, and wanting to bolster her self esteem. "I think you're very pretty."

The laptop suddenly went crashing to the floor, Tansy leaping off the seat and rushing across the room. "I'm not pretty!" she shouted, facing them both, angry and scared, arms wrapped around herself defensively. "Don't call me that!"

"I'm sorry," Heron apologised automatically, mystified by her distress. "I didn't mean to offend you."

"Why do people have to keep saying I'm pretty? I'm not, and I never wanted to be, so why can't you just leave me alone? I never wanted to wear those dresses, and I tried to cut my hair, so I wouldn't be, but he wouldn't let me have short hair!"

In a rush, Tansy ripped the elastic band out of her hair and ran out of the room.

Heron and Raniesha leapt up, dashing after her. They caught up to her in the kitchen, Heron letting out a startled cry as she saw the pair of scissors in Tansy's hands, but Tansy was too quick. In two or three decisive strokes, she'd hacked off her hair just below her ears. The long strands tumbled to the floor. She tossed the scissors carelessly onto the bench, then angrily grabbed the handfuls lying on the ground and shoved them into the bin. "I hate my hair! I hate wearing dresses." The destruction wasn't satisfactory, so she grabbed the scissors again, plunging them into the bin and massacring the hair that lay in a big clump, cutting and cutting until it was all in tiny pieces. "I hate him!"

"Okay, okay…" Heron approached her slowly, took her hand and gently removed the scissors, worried she would accidentally hurt herself with them, and then cautiously put her arms around her. While Tansy was understandably wary of anyone touching her, she seemed to accept physical contact from Heron well enough, and Heron was relieved when she sagged against her, breathing hard. But no tears were falling, and the girl seemed more angry than upset.

"I'm sorry, Tansy," Heron said, rubbing her back gently. "It's okay. No one's going to make you do anything you don't want to do."

But Tansy suddenly pulled away. "Don't call me that," she said angrily. "I hate that name. I hate the way the men said it, and my father... He always said it like it was an order. 'Tansy', like I was a dog or something. I want a different name."

"Okay." Heron nodded slowly. She was feeling out of her depth, but Tansy's reasons for disliking her name were sound. "What would you like to be called?"

Tansy stood still and thought for a minute. "Skip," she said finally, looking uncertain about it. "That's the name I go by online. And it doesn't matter what you look like online, because no one can see you anyway. And I'm good at stuff with computers."

"Then Skip it is," Heron agreed. "That's perfectly fine."

The newly appointed Skip nodded, though there was still an angry scowl on her face, and Heron waited patiently, Raniesha hovering just behind her.

"Can I ask you something?" Heron said carefully, once Skip had calmed down a little. "I don't mean to upset you, but... did your father used to tell you you were pretty? Is that why you don't like it?"

Skip nodded, her lips pressed together in an angry line. "His friends always said I was pretty. I hated them. But I wasn't allowed to go away. I had to stay with them, and they..." She stopped, lip quivering, a flood of dark memories overwhelming her, and Heron was suddenly fighting back tears at the stark reminder of what this precious young woman had had to live with for so long.

She stroked her hair softly. "You don't have to have long hair," she said firmly. "And you don't have to look pretty any more." Heron immediately resolved never to use the word again in Skip's presence, and also made a mental note to inform the rest of the Den of the need to avoid it.

Skip nodded, and wiped her nose on the back of her arm.

"Shall we go back and look for some more clothes?" Heron asked.

Back in the sitting room, the search went more successfully this time around. Heron found a jumper with a kitten on the front. "Oh, that looks very... girly," she said, fumbling for a word which showed her approval, but avoided the dreaded description of 'pretty'.

"Yeah," Skip agreed. "It's cute." With a click of the mouse, she added it to her selection.

"And I like this one," she added, finding a light blue t-shirt with a pale grey wolf on the front." She glanced up at Raniesha with a mischievous grin. "Cos wolves are awesome," she said slyly, then turned back to the screen.

After Skip's impromptu 'hair cut' that morning, Heron took her down to the local village to get it cut properly, a stern-faced Silas in tow. And, understanding the need for a bodyguard, Skip found she didn't really mind having him around. There was something oddly wounded about him, and while she was reluctant to get too close to him, he didn't scare her the way some of the other men did.

She struggled to sit still while the hairdresser did her hair, though not from any nervousness. She was getting a real haircut! For the first time in years. And as the ragged mess gradually took shape, fluffy on top, shaped nicely around her ears, Skip could barely contain her excitement. When it was done, she spent long minutes staring into the mirror. She could barely recognise herself. Short hair, bright clothes, the chunky necklace around her neck – not the sort of thing her father would ever have allowed her to wear – and the smile on her face… it had been so long since Skip had had a real reason to smile. On the way home, they'd stopped at a café and picked up a chocolate brownie for her and a muffin for Heron, and Skip felt like her world had been flipped upside down. So many things she was allowed to do now, that she hadn't been allowed to before. She made a point of thanking Heron for the unexpected gifts, and then turned to Silas, shyly thanking him too, for giving up his time to come with them. He looked startled at the display of gratitude, making Skip wonder why no one had been polite to him before, and she resolved to always remember her manners around him, delighted with the crooked, bashful sort of smile on his face.

Now, after a long day of so many new surprises, it was dinnertime, and Skip followed Heron down the stairs and along the hall. She was hungry, looking forward to another meal, so she wasn't really paying attention as they reached the dining room. She took two steps inside the door, glanced around the room… and froze.

Men. Everywhere. Twelve of them, and an automatic and uncontrollable panic set in, as twelve pairs of male eyes turned to look at her. "No…" It came out strangled, a desperate plea, and then she turned and fled, bolting down the hall until she came to a small cupboard. She flung the door open, scrambled inside and shut herself in.

Heron dashed after Skip as she ran from the room, Caroline right behind her. She wasn't sure what had startled the girl so badly, but she was willing to take her fears seriously, for all the lack of apparent threat. They were just in time to see the hallway cupboard closing, but rather than opening the door immediately, Heron instead came to a halt beside it, glancing worriedly at Caroline.

"Skip?" she called through the door, making an effort to sound calm and soothing. "Are you okay?"

"Keep them away from me!" Skip called back, vibrant alarm in her voice, and Heron crouched down beside the door.

"Sweetie," she said calmly. "No one is going to hurt you. I'm going to sit right beside you. And Caroline and Raniesha will be there. No one will touch you."

"I don't want to go near them."

Heron pictured the dining room in her mind. Twelve strong, athletic, confident men. And only a small handful of women. Damn it all, she should have realised the problem sooner. "Okay," she agreed immediately. It had been a big day, and she didn't want to push Skip into anything too soon. "You don't want to eat in the dining room? That's okay. You don't have to, if you don't want to."

Silence. And then a small, shuffling sound. The door cracked open a fraction. "They're scary," Skip told her, a small, timid voice from inside the darkness. "I don't want to touch them."

"You don't have to," Heron assured her, and she felt Caroline put a hand on her shoulder and give it a squeeze. Flashbacks and irrational fears were likely an ingrained part of Skip's psyche, and she was torn between wanting to assure her that there was no danger in the dining room, and allowing her the space and time to find her courage herself. "If you want, we can have dinner in the sitting room instead."

The door opened a fraction more, and Skip poked her head out. "But that would be rude," she said in dismay. "I'm sorry. I just... There are so many of them. I don't want to mess up dinner. And some of them are nice..." Skip had run into Kwan and Aaron in the foyer this afternoon, and had seemed eager to chat. She'd explained to Heron that she wasn't allowed to have friends at her old house, and Heron had been glad to see that she seemed interested in meeting people her own age.

"No one is going to be angry if you don't want to come to dinner," Heron said.

"Mark is scary," Skip confided softly. "And Luke. He's so tall..." Heron waited, while Skip thought the situation through.

"What about Simon?" Caroline said, when the stalemate seemed set to continue. "We told you about him earlier, remember? He likes working with computers, just like you do. He normally sits next to Heron, so what about if you sat between them? Then you could talk to him about programming, and maybe he can help you buy a new computer for yourself?" It was a blatant attempt at bribery, but one that came without the usual manipulation that the word implied. They had already promised Skip a new computer. Caroline's tactic was merely a lure to tempt her with the best possible machine, and while it wasn't a method Heron would have chosen herself, she was curious to see how Skip would react.

"Everyone's going to be looking at me," Skip said miserably, nudging her way an inch or two more out of the cupboard. "Cos I made a fuss, and…" She stopped, and then frowned. "I don't know the rules here," she said in confusion. "At home, my father would have been so mad if I'd run away from dinner. But you're all polite about it, and you're not mad or anything."

"No one in this house should ever be scared of living here," Heron told her firmly. She might have to repeat it a thousand more times before it sank in, but she was prepared to go the distance.

"Yes, but what are the *rules*?" Skip asked more insistently. "What does everyone else do at dinner?"

"Under normal circumstances," Caroline explained, "everyone is expected to come to dinner at seven-thirty. If Baron or Anna – Anna's the other person in charge here, but she's away at the moment. But if either of them have any news, then they tell everyone before the meal starts. And then we ask Sirius to bless the meal, and then, if anyone isn't hungry, they can leave, while everyone else eats dinner." They had briefly mentioned Sirius this morning, while they were explaining a few of the details of shape shifting to Skip, and she'd seemed to like the idea of a divine wolf spirit watching over her.

"Then I should come to dinner," she said firmly, picking herself up off the floor and closing the cupboard. "If that's what everyone else does, then that's what I should do."

Heron smiled down at her, feeling a wave of admiration for the girl. "You are the bravest young woman I have ever met," she said warmly. "Come on. Let's go back."

Inside the dining room, Heron was glad to see that the meal hadn't started yet. Knowing she had missed the start of it would only have made Skip feel more awkward. She was more relieved to see that everyone was being extremely tactful, avoiding staring at them as they returned to the room, and Heron led Skip to her seat, between herself and Simon.

Once they were settled, Baron tapped his fork against his glass, and the room fell silent. "I've received news from Anna. She's returning home tomorrow afternoon, flying into Carlisle by private jet. For anyone who hasn't heard yet, lockdown has officially ended. You're free to go about in wolf form as usual. Any other news?"

Silence, as everyone shook their head, and Heron was grateful for Baron's tact in not making a point of introducing Skip to the room. The attention would likely have given her another panic attack.

Baron raised his glass. "To those who still run," he said, repeating the nightly ritual toast.

"And to those who have fallen," the Den replied in unison. "May they be welcome at the table of Sirius at the setting of the sun."

With no further prompting, conversations sprung up all over the room, and everyone dug into the food.

CHAPTER SEVEN

October 25th

The next morning, Baron faced a sea of worried faces in the library. Almost half the Den had gathered to discuss Skip's future, to make plans for her schooling and education into shifter culture, her combat training, and to devise plans to help her deal with the trauma of her past. "Thank you all for making yourselves available on such short notice," he said, once everyone was settled. "First of all, I want to let you know that after Skip's panic attack last night, I took the liberty of speaking to the Council about her. They're sending one of their diplomats with Anna when she comes. Nia is trained in psychology, and while it's not normal protocol, they're willing to let her stay here for as long as Skip needs to get her head around things. I'm expecting a minimum of six months, possibly a year or more. We all know she's been abused, but none of us really knows the extent of that abuse, and we certainly don't have the skills to deal with it on the level that Skip is going to need."

"She's very smart," Simon commented. "And that's a good thing as far as therapy goes. Intelligent kids tend to respond to counselling fairly well."

"Something else I'd like to ask for at the same time," Heron added. "Therapy for Skip is essential, I agree, but it would be a great help if this therapist could spend some time with the rest of us. Let us know what we should be expecting from Skip, how to deal with her panic attacks, what to do in terms of discipline. I don't want to come down too hard on her, but in the long term, letting her have everything her own way isn't going to be good for her either."

Baron nodded. "Nia has been fully briefed on Skip's situation, and she's already said she'll need to have a few planning sessions with the rest of us. I know it's a little awkward having a stranger on the estate for that long-"

"It won't be a problem," Heron said firmly, and a chorus of voices agreed with her. "We all care about Skip enough to make allowances for a Council emissary."

"Thank you," Baron said, looking around the room. "Heron has volunteered to finish Skip's schooling with her, and I'm planning to take on a fair bit of her education into shifter culture myself, but I'll probably need someone else to fill in when things get busy. Raniesha, do you think you might have time?"

Raniesha nodded. "I'd be happy to help." She'd been in the Den for over a decade, and was well versed in the lessons Skip would need to master.

"But perhaps we shouldn't rush into that side of things too quickly," Heron suggested. "Skip's still fairly nervous around you, and around men in general. Maybe we should let her get used to the idea of living here a little more before we launch right into our complete history and culture."

Baron shrugged, not at all put out by the suggestion. "We have some time, so there's no harm in waiting a few weeks. I think her school work should start fairly soon, though. Having some sense of routine would help her settle in."

Heron nodded. "That should work nicely."

Next he turned his attention to Silas and Tank. Silas was their main instructor in combat training, teaching the new recruits everything from martial arts, to knife defence, to how to use a handgun. But since Tank had been recruited two years ago, and subsequently converted into a shifter just a few months ago, he'd proven himself to be on par with Silas as far as hand to hand fighting went. He'd been in the military before he was recruited, and Baron had recently assigned him to training Eric, their other new recruit. The results had been promising.

"Tank, I'd like you to have a think about training Skip in martial arts. By the time she's converted, she'll need to know how to fight at a fairly decent level. The Noturatii aren't picky about who they attack, after all. And Silas, I wanted to assign you to firearms training-"

"Uh..." Tank interrupted, looking uncomfortable. "I'm not sure me teaching her to fight is a good idea," he said carefully. Baron quirked an eyebrow at him. "Hand to hand training involves hitting the student," Tank explained. "Or at least pretending to. And with the way Skip feels about men right now, I really don't think having a man who weighs three times as much as her throwing a fist her way is a good idea."

Baron sighed. "I know it's not a great situation, but she has to learn to fight, one way or another. It's putting her own safety at risk if she doesn't."

"I understand the situation," Tank said respectfully. "But I'm going to have to say no."

Baron was surprised at the flat refusal. Up until now, Tank had always been amiable and cooperative, following orders promptly and taking a strong interest in the goings on around the Den. But given the situation, he could understand Tank's reasons for saying no, so he wasn't inclined to push the issue. He turned to Silas-

"The answer is no," Silas said, before Baron could even get a word out. "Tank's right. I'll teach her to shoot, no problem, but I'm not getting involved in anything that includes laying a single finger on her."

Baron snarled. "God damn it, we all know she has to be trained to fight."

"No argument there," Silas said grimly. "But throwing her in the deep end with trained killers is not the answer."

"Let's all think about it for a couple of days," Heron suggested diplomatically. "A solution will present itself. But she's only just arrived, and I don't like the idea of rushing her into anything that might do more harm than good."

"Fine," Baron conceded with a sigh. "We can discuss it with Nia when she arrives. She might be able to come up with a good solution that won't upset Skip."

"Moving onto another problem, then," Alistair said apprehensively. He was the Den's PR guru and kept a regular eye on the media to head off any news stories that might cause problems for them. "Skip's father has reported her missing. No surprises there, given who he is, but if we want to keep this as simple as possible, we need to get things wrapped up there fairly quickly."

"The original plan was to get Skip to do that for us," Simon reminded everyone. "From what Heron says, she ran away by choice, and given how she feels about what her father was doing, it shouldn't be hard to talk her into reporting him to the police."

"I'm not so sure," Heron said quickly. "Despite her dislike of him, he somehow brainwashed her into believing she's supposed to be looking after him – some kind of health problem or other – and she feels guilty enough about leaving him as it is. Accusing him of a crime may well be too big a step for her."

"We could always report him ourselves," Alistair said, weighing up the options. "But that doesn't explain why Skip suddenly went missing, and any report we file would have to be done anonymously. There's always the risk that, in the absence of further evidence, the police would fail to get a warrant to seize his computer."

"How about we talk to Skip about it before we go jumping to conclusions," Caroline suggested. "She's an intelligent girl. Some careful explaining would go a long way towards getting her to understand what's at stake."

Ten minutes later, Skip was sitting at the table with them. Silas and Tank had been sent away, so as not to overwhelm her, and Alistair had offered to make himself scarce as well, at least until they knew whether she would cooperate. If not, then he would need to concoct an alternative plan, but it was worth letting Baron and Heron try first.

Skip was staring morosely at the table, Heron having just explained to her that her father had reported her missing. "Do I have to go home?" she asked, her voice shaking slightly.

"No," Heron reassured her quickly. "We said you could stay, and we meant it. But because your father doesn't know where you are, the police are going to be looking for you."

"I don't want them to find me," Skip said, with just a hint of belligerence. "I don't want to go back there."

"Do you realise that what he and his friends were doing was illegal?" Heron asked carefully.

Skip shrugged. "Yeah, but the police won't do anything." When she noticed the frowns around her, she became slightly defensive. "He's a councillor. He's important. He said the police would think I was lying, and then I'd get into trouble. And then he was going to take my computer away."

Heron glanced at Baron, who looked as out of his depth as she was. "Well, he can't get you in trouble any more," she pointed out, not sure how to proceed. "And we're buying you a new computer. And even though he's an important person, that doesn't mean he's allowed to break the law. I promise you, the police aren't going to think you're lying."

"So… I could tell the police, and then he couldn't do it any more?" Skip clarified, making Heron feel a wave of relief that she seemed inclined to cooperate, even if she wasn't quite convinced that their plan would work.

"That's right," Baron confirmed. "He couldn't hurt you any more. Or anyone else, either."

Skip's face paled at that, and Heron wondered if Baron had just made a serious blunder. Perhaps the idea that her father might be hurting other children hadn't occurred to her. "Then we have to tell the police," Skip blurted out, her face alarmed. "Are there others? I thought it was just me. His friends… do you think they go to other people's houses and do the same thing?"

"We don't just think so," Simon said grimly. "We have evidence that he is already doing that."

"Then we have to stop him," Skip said determinedly. "How do we stop him?"

"I have everything you need right here," Simon said, opening a laptop and pulling up a file. "We'd need to take you down to a police station. You can show them your ID – you have a student card or something, right?" Skip nodded. "Okay, so you tell them that you left home voluntarily, you're

45

staying with a friend, and you don't want to go back. And then you can just give them this letter."

He turned the laptop around to show Skip the letter he'd composed earlier. It detailed the evidence they'd found on her father's computer that he had been hurting other children, then asked that the police investigate the matter further. It was straightforward, factual, and more importantly, left out anything about Skip being one of the victims of her father's crimes.

Skip read the letter slowly, her expression tight. When she'd finished, she nodded. "Yeah. That's good."

"Is there anything in there you'd like to change?" Heron asked, not wanting to manipulate her into doing anything she wasn't comfortable with. "Or do you have any questions about it?"

Skip shook her head. "No. That's pretty much what I would have said anyway."

"Okay," Baron said, relieved that that part, at least, was solved relatively simply. "Heron and Silas can take you to the station this afternoon. Don't worry, the police can't make you go home. And once they have that letter, they can start their investigation."

After they had all thanked Skip and sent her on her way, Baron turned back to the group. "I'll ask Alistair to monitor the news for anything on her father's arrest, and Simon, could you keep track of things via the police database? If anything goes wrong, I want an immediate heads up." Simon nodded. Hopefully, if the police did their job, this would be the end of it, but it was always a good idea to stay one step ahead of any problems.

"Is there anything else we need to cover now, or is that it for the time being?" Everyone shook their heads. There would be more to discuss later, but for now, the most important issues had been dealt with. "Then if you'll excuse me," Baron said, standing up, "I need to go and prepare for Nia's arrival. And given the mood Anna's been in lately, I'm expecting the mother of all shit-storms to start up the moment she sets foot inside the door."

"You've what?" Anna demanded, glaring at Baron as they stood in the middle of the foyer.

"We've recruited a new female," he told her blandly. "A young woman called Skip. She's sixteen-"

"How dare you! I am alpha of this Den," Anna snarled angrily, and Baron was grateful he'd had the foresight to ask Heron to take Skip for a long walk around the estate. There was no way she needed to be around to witness this. "You can't simply recruit new members without even letting me know!"

"But you can run off to Italy for six weeks at a time, with no regard for how the Den is running without you?" Baron pointed out in irritation. God, how he would love to get the woman booted out of her role as alpha. But the problem with that plan was that there were no other women in the Den currently willing or able to step into her place. So if anyone actually petitioned for a leadership change, and won, that meant the Council would have to send in a replacement, a high ranking female from another Den, and the current agreement among their own members was that the unrest that would cause would be worse than putting up with a sub-standard alpha. Everyone was aware of the tension Anna was causing, except for Anna herself.

"It's *Italy*, not the goddamned moon," Anna shouted. "I'm a phone call away!"

"And you didn't once phone us to ask how things were going in the entire six weeks you were away." Baron's tone was cool, almost bored. This was not an argument he cared about in the slightest. He'd long since given up trying to get Anna to care more about the Den, and was now resigned to simply chugging along as well as he could by himself, merely sidestepping any problems Anna tried to cause by sticking her nose in.

But Anna was not taking his dismissive tone well. "I won't allow it," she declared suddenly, ignoring the crowd that was gathering around them, drawn by Anna's angry shouts. "As alpha, I have the right of veto. And I refuse to let any new recruit join the Den without me being involved."

That got Baron's attention. But not in the way Anna might have hoped. Though it had been only two days since Skip had joined them, almost everyone in the Den had taken a shine to her. Silas, Kwan and Aaron were particularly fond of her, taking her under their wing as a little sister. Caroline would fight for her right to stay on principle, due to the serious lack of females in the Den. Simon would argue that they needed her – her hacking skills would be invaluable in future years. And Baron knew that he had held this Den together for long enough that, if push came to shove, every single person would fall in behind him, rather than Anna, no matter how unappealing the decisions he might have to make.

"If you exercise your right of veto to have Skip removed," Baron said slowly, advancing towards the woman, "then I will open a petition for a leadership challenge."

"The Council won't allow it," Anna said, but the expression on her face said she was well aware that they would. "You have no other females willing to stand as alpha."

"The Council doesn't determine who is alpha in any given Den," Baron pointed out. "The Den decides. And the lack of anyone to replace you doesn't mean the Council wouldn't have to listen to a vote of no confidence. So look carefully at the faces around you, and think about whether they'll really follow you, when you're trying to evict someone that they've all come to care about."

This wasn't the way he would have liked to have done this. He'd anticipated that Anna would be upset about not being consulted about a new recruit, but, aside from the fact that he didn't really give a shit what she thought, he'd been prepared to walk her through it. Concede to her security concerns. Introduce her to Skip and suggest she take a little time to get to know her. But as it was, with her threat to veto the girl, Anna had just backed herself into a corner that even Baron couldn't help her get out of. His ultimate concern was with the welfare of the whole Den. And in the long run, the Den would benefit from Skip's presence, despite the difficulties they might face in helping her adjust.

Anna seemed to realise she had lost this fight. She glanced around, her mouth opening and closing as she sought a way out that would allow her to save face. But after her bold declaration that she would evict Skip without even meeting her, even she realised she had nowhere to turn.

"So what's it to be?" Baron prompted, when Anna said nothing.

She glanced nervously around the room again. "Fine," she said eventually, after an awkward pause. "She can stay." She picked up her travel bag. "I'll be in my room, freshening up."

CHAPTER EIGHT

October 26th

Caroline was in the Den's gym, giving the punching bag a solid pummelling. Her self-imposed training regime was rigorous: weights, cardio, swimming, and martial arts, as well as running and agility training in wolf form. There was also weapons training, guns, knives and even sword practice, though the latter was more for fitness and agility rather than any real need to know how to use the weapon. It was standard protocol for every member of the Den to spend a minimum of ten hours a week in some form of training, but it wasn't unusual for Caroline to put in double that amount of time, and today, she was working on her boxing skills, as well as working off a little frustration, each punch a satisfying thud that helped keep her temper in check.

She stepped back for a moment, breathing hard, sweat dripping from her face, and then she heard a small scuffle from the back of the gym. She spun around, eyes sweeping the room for the intruder that she hadn't heard arrive, until her gaze settled on Skip, lurking near the door, watching her.

"Hey," she said, immediately relaxing her defensive posture. "Something I can do for you?"

Skip shook her head, edging towards the door. "No. Sorry. I didn't mean to interrupt."

Caroline scrambled for something to say that would call her back. She'd taken a firm liking to the girl, seeing in her a reflection of her own troubled childhood, though Caroline considered herself fortunate when comparing their respective pasts. She'd been abused by her father and brother, physically and verbally, but thankfully, neither of them had ever tried anything sexual. But even so, she could easily empathise with Skip's wary caution about the world. "Do you want to have a go?" she offered quickly, indicating the punching bag. The ongoing question of how to teach Skip fighting skills was still unanswered, but Caroline figured there couldn't be any harm in letting her hit the bag a few times.

Skip snorted, then shook her head meekly. "Me? No. I don't know how to hit things."

"Well... I could teach you," Caroline offered. When Skip had first arrived, she'd been looking forward to being involved in the girl's training, but with Heron handling her school work and Nia taking care of her psychological wellbeing, there had seemed little for Caroline to do.

Skip hesitated at that. She eyed the punching bag with a look of faint curiosity. "Really?"

"Sure," Caroline said. "Come over here." She stripped off her boxing gloves and wiped her face on a towel. Skip came closer, a shy smile on her face. "You've never hit anything before?" Skip shook her head. "It's not so hard. First you need to get your stance right. Feet apart, one foot in front of the other. Maintaining your balance is crucial. And then you need to get your fist right. Put your hand out," she instructed, holding out her own hand, palm upwards. Skip copied her, her hand tiny compared to Caroline's. "Now curl your fingers in," she said, demonstrating, "and then tuck your thumb over the top. Now, when you throw a punch, it's really important to keep your wrist straight. You want to make a straight line from the last knuckle of your little finger, right through to your elbow. If you bend your wrist up or down, you can sprain it pretty badly." Skip followed her instructions with care, then stepped up to the punching bag when Caroline waved her forward.

"Now pick a point you want to hit, make sure you keep your wrist straight, and..." Caroline flung out a punch, landing the blow with a thud that made the punching bag swing on its hooks. "Now you try it."

Skip did, a tiny hit that glanced off and didn't make the bag move at all. "I suck at this," she said dismally, far too ready to admit defeat. But Caroline was having none of it.

"No, no, just try it again. Tighten you abdominal muscles a little... now step in a bit closer. My arms are longer than yours. And don't aim for the point you're looking at. Imagine you're trying to hit something six inches behind it."

Skip did... and let out a startled cry of joy when her tiny fist connected with a thud, making the punching bag swing back a few inches.

"See?" said Caroline, a grin on her face at the girl's success. "Not so hard, after all. Now, let's try the same thing with your left hand..."

November 10th

Silas watched the sparring match going on on the back lawn with a smile on his face. Well, for him, it was a smile. For anyone else, it would have been little more than a tightening at the corner of the mouth. After the tense discussion in the library, the issue of Skip's training had swiftly and unexpectedly resolved itself. Caroline wasn't anywhere near experienced enough to handle the entire task herself, but given Skip's apparent enthusiasm for training with the woman, the solution was simple. Silas was to oversee her training sessions, evaluating Skip's progress, while Caroline handled the physical side of the sessions. After their first impromptu lesson in the gym, which had resulted in Skip lying on the floor in a giggling heap after missing a kick aimed at the punching bag and falling flat on her arse, she'd decided that combat training was a hilarious game, and was more than eager to pit her skills against Caroline, unafraid of the fight despite Caroline's greater height and weight.

With Caroline on the scene, there was also the added benefit that Silas could demonstrate any given move using Caroline as his 'victim', neatly sidestepping the issue of even pretending to throw a punch Skip's way. The girl was a fast learner, paying close attention to each new move, despite her playful attitude towards the whole thing.

But as he watched the lesson continue, a semi-contact sparring match, complete with padded vest and arm pads for Skip, his keen eye alerted him to a dozen errors in Skip's technique... which, on further consideration, were a direct reflection of Caroline's weaknesses. He sighed, the faint hint of a smile fading. While Baron seemed to be of the opinion that any training was better than none, Silas was taking the whole thing rather more seriously. For all their good intentions about protecting Skip, it was a fair call to say that one day she'd be front and centre in a fight with the Noturatii, and they weren't doing her any favours by taking it easy on her at this early stage, when bad habits she picked up now could cost her her life later down the track.

Once the session came to an end, Skip heading off into the house for a well earned shower, Silas called Caroline over. "A word?" he asked grimly, leading her away from the other onlookers, knowing Caroline wasn't going to like what he had to say, and wanting to spare her the humiliation of being dressed down publicly.

"What is it?" The pair of them had never got along particularly well – not surprising for two people who generally didn't get along with *anyone* – but where Skip's training was concerned, they'd both put aside their differences to try and give her the best teaching possible.

"You and me," Silas said without preamble. "We're going to do some extra training."

"Why?" Caroline looked offended – no surprises there.

"Because your fighting technique is not doing Skip any good." He wasn't trying to offend her – if anything, he was making an effort to be tactful, but his lack of practice at diplomacy was sadly evident. "You fight like a fucking bulldozer," Silas went on, cutting off the inevitable argument. "You're a tall woman, and a strong woman, and that's the way you fight. Skip has neither of those advantages. So if she's ever going to best a bigger, stronger opponent, she needs to use speed and technique to her advantage. And with all due respect, those are things you could certainly work at improving." No, definitely not the most tactful critique ever.

But to his surprise, Caroline didn't snarl back at him, didn't call him a bastard or punch him in the face or any of the other more volatile responses he might have expected. She glanced back at where Skip was disappearing into the house, and seemed to consider the idea seriously. "Fine," she said finally. "I'm not going to turn down something that helps me improve."

Silas shrugged, then led her off to a more secluded part of the lawn. He turned to face her, bowing respectfully to begin the lesson.

"New rules," Silas told her. "In light of Skip's physical limitations, you're not allowed to hit me anywhere above here." He held a hand up at the level of his solar plexus. "You're not allowed to physically throw me to the ground. And you're not allowed to use any holds or grabs that required physical strength to maintain."

"That's fucking stupid!" Caroline spat at him.

"And that is Skip's reality," Silas reminded her. "She's short, she's small, and she lacks any real degree of upper body strength. And yes, we can certainly work on that for her, but she's never going to be able to hit above her weight like you can."

Caroline scowled, but made no further protest.

"We'll begin with taekwondo," Silas said, falling into a defensive stance. "Your first task: attack me, assume that both of us are unarmed, and you win the fight when you succeed in kicking me in the balls." He wasn't wearing a cup, so he had no intention of making it easy for her.

Caroline grinned, a sardonic look full of glee. "It would be a pleasure," she replied, adopting her own fighting stance.

"Begin."

December 22nd

Six weeks passed in what seemed like the blink of an eye. Skip settled into the estate easily, getting to know everyone and forming opinions on who she liked to spend time with, and who she would rather avoid. Simon rapidly became one of her favourite people, no doubt due to the long hours he spent with her poring over various computer programs. The women on the estate became her confidants, with Heron stepping eagerly in as a mother-figure, a role that had been sorely missing from Skip's life for far too long. Baron slowly earned her trust, treating her with unwavering kindness and respect, while she maintained a wary distrust of some of the other men – Mark, Luke and Alistair in particular. While the young men were disappointed with the distance she maintained from them, they respected her boundaries, and never imposed on her time or space. But Kwan and Aaron had become her new playmates, the three of them spending long afternoons roaming the forest or playing video games in the television lounge. Skip had been deprived of real friends for a long time, and seemed more than eager to make up for it now.

For their part, the two boys took an instant liking to her, treating her as the younger sister they had never had. She had the pair of them wrapped around her little finger, and there was nothing they could deny her, whether it was shy requests for another teddy bear, or mischievous demands that she be allowed to choose her character first in the video games. So when, on a quiet afternoon, Skip cheerfully invited the two of them to go for a walk up the hill, they both eagerly agreed.

Winter was well underway, and they were all dressed warmly as they took their usual route up the hill through the trees, heading for the top of the hill where they could get a view of the surrounding estates and where Skip loved to stand with the wind in her face. Aaron had shifted, Skip uniformly delighted whenever anyone took on their wolf form, and her lack of fear of the large animals had reassured Baron and Heron that the decision to bring her here had been a good one.

"Hey," Kwan said suddenly, after they'd spent some time at the top of the hill and were on their way back down. "Do you want to try climbing a tree?"

Skip paused, looking up warily at the tall pine he'd stopped beneath. "I don't know," she said, slightly breathless. "How do you... Isn't that too high?"

Aaron shifted back into human form and grinned at Kwan. "Not if you know how," he said with a smirk. "Do you want to learn?"

Skip stared up at the tree, a look of consternation on her face. "Are we allowed?" she asked uncertainly. In the past weeks, she'd asked the question again and again, and Kwan had learned not to be surprised at her hesitation. After his own strict upbringing, nothing so traumatic as Skip's, but confined by rules and regulations nonetheless, he'd been surprised at the level of freedom he'd been allowed when he'd first joined the Den, and could relate to Skip's surprise at the things she was allowed to do.

"Of course," Aaron said, sounding confused. "Have you really never-?"

Kwan nudged him sharply, and Aaron immediately shut up. "Yes, we're allowed," Kwan said instead. "But you need to be careful. We don't want you hurting yourself."

"But it's way cool," Aaron added, not minding the interruption. He had the best of intentions where Skip was concerned, but occasionally said things that came across as a little tactless. And he was aware enough of his own shortcomings to not mind when Kwan pulled him into line.

Skip stared up at the tree some more. "But it's not..." she said, and then stopped.

Kwan waited, then when she didn't continue, prompted her, "It's not what?"

"It's not... *dignified*."

Kwan didn't know what to make of that one. He glanced at Aaron, who shrugged. "What do you mean, it's not dignified?" he asked finally, hoping the question didn't upset Skip. He, like everyone on the estate, knew the bare bones of Skip's past and the reasons behind her occasionally out-of-place behaviour, but if he was honest about it, he didn't really understand what she'd been through.

"That's what my father always told me," Skip said, sounding unhappy. "A proper young lady shouldn't sit on the floor, or climb on things, or go barefoot, or go outside without her hair done properly, or..." She smacked the trunk of the tree suddenly. "I hate him! Fuck... he never let me swear, either. Fuck, fuck, fuck!"

Kwan grinned at that one. Goodness knows there was enough swearing around the Den for Skip to have picked it up fairly quickly.

"I don't know who I am!" Skip told him suddenly, plaintively. "I was supposed to be all polite and proper, and dignified, and then you want me to climb trees and run around on the grass barefoot, and I don't know what I'm supposed to be!"

That, at least, Kwan could relate to. His own parents had assumed he would be a doctor. No asking him what he thought of the idea, or if there was something else he might have preferred to do with his life, and coming to the Den had been an eye-opening adventure into a staggering range of possibilities. From the sounds of it, Skip had been experiencing something very similar, a round peg being shoved into a square hole.

"Okay," he said, thinking fast. "How about this..." He crouched down on the ground, gesturing Skip and Aaron down with him, and they huddled together at the base of the tree like children about to share a closely guarded secret. "You know how caterpillars have two lives," Kwan said. "They start out as little green worm things, and crawl around and eat and eat and eat... and all the while, they have no idea what they're going to turn into. And then one day, they suddenly come out of their cocoon, and discover they have wings. But," he said, in a conspiratorial tone, "I don't think they realise what those wings are for. Not straight away. Can you imagine it, a bright new butterfly, sitting on a twig, thinking he needs to crawl around and eat leaves like he's been doing his whole life? I think when they come out of the cocoon, they're all horribly confused, and maybe they only learn to fly by accident. Like, a strong wind comes along, and knocks them off their twig, and then suddenly they discover what their wings are for. But then," he went on, looking Skip in the eye seriously, "they discover how much fun flying is, and they can hardly stop themselves from doing it. So maybe you're like that," he suggested hopefully. "Maybe you've just turned into a butterfly, but because it's all so new, you haven't quite figured out how to be the new you. And that's okay, because everyone goes through that. We all have to grow, and learn, and try new things to see who we're supposed to be.

"So try doing some new things. Try climbing a tree. Maybe you'll like it, and want to do it some more. Maybe you won't like it, but that doesn't mean there's anything wrong with it. It just means you're not a tree-climbing butterfly. Maybe you're a swimming-in-the-lake butterfly. Or a rolling-in-the-snow butterfly. But unless you try, how will you ever find out?"

Skip stared up at the tree, thinking the idea through… and a slow smile spread across her face. "Okay," she said simply. "So let's try climbing a tree."

With a grin, Kwan stood up. "Watch carefully," he said, lacing his fingers together and offering his hands to Aaron, who carefully placed his foot in the support. And then Kwan hoisted him up onto the first branch. He scrabbled about, trying to find hand and foot holds, and then he was standing on the branch, grinning down at Skip as she watched on in excitement. "Make sure you're always holding on with at least one hand," Kwan told her, readying himself to hoist her up the same way. "Don't stand on any branch that's dead, even if you think it looks stable. And most importantly… remember to have fun."

CHAPTER NINE

April 20th

Silas was waiting in the foyer for Skip and Simon to join him. It was six months since Skip had joined the Den, and lately, Simon had reluctantly admitted that she was rapidly surpassing him in regard to the various hacking and security tasks he was in charge of.

The latest discussion the pair had apparently had involved Skip's growing concern that the Den's computers were in serious need of an upgrade. After a prolonged discussion with Baron and Anna, they'd been given leave to replace them with faster and more powerful machines. The Noturatii were doubtlessly employing the latest and greatest computer gadgetry in their quest to exterminate the shifters, Simon had pointed out, and so if they were going to hold their own in the Endless War, Il Trosa was going to have to make a few serious investments into technology themselves.

Today was the big shopping trip. Simon had located a computer warehouse in Manchester that was likely to have everything they needed – the sort of place frequented by computer nerds and people buying company supplies, rather than by the general public – and Silas was going along as their bodyguard. Skip had been bouncing off the walls for days in anticipation of the excursion, and Silas had to smile as she came dashing into the foyer now. She skidded to a stop, smiling at him gleefully, then hovered near the door. It was likely both a sign of her eagerness to be on their way, and her normal wariness around him. While she was always friendly and polite to him, he'd also noticed that she always made a point to give him a wide berth, and in return, he made an effort not to impinge on her space.

Five minutes passed, and Silas checked his watch. No sign of Simon, so he took out his phone and dialled his number. In a house as big as this one, it was usually quicker to call a person than run around trying to track them down. And two minutes later, he had his answer.

"Bad news," he said to Skip as he hung up. "The server's just crashed. Simon's working overtime to try and get it working again, so he said he's going to have to take a raincheck on the shopping."

Skip's shoulders sagged almost comically. "Damn server," she complained. "Couldn't have waited two more days until we got a new one." She pouted and let out a sigh. And then she pulled out her phone, quickly getting Simon back on the line. Another brief chat, in which Skip seemed to be trying to convince him to come, and then she passed the phone to Silas.

"Hey, what's happening?" he asked, putting it to his ear.

"Skip has a point," Simon said, his voice muffled as if his phone was tucked under his chin while he continued working. "We're going to need the new server sooner or later. But Skip knows enough about what else we need to find the right stuff. So if she's okay with it, you may as well take her without me, and then at least I can just load the data onto the new server, rather than trying to get this pile of shit to work again."

After he'd hung up, Silas handed the phone back to Skip. "So how about it?" he asked, assuming Simon had already told her she could go without him. "Just you and me?"

Skip nodded. "No problem." She was out the door in an instant, bouncing down the steps towards the garage. Silas did one last check of his guns and knives, and headed after her-

"I'm coming with you," Caroline declared, appearing out of the sitting room where she had apparently been listening in on the conversation.

"What? Why?"

"Skip spending half a day alone with a man? Are you nuts? She'll feel better with a woman along."

"Skip said she was fine with it," Silas argued. "And even if Simon was coming, it would still be her on her own with two men, so no big difference there."

"I'm coming," Caroline said, folding her arms defiantly.

"Not unless you can give me one good reason why."

"Because Skip is scared of men," Caroline said, slowly, as if she was trying to reason with an idiot.

Silas raised an eyebrow. "And yet she spends hour after hour closeted away with Simon in that dim little IT office, and no one bats an eyelid. I don't think you're worried about her spending the afternoon with a man. I think you're worried about her spending time *with me*."

Caroline didn't deny it. Instead, she stepped closer, pointing a finger at his chest. "I've heard the rumours," she said coldly. "I've heard what you did back in Afghanistan. Baron seems to think you're harmless as a day old puppy, but I disagree. So know this: if I find out you've laid so much as one little finger on her, I will *gut* you."

Silas's mild scowl deepened into one of genuine menace. He closed the distance between them, so they were standing chest to chest, barely an inch of air between them.

"You listen to me, you mangy upstart. You know *nothing* of what I went through before I came here. Skip is a part of my family. This is the family I fight for. The family I bleed for. And the family I kill for. So I will *never* hurt her. Nor will anyone else, so long as I am breathing. You understand me?"

The battle of wills went on a moment longer, each of them trying to stare down the other. At last, Caroline gave a nod. Looked away. Stepped back. "Good," she said simply. Then she turned and stalked away.

Four hours later, Silas was feeling totally exhausted. Simon had called ahead, and the warehouse had set aside the model of server they were after, but Skip had taken her time perusing the rest of the toys on offer. Laptops, monitors, wireless routers, a scanner, two printers, nine different types of cables, gadgets and widgets galore as more and more things that Silas had never even heard of were added to their pile of purchases.

The sales assistant had seemed surprised at the size of their haul, so Silas had felt compelled to explain. They worked for a company in Italy, he'd said conversationally, while Skip went about her work, but they were opening an office in England and needed the full set of computer equipment for their new staff.

"She seems a little young for this," the assistant had said softly, not wanting Skip to overhear, and Silas had forced a laugh. "Would you believe she's nineteen?" he said, lying through his teeth. "Something of a genius, as I'm led to believe. Finished a computer science degree in two years, and was snapped up the moment she graduated. I don't know anything about this shit myself," he said with a smirk, gesturing to the rows of machines around them. "I'm just here to pay the bills." The assistant had laughed at that, and asked no more questions, much to Silas's relief.

And so, after two hours of traipsing around the shop, Silas had brought the van around to the rear door, helping the delivery men load their numerous boxes into the back of the van. When the last box was loaded, he slammed the door and joined Skip inside the van. It was getting late, and if they didn't hurry, they would hit peak hour traffic. With a two hour drive as it was, Silas wasn't inclined to waste any more time.

The lane was deserted, numerous warehouses backing onto the narrow road, and he eased back towards the main road carefully, large bins and blind corners making it a tight squeeze to get out-

Silas slammed on the brakes as he rounded a corner, and cursed blackly.

"Get down," he snapped at Skip, already drawing his gun. "And stay in the car." There were four men standing in the middle of the road waiting for them, and though he couldn't imagine how they had found them, Silas would have bet a year's pay that they were from the Noturatii. Damned vermin had a knack for showing up in the most unlikely of places. Which was why it was a rare thing for anyone to leave the estate without a bodyguard.

"Gentlemen," he said grimly, as he climbed out of the van. "Mind stepping out of the way? We were just leaving."

The men grinned. Drew their own weapons with a casual confidence that said they didn't expect one man to be much of a challenge. And then Silas was launching himself into a fight for his life, as the men attacked as one.

Silas stared around himself, breathing hard. The carnage was complete. The four Noturatii men lay dead on the floor. One was missing a hand, though Silas didn't remember cutting it off. The bloody knife in his hand confirmed that he must have done.

One of the men was all but gutted, his insides spilling out over the concrete. Another was unrecognisable, a bullet to the head leaving him with only a pulpy red mess where his face had been.

Silas himself was covered in blood. It coated his hands, was splattered over his face and shirt. Dripped onto his boots. He was uninjured – years of training to become the most efficient killing machine had seen to that…

Where the hell was Skip? He looked around in a panic. In the middle of the fight, one of the men had broken away and gone for the van, ripping the passenger door open and Silas's heart had been in his throat as he'd heard Skip's terrified scream. He'd elbowed one man in the throat, stabbed another in the leg as he fought to get to her, but then she'd somehow managed to kick the man in the balls and darted for cover… and he'd lost track of her, as the fourth man had swung at him with a knife, forcing him to defend himself.

"Skip! Where are you?" He felt his heart lurch, both in dismay and relief when he saw her. She was curled into a ball, huddled behind a bin against a brick wall, arms around her knees, rocking slowly. But her eyes were fixed on him, wide and shell shocked, and he felt sick. Fucking hell. He'd been sent to protect her. To look after her and keep her safe. And while he might have succeeded physically, he'd clearly done a hatchet job on her psyche.

Heron would never forgive him.

God, he'd never forgive himself.

He wiped his hands on his jeans, leaving red smears, and tried to relax, to tone down his body language so he looked less like a maniacal killer and more like the sort-of-friend-slash-older-brother that Skip seemed to have accepted him as.

"Skip? Sweetie?"

Like a shot, she was up off the floor, moving so fast she caught even him by surprise. But she wasn't running away. Instead, he felt the impact of her small body before he'd even registered that she had moved. And he braced himself for the flailing of tiny fists, for curses and accusations...

But then instead, he instinctively wrapped his arms around her to catch her as she caught him in a full body hug, her arms squeezing tight around his shoulders, legs clinging tightly to his waist like she was drowning and he was a life raft.

They stood like that for a long moment, both of them shaking, and then he caught the tiniest whisper, murmured into his neck.

"Thank you."

What the hell?

He held her tighter, rubbing a soothing hand up and down her back, aware that he was leaving red smears of blood in the process, aware that the hand on her thigh would have left a bloody, macabre handprint just below her buttocks.

"Thank you," she said again, and Silas felt his world sway. What the fucking hell? She seemed to think he was the hero here. He'd just massacred four men in front of her. Dismembered. Gutted. And she'd decided he was some kind of saviour? There was no way in the world he could process that...

And yet, in that same moment, he felt his heart simultaneously break and knit itself back together again.

He was no hero. He'd failed a woman before, back in Afghanistan. He'd let his CO kill an innocent civilian in front of him. He'd arrived too late to prevent her from being raped, then stood by while a violent man whom Silas had trusted with his life had slit her throat, too shocked to do anything to stop him. Later, of course, he'd repaid the crime in full, murdering his CO and earning himself the scar that had nearly cost him his left eye. But it had been too late to save the woman.

And yet this time, he'd somehow succeeded. Saved her life, and apparently saved her sanity in the process.

What a damn, God-forsaken, fucked up mess.

"Shall we go home?" he asked softly, and felt Skip nod.

"Here..." He tried to set her down, prepared to lead her back to the van, but she clung on, determined to hold on to the only rock she could find in her crazy, messed up world.

And so he carried her. Carried her slowly back to the van. Eased the door open with two fingers. Set her on the seat, and then waited a moment longer until she saw fit to let him go. She curled up on the seat immediately, and he closed the door, hurrying around to the driver's side. He was half expecting her to panic when he opened the door and climbed in, but she didn't, merely leaned towards him, then uncurled her legs a fraction at his prompting that she do up her seatbelt.

It was daylight, a long drive back to the estate, and he prayed to a God he wasn't sure he still believed in that they make it back without incident. He didn't want to take the time to clean up now – didn't have the means to anyway, with no change of clothes or towel in the car to wipe the blood away. But if the police pulled him over for any reason, he'd likely be arrested for both murder and kidnapping. How else did you explain a man who looked like a violent thug, covered in blood and driving a van with a terrified teenager in the passenger seat?

After a time, staring at the road and taking care to take the turns smoothly, he reached for his phone. Sent a message to Baron, in code, as was their protocol. 'E90. 2IB. 4XN. 0J.' In translation, it meant 'ETA 90 minutes. Two people inbound. Four Noturatii members dead. Zero injuries.' In general, neither Il Trosa nor the Noturatii liked to leave dead bodies lying around, and both sides of the war tried to clean up whenever a fight went down. So if Baron wanted to know where the men had been killed, it would be a simple matter of looking up the GPS records of the van. The last point where they'd stopped would be the location of the bodies. But Silas put the mess he'd left behind out of his mind. Let the Noturatii deal with the fall out. Right now, he had exactly one job: take the girl he looked at as the daughter he'd never had, and get her home safely.

There was a reception waiting for him at the steps of the manor, and Silas pulled the van to a stop, glancing worriedly at Skip as he did so. She'd been silent for most of the drive, responding with single word answers to his enquiries about whether she was hurt. He'd explained that the men he'd killed were Noturatii, the shifters' sworn enemy, and she'd nodded, but said nothing.

Baron was front and centre outside the manor, Tank and Caleb beside him. Heron was there, a look of horror on her face, and Caroline, who looked like she wanted to kill someone. Probably him, but that was the least of his concerns.

He got out of the van and went around to the other side, opening Skip's door for her.

"She's not hurt," he said to Heron, as she came forward quickly, then turned to Baron. "Didn't have time to clean up," he said grimly, "so there'll likely be a report on a multiple homicide on the news. Get Alistair on it. It'll take some serious explaining to make this one go away." Simon arrived out of the front door, but when he saw Heron attending to Skip, he sighed, and left her to it. "Gear's in the back," Silas told him, aware that he looked a wreck, and seeing there was nothing else useful for him to do, Simon opened the door and set about unloading the equipment.

"Skip?" Heron was saying, trying to coax the girl out of the van. "Can you come out? I'll take you inside, and you can take a shower, or you can go to bed… You're safe now, sweetheart. Please, come on out…"

Skip shook her head, and her wide, fearful eyes met Silas's over Heron's shoulder. The look seemed to plead with him, and, astonished by the silent request, Silas went over, gently guiding Heron out of the way. "Come here, sweetie," he said, astonished all over again as Skip finally let go of the seat and eased towards him. He slid an arm around her back, and then she launched herself into his arms, legs wrapped around his waist as he picked her up again, much as he had the first time.

Beneath Heron's astonished gaze, and Caroline's outraged one, he headed for the house, carrying the girl up the stairs and into her bedroom. He set her on her bed, aware that he was probably leaving blood stains on the sheets, and gently unwrapped her limbs from around himself. "Sweetie? You're home. You're safe now. Heron's here. She's going to take care of you, okay?"

There were tears now, when her eyes had been dry for the entire trip home, and she nodded, wiped her nose on her sleeve and transferred her grip to Heron's arm, instead of Silas's.

"Don't go away," she whispered, as Silas eased off the bed.

"I'll be right down the hall," he said gently. "I'm not going far. And Heron's going to stay with you."

Another nod, then Silas let himself silently out of the room.

Caroline was waiting for him in the hall, and he braced himself for an earbashing about how he could have exposed Skip to that kind of danger.

Caroline looked him up and down, then glanced at the closed bedroom door, no doubt imagining what Skip looked like, curled up in a ball on her bed, hot tears running down her cheeks.

"It seems I was wrong about you," Caroline said finally. "I won't make that mistake again." With a wry kind of a smirk, she turned and walked away, leaving Silas with the feeling that this was the weirdest fucking day of his entire life.

CHAPTER TEN

May 11th

"Nine…" Silas counted slowly, as Skip fought to complete the last few push ups in the set. "And ten. Excellent. Well done." He helped her to her feet, giving her a moment to recover as she caught her breath. "Enough for today?" he asked, as she stretched the tired muscles in her arms, and Skip nodded. Since their run-in with the Noturatii, she had suddenly started taking her training a whole lot more seriously. Rather than the playful laughter of her previous sessions, she now fought against Caroline with a hardened focus that left even Silas impressed. It was now a regular routine that he worked with her on strength training twice a week, took her for long jogs up the hill, keeping his pace slow as Skip struggled to keep up, took her through sets of push ups, sit ups, lunges, until her muscles were screaming for a rest, but her mind refused to give up, pushing her on until she was wilting with exhaustion. He'd made an effort not to push her too hard at first, but had quickly realised that if she didn't feel she'd done enough for the day, she'd just go back to her room and do more, another set of push ups, ten more squats, more practising her kicking from her martial arts lessons.

To give her a break from the more physical side of her training, Silas had another plan in mind now, one that he'd cleared with Baron just that morning.

"I have a surprise for you," he said, leading Skip out of the gym. But instead of heading upstairs to the foyer, he led her down the long hallway and into the old cellar that the Den used for their firearms practice. The dirt walls insulated the sound, keeping the neighbours from getting alarmed, and also provided a safe place for practice without the need to spend a fortune on a custom built facility.

"Now, this," he said, unlocking the gun cabinet and selecting a weapon, "is a twenty-two calibre semi-automatic handgun." Skip's eyes opened wide, utterly captivated as she stared at the weapon. "In normal everyday use, this is not powerful enough for anything we'd need it for. But it's an ideal gun to learn on, because it's light and it has minimal recoil." He spent a few minutes going through some basic gun safety, showed her how to hold the gun and explained how it worked, and Skip listened with solemn attention all the way through. He showed her how to load it, and re-emphasised the importance of not aiming it at anything that she didn't actually want to shoot. Then he took out two pairs of earmuffs, handing her one, and putting the other on himself.

Skip looked torn between fascination and fear as she took the small gun in her hands and stepped up to the firing line. She lined up the shot carefully, as he'd shown her, bit her lip, held her breath… and pulled the trigger.

A squeal of glee left her mouth, and she put the gun down and ripped off her earmuffs, bouncing up and down in excitement. "That's so awesome!"

Silas brought the target forward. The shot was well off centre, not surprising, given this was her first shot, but Skip was excited at seeing the results of her work nonetheless. "Not bad for a first try. Let's give it another go."

May 12th

Caroline was aware of Silas watching her and Skip in their latest sparring session, and for once, he looked pleased with the girl's progress. Skip had gone from a timid, awkward girl to a poised fighter, her stance becoming more grounded, her focus sharper, each of her blows being made to count. And while she still had a long way to go, Silas had told her just yesterday that he was confident that one day she'd be able to hold her own in a fight against the Noturatii.

"She's improving," Silas said to Caroline, once the lesson was over and Skip was heading back towards the house. "As are you."

"I have a good teacher," Caroline said gruffly. Since the incident at the computer warehouse, she'd lost some of her usual antagonism towards Silas, and their regular training sessions had progressed more quickly because of it. And if she was honest, Caroline was finding that her skills had improved considerably. Since beginning the extra training, she'd challenged both Luke and Simon to status fights, and won both rounds. Now she was ranked just below Raniesha. But Raniesha was a firecracker, tough, determined, and every bit as gutsy as Caroline. And given that the fight wouldn't affect the ranking of any of the males in the Den, Caroline was in no rush to challenge the woman.

But as she wiped herself with a towel and gathered her things, she caught Silas watching her, an odd expression on his face. "With the number of new recruits we've got going on, there are bound to be a few reshuffles in the ranking over the next year or two," he said speculatively. "It would be as well to see how far you could climb the ranks now. Just to escape some of the squabbling later."

Caroline tilted her head, suspicious as to his motives. Why did it matter to him where she was ranked?

"You could easily best Raniesha," he mused, feigning disinterest. "Possibly even Heron."

And then Caroline saw where he was going with this. She glanced around to check that no one else was nearby. Conversations like this could easily lead to trouble, and since she was nowhere near ready for what Silas was talking about, there was no sense in making waves. "I'm not challenging Anna for alpha," she hissed, annoyed that he would even bring it up. "No one would support me. And besides which, I'd have to beat *you* in a fight to get there, and we both know that's not going to happen."

"I'm not saying you should go all gung-ho and head for the top job right now," he said, rolling his eyes at her. "A little realism, please. But Anna's not going to be alpha forever. So sooner or later, there's going to be a gap at the top of the ladder. And *someone's* going to have to step up."

Caroline was reluctant to admit it, but Silas was right. She glanced around again, seeing Raniesha loitering near the edge of the lawn. She was a tall woman, but lighter than Caroline. She had refined skills with explosives and guns, but her combat skills, particularly in wolf form, had never been her strong suit. Perhaps Silas had a point after all. It would be nice to sidestep some of the status fights that would be inevitable later in the year. And if nothing else, it would be nice to test out her new skills, to see just how far she was able to go.

"I'll think about it," she said, not wanting to make any firm promises, and particularly not willing to weigh in on the debate about their current alpha for the time being. But later tonight, or maybe tomorrow... it wouldn't do any harm to track Raniesha down and challenge her to a fight...

CHAPTER ELEVEN

October 20th – 17 months later

Skip stood in the centre of the circle of shifters, shaking with fear. It was two years since Heron had found her in the park, two long, blissful years in which she'd lived with her new family, learned the lore of the shifters, developed new skills and confidence, and put some of the ghosts of her past to rest. Nia, her therapist, had stayed on for just over a year, holding therapy sessions three times a week. Skip's panic attacks had decreased from once a week, to once a month, and then to once every two months, and it was now four months since she'd had one at all. She'd drawn pictures and written stories about her old life, breaking down the shame and fear she felt about her past and the things she'd had to do to survive.

And now, after two years of training and education, the night had finally arrived when Skip was to take the final step in becoming one of her pack, being converted into a shape shifter.

The idea itself was thrilling. Skip had seen enough of the skills and tricks of the wolves over the past two years to embrace the conversion wholeheartedly. The shifters had performed a beautiful ceremony, with chants, incense, storytelling and the sharing of spiced mead, along with prayers to Sirius, the Wolf God. Skip had actually been brought to tears a few times throughout the ceremony, touched by the deep care the pack showed for its members and the intricacies of their spiritual life.

But now it was time for the final part of the ceremony, and Skip was terrified.

Silas and Caleb had set up the conversion machine around her, a wide circle of wires and metal pillars that was going to inflict a small electrical shock to her wrist. Tank stood beside her, her chosen sire, whose blood was to be mixed with her own in order to catalyse the conversion. And

Heron stood before her, holding a long, sharp knife in her hand, waiting for Skip to acquiesce to the final trial before she could become a wolf. Heron was going to slit her wrist, a long, deep cut that would let her blood flow freely, mingling with a matching cut on Tank's wrist.

Thinking about how much it would hurt was horrifying.

Skip stood still as a statue, breathing hard, trying to work up the courage to offer her wrist to the woman who had become her adoptive mother. Without being cut, she couldn't become a wolf…

The shifters stood silently around her, waiting patiently. Not one of them made any attempt to hurry her up. This ritual had been explained to her in detail. She'd even seen it done before, when Eric had been converted, and she'd firmly declared her intention to go through with it. But now that it was time to actually do it, she found it harder than she had imagined.

"Courage, little sprite," Tank murmured to her, waiting to take the knife from Heron and cut his own wrist. "It'll all be over soon."

That was the key, Skip realised. The anticipation was almost worse than the cut itself, and so she held her breath, closed her eyes and thrust her wrist forward. Heron wasted no time, just held her wrist firmly and made the cut quickly and cleanly, while Skip clenched her fists and gritted her teeth. A moment later, Tank had repeated the action, and placed his wrist over her own. Heron wrapped a wide cuff around their joined arms, then retreated out of the circle. Skip felt a sharp zap of electricity, and then the cuff was being removed… and she dared to open her eyes for the first time. Heron was back beside her, Silas and Caleb already packing up the machine, and Skip waited, nerves taut, trying to detect any change within herself. The conversion worked ninety-nine percent of the time, but there was still a small risk something could go wrong…

What the hell was that? Skip felt a surge within herself, a sudden wave of courage, a fierceness at odds with her own tremulous fear… and an odd sense of protectiveness that came from within, and yet was not a part of her.

The wolf. She had to merge with it, she knew, accept it wholeheartedly and embrace its desires and demands as her own. But that was impossible, when the wolf was wild and confident and powerful, and she was so small and timid and fearful.

She felt a wave of electricity creep up her spine, a strange presence entering her mind, and felt an odd sense of reassurance from a much more powerful being. Peace, the creature seemed to say. Courage. Embrace the night, and become one with the wind and the trees and the stars.

The stars were bright tonight, Skip realised, looking up. The air was crisp, the leaves beautiful in the dim light of the dozen torches that burned all around them. The power was not her own, she knew, but she could accept it, embrace it as it covered her, protecting her, promising to hold her safe. Her hands touched the grass, and Skip realised they had become paws. She scented the air again, receiving a thousand subtle messages on the slightest breeze, her new wolf senses a hundred times sharper than her human ones. And as she looked out into the darkness, she could feel the shifters around her, feel their very souls with her own, deeper and more complex than they had been before.

The wolf wagged its tail, bounded over to Heron and barked once, a joyful sound full of strength and richness. The Chant of Forests started up around her, a solemn pledge from her pack to guide her and protect her all the days of her life.

An unspoken question from the spirit of the wolf, and Skip replied with a wholehearted 'yes'. Welcome, wolf-kin, she told the spirit. Welcome to the night, to the wilderness, to the Endless War and the quest for a brighter future.

SHIFTERS OF THE LAKES DISTRICT DEN
PRESENT DAY

Rank	Name	Age
1	Baron	38
2	Caroline	35
3	Tank	34
4	Silas	46
5	Andre	40
6	Heron	61
7	John	Unknown. Mid twenties.
8	Raniesha	43
9	Dee	27
10	Simon	38
11	Alistair	35
12	Kwan	26
13	Cohen	33
14	Skip	24
15	Aaron	25
16	George	72
17	Mark	28

PART TWO
PRESENT DAY

CHAPTER TWELVE

Jack Miller sat on his couch in his flat in east London, a glass of whiskey in his hand and a sick feeling in his stomach.

The past few days had been an unmitigated disaster, and he'd been granted two weeks' leave from his job as security guard for the Noturatii as a result, time to regroup and deal with the serious losses the organisation had sustained. Losses that were a direct result of Miller's actions.

A few days ago, Jacob Green, the head of the organisation's British Division, had found evidence that one of the shape shifters on their records was in Scotland; a man whom the Noturatii had captured early in the year, and who had subsequently escaped during a violent raid by the rest of the shifter pack. Eager to recapture their escapee, Miller had put together a team and launched an attack on the remote property, expecting it to be a relatively straight forward exercise. They'd taken fourteen men on the raid, more than enough for the anticipated handful of shifters they were likely to find.

Instead, they'd stumbled into a god-damned shifter convention, fifty wolves banding together to defend their territory with relentless force, and Miller's entire team had been slaughtered. Thirteen men, some with wives or families, dead because of his mistakes. Miller himself had only escaped with his life due to another tragedy – the death of a young hiker who had wandered onto the property and been caught up in the battle, and he'd been allowed to leave so that he could use his connections in the Noturatii to sweep her death neatly under the rug.

Guilt at all the deaths on his hands had been gnawing at him, and he'd requested leave on the official grounds that he needed time to come to grips with his own mistakes.

But the truth was far more complicated than that. In addition to the guilt of the loss of his team mates, he'd been harbouring doubts about the

Noturatii's agenda for months, small clues as to the shifters' true nature adding up to weigh heavily on him. In Scotland, he'd seen convincing evidence that, far from the mindless beasts and dangerous terrorists that the Noturatii painted the shifters to be, they were, in fact, kind, intelligent and compassionate people. Which brought Miller's entire future into question.

The Noturatii worked underground, a covert organisation with the highest levels of secrecy, and once a member of staff knew the truth about the existence of the shape shifters, the only way anyone ever left the organisation was in a body bag.

But knowing what he did now, Miller couldn't continue to work for them, his conscience plaguing him, his nights sleepless, his days a quagmire of doubts and guilty thoughts.

So now he had two weeks in which to concoct a plan that would allow him to escape the organisation's clutches. An organisation who treated detractors with a brutal policy of torture and bloodshed. An organisation with access to some of the most highly trained assassins the world had ever seen. An organisation who had a long reach, with offices right across Europe and extending into Russia, China and the United States.

Miller downed the remainder of his whiskey, and reached for the bottle to refill the glass. Unless he came up with a solid plan soon, one that would disguise his treachery and outwit some of the most intelligent minds in the world... he was a dead man.

CHAPTER THIRTEEN

Dee rushed to keep up as she followed Eleanor up the steps into the villa that the Italian shifters called home. They'd landed in Venice just over two hours ago, after flying in from England that morning, and the drive to the Italian Den in Agordo had been silent and fraught with tension.

Caleb, one of Dee's Den mates, had also been on the flight, having recently been recruited to serve the Council as a historian, keeping records of their species and translating the ancient texts from the old language, and he'd been collected at the airport and taken directly to the Council's villa in Cison de Valmarino.

Dee, unfortunately, had a much grimmer task ahead of her: she was going to kill someone. The Italian Den had a new recruit who had been converted into a shifter a couple of days ago, and the conversion hadn't taken. The woman had been unable to merge with her wolf, and the pair of them were now headed down the slippery slope of insanity, the wolf turning rogue, the human going mad. At the request of the Council, it was now her job to remove the human half of the shifter, killing the woman, but allowing the wolf to live. The wolf would then be taken to Romania and looked after in a wolf sanctuary that was being set up there.

It was a unique skill that Dee had, one that she had discovered earlier in the year. Most shifters were a seamless blend of their human and wolf sides, one mind, with two bodies. But soon after her conversion, Dee had realised she was different. Her wolf was a separate personality, a distinct consciousness; they were two minds, each with their own body to inhabit, albeit that only one body could be present at a time. Faeydir, as her wolf was known, was the reincarnation of an ancient wolf, Fenrae-Ul, the Destroyer, prophesied to bring about the extinction of the wolf shifters. She alone held the ability to separate human from wolf.

It was a horrible task, and Dee had only agreed to it because she knew the alternative was for both human and wolf to be put down. A rogue wolf was insane, aggressive, violent, no longer a sapient being, but a violent force of nature. As unfortunate as it was, the rogue shifter could not be allowed to live.

Aware of her distress, Faeydir gave her a mental nudge, then sent her an image of a female wolf, strong and healthy, running through a snow-covered forest; a clear reminder that one half of this story would have a happy ending, even if the other was a stark tragedy, and Dee tried to focus on that more positive outcome of the situation.

She and Eleanor were clearly expected, Antonio, the Den's alpha meeting them at the door. After a brief introduction, they followed him through the villa, out the back door and across the lawn to a stone building, a little larger than a double garage. Antonio wordlessly opened the door and ushered them inside.

There were six people already inside the building, three men and three women. One of the men was clearly a guard, standing beside a large cage with a gun in his hand and a look of sorrow on his face. Inside the cage was a woman, curled up in the corner, and as the three of them hurried inside, she snarled and wailed at them, beating on the bars with her fists. There was no doubt she was a rogue, Dee observed grimly, incoherent sounds coming from her throat, her eyes wide and fearful, her movements jerky and uncoordinated.

But before she could concentrate on the woman too much, Eleanor turned to the others, waiting quietly by the wall.

"Dee, this is Feng," Eleanor introduced her quickly, indicating an Asian man. "And Rafael," – a man who looked to be of South American descent, "and Paula," – a woman with pale blonde hair. "They're from the Council. And this is Mirela," she said, turning to the last woman. "She's an assassin." Of course, Dee thought, offering the woman a tight smile. No doubt she was charged with putting the rogue down, if anything went wrong.

"She's been getting worse," Feng reported, glancing at the caged woman. "I'm afraid we're running out of time."

"I'll get things set up," Mirela volunteered immediately, and for a moment, Dee wondered just what preparations were necessary. When she'd done this before, it had been as simple as reaching out with a kind of psychic energy to feel the two halves of the shifter and pulling them apart. But then her stomach lurched as she saw Mirela take an object out of a box in the corner and realised that it was a camera.

"What's that for?"

"We'd like to film the separation," Rafael said apologetically. "Seeing it in person is one thing, but the rest of the Council will want to see how it was done, and we may need to analyse the footage later. It seemed a prudent step to take. There are also receivers set up around the room to record any fluctuation in electromagnetic radiation."

Dee was disgusted at the frank explanation. "You all seem to think this is a fascinating experiment," she snapped, irritated by their calm curiosity. "I'm about to kill another human being. You could show a little compassion." In general, speaking to the Council in such a tone was a gross breach of protocol. But given the circumstances, Dee didn't feel inclined to go through the usual process of fawning over the shifters' version of aristocracy.

"We are certainly not without concern for Claudia," Eleanor said gently. "But you also have a unique and dangerous skill. That is the other purpose in you coming to Italy, after all – for us to develop a better understanding of your talents."

"We care for each and every one of our brethren," Paula said, her tone a touch sharper than Eleanor's had been. "But none of us can forget that we also have the responsibility of safeguarding our entire species. The opportunity to study your talents cannot be overlooked."

Dee was not the slightest bit mollified by their words. "At the expense of the dignity of one of your own? That's hardly reassuring."

"It must be a happy luxury to have only one life to worry about," Mirela said condescendingly, as she finished her preparations, "rather than the weight of three thousand resting on your shoulders."

Dee bristled under her disdain. It was not at all what she had expected from an assassin. Andre, another of the Council's assassins, had spent the past few months with Dee's Den in England, and after seeing his genial ways and almost excessive politeness, the reprimand was a rude shock. But to Dee's dismay, she quickly realised that Faeydir didn't share her offence over the assassin. She was a high ranking wolf, Faeydir pointed out. If she wanted to tell them off, she was well within her rights to do so.

Dee sighed. Okay, so maybe they had a point. This wasn't a display she could easily repeat, after all, not without killing someone else, and she grudgingly had to admit that recording the event held a certain logic. Even if it seemed disrespectful to Claudia at the same time.

She glanced at Claudia, who was now huddled at the back of the cage, whimpering, and realised an immediate obstacle to her task. "If I'm going to remove the human, then she's going to have to be in wolf form," she explained to the waiting Councillors.

The men and women around her seemed surprised – no doubt they would be asking plenty of questions about this later – but Antonio didn't bat an eyelid. He went to a fridge nestled in the corner and took out a bowl containing a steak.

He crouched down near the cage, holding out the steak and muttering soft words in Italian to Claudia. She seemed to calm for a moment, eyes fixed on the meat, and licked her lips. Antonio kept talking to her in soft, gentle words as he eased closer, Claudia slowly coming forward... and then the woman shifted.

The instant she was in wolf form, her entire demeanour changed. Instead of focusing on the steak, she put her head down, hackles up, teeth bared as she snarled at Antonio. He tossed the steak into the cage, snapping his hand back as sharp canine teeth tried to take a bite.

"Stand back," Dee said sharply, not knowing how long it would be before the woman decided to shift back. And given the strength of her abilities, she didn't want anyone else in the way, getting caught up in the magic.

She stepped forward and reached inward, letting Faeydir come to the fore. Invisible hands seemed to reach out in front of her, two waves of energy which felt for the two halves of the shifter, took a firm hold of them both, and yanked...

The wolf let out a scream, flailing about the cage in a panic. Faeydir lingered a moment longer, Dee's skin crackling with static electricity, and then she retreated. Dee felt something warm and furry brush her neck – not a real sensation, but the memory of one – and thanked Faeydir for the gesture of concern. She would be fine, she told the wolf, even as tears gathered in her eyes.

After a moment or two of whining and struggling, the wolf went still, collapsing onto the floor of the cage. Her rapid breathing gradually evened out, and eventually she lifted her head. Looked around. Saw the people watching her, but oddly, didn't seem at all alarmed by the audience. She sat up, sniffed around... and delicately picked up the steak with her teeth, setting about devouring the meal with a huff and a wag of her tail.

The Council members were staring at her, seeming surprised that it was over so quickly. "Is that it?" Feng asked.

But Dee didn't hang around to explain. She couldn't stand being in this room a moment longer, and she quickly headed for the door, rudely pushing Eleanor out of the way when she didn't move fast enough, and escaping into the afternoon air. The sky was a brilliant blue, the sun out, but Dee felt like she was smothered in a dark fog, tears spilling out of her eyes as she dashed across the lawn and sought refuge in a thick pocket of bushes. She sank down onto the ground, gasping for breath, grief and guilt warring in her mind. She felt her skin crackle, and she retreated willingly as Faeydir emerged. The wolf was closely attuned to her emotions, and was willing to take over for a while, to give Dee time to recover from the awful task.

Eleanor was right behind her, arriving just in time to see the end of the shift, and she slowed to a halt with a sigh.

"I'm sorry," she said, sinking down beside Faeydir. "I know that was unpleasant. But it was by far the lesser of two evils, and-"

Eleanor trailed off as Faeydir picked herself up and gave her a short bark. Tail high, she retraced Dee's steps back towards the shed, then slunk inside, going right up to the cage. Eleanor followed, baffled by the wolf's behaviour.

Faeydir sniffed the cage and the captive wolf, then rose up on her hind legs and batted the lock. She glanced back at Eleanor and barked again.

"What? You want me to let her out?"

Faeydir nodded, recognising the confusion in the humans as they glanced at each other. Baffling creatures, they were, always making things more complicated than they needed to be.

"Let's see what she does," Mirela suggested, coming forward with the key. Faeydir whined and licked her leg as she opened the lock, a gesture of respect for the powerful wolf.

Claudia – or the wolf that remained of her – put her head low and slunk towards Faeydir. She was a weak wolf, newly created and not sure of her surroundings. But Faeydir wagged her tail, bounced her front end down slightly – an invitation to play – and darted off a few steps towards the door.

Claudia followed, cautious until she got to the door and saw the wide lawn and the bright sun. Her whole body relaxed at once. She bounded out the door, giving chase as Faeydir ran across the lawn, tongue lolling out, tail high, and the pair of them dashed off into the bushes, newfound friends bent on adventure.

CHAPTER FOURTEEN

Eleven Council members were gathered around a long meeting table. Normally there would have been twelve of them, but after one of their members had died earlier in the year, the careful process of selecting a replacement was still ongoing.

After witnessing the shifter's separation in Agordo, the four attending Councillors, along with Dee, had returned to the Council's villa in Cison de Valmarino. Now Dee was resting, while the Council discussed her unusual talents.

"I must say," Feng began, "I'm rather baffled by her reaction to the separation, considering what the prophecy says about her. She was grief-stricken after killing just one person. It's hard to see how we go from there, to Dee wiping out the entire species."

"Don't discount her so quickly," Paula said. "A year ago, if anyone had asked her, no doubt she would have scoffed at the idea of abandoning her family and becoming a wolf shifter. She was converted by force, thanks to the Noturatii, but since then, she's wholeheartedly accepted the conversion and her new life. She's shown extreme resilience under the most trying of circumstances. Who's to say what could happen in the future that could cause an even more dramatic change in her."

"Only a few months ago, we were contemplating having Mark put down," Elise added, the youngest member of the Council, referring to Dee's boyfriend, who had betrayed his Den and faced serious punishment as a result. "If we'd gone ahead with his execution, Dee might well have let her grief open the way for a long campaign of revenge. It's entirely possible that some other similar dilemma in the future might cause her to rethink her compassionate ways."

"I think we're missing an important detail here," Rafael interrupted. "Dee herself seemed quite distressed with the separation. But her wolf half was remarkably unaffected by it. Faeydir took Claudia off to play and seemed rather delighted by the whole thing. And we must keep in mind that they're two separate people, for all that they share a body. Perhaps it's not Dee we need to worry about, but Faeydir."

"It's a valid point. Prophecies can be a tricky thing," Feng agreed. "Faeydir is indeed the reincarnation of Fenrae-Ul, but the prophecy doesn't mention Fenrae's new host. It simply says that Fenrae shall be restored to life, and *'under her reign, the shyfters shalle be restor'd to the natural order.'* Under Fenrae's reign, not Dee's. It's entirely possible that Dee may object to the whole thing, but Faeydir, as Fenrae's reincarnation, has every intention of destroying us."

"We need to find out more about Faeydir," Eleanor said. "Dee maintains that she's a peaceable wolf with no grudge against us, but we have only her word on the matter. And Dee herself has admitted that at times she has trouble understanding what the wolf is saying."

"Then we should also concentrate on helping her understand the wolf better," Feng added. "She's our only link to being able to communicate with Faeydir."

"I agree," Eleanor said, and the other Councillors murmured their support for the idea. "For the moment, Dee's resting – she's still quite upset about Claudia. But in the meantime, we also need to finalise our selection of the new Councillor. Even once someone is chosen, it'll take weeks before they've completed their initiation. And given the challenges we're going to be facing in the near future, I, for one, don't like leaving the position vacant for any longer than necessary."

Dee sat on a cushion in the villa's wide living room, in the middle of her first session with the Council as they began their investigations into her unusual wolf. There were four Councillors seated on the floor around her. She was aware of the camera set up at the side of the room, recording the entire conversation, and she tried not to feel self conscious about it. It was necessary, she understood, for the rest of the Councillors to be able to review the conversation and compile a list of questions later, as they hadn't wanted to overwhelm her by having the entire Council in the room all at once.

At the moment, they were discussing Faeydir's unexpected reaction to the separation they'd performed yesterday. And Dee had been rather dismayed to hear that the Council were concerned about Faeydir's apparent joy in the act. "All she was doing was trying to cheer me up," she said earnestly. "She's very in tune with my emotions, and knew I was very upset. She wanted to show me that the wolf was happy and unharmed, not revel in the fact that a human had died. I'm sorry if that came across as enjoyment of the act. Faeydir takes the separation as seriously as I do."

Eleanor nodded. "I see. And I'm sorry for the insensitive questions. This is new territory for all of us. As I'm sure you're aware, it can be difficult to understand the motivations of a creature who can't speak or explain herself directly."

Dee nodded, not inclined to take offence. The day before had been trying for all of them, and it was to be expected that the Councillors were feeling rather tense about the whole thing.

"Okay, let's move on then," Eleanor said gently. "We'd like to discuss the prophecy of Fenrae-Ul with your wolf, to see what her perspective on it is. Does she know the details of it?"

Dee nodded. "Yes. I read it in our library a while ago, and Faeydir remembers what it said."

"Excellent. The prophecy begins, *Thus be the truth of the wolfe Fenrae-Ul.*' Does Faeydir agree that that's her? Is she aware of being a reincarnation of another wolf?"

Dee concentrated, tuning in to the responses from her wolf, and she nodded. "Yes. She's aware that she's lived before. A long time ago. And she..." Dee paused, working to unravel the message, delivered to her in a blend of images, scents and emotions. For all that she was merged with a human, Faeydir had never taken to communicating in words, finding the language overly limiting – much as Dee would have had trouble trying to convey all her thoughts in simple mental images. "She's been waiting a long time for an opening in the spirit world, and is very pleased to be back in this world now."

"Remarkable," Eleanor said, a note of wonder in her voice. "The next part reads, *The daughter twice removed from Faeydir-Ul.*' In what sense is she the daughter of Faeydir-Ul? Shifters aren't able to have children, after all. Did Faeydir have a daughter before she was converted?"

Faeydir-Ul, or Origin Wolf, had been the first wolf shifter to ever exist, according to their mythology. Debate had raged for centuries about whether Faeydir-Ul was a real wolf, or a metaphorical figure, and Dee found herself rather curious about getting an answer to that question. "Yes... oh wow," she interrupted herself, the images coming from Faeydir detailed and vivid. "Yes, Faeydir-Ul was a real person. Fenrae was not her natural daughter." Dee closed her eyes, then pressed her fingers to her temples, fascinated by the story that was slowly being revealed to her. "After Faeydir-Ul was converted, she was used to convert a man. One of the men in her tribe. Apparently she wasn't happy about it – the tribe had to force her to complete the ritual. But a male shifter was created, and then he created more female shifters. So when did you...?" she said, directing her words to her wolf half the time, and to the Council the other half. She hoped they could follow her ramblings – she'd found it far easier to communicate with the wolf by voicing her side of the conversation aloud. "Oh, okay. Fenrae was converted ten years after Faeydir-Ul's conversion. So 'twice removed' means Faeydir-Ul converted the man, then the man converted Fenrae."

"So Faeydir-Ul was a real wolf?" Eleanor said. "Fascinating… And the next part: *The cause of the death of her mother's unhappy tale.*' We take that to mean that Fenrae will be the one to eradicate the shifters from the earth-"

"What?!" Dee suddenly exclaimed, shocked and alarmed at the sudden image in her mind of her wolf grinning happily, wagging her tail. "How the fuck is that a good thing?" she demanded, aware of the Councillors sitting around her in a sudden grim silence. An image in her mind, a woman, a shifter, then the wolf half separated out, moving to stand beside the woman. More tail wagging, along with a profound sense of satisfaction. "You want to kill people?" she demanded of the wolf, aghast by the idea.

Faeydir responded swiftly with the image of a wolf puppy, which tripped over its own feet and fell over. *You're as stupid as a new born puppy.* "Sorry," Dee apologised aloud. It wasn't the first time Faeydir had tried to tell her something, and Dee had misinterpreted her message, or failed to understand it at all. "But I don't understand. Please, explain that again." The Council were silent, patiently waiting for her to tease out the meaning of her conversation with the wolf, and privately, Dee was impressed by their self restraint. After her sudden outburst, she could well imagine that they had a thousand questions to ask.

Faeydir repeated the image – a woman, clad in buckskin, feathers in her hair. The wolf, separated, standing beside her. And then the woman collapsed to the ground, dead. A wave of satisfaction at the achievement.

Dee pondered the image for a long moment, knowing there were details she wasn't understanding. The image came again. A woman… *one* woman, Faeydir emphasised. This particular one, not all the rest.

"Who is she?" Dee asked, and Faeydir repeated the image she'd shown her before, of the first conversion Faeydir-Ul had performed. A young woman locked in a cage, angry and screaming abuse at those around her. Three strong men, dragging her out of the cage. A man, waiting nearby. Their wrists were cut, the wounds placed together, and then the man became a wolf. And then Faeydir very deliberately took the image of the woman – the original Faeydir-Ul – and superimposed her onto the image of the woman lying dead on the ground.

"Faeydir-Ul?" Dee asked in surprise. "You killed her?"

Faeydir shook her head. An image of a wolf, running free in the forest.

"You separated her?" Dee asked instead, no less shocked at the admission. "But why?"

Faeydir paused at that. It was a long story, a complex one, she seemed to say, and she wasn't sure if Dee wanted all the details now.

"Tell me," Dee said, knowing the story was too important to wait for another time. The Council would be interested, she was sure, and wouldn't mind waiting a while for the story to be told.

Faeydir walked her through it slowly, making sure she picked up on every important detail along the way, and as she did, Dee narrated what she saw to the people sitting around her. "Faeydir was a woman. A teenager. She lived with a tribe in ancient Europe. It looks... maybe stone age? Maybe a bit later. A shaman came to their village. He looks African. He offered the tribe magic. They accepted, and chose the girl for the ritual. She didn't want to do it... Oh God, that's horrible..." Dee paused, taking a deep breath as she tried to control her emotions, the images stark and confronting. "Did you actually see all of this?" she asked her wolf. Her human had, Faeydir replied, before she was converted. Fenrae the wolf hadn't been born yet, her being coming into existence when her first human partner had been converted. But that human had been a part of the tribe, had witnessed the original ritual.

"They trapped a wolf in the wild," Dee went on, as Faeydir picked up the story. "Brought her to the shaman. He used his magic to join their forms, creating the first shape shifter. He'd come from very far away, and was very powerful. The woman tried to resist, but the tribe overpowered her. But she couldn't merge with the wolf. That part of the story is true, at least," she added for the Council's benefit. "Faeydir-Ul lived at war with her wolf. She was a rogue. She went mad, and they put her in a cage, kept her locked up so she couldn't hurt anyone. She had a terrible life. Okay, fast forward ten years," she said, as Faeydir skipped over to her own creation. "Fenrae was created from a human who volunteered for the ritual. The shifters were multiplying and spreading at that time. The woman who became Fenrae-Ul was a healer. She used herbs to treat illnesses in her tribe. And after she was converted, she felt sorry for Faeydir-Ul, hated the way she was locked up, and the way the ritual had been forced upon her in the first place. So she used her abilities to remove the human from the wolf. Faeydir-Ul returned to being just a wolf, and Fenrae let her go, let her run off into the forest. It's not entirely clear what happened after that, but Fenrae saw her again, a few years later. She was doing well, healthy, happy. So it's likely she found a pack to join, and went back to living her life as a wild wolf." Dee opened her eyes, meeting the fascinated gazes all around her. "So Fenrae was *'the cause of the death of her mother's unhappy tale.'* She killed the human, so that the wolf could live, because Faeydir-Ul was rogue. The end to a most unhappy existence."

"Amazing." The four Councillors were staring at her with rapt attention. "Our myths say that Faeydir-Ul was originally a wolf – that the wolf was the instigator of the ritual to create the first shifter. You're saying it was a human? A shaman of some sort?"

"Or a god," Dee said, picking up on Faeydir's deep awe and respect for the man. "Faeydir suggests he might have been Sirius. Whether he was actually a human, or the incarnation of some spirit isn't clear, but he could well have convinced the people of that time that he was a deity. And as he created the first wolf shifters, perhaps they took his name, and turned him into a god, through generations of story telling."

The Council members looked stunned. "So we've had this completely wrong," Elise spoke up, after a heavy silence. "Fenrae isn't going to cause the death of her mother's entire people, because she's already killed Faeydir-Ul herself."

"I wouldn't jump to that conclusion quite so fast," Eleanor interrupted. "The rest of the prophecy still indicates a change in our current form: *'And under her reign, the shyfters shalle be restor'd to the natural order.'* What's Faeydir's take on that? Does she see shifters as somehow unnatural?"

Dee turned her attention inwards again, waiting for an explanation from her wolf… and was surprised to receive absolutely nothing in reply. She repeated the question, and felt a faint thread of puzzlement. "She doesn't know anything about it," Dee said, thoroughly confused herself. After the wealth of information Faeydir had flung at her so far, it was startling to find such a huge gap in the wolf's knowledge. "She has no idea how that's supposed to happen."

"How strange," Eleanor mused, watching Dee speculatively. The woman didn't believe her, Dee realised all of a sudden. She thought Dee was hiding something, lying to protect her wolf, perhaps. And Dee's easygoing attitude suddenly vanished. They had her here under false pretences, she realised, and Faeydir immediately agreed. All the platitudes about curiosity and helping her control her own abilities were a ruse designed to get her to cooperate, when they had actually brought her here to assess how great a threat she was to their species.

"Why don't you tell me why I'm really here," Dee said suddenly, not willing to be a pawn in the Council's game. "Because if there's one thing I really can't stand, it's being lied to."

CHAPTER FIFTEEN

Two Weeks Later

Silas pulled the sedan up beside the curb, glancing at the large hall where Skip would be spending the afternoon. "You sure you're going to be okay?" he asked, for the fifth time, as she gathered her things and got ready to get out of the car.

"I'm *fine*!" Skip insisted. "I'm going to a computer seminar, not a boxing match. Public place. College campus. No big deal."

"I should be staying with you."

"And how would it look for me to be sitting in there with my bodyguard? No one would talk to me. They'd all think I was totally weird. I mean, weird even for a computer nerd," she amended, knowing she probably came across as fairly weird anyway. "I'll be fine," she said again, opening the car door. "It finishes at nine, and I'll meet you right back here. So stop worrying."

Silas wasn't convinced, but there was little he could do about it at this point. "Be careful," he called, as she shut the door, and then she was gone, disappearing inside the hall where dozens of other students were going to spend the next few hours talking jargon and generally being nerds.

He waited a moment or two, making sure she made it inside okay, and then glanced around the area, looking for any suspicious types, men who seemed a little too watchful, jackets that could be hiding weapons. He was almost disappointed when he found nothing that he could justifiably be concerned about.

Checking his mirrors, he pulled out onto the road again and headed back to the estate. And began counting down the hours until it would be time to pick her up again.

Deep in the Kielder Forest in northern England, in the Grey Watch's eastern camp, Genna heard yelling from inside the tent, and quickly slunk out of the way, heading for the edge of the clearing, finding a dark patch of scrub to hide in. Sempre was in a mood again.

Moments later, the flap of the tent was flung open and an anxious looking male was forcefully ejected through the gap. "Get out!" Sempre snarled, appearing in the doorway, only half dressed. "If you can't perform, then I may as well geld you."

The male shifted immediately and scurried away, back to the other males waiting at the edge of the camp. Genna winced, feeling sorry for them. They were treated more as slaves than as shifters, able to be called upon at any time to service the sexual desires of any of the women, and this one had clearly failed to satisfy Sempre. It was hardly a surprise. With the woman constantly berating the men and criticising their skills in bed, it was no wonder they would develop a case of performance anxiety. Some of the other women were more considerate, but none of them really treated the men as people, as equals. They were pets, there to do the women's bidding, and nothing more.

Sempre disappeared back inside the tent, emerging a few moments later, her clothing straightened, her face wearing a harsh scowl. Genna looked away, not wanting to attract any attention to herself... but she was too late. Sempre stalked over, eager to give the pack's newest member another earbashing.

"Don't you have anything useful to do?" she snarled, seeing Genna lurking beneath the bush. She reached in and grabbed her by the scruff, dragging her out into the open. "Lying around all day like a fucking lump of dirt. You should be off catching some prey. Or doing some chores around here. The water tank's empty again. You could get a bucket and fetch some from the creek."

Yes, she could, Genna agreed. But if she did, then she would be scolded for spending too much time in human form. She could prepare some food, bake a new loaf of bread perhaps, but then be told off for being gluttonous. Or she could slink off into the forest and mind her own business, and then be accused of not caring enough about her pack. It was a constant lose-lose situation with this lot, so she tried to ignore Sempre now, while at the same time trying not to look belligerent about it.

"Human form," Sempre ordered suddenly. "I want to talk to you."

Wanted to yell at her was more likely, Genna thought blackly as she shifted. And she hardly needed to be in human form when Sempre wouldn't let her get a word in edgewise. But the opportunity to be out of wolf form was welcome, even if it was only for a few minutes, so she complied, waiting meekly for Sempre to say whatever it was that was on her mind.

"You've been here for more than six months now," Sempre began, eyeing Genna suspiciously. "And that's the time when most wolves develop their extra abilities, if they're going to. You've been keeping an eye out for that, haven't you." It was more an accusation than a question, and Genna kept her eyes down, not willing to interrupt her angry alpha. "No odd events you'd like to tell me about? No strange urges to seek out water? To go out in a lightning storm? Restless twitching of the skin?"

"No, ma'am," Genna said, keeping her eyes fixed on the ground. It wasn't out of respect, or even the desire to pretend that she bowed to this woman's rule. Rather, her display of submission was born of a sudden and stark terror, and she tried to stay calm, praying that Sempre wouldn't see through her deception. The truth was, she had indeed developed an unusual ability. Roughly one in five shifters did, sometime within their first two years after conversion. Some could call down lightning. Some could detect prey, far off in the forest. And others could perform sacred rituals, tapping into the raw, elemental power of the shifter magic.

Genna had discovered her own talent quite by accident, and knew two things as a result: firstly, her ability was one of the rarest of all shifter talents. For most shifters, objects like clothing or weapons that were strapped closely to the body vanished when the shifter changed forms. But Genna had the ability to make objects disappear without completing the shift, a rare and treasured skill that was also extremely dangerous. It could be used to steal things, to break into buildings, to render guns or other weapons useless by 'deleting' vital components of the equipment.

But the second thing she knew was that if Sempre ever discovered her abilities, her life was effectively over. She would be enslaved to Sempre's whims, used as a tool to complete her macabre schemes, her talents pushed beyond their limits, slowly draining her life and leaving her as a hollow shell.

"Nothing, hmm?" Sempre asked, disdain thick in her tone. "No little sparks of promise? Nothing you could use to help your pack?"

Genna shook her head. "No, ma'am."

"Fucking useless girl," Sempre snarled, stalking off across the clearing, and Genna breathed a sigh of relief as she left. Now it was just a choice as to what to do next, and while being berated for being in her human form for too long was unappealing, she had also reached the point where staying in her wolf form for much longer was going to start becoming decidedly uncomfortable. She headed for the stream, snatching up a bucket along the way, deciding to go with Sempre's suggestion to cart water to the tank in the centre of the camp.

Miller gritted his teeth and tried to concentrate as he drove the SUV along a winding road. He had two men in the car with him, who had been assigned to him in the short term until he could put a new team together to continue searching for the shape shifter pack in the Lakes District.

It was his first day back at work after his two week break, and he'd woken this morning with a feeling of dread. Despite long hours of thinking, of weighing up contingencies and teasing out details, his entire break had only served to confirm what he already knew: there was no way out of the Noturatii that wouldn't end up costing him his life.

And so he'd shown up this morning and done the first thing he could think of that would look like purposeful work, yet would pose the least possible threat to the shape shifters: he'd volunteered to continue the quest to find the hidden pack.

Actually finding them, of course, would spell disaster for the group, but at this stage, he was simply buying time, counting on the fact that they still had large areas of the Lakes District to cover, and the chances of actually finding the right property in the next few weeks were slim at best.

At first, he'd been planning to go on the scouting trip alone, as he'd been doing before the disaster in Scotland. But Jacob had pulled him up, told him that the shifters would be out for his blood, that he would be in mortal danger if they happened to catch sight of him, and so he'd been assigned the two other men. There was safety in numbers, Jacob had told him, before slapping him on the back and declaring that it was good to have him back on the team.

And so they'd spent the day driving from property to property, asking questions, on the lookout for any suspicious activity, and now, as the day was drawing to a close, Miller was entirely relieved to note that in terms of real progress, they'd achieved absolutely nothing.

But tomorrow was another day, and they were going to be spending the night in a hotel, the Lakes District too far from London to keep driving back and forth all the time. Sooner or later, Miller knew, they were going to run out of ground to cover, and whether through diligence or blind luck, they were going to find the shifters' home.

God help them all, when that day came.

It was six-thirty when Skip stepped out of the hall and stretched. The seminar was going fantastically, new ideas being shared, lots of technical talk, with plenty of the students proving they were just as smart as the lecturer, asking questions, tossing out new ways of doing things. Skip was loving every minute of it, and couldn't wait to get back in there for the next session.

For now, though, the group was taking a half hour break for dinner. The hall was right on the edge of the college campus, and there was a café across the road, so Skip headed over to get a bite to eat. The street was mostly deserted, but there were a dozen or so students loitering outside the hall, some eating, a couple of them using the break to smoke a cigarette, so she figured she wasn't going anywhere too isolated. The café had a good range of things to eat, sandwiches, lasagne, quiche… She stared at the counter, trying to choose, eventually deciding on a mushroom pie and a fruit smoothie. Then she settled herself at one of the tables and opened her laptop – not the usual one she used, as that one contained too much sensitive information, but the spare the Den kept for excursions like this, good functionality but nothing that could get them into trouble if it somehow got lost or fell into the wrong hands. She pulled up the notes she'd been making in the seminar and began rereading them, making a list of questions to ask the lecturer later on.

Miller sighed as he drove the SUV into the centre of the town. His team mates were hungry, and though Miller had no appetite himself, he'd brought them here to search for a quick dinner.

He slowed the car as they reached a row of shops. A few still had lights on, and he spotted a small café that looked like a good place to get a simple meal, so he pulled in to the curb. "Will this do?" he asked his two companions. They were amiable enough men, but with Miller's ongoing crisis of conscience about his current line of work, he'd been having a hard time keeping his temper in check today. Everything seemed to be annoying him more than usual, and he was hoping that neither of them would object to the simple café. After a long day, he had little desire to drive all over town looking for a place to eat.

"Good enough," Daniel said, unclipping his seatbelt and hopping out of the car. Steve just shrugged.

There weren't many people around, one or two inside the café, another couple hanging around outside the hall across the street. Miller hoped that that meant they would get served quickly, and could get out of here. He was sorely longing for a little time to himself in his hotel room.

Steve opened the door to the café, just as a young woman on the other side of the door went to do the same. She stepped back, politely letting them pass, and Miller smiled at her, opening his mouth to say thank you…

And froze in his tracks. It was the girl from Scotland, the one he'd seen at the start of the battle with the shifters. His shock at seeing her here was eclipsed only by his relief that she was still alive. She'd vanished by the end of the battle, and he'd had no idea whether she'd escaped, or been killed.

The girl looked up at him, recognising him in the same instant, and if he'd had any doubt as to her identity, the immediate look of horror on her face did away with it.

He didn't want to hurt her, had in mind to just ignore her and keep walking, but in the split second between recognising her and making that decision, Steve had seen the look on his face, registered the shock on the girl's, and reached the completely obvious conclusion: she was a shifter.

Moving with a speed that startled even Miller, Steve spun around and grabbed the girl, slamming a hand over her mouth so she couldn't speak, and hauled her out of the café. He was twice her size, the girl just a tiny slip of a thing, and her struggles were useless against his greater strength.

"Shifter," Steve hissed at Daniel, and his other companion wasted no time in helping to subdue the girl. It was a few short steps back to the car, not nearly a long enough time for Miller to come up with a plan B, a strategy for letting the girl slip out of this unexpected trap.

"Open the door," Steve snapped, and, not knowing what else to do, Miller did. He could hardly protest that they shouldn't take her, after all. Officially, he was still working for the Noturatii, and hadn't got anywhere near close enough to formulating an exit strategy to think of anything useful to do now.

Steve hauled her into the back seat, while Daniel slammed the door then jumped into the passenger seat. Feeling numb, Miller got into the driver's seat.

Daniel pulled out his gun and pointed it at the girl's head. "Sit still, or you'll have a bullet in your skull." The girl went still, glaring daggers at them all while Steve kept his hand over her mouth.

"You know this girl?" Steve asked Miller, still keeping a tight grip on her. "She's a shifter, yeah?"

Miller nodded, his mind not working fast enough in his shock to come up with a plausible denial. "Saw her in Scotland," he said shortly, feeling his gut churn.

"Hand over your phone," Daniel barked at the girl, and after a moment's hesitation, she did.

"We need to drug her," Steve said pragmatically. Taking a conscious and struggling captive all the way back to London was going to be a nightmare, but Daniel shook his head.

"Can't. We don't have anything. This was supposed to be a simple recon mission."

"Fuck," Steve swore. "We've at least got some handcuffs, right?" The girl struggled at that, causing Steve to tighten his grip on her, pressing his forearm against her throat until she was struggling to breathe. "In the glove box?" he suggested, and moments later, Daniel came up with a set. He tossed them onto Steve's lap and pointed his gun at the girl again.

"You stay still, or you're dead. Got it?"

The girl glared at him, but didn't move as Steve released her carefully, then locked the handcuffs around her wrists, her hands secured behind her back. "Miller! Move it! We can't hang around here all day," Steve snapped, and Miller obediently started the car and put it into gear. Steve shoved the girl into the seat behind Miller's, reaching over to pull the seatbelt around her and do it up. "Don't want you getting any ideas about leaping out of the car," he growled at her, then slid into his own seat and pulled out his gun, taking over guard duty from Daniel.

"Stop here," Daniel barked suddenly, and Miller did. Daniel hopped out of the car and dashed over to a nearby rubbish bin, dumping the girl's phone inside, then raced back to the car. It was another pragmatic move, as they could easily assume that the shifters' phones were traceable via GPS chips, much as the Noturatii's were. "Now, let's get this piece of filth back to London," he said to Miller, a look of triumph on his face.

Keeping most of his attention on the road, Miller programmed their new destination into the GPS, and minutes later, they were heading out of town, along a series of winding roads that would lead them back to the motorway.

"What's in the bag?" Daniel asked, referring to the small backpack the girl had been carrying, and he reached for it, checking inside. "Water bottle. Jumper. Booking form for… hmm, a computer seminar. Fascinating," he said drily. "And what have we here? A laptop." He smirked at the girl, who said nothing. "I wonder what little gems will show up on this one." He opened it up, but it was immediately apparent that the computer was not only password protected, but also encrypted in some way.

"No matter," he said, closing the thing and putting it back in the bag. "The lab will be able to get into this later. And then all your secrets will be ours."

Miller glanced at the girl in the rear view mirror, just in time to see her roll her eyes, and he concluded that there was nothing of value on the laptop. It wasn't likely she would just be wandering the streets carrying confidential information, after all.

The girl stared out the window, ignoring the gun still pointed in her direction. She was gutsy, Miller had to admit, calm under pressure, able to maintain her self control. She hadn't spoken a single word after they'd got her into the car. And as the miles slid by, he had to wonder what she was thinking. Praying someone would come and rescue her? Regretting the decision to attend the seminar? Or plotting her imminent escape?

CHAPTER SIXTEEN

As the minutes dragged by, Miller's mind was running double time. After his initial shock had worn off, the reality of his situation had sunk in. What a fucking cock-up. He'd requested this assignment specifically because he'd thought it a good way to avoid doing any immediate harm to the shifters, and instead, he'd accidentally kidnapped one of them, the very one that he had been most eager not to harm.

What the hell was he supposed to do now? He drove slowly, and not just because the road was narrow and winding. They were out in the countryside, stone walls lining fields on either side of the road, but they hadn't reached the motorway yet, and he scrambled for some ploy that would give the girl a chance to escape. A stop for fuel? No, the tank was more than half full. A bathroom break? If the girl asked for one, it might wash, but he could hardly suggest it to her off his own back. What other excuse might there be for stopping the car? It was drizzling, ominous clouds gathering in the distance, and he turned the wipers on, feeling the seconds ticking by with each swipe of the blades across the glass.

And with each passing moment, his thoughts became bleaker. It was bad enough that he'd helped these thugs for this long, under the honest but misguided belief that he was doing the right thing. But to continue to do so now, when he knew it was wrong, when he knew exactly what kind of nightmare he would be condemning this girl to... No. If he didn't find a way to help her, he would be damning himself straight to hell.

As he desperately sought a solution, his eyes wandered over the road ahead. At the next bend, the stone wall curved to the right, with the line of the road. And in a split second, his racing mind analysed a thousand tiny details.

The two other men were seated on the left hand side of the car, the woman sitting directly behind Miller. She had her seatbelt on. This car was

90

an older model, with no airbags fitted. A side impact would likely kill whichever passengers were on the side of the collision. And shape shifters were generally more difficult to kill than ordinary humans. He wasn't sure how they did it, but there were dozens of stories in the Noturatii's files of shifters who had been mortally wounded, only to change forms, pick themselves up and carry on fighting.

And in that moment, the decision was made. He was not going to hand this woman over to be tortured at the hands of the Noturatii. His own death was preferable to the guilt that that act would heap upon his soul.

Miller put his foot down, increasing the car's speed. He stared straight at the wall, waited for the last moment, then spun the wheel so that the car swerved, slid; it hit the barrier side on, crushing the two men on the left of the car. And as he felt the jarring impact, there were only two thoughts in his mind. 'God forgive me', and 'Please let her survive.'

Skip felt the impact of the crash without warning. She was flung sideways, her seatbelt snapping taut, a scream escaping her involuntarily as the car groaned, screeched and buckled. It seemed to take forever to stop moving, for the shaking to end, but the instant it had, Skip forcibly pulled herself together, glancing around, mind racing as she rapidly assessed the situation.

The car was a wreck, the left side a crumpled mess of twisted metal. The man beside her was injured, bleeding profusely. The one in the front passenger seat was dead, and the one driving seemed to have hit his head, perhaps suffering from concussion as he made no attempt to move.

Twisting around, she tried to reach the seatbelt release with her restrained hands. There were tiny shards of glass all over the seat, the window shattered, and she cut herself on the sharp edges, but ignored the pain. Then she felt the clip, and pressed the button, the seatbelt retracting obediently, and she was free.

Now to be rid of the handcuffs. Shifting was the quickest, easiest way to deal with that, but with her heart racing and adrenaline pumping through her, she was finding it hard to focus enough to manage it. Calm down, she told herself firmly. Take a deep breath. And concentrate…

Miller fought back a wave of dizziness as he realised the car had stopped moving. A scrabbling sound from the back seat alerted him to the fact that the girl was alive and fighting to escape, and he felt a rush of relief that she had survived. He unclipped his belt and searched Daniel quickly for the keys to the cuffs, trying not to look at the way the side of his head had caved in with the impact. He found the keys in his shirt pocket and scrambled out of the car, desperate to see if the girl was hurt.

Knees shaking, he opened her door and saw that she'd undone the seatbelt. She recoiled at his arrival and bared her teeth, so he backed up a fraction. "Hey, easy. It's okay. I'm going to get the cuffs off you." He leaned in again, and she allowed him to tug her hands towards him, eyeing him distrustfully, but saying nothing. A moment later the cuffs were undone. "Are you-?"

The girl elbowed him in the throat, knocking him back from the car, and he felt hands fumbling at his waist as he lurched backwards, hand to his throat as he coughed and winced.

"You stay away from me!" she snarled, and Miller realised that in his moment of inattention, she'd leapt out of the car and... taken his gun. Fuck. She brandished it at him now, backing slowly away down the road, and he held up his hands in surrender. "I'm not going to hurt you," he said, eyes on the gun, trying to sound calm.

"Damn right you're not."

She was bleeding, he realised quickly, as she stumbled away down the road, a dozen shallow cuts on her hands from the broken windows, much the same as Miller had received. But nothing serious enough to kill her.

Without another word, she shifted into wolf form and took off. Thank God, she was safe... but his relief turned to terror when a gunshot split the air and he heard a pained yelp from the wolf. He spun around to see Steve staring out the back window of the car, the glass completely shattered, a gun in his hand. Fucking hell, he'd survived. And shot the girl.

Without even thinking about it, Miller dived through the still open door and punched Steve in the face, then grabbed the gun out of his hands and shot him in the head. He stared at the bloody mess, stunned by his own actions, but not quite able to regret them.

He scrambled out of the car again to check on the wolf. She was staring at him, whining and struggling as she dragged an injured back leg, blood pouring from the wound, and his heart lurched in his chest as he realised he might not have saved her after all. The wound looked bad, blood pumping, painting the road red.

But then she shifted again, a panicked look in her eyes as she regained her human form. The rain was falling heavier now, and they were both getting rapidly drenched. She glanced from Miller to Steve and back again, not seeming to believe what she was seeing.

"Why did you do that?" she asked, fear and astonishment in her voice.

"You're hurt," Miller said, taking a step forward. "You need to get to a hospital." Or a vet clinic, maybe? How did the shifters deal with injuries to their animal forms?

"I'm fine," the girl snapped, climbing slowly to her feet. "Why did you shoot that man?"

Miller glanced at Steve. "I'm leaving the Noturatii," he said simply.

"Put the fucking gun down!" she ordered suddenly, lifting her stolen gun again and pointing it at him, and Miller realised that Steve's gun was still in his hand. "I'm not going to hurt you-"

"Gun down!"

Not keen on getting shot, he carefully bent over and set the gun on the road. "Now slide it over to me," she demanded, and Miller did, giving it a solid push so that it slid across the wet bitumen and landed at her feet. Not taking her eyes off him once, she reached down, picked up the second gun, put the safety on and slid it into the waistband of her shorts. And then she sneered at him, picking up their conversation where it had left off. "Nobody leaves the Noturatii. Not unless it's in a body bag."

"I know. But what they're doing is wrong. So I'm leaving." Odd, how it sounded so simple now, when he'd spent the past two weeks agonising over the idea like he was contemplating the meaning of life itself.

Skip stared at the man, feeling totally confused. She should shoot him. He was Noturatii, dangerous, a threat to her continued survival. Silas had been quite thorough in his lessons on firearms. She had a steady hand and good aim. She imagined the man's heart beating beneath his chest, a palm-sized target that would be an easy shot from here.

But the sad truth was that, in all her years in the Den, in all the battles with the Noturatii, she'd never actually killed someone before. And she found that now, when it came down to it, it wasn't quite as easy as Silas had made her believe. Ever since she'd joined the Den, the more senior wolves had taken it upon themselves to protect her from danger, and so, aside from her training in the Den's shooting range, she'd never been in a position to have to pull that trigger.

"That's bullshit," she snarled at him, not believing he was serious. "You were in Scotland. You shot a whole bunch of my friends, two fucking weeks ago, and now you say it's all bad and evil and you're just leaving? That's fucking bullshit." She was backing away slowly down the road, and the man followed, matching her pace.

"I deeply regret what I did in Scotland," he said, the admission sounding heartfelt. "I'm so sorry for the loss of your friends."

He was lying, Skip told herself firmly. She let her wolf senses come to the fore, the shifters' canine sides extremely adept at detecting lies, and tested his body language, his tone, his facial expression... which left her even more confused when everything checked out. By all indications, he was telling the truth.

She glanced at the dead man, his bloodied face just visible through the shattered back window. The man had just shot his friend, right in front of her, because the other man had shot her. Her bullet wound was going to be a serious problem, but for as long as she stayed in human form, it wouldn't kill her. Once she got back to the Den, they could arrange for a doctor to do surgery... She squashed the creeping fear that told her the wound was bad. She'd been bleeding heavily, the bullet catching her at the top of her left leg, and she wondered whether it had gone straight through and into her abdomen. If that was the case, she could be in serious trouble...

But that would all have to be dealt with another time. Aside from the inconvenience of not being able to use her wolf form at the moment, it was a problem that could wait.

The man was still standing there, hands up in surrender, a look of concern on his face. Her finger tightened on the trigger as she seriously considered shooting him. He'd led a team of soldiers right into their home, killed eight of her friends, injured a dozen more...

But less than a minute ago, he'd saved her life. He hadn't tried to shoot her. He had *given her his gun.*

And if what he said about wanting to leave the Noturatii was true... Well, it was hard to shoot a man, regardless of his past, if he'd just realised the error of his ways and wanted to make amends.

But he was Noturatii, and not to be trusted...

Miller waited as the girl seemed to be weighing him up, assessing the truth of his words. He stood still, knowing there was a very real risk that she would decide to just shoot him. And if she did, he acknowledged to himself, then he would deserve it. Justice, albeit too late to save her friends, for years of violence committed against them. But he'd saved *her.* So perhaps he wasn't headed straight for hell, this last, desperate attempt to make amends surely worth something on the cosmic scales.

"You killed my friends," she said finally. "But then you saved my life. So I'm going to call that quits." What? Was she serious? "I'm leaving now," she added, backing away. "So you stay away from me."

"You're hurt!" Miller insisted. "You just got shot. You need a doctor-"

"I'm fine," she said, through gritted teeth. "Fuck, what is wrong with you? You're supposed to kill us, not care about us!"

Miller stepped forward, hoping he could reason with her, make her see she needed help... but then he glanced back at the car, another part of this equation nagging at the back of his mind.

Despite the impulsiveness of the whole thing, this was the perfect set up to fake his own death. The Noturatii would find the wrecked car and the dead bodies, assume the shifters had come after their captive and run the car off the road, shot Steve... and if Miller was lucky, they might believe that the shifters had taken him with them, perhaps to be interrogated, and then later killed.

But there were a few things still to be done before he left his old life for good. "Wait a second," he told the girl. Then he dashed back to the car, left a bloody hand print on the steering wheel where the rain wouldn't wash it away, his palms bearing dozens of cuts from the broken glass. Then he grabbed the girl's backpack – just in case there was something of use on the laptop after all – and left another handprint on the door as he got out again. And then the pair of handcuffs on the back seat caught his eye. He picked them up and put them in the backpack, so that no one would ask questions about how their shifter captive had escaped from them.

There. Signs of his own injuries, which would stand up to scrutiny if the Noturatii decided to check the fingerprints or run a DNA test on the blood. Plenty of violence to implicate the shifters. His head was throbbing, and he put a hand to his forehead, finding a bloody wound where he must have hit his head in the crash. It was bleeding, but it wasn't too serious, so he put it out of his mind for the moment. Then he pulled his phone out of his pocket and dropped it on the road. They all had GPS trackers in them, and he had no intention of allowing the Noturatii to accidently find him again; the last connection to his old life, slowly drowning in the rain.

He looked up... and cursed as he realised the girl had vanished. "Fuck!" He dashed back to the last place he had seen her. No one on the road. On one side, the hillside sloped downwards, empty fields providing little cover. But up the hill, there was a thin forest, and he scanned the trees in the fading light... There! Movement!

"Wait!" he shouted, taking off after the girl. The urgent need to protect her, to make sure she didn't die after he'd taken such reckless steps to try and help her, was clawing at him. She glanced back, saw him following, and increased her speed. She was surprisingly fast for someone so small, and he had to sprint to catch up, hard work when it was uphill all the way. But just as he was closing on her, she spun around, hair plastered to her face in the rain, and pointed the gun at him again.

"Stay away from me!"

"You're hurt!" he said again. "There's a storm coming, and it's going to be dark soon. Where are you going, anyway?"

"Putting some distance between me and that car," she said pragmatically. "Your friends are going to be coming for it, and I don't want to be anywhere near it when they arrive." It was getting harder to hear her as the wind gathered strength. A shaft of lightning arced out of the sky a few miles away, then a deep, rolling wave of thunder broke over them.

"You can't stay outside all night," he told her. "We need to find shelter."

"Well, I wouldn't have to stay out here if you hadn't stolen my fucking phone!" the girl yelled at him. "We're in the middle of nowhere. Where the hell do you think we're going to go?"

Miller glanced around. Up the hill there was a tall outcrop of rock, large boulders, then a small cliff. "Up there," he said, pointing. "There might be a small cave or something we can shelter in."

"We?" the girl spat. "I'm not going anywhere with you."

"I'm not going to hurt you," Miller tried again, realising he was on the losing side of this argument. "If I wanted to do that, I wouldn't have shot Steve. Or given you my gun."

That made her pause. "Maybe this is a trick," she insisted. "You want to spy on us, so you're trying to make it look like you're leaving the Noturatii, when you're really just gathering information for them."

Miller actually had to laugh at that. "By kidnapping you and then crashing my own car? By killing two of our own men? That's a pretty desperate strategy, even for us."

The rain was falling heavily now, both of them soaked. The girl glanced up the hill to the rocks. Frowned. And sighed. "Fine," she said reluctantly. "Let's go."

Another shaft of lightning lit the sky, the black clouds blocking out the last of the evening's light, and it was difficult to see as they both scrambled up the hill, the slope slippery and low bushes making it hard to find a path. They reached the rocks, and Miller scouted around while the girl watched him distrustfully. At first glance, there wasn't much shelter to be had, but he climbed up on the first row of boulders and looked around… Thank God. There was a cave, low but long, and large enough for them both to squeeze inside, with an overhanging lip that kept the rain out.

"There's a cave," he called down to her. "Can you climb up?"

She tried, scrambling on the rocks, not quite tall enough to make the climb as Miller had done, and so she was forced to put the gun away, tucking it carefully into her shorts after putting the safety on. But the rain was making it hard to get a grip on anything, and he saw that the effort had reopened the cuts on her hands, leaving pink trails of blood amid the pouring rain.

"Here…" He reached down, offering his own hand, and with a fierce glare, she reached up and took it. She was as light as she looked, and it took little effort for him to haul her up the rock face, desperate to get inside the shelter as he felt his skin tingle with static electricity-

A bolt of lightning hit the ground not twenty metres from where they stood, the clap of thunder deafening as he felt it vibrate right through his body. The girl flinched, but otherwise didn't react, while Miller recoiled violently and had to fight to keep his balance.

But he didn't let go of her hand. Cursing darkly, he dragged them both into the cave, ducking his head to fit inside, and collapsed against the back wall.

CHAPTER SEVENTEEN

Silas pulled the car up outside the hall where he'd dropped Skip off. It was a few minutes to nine, so he waited, scanning the street for anything suspicious, then listening to a song on the radio.

The doors of the hall opened, and people started to file out. It was raining heavily, thunder rumbling in the distance, and none of them lingered, dashing over to waiting cars, or heading for the shelter of nearby shops or bus stops.

The initial flood of bodies thinned to a trickle, and Silas switched off the radio, waiting for Skip to emerge, no doubt brimming with excited news about everything she had learned today.

He waited... and waited some more, as the last of the people scurried away into the night.

Where the hell was she?

Figuring she might still be inside, maybe asking questions of their instructor, he got out of the car and ducked inside the entrance. Sure enough, there was a small group gathered at the front of the room, attention fixed on a computer screen, but a quick glance told him that none of them was Skip.

Was she in the bathroom? He went over to the door, knocked, waited, and when there was no reply, eased it open and stuck his head inside. "Skip?"

No reply.

He headed outside again, checked the car – no Skip – then pulled out his phone and dialled her number. He waited while it rang... and then it switched over to voicemail. He hung up and called again, cursing when he got the same result.

A cold weight settled in his chest, and he tried to tell himself not to panic. Skip had spent the entire afternoon in a public place, surrounded by people. There was likely a rational explanation for this...

Fuck it. He quickly dialled Simon, back at the estate, and was grateful when he answered after the first ring. "Skip's not outside the hall," he explained quickly. "I need you to track her phone for me."

"Sure thing," Simon replied, then there was the sound of booted feet on wooden floorboards – he was likely running up the stairs to the IT office – then the faint 'tap tap tap' of fingers on a keyboard.

"I've got her signal," Simon said a few minutes later, while Silas stood in the rain, continually scanning the street. "And I've got your location, too. She's less than a hundred metres from you." He gave Silas directions, down the road, around a corner, past a handful of shops...

"She's not here," Silas said sharply, when he reached the place Simon said she should be. "Where the hell is she?"

"Hold on, I'll call her phone," Simon said, and Silas waited... There! Faint ringing... from the rubbish bin? He grabbed food wrappers and coffee cups, tossing them aside... and there it was, Skip's phone, in its pink case, cheerfully chiming away amid discarded newspapers and greasy burger boxes.

Silas felt his heart all but stop, his hands shaking as he forced his throat to speak the next words – words he had hoped he would never have to say. "Get Baron," he growled. "Skip's been kidnapped."

Skip sat shivering at the back of the cave, catching her breath as she stared at this most peculiar man in front of her.

"We should start a fire," he said pragmatically, raindrops dripping down his face. The overhanging rocks had gathered a fair pile of debris over the years, and some of it was dry enough to burn, so after carefully setting Skip's backpack against the wall, he set about laying a fire near the entrance of the cave. His hands were bleeding, she noted as she watched, his palms cut from the glass in the car. He pulled a lighter out of his pocket and lit the kindling, coaxing the small flame to life as the larger pieces of wood caught.

"There," he said, a few minutes later. "Try to get dry. It's going to be a cold night."

Skip retrieved the two guns from her shorts and quickly unloaded one, storing the gun in her backpack and the bullets in her pocket. The other one she left loaded. She huddled closer to the fire. The storm was still raging outside, thunder booming against the hills with each flash of lightning, but she wasn't the slightest bit afraid. Not of the storm, at least. Shifters had a natural affinity with lightning, and the storm was actually rather comforting.

The man, on the other hand... "Why did you help me?" she asked, keeping the gun within easy reach as she warmed her hands.

He wiped his face, brushing away stray drops that trickled out of his short hair, and sighed. "Like I said," he told her, sounding tired. "I'm leaving the Noturatii."

"They'll kill you," she said pragmatically.

"Not if they already think I'm dead."

She snorted at that. "So this wasn't about helping me at all, was it? It was just some bullshit attempt to help yourself. That crash could have killed me," she complained, knowing the accusation was a little hollow. From the stories she'd heard, death would be preferable to imprisonment at the hands of the Noturatii.

"It was a calculated risk," he said apologetically. "I was taught some advanced driving techniques during my training, and I tried to crash the car in a way that gave you the best chance of survival."

"But *why?*" she insisted. This was making no sense...

The man looked at her sadly, regret heavy in his eyes. "When I joined the Noturatii, I thought I was protecting people. Stopping terrorists. Killing people who were killers themselves. But hurting little girls was never part of the job description, and I guess my conscience finally caught up with me."

"I'm not a little girl," Skip protested, annoyed at the description.

He looked at her again, seeming to re-evaluate her in the dim light of the fire. "No, you're not," he admitted, a hint of wry humour in his voice. "You're fierce! Far more fierce than I imagined you would be."

Despite her reservations about this man, Skip found herself blushing... and then blushed harder at the realisation. She had always wanted to be fierce, ever since she'd been converted into a wolf and handed a power that ordinary men would kill to acquire. But she'd never felt she was. Silas was fierce, the seasoned warrior who protected them all with lethal force. Tank was fierce, with his awesome combat skills and propensity to hurl himself into danger. Caroline was fierce, with her black leather and fiery attitude. Skip had never measured up.

But here she was, stuck in a cave with a Noturatii operative, a man twice her size, her sworn enemy... and he thought she was fierce! The surge of pride she felt was as ridiculous as it was heartening, and, to hide her pleasure at the description, she frowned and glared at the fire.

"You're really leaving the Noturatii?" she asked, a little while later, and the man nodded.

"I really am."

"Sucks to be you," she said sympathetically. If they realised he was alive, they weren't just going to kill him. They were going to gut him slowly, and laugh while he screamed in pain.

"What's your name?" he asked, after another moment of silence.

"Susan," Skip said automatically. It was the false name she'd used to sign up for the seminar.

"Is that your real name?" the man asked, and Skip snorted.

"No, of course not. But it's a step up from 'Hey, you', so it'll have to do for now."

"I'm Jack," the man said. "Jack Miller."

"I would ask if that's your real name," Skip said, a sardonic edge to her voice, "but I don't really care."

"It's my real name," Miller said. "I don't know if you're going to believe that, but I've spent too long lying to people. It feels good to tell the truth once in a while."

They both fell silent after that, the small fire slowly turning their clothes from wet to damp, and inside this cosy nook, Skip was relieved to find it wasn't all that cold. After a while, the rain let up, returning to its usual drizzle, while the storm moved off to the east.

And all the while, Skip was pondering this most unusual man. Men in general were dangerous, she had learned at an early age. Men of the Noturatii more so. She contemplated a long night in an isolated location with this powerful man, thought of the shifters he had killed, the attack on the estate in Scotland, the way he had shot a man in the head in cold blood just half an hour ago. He was dangerous, that much was obvious. He had hurt people, some of them people she cared about. But the thing playing on her mind, as she watched him through the dim light, was that he hadn't hurt *her*.

He'd had the opportunity. He'd had a gun, when the car had crashed. He was stronger than her, and could no doubt handle himself in a fist fight. But he hadn't hurt her.

Odd.

He wasn't the first man to not hurt her, Skip reminded herself. Silas had never hurt her. He'd killed people to protect her, he had fights with other people in the Den, but he'd never hurt *her*.

But Miller was from the Noturatii. There was no way in the world he could be anywhere near as nice as Silas.

Time to put the theory to the test.

She leaned closer, peering intently at the wound on his head. It was still seeping blood, a thin trickle of it running down his face into his collar. "You hit your head," she said, trying to sound concerned.

"I don't think it's too serious," he said, bending his head down so she could get a better look at it.

Skip lifted her hand to wipe some of the blood away... and then jammed her fingernails into the wound.

"Fuck!" He leapt back like she'd stuck him with a red hot poker. "What the hell did you do that for?" He put his hand to the wound, scuttling away from her, disbelief and outrage on his face.

Skip shrugged. "I don't like you," she said simply. There was no remorse in her voice at all. And then she waited, curious to see how this strong, powerful man from the side of evil would react.

"Bloody hell... you're a crazy shit, you know that?"

Skip shrugged again. Yeah, she was crazy. But where she came from, that was a compliment. She waited some more.

Miller settled back down, further away than he had been before, probing the wound and then seeing the blood on his fingers as it started bleeding again. "Look, I said I wasn't going to hurt you, and I meant it. So can we just call a truce? I don't hurt you, you don't hurt me, and we both get out of here alive. Okay?"

"Okay," Skip agreed easily.

"Okay?! So why did you just scratch me?"

"You've hurt a lot of my friends. A little retaliation seemed appropriate." Skip settled back down, feeling more confused than ever. Why hadn't he hurt her back? He could have hit her, tried to grab the gun to shoot her, slapped her across the face? *Why was he refusing to hurt her?!*

Miller shuffled around uncomfortably. His head was throbbing again, the ground was cold and hard, and his clothes were clinging to him, damp against his skin. It was going to be a long night, with little expectation of getting any sleep, and he was starting to realise that his problems were far from over. Despite the agreed truce, he didn't quite believe this girl wasn't going to do him further harm during the night, and he eyed the gun at her side apprehensively. An hour ago, death had seemed a viable option, but with the girl's apparent declaration that saving her life was fair payment for his crimes, he'd started to believe he might get out of this mess alive. His life would never be the same, of course. He'd have to leave the country, bribe smugglers to move him across borders, and head for somewhere where the Noturatii didn't operate. South America, maybe, or Australia. But there was a chance – slim but realistic – that he might be able to get away from his past and start again somewhere new.

Susan was huddled up near the fire, her short hair curling as it dried, and he took the time to look at her more closely. She wore a bright pink t-shirt with a unicorn on the front, a pair of baggy shorts, and trainers covered in glitter.

But her fiery attitude and grim expression contradicted the impression of a young girl, and he reassessed his estimation of her age. Perhaps she wasn't a teenager after all, but in her twenties. She'd reacted without hesitation after the crash, level-headed enough to steal his gun and get herself out of there without panicking, no screaming, no reaction to her wounds. And he felt a fresh wave of guilt at the thought that she must have been through enough emergencies to have developed the skills to deal with them. She was actually quite beautiful, in a wild sort of way, her pixie-ish face golden in the firelight, her body toned and trim, and despite her odd choice of clothing, the look suited her.

She looked up, caught him staring at her, and her glare returned. "What?" she asked gruffly, and Miller shook his head.

"I'm sorry. I just think you're..." He had been about to say pretty, but the word didn't really fit. There was nothing classically 'pretty' about the girl. He shrugged. "I think you're nice to look at."

Susan looked at him strangely, and he had to admit it must have sounded like an odd sort of compliment, coming from a man who worked for an organisation that had tried to kill her.

"I'm going to get some sleep," she said, sounding almost petulant. "And don't try to take my gun," she added, tucking the weapon beneath her arm as she tugged the backpack over as a makeshift pillow and lay down, making herself as comfortable as possible on the cold ground. 'Her' gun now, rather than his.

Miller sighed and set about creating his own makeshift bed – a rough depression in the dusty ground, his arm curled up for a pillow. His body felt odd, tight and tingling, an uncomfortable feeling like he wanted to yawn, but couldn't quite figure out how. He had the strange sense that there was something he needed to do, but couldn't think what it could possibly be.

It was likely just the stress of the car crash, he told himself, closing his eyes. He didn't expect to sleep, but was determined to try. And then after the crash, he'd nearly been struck by lightning. It was only to be expected that he was feeling rather on edge. His legs felt odd, like they were too long, like his feet worked the wrong way. And his mouth felt strange, like his tongue was too big. Go to sleep, he told himself firmly. It was just stress, adrenaline, his imagination playing up over a day of too much excitement. He just needed to get a little sleep, and then it would all look better in the morning.

It was dark when Skip woke up, still the middle of the night, but the sky had cleared and the moon was bright, shimmering beneath faint wisps of cloud. The fire had gone out, but Skip's night vision was excellent – a benefit of her wolf side – and she immediately remembered where she was, and with whom.

Her first thought was to check the gun... yep, still there, beneath her arm. And then she glanced over at Miller... and choked back a startled cry before it could escape.

He was... holy fuck... how the hell...??

Instead of sharing a cave with a dangerous, confusing man, Skip felt a rush of disbelief as she looked over to the other side of the fireplace and saw a large, black wolf, sound asleep on the ground.

A wolf?! What the hell?

Miller wasn't a shifter. Couldn't be. He worked for the Noturatii! If they'd known he was a shifter, they would have killed him. Or tortured him. They would certainly never have let him wander around the countryside on his own.

But as she shuffled around in the dark, trying to stay as quiet as possible, Skip felt the sting of the cuts on her hands, and looked down at her palms in consternation.

No. It wasn't possible…

But there was no other explanation. Miller had the same cuts on his own hands. In the storm, he'd grabbed her hand to pull her up the rocks, both of them bleeding, and then the lightning had struck, a stone's throw from where they were standing.

It wasn't possible…

"Oh, Sirius, what have you done this time?" she breathed, her words barely audible. A Noturatii man had just been converted into a shape shifter.

And aside from the staggering irony, Skip felt a jolt of fear as she realised the dire situation she was in. He couldn't be allowed to leave. If he actually was a spy, unlikely though that seemed, then he could take their secrets straight back to the Noturatii, giving them even more fuel with which to fight this hideous war.

But even if everything he'd said was true, and he really was intending to leave the organisation, Skip still couldn't let him walk away. A stray shifter on the loose could expose their species to the public, put the whole of Il Trosa at risk.

Bloody hell. She considered shooting him… but despite her concerns, she knew she would never be able to do it. He had saved her life, after all, had helped her survive the storm, had sat with her all evening without once trying to harm her. Killing him would only make her a murderer.

But there was only one alternative, and that was to somehow convince him to follow her back to the Den, where he could be assessed properly, to see if he could merge with his wolf, to see if he really was breaking off his loyalties to the Noturatii.

Baron would have a fit. Silas would likely shoot him on sight. Tank… God, she dreaded to think how Tank would react, given what he'd been through that time he was captured and held in a Noturatii lab.

Did Miller even know he was a shifter? He hadn't seemed to, all that time they were sitting in the cave. Did he know now? The wolf was asleep, and it wasn't uncommon for a shift to occur while someone was sleeping. Maybe he'd just shifted in his sleep, and was completely unaware of the extra passenger he was now carrying.

Skip shook her head, abandoning any thoughts of more sleep tonight. She would have to keep an eye on her strange companion, make sure he didn't try to sneak away in the morning without her noticing.

And somehow she had to come up with a plan that would make sure he followed her home, and at the same time, convince Baron not to just shoot him when they arrived. The world had just got a little more crazy than usual.

CHAPTER EIGHTEEN

When Miller woke up in the morning, Susan was already awake. She was sitting huddled up beside the long-dead fire, staring at him with an odd look of contemplation.

"Morning," he said shortly, sitting up and trying to stretch his stiff muscles in the small space. He was surprised at how well he'd slept, not stirring from the time he'd lain down to just now.

The rain had stopped, leaving the sky grey and cloudy, and he wished they had something to eat. He hadn't had dinner the night before, and all indications were that he wasn't going to get breakfast either. He idly wondered how much money he had on him, knowing that now he was on the run, making use of his credit card was out of the question.

"I've been thinking," Susan said suddenly, not taking her eyes off him. "You said you want to leave the Noturatii. And that means you think the shifters aren't evil incarnate any more, right?"

"Right," Miller confirmed.

"Which also probably means you think the Noturatii are pretty shit, am I right?"

That one was a harder question to answer. "I'm certainly against what they're doing, and I have no intention of helping them any more. But I've got a few friends working for them as well. Good people. Just maybe misguided, like I was." Susan didn't look impressed with that, so he went on, "We get lied to a lot. There's a lot of propaganda, a lot of the higher-ups running around making sure everyone believes the right story. I'm not saying I agree with any of it, but when you're at the bottom of the ladder, it can be hard to tell the truth from the lies."

Susan thought about that. "Makes sense," she conceded after a moment. "But there's still a lot going on in the upper levels that you don't like, right?"

"Right."

"So I have an idea." She peered up at him, giving him a hopeful, speculative look. "You should come home with me."

It took Miller only half a second to catch onto her plan. "You want me to play informant. To give the shifters the information I have on the Noturatii's operations."

"Right," Susan said, sounding almost cheerful about the idea. "You said you were sorry for what happened in Scotland. This would be a perfect way for you to make up for that."

Miller let out a laugh in disbelief. "I don't think that's a good idea," he said wryly. "The instant I set foot on shifter territory, there are half a dozen people who would shoot me on sight."

"Not necessarily," Susan insisted. "Not if you're with me. Not if I tell them not to. They'd probably rough you up a bit, yeah," she admitted with a grimace. "But they're not going to do too much damage if they know you have some good information for us. Besides," she went on quickly, "where else are you going to go? Your escape seems fairly spontaneous, so I doubt you have a big pile of cash on you. And you can't access your bank account without letting the Noturatii track you. We know people who know people. If you want to skip the country at some point, we can point you in the right direction."

Miller narrowed his eyes in suspicion. "You're offering to help me escape from the Noturatii?"

Susan snorted. "No. I'm trying to get you to come with me so we can tap your brain for useful intel. But the fact remains, we know people who deal in various illegal trades, so once you're done helping us, we might decide to scratch your back in return. I'm not doing this as an exercise in altruism. I don't owe you anything. But unlike *you know who*, we don't tend to stab people in the back after they help us."

Miller thought about the idea. On the one hand, it was crazy. Regardless of what Susan said, there was a high chance the shifters would take one look at him and put a bullet in his skull. But on the other hand, he was rather short on options. As she'd pointed out, he had little money on him – certainly not enough to bribe people smugglers. And while he knew a few people with interests in that area, they were all linked to the Noturatii in one way or another. Not a great plan, when he was doing his best to play dead and not get caught.

"Okay," he said finally. "But you have to promise me you'll do everything you can to make sure they don't kill me."

"You saved my life yesterday," Susan said firmly. "That's not something I'm going to forget in a hurry."

Jacob Green strode into the Noturatii's main base in London, in a better mood than he'd been in for weeks. "Morning, James," he greeted one of the guards as he headed for his office. "How's our new captive this morning?"

The guard looked at him blankly. "Captive, sir?"

"I got a message from Steve last night," Jacob said, setting his briefcase on the desk. "He said Miller's team from the Lakes District had captured a shifter girl. They were bringing her in."

The guard shook his head. "I'm sorry, sir, but I haven't heard anything about a new captive. Just a moment. I'll call Science and Research." A minute later, the man was ending the call and looking baffled. "Sorry sir, but there's only one shifter in the cages – the one we've been experimenting on. No one's seen Miller since yesterday morning."

"Hmm." With a frown, Jacob pulled out his phone and called Miller's number. It rang out, and then switched to voicemail. He tried again, with the same result. Then he called Steve, and then Daniel, the other man who'd been sent on the assignment. No one answered either phone.

"Excuse me," he muttered to the guard, hurrying off down the hall to the communications office. "Which car did Miller take yesterday?" he snapped to one of the staff when he arrived. The man in front of the computer sat up straight and set about looking up the logs immediately.

"The blue jeep, sir," he answered. He brought up the tracking system on the screen. "According to the GPS, it's stationary." He pulled up a map and turned the screen so Jacob could see. "Right here, sir. South of Kendal. And according to the logs, it's been there since yesterday evening."

Jacob stared at the blinking red dot on the screen, his mind working quickly. Three staff MIA and a car stuck in the middle of nowhere? "Give me a list of who's rostered on for security this morning. And forensics staff, as well. I want to get a team out there and find out what's going on."

Skip thanked the driver of the car she and Miller had hitched a ride in and climbed out. They were in front of a wide driveway leading up to a big old farmhouse – one of the Den's neighbours – and she shouldered her backpack, waiting until the car drove off.

"So this is home?" Miller asked, looking up the hill towards the farmhouse in surprise.

Skip snorted. "No. Of course not. I'm not going to lead some random stranger right to our door. Geez, you're not too quick on the uptake, are you?" Miller looked faintly embarrassed. "Come on," she said, turning left and heading off down the road. "It's this way."

They walked along in silence, both of them having a lot on their minds. Skip had been profoundly relieved when Miller had agreed to come with her this morning. When she'd told him her plan, she'd made an effort to make it sound practical, workable, but not overly generous, lest Miller get suspicious about her motives. And his reluctance to join her had only served to convince her even more that he was serious about his decision to leave the Noturatii.

By all indications, he was still unaware that he was a shifter, and that in itself was odd. Usually the wolf made itself known fairly quickly after the conversion, demanding a rapid shift, expressing desires that were at odds with the normal, human way of thinking. But Miller's wolf seemed strangely quiet, and Skip wondered if it had somehow picked up on the danger he was in, and was biding its time.

Or perhaps it was simply content with his mindset the way it was. Miller was a soldier, after all, a hunter of sorts, with a strong personality and plenty of skills in self defence. Perhaps the wolf recognised that it didn't need to make any excessive demands about embracing the wilder side of his nature.

But the other thing on her mind was wondering what she was going to say to the others when they arrived at the estate. They would be furious at having a Noturatii operative show up at their front door, and despite her assurances to Miller, she wasn't entirely convinced she could persuade them not to shoot him on sight.

But it was too late to back out now, and in all honesty, she didn't think there was a viable alternative. She would just have to make the best of it she could.

Twenty minutes later, the estate came into view, and Skip felt her heart kick up a notch as nervousness took over. "Wait," she said, coming to a stop before they reached the gate. "Do you have any other weapons on you? Because they're going to search you, and they won't be happy about finding you armed."

Without a word, Miller reached down and withdrew a knife strapped to his ankle, handing it to her handle first, and then fished through his pockets. He pulled out a pocket knife, an extra clip of ammunition, and handed them both over. Skip stowed the items in her backpack, then looked Miller over. "Anything else?"

"That's all."

"A word of advice? Do whatever they ask. Go wherever they tell you to go. And don't say anything that's going to antagonise them. There are going to be plenty of insults coming your way and they won't be inclined to put up with any backchat."

"Got it," Miller said, looking apprehensive. "How much further is it?"

Skip nodded to the gate, just visible at the next bend in the road. "We're here."

Miller's eyebrows rose. "Are you serious?"

"Yeah. Why? What's the problem?"

"I've been here before," Miller said, a strange kind of awe in his voice.

"We received some unusual intel and I came to take a look. The whole place checked out. One thing I'll say for you; you know how to cover your tracks."

"You sound surprised," Skip commented drily, leading the way over to the gate.

"My mistake," Miller muttered softly.

When they reached the gate, Skip didn't even consider entering the code to open it. Having Baron and the others meet a Noturatii operative at the gate would be bad, but if they found him already inside the estate, they wouldn't hesitate to kill him. So instead, she went over to the intercom and pressed the call button.

"Good morning. How can I help you?" Silas's voice came through the speaker, and Skip felt herself relax. It was so good just to hear a familiar voice again.

"It's me," she said, making sure not to use her own name. She didn't trust Miller, and he wasn't anywhere near contained yet, so letting him know her name was an unnecessary risk. "I'm down by the gate. I need-"

"Fucking hell, Skip?" Silas yelled. "Are you all right?"

Skip sighed. So much for remaining anonymous. "I've got someone with me," she blurted out, knowing that she had a very small opportunity to explain herself, "and you have to not shoot him."

Silence. "Who's with you?" From his tone, it sounded like Silas was already imagining gutting whoever it was.

"You won't like him," Skip said, trying to buy enough time to make Silas listen to her. "But you can't shoot him. It's really important."

The intercom shut off suddenly.

"Oh God, they're going to shoot you," she groaned. "Quick. Hide in the bushes."

"What?" Miller asked in alarm.

"Hide in the bushes," she repeated, waving him back urgently. "If they see you, they'll shoot you, so I need a little bit of time to talk them down."

CHAPTER NINETEEN

Skip held her breath as Miller darted over to the thick bushes beside the gate and dived inside. The sun didn't reach the deep pocket of leaves, and with his dark skin and clothing, he was all but invisible.

She could well imagine the chaos going on inside the manor. Silas would be yelling that they were under attack. Baron would gather a team of armed soldiers, arrange a line up of the less experienced wolves in the foyer to defend the manor, and bring the stronger ones with him to meet their foe head on. Skip stood patiently, long minutes ticking by, and then the heavy thud of multiple sets of boots could be heard coming down the driveway.

"Hi," she said simply, when they arrived, and yep, there was quite the line up. Silas, Tank, Andre, Caroline. Raniesha was there too, and Heron, with a look of profound relief at seeing Skip alive and unharmed. She was a little relieved that Baron hadn't brought John along. Given his past, he was just as likely to shoot Miller, regardless of any orders to the contrary.

Baron marched straight up to the gate and tapped in the code. The gate began to open. "I've got-" Skip tried to say, but before she could get any further, Silas grabbed her arm and hauled her inside the gate. He stepped through the gap, gun at the ready, Andre and Baron quickly following him, and then Tank closed the gate behind them. They scanned the road, looking for any sign of danger.

"Wait! Listen to me!" Skip told them insistently, struggling from where Heron had grabbed her and was holding her back. "You can't shoot him. It's really, really important."

"Who is it?" Silas asked, continuing to scan the road.

"He's from the Noturatii. But he's leaving them. He wants to help us. He's got intel that we can use."

"It's a trap," Baron declared flatly. "Fucking hell, Skip, are you really that stupid-"

"You fucking listen to me," she snarled, breaking free of Heron and marching forward to stand at the gate, knowing she had mere seconds to save Miller's life. "I am not some five year old idiot! I know what war we're fighting, I know who our enemy is, and I'm not going to believe some Noturatii arsehole just because he smiles and tries to sweet talk me. Things happened last night that you know nothing about, and I have *very* good reasons for what I'm doing. So pull your head out of your arse and listen for a change."

The outburst had the desired effect. Baron stopped cold, staring at her like she'd grown a second head. He glanced up and down the road one more time, and then lowered his gun, motioning for Silas and Andre to do the same. "You brought a Noturatii operative to our very doorstep," he snarled at her, his eyes never leaving hers. "So you'd better have a *fucking good reason* for that kind of lunacy."

"I do," Skip said firmly. She didn't bother being surprised at her own outburst, or at the odd courage currently pulsing through her veins. After her conversion, she'd rapidly learned that her wolf's personality was rather different from her own, confrontational where she was timid, stubborn where she gave ground, and over the years, there had been half a dozen occasions where the wolf had sprung to the fore, driving Skip to do things that she would normally have found terrifying. And after surviving a car crash and a night in the wilderness with a Noturatii man, she was feeling rather bold. "So are we going to play ball, or are you going to shoot us in the foot when I'm doing everything I can to help us?"

Baron hesitated a moment longer... then let out a long-suffering sigh. "Fine," he said, though it was clear he was far from happy with the situation. "Come out," he called. "No one will harm you."

"Wait," Skip said, eyeing Silas and Andre. "He's not just a Noturatii."

"Then who is he?"

"You promise you won't shoot him?"

"I promise I won't shoot him until after I get the full story from you. After that, all bets are off."

It was as good a reply as she was going to get, so Skip took a deep breath and blurted out the rest. "It's the guy who led the massacre up in Scotland. The black one who took the dead hiker away." While Skip hadn't been present at the end of the battle, she'd been there when the attack had begun, and had heard the story of how the fight had ended.

"You have got to be fucking kidding me." It was Silas who made the exclamation, his face turning pale at all the possible implications of her statement.

"He saved my life last night," Skip told him. "So that at least earns him the chance to explain himself."

"You had damn well better be right about this," Baron growled, looking like she'd just asked him to eat a pile of his own vomit. He holstered his gun. "Come out," he called again.

There was a pause, and then a rustling sound from the bushes. Miller came out slowly, keeping his hands visible, and stood quietly beside the drive.

Baron wasted no time in spinning him around, pressing his hands up against the stone wall and patting him down.

"He gave me all his weapons," Skip told him.

"Smart move," Baron said, coming up with nothing. "What the fuck are you doing here?"

"I'm leaving the Noturatii," Miller said, not moving from the wall. "The young lady said you'd be interested in the information I have on them."

"And what the fuck happened last night that's got Skip so excited?"

Miller told them the bare bones of the story; the kidnapping, the car crash, his two team mates both killed, the thunderstorm, sheltering in a cave overnight, and then hitching a ride back here this morning. Silas and Andre were both standing by, ready to leap into action at the slightest sign of danger, but Skip was relieved to see that they seemed satisfied with the explanation. For now, at least.

Baron pulled out his phone and dialled a number. "Simon?" he said, after a moment's pause. "Find Kwan and get down to the gate. I've got a Noturatii operative I need you to scan for bugs."

The group waited in tense silence after he hung up, and then, minutes later, more footsteps came hurrying down the drive. Simon was carrying a case of equipment, and he wasted no time in slipping through the gate and setting up what he needed. "Any metal on you?" he asked.

"Belt buckle," Miller said, still not moving. "Steel caps in my boots. Wallet in my back pocket." Baron set about removing the items, undid the laces on Miller's boots and told him to toe them off, and then Simon did a full scan of him, not just for metallic objects, but for anything with an electrical signal, listening devices, hidden cameras.

"He's clean," he announced a while later, stepping back and packing up his equipment.

"Kwan? You're up," Baron announced, and Kwan stepped forward. His scan of Miller was a lot slower, and a lot more unorthodox. After his conversion, Kwan had developed the unusual ability of being able to detect and manipulate electric currents, and he carefully performed a full sweep of Miller now, hands hovering just over his clothes as he scanned every inch of his body, checking for any kind of tracking device that might be too subtle for Simon's equipment to detect.

"Nothing," he announced, some time later. The look on Baron's face was almost comical, as if he couldn't believe that Miller was actually clean. Skip couldn't really blame him for his scepticism, though. But for the events of last night, she herself would never have believed that a man like Miller would dare to show up here, unarmed and without even one tiny bug on him.

"Now what?" Silas asked, looking as baffled as Baron.

"I thought you could put him in one of the cages," Skip suggested, watching from the gate. "Don't worry," she added, when Miller looked apprehensive about the idea. "It's not as bad as it sounds. And it's not like we can just let you wander around the estate on your own."

"Take him through the cellar door," Baron said, opening the gate once more. "And I want two guards on him at all times. Skip? You and me are going to have a little chat about this."

Skip nodded. She had expected as much.

"And Tank? Do a full sweep of the estate. I want to know there's nothing else going on around here that shouldn't be."

Ten minutes later, Skip was pacing the library, four pairs of worried eyes staring at her expectantly; Baron and Caroline, as the Den's alphas, Andre, who was always a good choice when strategic decisions needed to be made, and Heron, who Skip suspected was just unwilling to let Skip out of her sight for the time being.

"Jack Miller," Baron said, repeating the name she had just given them. "Why would you bring him here?" He was clearly making an effort to rein in his temper. "Okay, so he saved your life, but he's a Noturatii. If he wants to leave the organisation, you could have just let him walk."

"No, I couldn't," Skip explained. "See, there's something else you need to know... Jack's been converted. I don't think he realises it yet, but he's become a shape shifter." She explained it quickly, the thunderstorm, the cuts on their hands, the lightning strike, and her shock at waking up to find she was sharing the cave with a wolf. And if she had been surprised, it was nothing when compared to the shock on the faces around her. "So I couldn't just let him go," Skip concluded. "He could have exposed us all. Or taken those secrets back to the Noturatii. And given that he saved my life, I couldn't just shoot him, either. I know this is bad, and it certainly wouldn't have been my first choice, but I didn't know what else to do."

"It's okay," Heron said gently. "You did the best you could under the circumstances." She levelled a firm glare at Baron, as if daring him to contradict her.

"Fuck," Baron muttered, and Skip was already anticipating the extended argument that was going to happen about what to do with Miller next.

But she had another, much more urgent issue to discuss, and so she interrupted Baron before he could begin his next rant. "I have another problem," she said quickly, but Baron was already not listening.

"We can't just let him go. Get Tank in here," he said to Caroline. "No, scratch that. He saved Skip's life, so we're going to have to think about this one carefully for a while. Maybe we could-"

"Baron! There's something else you need to know."

"Did he harm you in any way?" Baron asked, turning to her quickly. "Because the only reason he saved your life was because he kidnapped you in the first place, so if he's-"

"I've been shot."

Baron stopped immediately. His eyes ran over Skip's body, looking for any signs of injury. "Where? I'll get Silas to remove the bullet. Or did it go straight through? We've got plenty of local anaesthetic, so he can stitch you up-"

"No. He can't."

And finally, she had Baron's attention.

"Where were you shot?" Heron asked, her face turning pale.

"In the leg. As a wolf." Skip swallowed, remembering the pouring blood, the searing pain.

"How bad?" Caroline asked.

"Bad," Skip said simply, knowing they would know what she meant. They were all well versed in the consequences of bullet wounds, and Skip had seen enough herself to know how much blood meant it was ugly but manageable, and how much meant a serious problem. It was remarkable how much a person could bleed before their life was seriously at risk, and it was common for new recruits to panic a little at some of the wounds that were presented. The older, more experienced wolves had a much better grasp on the intricacies of life-and-death situations. "It hit me in the leg, and possibly went through into my abdomen. I'm not sure about that part, but it definitely hit an artery." Arterial blood was a much more vivid red than blood from the veins, and instead of seeping, it pumped, the waves of pressure often visible with each beat of the heart.

"How long have you been in human form?" was Baron's next question, and Skip glanced at the clock on the wall.

"Coming up for twenty-four hours. I was in wolf form for less than a minute when I was shot, and aside from that, I haven't shifted since about midday yesterday."

"Fuck."

The timing of her last shift was critical. In general, shifters needed to spend roughly half their time in each form. Spending longer than twenty-four hours in one form became uncomfortable, and after three days, a shift was all but inevitable. And Skip knew everyone had grasped the implications of her injury. They needed to find serious medical help within the next forty-eight hours, at an absolute maximum, or she wouldn't be able to control her next shift, and she would likely bleed to death the moment she was in wolf form.

"I'll call the Council," Baron said, stalking from the room, the problem of a Noturatii operative locked in one of their cages suddenly forgotten.

It was mid afternoon when Jacob's phone rang, and he answered it immediately. "What?"

"We found the car, sir," one of his security personnel reported. "And it's bad news. It crashed into a stone wall. Steve and Daniel are dead. Miller's body isn't here, but there's blood on the driver's side door and his phone was lying on the road. There's no sign of the shifter girl."

"So what the fuck happened?"

"Forensics are going over the scene, but I'd be willing to make a few educated guesses until we get the official report back. Looks like they were heading back to the base with the girl in the car. Maybe the other shifters caught up with them, ran them off the road, and took the girl back. If Miller was injured, but still alive, it's likely they'd have taken him with them for interrogation. I don't like his chances of survival if that's the case."

Jacob swore fluently, rubbing his eyes, then thanked the man and hung up. The shifters were getting far too dangerous; they'd lost dozens of staff to them in the past year, and now Miller as well? He'd been one of the best, level headed, devoted, as reliable an operative as Jacob had ever known. He would be damn hard to replace.

But despite the security guard's assessment of the situation, Jacob wasn't prepared to close the case until the official forensic report came in. Miller had a sharp mind, a strategic way of thinking, and it was entirely possible he'd managed to escape, perhaps hiding somewhere nearby, perhaps even managing to hitch a ride back towards London. There were dozens of questions about the crash that needed investigating, and Jacob wasn't going to give up on Miller until he had answers.

CHAPTER TWENTY

"Feng!" One of the Council's administrative staff came dashing into the foyer, almost running into Feng in her hurry. "Video call for you, sir. It's Baron, from England."

Feng swore softly to himself. The Council was currently snowed under dealing with a major crisis, and he'd been on his way to an urgent meeting. "Can it wait?" he asked sharply, continuing on his path towards the library. But the woman shook her head.

"No, sir. It's urgent. A matter of life and death, he says."

"Shit..." Feng swiftly changed direction, following the woman back into the IT office. As if he didn't have enough on his plate at the moment. "Baron," he said, once he'd taken a seat and put on the headphones. "What's up?"

"We've had a run-in with the Noturatii," Baron said, wasting no time on pleasantries. "One of our wolves has been shot. Possible abdominal wound. We're going to need Nadia to get over here and do surgery." Nadia was the Council's physician, and the only person in Il Trosa currently with the skills to perform that kind of operation. Every Den had a few members skilled at treating wounds on the extremities, bullets or knives the usual culprits, and they were all equipped with a good supply of local anaesthetic, suture materials, antibiotics and the like. But abdominal surgery was a totally different ball game, with the risk of severe infections or damaged internal organs requiring the most skilled of hands for the task.

But recent complications made it impossible for Feng to meet Baron's request. "Can't do it," he said apologetically. "I'm sorry. One of the Dens in Russia was attacked. They've got a dozen casualties, and Nadia's on the plane heading over to them as we speak."

Baron swore. "Can you send the plane around? You could pick up Skip here, and send her over to Russia. She's not critical at the moment, but the clock is ticking."

"How much time?" Feng asked.

"We've got forty-eight hours, tops."

He closed his eyes, sighed, and shook his head. "Sorry. After Nadia gets to Russia, we're sending the plane to Berlin to pick up a couple of assassins, then sending them over to help out with the Russians. It was a full scale attack on their home estate. We're going to have to relocate the survivors, and we need backup so that the Noturatii doesn't come back and finish them off before we can move them. At this stage, it's just a numbers game," he said, cringing at how heartless that had to sound. "We can save more lives by focusing on Russia than by diverting the plane for one wolf."

More swearing from Baron, and Feng apologised profusely, though he wasn't sure Baron was listening.

"So what the fuck are we supposed to do?" Baron demanded. Given the extreme need for secrecy and the Noturatii's way of picking up on anything unusual going on, making use of local hospitals or veterinary services was out of the question. It was one of the bleaker parts of their existence, unable to access the normal, everyday services that humans took for granted.

But then Feng remembered something the Council had discussed a week or so ago. After her trip to England to visit the Den there, Eleanor had returned with some profound news. Andre, one of their former assassins, had devised a strategy to end the war with the Noturatii through a detailed and extravagant plan to expose the shifter species to the public.

Even if the Council accepted it, the plan would take years to accomplish, and it came with significant risks. There was a myriad of details still to be discussed, and there was currently no firm commitment to proceeding. But even so, several of the ideas had been surprisingly promising, one of which was to test out public sentiment about the shifters by revealing their secrets to a few select people, doctors, police or the like, who could offer the shifters valuable services. The response from the Council to the idea had been cautiously optimistic. And that was possibly something Baron could make use of now.

"Do you know of any decent vet clinics near you?" Feng asked, a cautious undertone in his voice.

"There are a few," Baron said impatiently. "But we can hardly just show up on their doorstep with a wolf with a bullet wound. People are going to ask questions about that sort of thing. And Skip's only going to have minutes to spare before she bleeds out once she shifts."

"I understand the problem," Feng said slowly. "But there's another angle we can approach this from…"

Dr Jamal Nagi bolted awake as his emergency phone rang shrilly. He grabbed it off the bedside table and answered it quickly. As a vet with his own successful practice, he was often on call for late night emergencies, and while getting dragged out of bed was never fun, he accepted it as a necessary part of his job. "Doctor Nagi," he said into the phone. "How can I help you?"

"My dog's been hit by a car," the urgent voice on the other end of the line said, a man with a deep voice. "I think she's going to need surgery. Can I bring her into the clinic?"

The news brought Jamal fully awake, and he sat up, flicking on the lamp and fumbling for a notepad and pen. "Of course," he replied quickly. "What's your name?"

"Henry Simms," the man said. "We haven't been to your clinic before, but we've just moved into the area. Our last vet was in London."

"No problem. You understand there are fees for an after hours call out?" He quickly outlined the likely costs, the call out fee, the hourly surgical rate – he was hoping that the dog could be stabilised and surgery performed the following day, as he didn't like performing difficult operations in the middle of the night without his nurses there to assist – and an additional fee for any medication the dog might require. Henry agreed to all the charges easily, stating that he would bring cash with him.

"What sort of dog is it?" Jamal asked next.

"Husky crossed with border collie."

"And where is she injured?"

"Her back leg," the man said. "And she's got a tear in her abdomen. It looks like it's gone right through."

Jamal held the phone away from his ear, swearing softly to himself. Abdominal wounds were nasty, the risk of infection high, and bore the possibility of further complications down the track. "Okay, I can be there in ten minutes," he said, already searching for his trousers.

"Okay. Thank you. See you soon." The man hung up, and Jamal finished dressing quickly, grabbed his keys and headed for the door.

But he paused a moment in the dim light of the lamp, glancing at the empty side of his double bed. It was both a blessing, and a curse that there was no one else in his flat who could be disturbed by his irregular late night calls. He'd divorced his wife five years ago in a messy break-up, and they'd never had any children. He'd poured all his energy into his business after the divorce, finding a certain satisfaction in the work, the joy of healing people's four-legged companions, the fascination of treating a range of wildlife from time to time... but there were still nights when waking up alone seemed to startle him, as if he had never quite adjusted to the lack of another human presence sleeping beside him.

Perhaps it was time he got another cat, he thought as he hurried out the front door and into his car. It was so much nicer to come home from these late night adventures to find *someone* waiting for him. As it was, he rather thought that if he didn't come home at all, no one would actually notice…

Baron pulled the van up outside the vet clinic. Silas had been watching the building since before they had called the vet, and had phoned Baron just moments ago with the report that the man had arrived at the clinic, that he was alone, and that there were no other people in the vicinity. They were good to go.

When they'd broken the news about Russia and the Council's surgeon to Skip, she'd turned pale. But then, when Baron had outlined the rest of Feng's plan, she'd taken on a determined look, and immediately scurried off to the IT office. "I have a database of humans who might be persuaded to help us," she'd said, rapidly typing on her treasured laptop. "Contingency plans, in case of emergency and all that," she'd added, no doubt aware that, in the normal scheme of things, exposing the general public to their secrets was absolutely forbidden. "There's a vet clinic in Carlisle. An unusual sort of vet. He does a lot of work for wildlife – birds, moles, hedgehogs. And he's a member of a medieval re-enactment society. It doesn't make him a sure thing, but it at least ticks one of the boxes, if he's into mythological sorts of things."

Skip had done her homework, Baron was relieved to see, a full background check on the man, with nothing showing up that would immediately discount him from being enlisted to help them – no immediate family, no criminal convictions, no signs of any link to the Noturatii.

And so they'd put their plan together. Taking a wolf to the clinic in broad daylight was definitely out, but if a midnight meeting could be arranged, by way of an 'emergency', then it would minimise any potential bystanders. They had decided not to tell the vet too much over the phone, Alistair helping them come up with the story that their 'dog' had been hit by a car in order to lure him to the clinic, and now it was Baron's job to meet the man in person and explain the rest of the situation – or a version of it, at least, one that would sound plausible to a man who was doubtlessly intelligent and discerning, but which also kept as much of their world a secret as possible. He would no doubt have questions, and despite their carefully constructed lies, there was a very real risk that something could go wrong – Skip shifting while waking up from the anaesthetic, for example – which would mean their cover was blown and their secrets exposed. While the good Doctor Nagi seemed like a decent enough fellow, they hadn't had time to do anything like their usual level of investigations to ensure that he was both willing and able to keep the kind of secrets he could become privy to.

Skip was still in human form, waiting in the back of the van with Heron, nervous and pale as she was entirely aware of everything that could go wrong with this plan. Baron would go inside, explain their requirements and make sure everything was set up for urgent surgery, and then at the last possible moment, she would shift, they would carry her inside and, if Sirius was smiling on them today, the vet would remove the bullet and save her life.

Baron was feeling almost as nervous as Skip. Due to their time limitations, this exercise had been planned in a rush and he knew there were almost certainly details that they had overlooked. But, as he'd acknowledged in his earlier conversation with Feng, they were out of options. Risking a human finding out about them was dangerous, but not entirely out of the question, given the Council's recent discussions on the possibility of going public – an announcement that Baron had found rather startling, if he was honest about it – and simply allowing Skip to die was not an option. With one final, grim nod to Skip and Heron, he climbed out of the van.

Caroline and Andre were right behind him, and he was relieved to see Silas appear from out of the darkness, heading straight for the van. As the most experienced of them all in terms of surgery and the treating of wounds, it would be his job to control the bleeding until Skip was on the table and the vet had taken over. Caroline immediately headed off into the shadows, charged with keeping an eye on security while the rest of them were inside, and Andre had been brought along because of his unusual abilities in hypnosis. If the vet decided to panic or get too curious about any of the details, it was Andre's job to calm him down and make sure he was in a suitable frame of mind to perform the surgery.

"Ready everyone?" Baron asked, glancing at the team around him. They were some of the finest wolves he had ever met, and he couldn't have asked for more in an undertaking as stressful and risky as this one.

A chorus of agreement came back at him, so he marched quickly towards the building, bracing himself for a very odd conversation to come.

Jamal had just finished checking there was enough liquid in the anaesthetic machine when he heard a knock at the door. He hurried out into the waiting room and saw the two men standing there. His first impression was of a couple of thugs, both of them large men, wearing dark coats and darker scowls, but when he appeared, the taller of the two looked relieved and waved at him through the glass. He unlocked the door and let them in.

"Thank you so much for coming," the man said without even introducing himself. "The dog's in the van. She's been bleeding pretty badly, and we've got her more or less stable, but the moment we move her,

I think the bleeding's going to start up again."

"Perhaps I should take a look at her in the van first of all then," Jamal volunteered immediately, reaching for the stethoscope on the reception desk, but the man shook his head.

"Before we do any of that, there are a few things I need to explain. She's not a normal dog, and… I'm afraid we haven't been entirely honest about her injuries."

That got Jamal's attention. He wasn't a small man, and had seen enough of life in his fifty or so years that he didn't scare easily, but the look of grim determination on this man's face was enough to give him pause.

"If you've come here to rob me, you've come to the wrong place." It wouldn't be the first time weirdos had shown up at the clinic, hoping to score some morphine or wanting a supply of syringes for various nefarious purposes, and Jamal had learned to be firm and direct in his refusals, not hesitating to call the police should anyone get out of hand.

"No, no, nothing like that. We have no intention of threatening you. We need your help," the man said sincerely. "I'm sorry, I should at least introduce myself. My name's Henry. I spoke to you on the phone. And this is Andrew," he added, pointing to the man beside him. "We have a badly injured dog, and she's going to need urgent surgery to save her life. The problem is more in the details."

"Go on," Jamal said, curious, though also cautious about these imposing men.

"I'll try to keep this short and simple," Henry said. "We are a covert operations unit within the military. Our usual vet is away overseas, and we had a run in with a terrorist group who decided to shoot first and ask questions later. The dog hasn't been hit by a car; she's been shot in the back leg, and the bullet has ruptured an artery and passed through into her abdomen. I need you to control the bleeding, remove the bullet, and see to any internal injuries. I'm sorry I couldn't tell you this on the phone, but given the nature of our operations, all information about ourselves and our animals is on a strict need-to-know basis."

Jamal was listening carefully, perplexed by the secrecy and subterfuge, but with an injured animal needing medical attention, he wasn't inclined to play twenty questions about the exact circumstances of her being injured. "I can do my best," he said in reply, "but bullet wounds aren't the usual fare of a vet clinic. I don't have anything like the kind of medical facilities that would be available in a human hospital."

"Okay, then let me put this in context for you," Henry said, calm but firm, his eyes never leaving Jamal's. "This dog is the product of generations of careful breeding. She has undergone years of specialist training, she has saved the lives of several members of our team, and all up, she's probably worth close to a hundred thousand pounds. Money is no object. Whatever treatment you think she needs, you give it to her. Here's five hundred pounds for starters, and I'll pay you the rest once you know what the exact costs are." He retrieved a wad of cash from his pocket and handed it to Jamal. "We've brought one of our medical support staff with us, who can act as surgery nurse, and the rest of us are willing to lend a hand in whatever way is necessary." Jamal saw a tremor cross the man's face, and had the odd impression that he was fighting back tears. "I need you to save her life," he said simply, by way of conclusion, and Jamal took a deep breath, and then nodded his agreement. If he was reading the guy correctly, then it wasn't just a question of the dog's monetary value. He'd treated working dogs before – police dogs, military dogs, guide dogs – and had seen the extreme emotional bonds that soldiers and officers often formed with their animals.

"I'll do everything I can," he promised them.

"It's a foregone conclusion that she's going to need surgery," the second man said, the first time he'd spoken since he'd entered the room. "So how about we help you get everything set up and ready to go, because like Henry said, the moment we move her, she's probably going to start bleeding again. We're not going to have much time to mess about."

Jamal led them through into the surgery room and picked up his preparations where he'd left off. Surgical kit, sterilised and ready to go. Gloves for himself and an assistant, an IV line set up for fluids, a syringe full of intravenous anaesthetic to put the dog under, suture material, antibiotics; he prepared everything he could think of that he might need. And when the preparations were complete, he turned back to the waiting men. "Okay, all set. Bring her in."

"It might take a few minutes," Henry said, heading for the door. "We want to make sure we don't do her any further damage by moving her."

Jamal nodded, and watched the two men leave. It was going to be difficult surgery, but he was surprised to find he was feeling rather calm about the whole thing. For all his military air, that second man, Andrew, seemed to have a rather soothing air about him. It was going to be fine, Jamal recited to himself, mentally preparing himself for the long operation to come. It was all going to be fine...

Back at the van, Baron opened the side door, seeing Skip sitting on the floor. Heron was beside her, holding her hand, while Silas had set out a range of medical supplies to take care of the wound.

"All set," Baron reported. "Ready whenever you are."

Silas turned to Skip and gently took her hand. "Don't fret, little sprite," he whispered to her, and then recited a portion of the Chant of Forests, the shifters' solemn vow to defend each other to the death. "*I will not sleep until you rest safely. If you call me, I will come. If you fall I will carry you. I will measure your steps this day that you run."* And then he added a final line, not part of the chant, that elicited a wobbly smile from his young patient. "The sun will not set upon you this evening."

"Let's do this," Skip said, trying to sound brave, and then she lay down on the pad of towels that had been laid out for her. The shift was smooth and fast, and the instant she was in wolf form, Silas leapt into motion. A quick check of the wound to assess the damage, then a thick dressing, pressed down firmly to slow the bleeding. A rapid assessment of her vitals. "Pulse is strong. Breathing's steady. Colour's good. It's as good a starting point as we could ask for."

"You ready to move her?" Baron asked, and Silas glanced at Skip, who nodded.

"Let's go."

She was clearly in pain, Baron could see, as he carefully slid his arms beneath her body and lifted her as gently as he could. Silas was keeping pressure on the wound, trotting along beside him as he made his way back to the clinic, then there was an awkward sideways shuffle as they made their way into the surgery room.

"Let me see the wound," the vet instructed, once she was settled on the table, and a quick peek under the dressing had him swearing softly under his breath. He quickly took her vitals, and then said, "All right, let's put her under." He reached for a set of clippers to prepare an IV site on Skip's foreleg, and Baron hoped he wasn't going to say anything that would unduly worry Skip before she was under. He would have liked to warn the doctor to watch what he said, but for the life of him, he couldn't think of a sensible way to explain the fact that their dog could understand English.

"I'm going to need someone to hold her head while I intubate her," the vet said, once the IV line was in place, and Baron stepped forward.

"I'm on it."

"Usually I don't do this unless the animal has had a sedative first, so the induction might be a little rough. If she struggles, I'll need you to hold her down."

"Hang on tight, sweetheart," Baron muttered to Skip, as the doctor began injecting the anaesthetic into her vein. "It'll all be over soon."

An hour and a half later, Baron was pacing the room. The vet had done a marvellous job so far, giving clear instructions to Silas while he prepped the wound sight, controlling the bleeding rapidly and closing off each blood vessel with neat, precise stitches.

Silas had been monitoring the anaesthetic, Skip's blood pressure, reflexes and breathing, and there'd been a few minutes of tense alarm when her blood pressure had dropped dramatically low. As predicted, she'd lost a lot of blood during the process of closing the leg wound, and Jamal had left off the surgery for a moment, giving curt instructions to Baron about increasing the rate of her IV fluids, administering various medications to try and stabilise her. It had worked, to a degree, but Jamal remained anxious about her vitals, asking Silas for updates every few minutes in case she took a turn for the worse.

A few minutes ago, Baron had helped him move Skip onto her back, ready for the next part of the surgery, and he'd watched with apprehension as Jamal had cut a long, straight line along her middle, opening up her abdomen in order to remove the bullet.

Jamal was wrist deep in her innards now, portions of her guts hanging out, and Baron fought back the urge to vomit. For all his hefty experience in treating wounds, he'd never had to stand there and look at the intestines of one of his Den mates before, and the view was more than a little confronting. How the hell vets and doctors did this on a daily basis, he would never understand.

He was about to ask Jamal if it was okay if he stepped outside for a short breather when the vet suddenly swore, his hands a flurry of motion as he grabbed surgical instruments and swabs and pulled a large section of Skip's bowel out of her body.

"What's up?" Silas asked, sounding far calmer than Baron was feeling.

"The bullet perforated her gut," the vet said grimly. "There's been some leakage into her abdomen. I'm going to need to lavage the abdomen and put her on some strong antibiotics, or she's likely to end up with a serious infection."

Baron gritted his teeth and sent a fervent prayer skyward to Sirius. *Save her life,* he asked of the divine wolf god. *This is your daughter. Your creation. Don't take her from us now...*

CHAPTER TWENTY-ONE

Miller sat on the narrow cot in his cage in the shifters' dungeon, watching the guard who was watching him back. There were two guards, actually, the second being a dark skinned woman with a predatory stare, but the one who held his attention was the man.

It was the shifter they'd captured back before the lab explosion at the beginning of the year. The one he'd seen in Scotland, playing with the young woman he now knew to be Skip.

The one who had promised to kill him one day.

In all honesty, he was feeling a little confused about his captivity. After being bundled into the cage, he'd expected to be interrogated, asked for more details on the men who had helped him capture Skip, his job, the Noturatii's operations, the other staff members he worked with.

Instead, they'd brought him lunch. Then a change of clothes and a towel so he could have a shower, and then a small medical kit so he could clean the wound on his head.

After that, he'd expected the leader of the pack to come down and start the interrogation routine, or perhaps the warrior woman he'd seen back in Scotland, the one who habitually wore black leather. But neither had appeared, Miller being left alone, aside from the two guards, until dinner had arrived. He wondered if the delay in the leader coming to see him was a simple psychological tactic. If so, he was prepared to wait. The longer they took to interrogate him, after all, the longer he got to keep breathing.

But despite looking after him physically, the guard had made no secret of his loathing for Miller, glaring at him like he'd be more than willing to gut him while Miller screamed. It was an obvious intimidation tactic, but being as well versed in the various methods of dealing with prisoners as he was, Miller had succeeded in ignoring him for most of the afternoon.

Now, it was coming up to 1am, but despite the dramas of the day, Miller wasn't feeling inclined to sleep. There were too many unanswered questions plaguing his thoughts.

Arriving at this estate had been startling in and of itself. He'd been right here, earlier in the summer, during his quest to locate the second shifter pack. He'd talked to that 'caretaker' and fallen for the disguise, hook, line and sinker, dismissing this estate from the list of those that could potentially be connected to the shifters. But despite his embarrassment at being fooled, it was something of a relief that he had been. Otherwise all of these people, along with himself, would be in a whole lot more trouble than they were already in.

And then there was the realisation that the entire group of them were living together in one place, under one roof. They'd been here for years, decades, and yet even now, the Noturatii were none the wiser. Hiding in plain sight, as it were, and they were far, far better at it than he would ever have believed, given the Noturatii's insistence that the shifters were little better than dumb animals. How many of them were here? How did they keep the peace, with so many people living in the same building? What sort of facilities did they have, to keep all of their members trained in combat so well?

The questions were endless, and many of them would likely never get answered... but as he sat there, he glanced at the guard, wondering if he could answer at least one of the swirling concerns in his mind.

"How's Skip?" he asked, breaking the tense silence.

"None of your business," the guard replied shortly.

"She was shot, just after the car crash," Miller persisted. After his efforts to help the girl, it would be nice to know whether she was going to suffer serious complications from the wound. He couldn't quite bring himself to entertain the idea that she might die from it. It had been bad, certainly, but he was sure that the shifters would make every effort to look after her.

The guard paced over to the front of his cage. "Mind your own damn business," he said harshly, and Miller fought back a sigh of frustration.

"What's your name?" he asked next, changing tactics.

"You just don't quit, do you?" the guard snapped at him. "Sit down, and shut up."

"Look, I know you hate me. And with good reason. But I'm serious about leaving the Noturatii. And I'd like to help you, if I can. You don't deserve the shit they've been doing to you." It was an attempt to appease the guard, to open a more meaningful conversation, though there was a good chance he was wasting his time. "I know it doesn't make up for much, but I owe you an apology."

"You owe me a hell of a lot more than that," the guard said darkly. "But don't worry. I have every intention of collecting."

"I just want to know if Skip's okay. She was bleeding pretty badly-"

126

"What I want to know," the guard snapped, standing less than an inch from the bars, "is what the hell kind of fucked up arsehole thinks that what your mob of bastards was doing could ever have been right? You kidnapped innocent women. Tortured them. Killed them. You wanted to kill shifters, yeah, I kind of get that. But random bystanders who had never done you any harm? There was never a point when you looked at that and thought 'hey, maybe this isn't such a great idea, after all'?"

The guard had a point, and Miller felt a fresh wave of guilt that he hadn't realised the error of his ways sooner. But in the next instant, a strange instinct rose up inside him, an irrepressible urge to answer the challenge the man was presenting him with, the urge to protect, to fight, to defend, and he found himself on his feet a moment later, facing the man through the bars. "So you've never made a mistake? Killed an innocent bystander? Pulled the trigger a little too soon when you should have been finding out what the real situation was? I'm not perfect. I've made plenty of mistakes, and I regret a lot of them, but don't get on your high horse and pretend you've never hurt anyone who didn't deserve it."

"We've never tortured anyone," the guard growled, and Miller felt the oddest sensation along the back of his neck, like a crackle of static electricity, his hairs standing on end.

"Oh, so it's fine to kill people, so long as you don't let them suffer in the process? That mentality is just as screwed up as the Noturatii's." Where the hell was this aggression coming from? Until now, his philosophy had been simple. Sit down, shut up, and don't do anything to antagonise the people who were no doubt more than willing to put him in an early grave.

The guard moved then, and in a flash, he had unlocked the cage door, flung it open, grabbed Miller by the collar and hauled him up against the wall. And despite his own size and weight, Miller was rather astonished by the strength of the man. "Much more of your backchat, and you're going to find out just how angry I can get," he promised grimly.

"Tank!" the other guard yelled in alarm, drawing her gun and dashing forward. "What the fuck are you doing? Baron told us not to kill him!"

So his name was Tank, Miller thought as he wondered what was going to happen next. There was an odd satisfaction in finally knowing the man's name. And it couldn't have suited him more.

With a predatory leer, Tank stepped back, set Miller back on his feet, and slowly drew his gun. Miller braced himself, hoping his death would be fast and painless... but instead, Tank handed his gun to the woman.

"Hold this," he said, then grabbed Miller again and hauled him out of the cage. "I promised you a fair fight one day," he bit out, stepping back and falling into a fighting stance. "Just you and me, no wolves, no guns... and I'm about ready to deliver on that promise."

"I don't want to fight you," Miller said, automatically bringing his fists up to defend himself.

"Then stand there like the wet cunt you are, and let me kill you."

Raniesha gasped in horror as the two men threw themselves at each other. This was supposed to be simple guard duty, keep an eye on the prisoner until Baron and Caroline got back from dealing with Skip, and then their alphas could sort out the mess. She glanced down at the gun in her hand, then pointed it almost desperately at the two brawling men. "Stand down!" she ordered sharply. "Pull your head out of your fucking arse and put him back in his cage!"

Both men ignored her, and Raniesha frantically tried to think what she should do next. Actually shooting either of them was out of the question – Tank was their 2IC, and the ranking wolf on the estate while Baron was away, and Miller was a hostage who could have vital information to help them fight the Noturatii.

Swearing to herself, she pulled out her phone and dialled John's number. There was no way she could take Tank on by herself, as he was not only bigger than her, but a far more experienced fighter, and John was the only person currently on the estate who had the skills to separate the two men without getting badly hurt in the process. "Get down to the cages," she snapped, when he answered the phone. "Tank and Miller are fighting!"

The phone went dead, and moments later, heavy footsteps came thudding down the stairs. John threw the door open and took one look at the two men – Tank currently had Miller in a headlock and was trying to choke him, while Miller had sunk his teeth into Tank's arm and was clawing at his face, trying to go for his eyes – and John promptly burst out laughing.

"It's not funny!" Raniesha snapped. "Help me get them apart!"

But John kept laughing, then had the audacity to lean nonchalantly against the door frame. "Oh, thank you for letting me see this," he said to no one in particular. "I only wish I'd had time to make popcorn."

Miller had succeeded in extracting himself from Tank's grip now, and they were facing off like a pair of boxers… until Miller kicked Tank in the groin, and slammed his fist into his face in the moment of distraction that followed. Tank's response was to body-slam his opponent into the wall, Miller cracking his head on the concrete with a loud thud.

"Fuck you," Raniesha said to John, then dialled Simon instead. Where the hell were Andre or Silas when she needed them?

Less than a minute later, there were more footsteps on the stairs, and she breathed a sigh of relief as not just Simon, but Alistair and Mark both came charging into the room.

"Tank!" Simon barked. "You let him go right now!" Tank had Miller pinned up against the wall, his forearm slowly crushing his throat and Miller's face was turning red, then purple as he tried to breathe.

When his shouts got no response, Simon stalked over to Raniesha and took the gun out of her hand. "You can't shoot him!" she said, sounding uncertain. But how the hell else were they going to get the two men apart?

But Simon was nothing if not a strategic thinker, and rather than aiming the gun at Tank's head or chest, he instead pointed it at his leg. "So help me God, I will shoot you in the leg if you don't let him go."

The cold steel in Simon's voice broke through Tank's rage, and he seemed to realise that Simon was absolutely serious in his threat. He eased the pressure off Miller's neck, then stepped back, letting the other man slide to the floor as he gasped for breath.

"No problem," he said darkly. "I think I've made my point."

"Get back in the cage," Simon said next, turning the gun on Miller, and Miller nodded, then dragged himself upright and staggered back inside the cage, Simon slamming the door shut behind him.

An awkward silence settled on the group.

"Mind if I have my gun back now?" Tank asked smoothly.

"Are you done being a fucking idiot?" Simon asked, not at all intimidated by the larger man.

"Like I said. I've made my point."

Simon rolled his eyes, but handed the gun back anyway. Alistair and Mark were still hovering in the background, while John looked almost disappointed that the show had ended so soon.

"Want me to take over guard duty for a while?" Simon offered, which made Tank chuckle.

"I think I can handle it." Simon lingered a moment longer, then turned and headed out the door, the rest of them following behind. Watching from the side of the room, Raniesha wasn't entirely happy with the arrangement, not convinced that Tank wouldn't try some other reckless stunt the next time his anger got the better of him, but since he was the ranking wolf, there was little she could do about it for the moment. "If you've got any sense," she snapped at Miller, "then you'll keep your thoughts to yourself for the rest of the night. Got it?"

"Got it," Miller agreed, hunched awkwardly on his bed as he caught his breath. "No problem."

It was approaching three o'clock in the morning when the surgery was finally over. Skip was recovering from the anaesthetic, laid out on a pad of towels on the floor, whimpering and shivering as she slowly came to, with Heron and Silas sitting protectively beside her.

Jamal had performed as well as anyone could have expected, removing the bullet, closing off the hole in her intestines and cleaning out her abdomen as thoroughly as he was able, though he still had grave concerns about her recovery.

"She'll need to stay at the clinic for a few days," he said to Baron, once he'd cleaned up the bulk of the surgical equipment. "There's a strong likelihood she'll develop an infection. I've given her some IV antibiotics, but I'd like to monitor her for a few days-"

"It's not going to happen," Baron said firmly, respecting the doctor's opinion, but unable to consent to his request. "We'll be taking her with us tonight, as soon as she's awake enough to travel."

Jamal frowned at that, glancing over to where Skip lay on the floor, then over to Andre, and back to Baron. "I'm afraid I can't let you do that," he said, as politely as possible. "It puts her life at risk, and if she's as valuable as you say she is, then-"

"Step into the waiting room with me," Baron instructed, then headed out the door without waiting for a reply.

Jamal followed him, unhappy with the way the conversation was going, and from the look on his face, ready to make an issue of it.

"I understand the risks to her health," Baron said, once they were alone. "But in this case, there are extenuating circumstances that mean it's impossible for us to leave her here. What I said about her being valuable is true. But our work tends to attract the attention of some extremely nasty people, and there are those who would kill – literally – to get their hands on one of our dogs. So it's not safe for her to stay here, either for her, or for you."

Jamal considered that idea carefully. "You're saying it's possible that if anyone found out about this, they could take exception to me helping you out?"

"It's unlikely anyone will find out, but it's a possibility, yes. So I would recommend not keeping any records of what went on here tonight. But if you really have to, then make up a name, both for me and the dog, say that the surgery was what I said the first time – a dog hit by a car – and then do your best to pretend you never saw us."

"Not exactly the result I had in mind when I was called in for a dog in a car accident," Jamal said wryly, then he sighed. "Fine. I guess you're taking her with you, then. What sort of medical equipment do you have back at your base?"

"Plenty. And we have some trained medical staff. They're just not qualified to do the kind of surgery you did here tonight."

"Then I would strongly recommend monitoring her closely for the next few days, including keeping track of her blood pressure and temperature. I'll give you some antibiotic tablets to take with you, but if her temperature spikes, for God's sake, bring her back. Do you have some IV fluids?"

"Yes."

"Then I'll leave the cannula in. Give her another bag over the next twenty-four hours. Or better yet, a blood transfusion, if you have another dog who can act as a donor, and have the facilities for that sort of thing. Her blood pressure's still low, and that's not going to help her fight off an infection."

Baron nodded. "We'll be in touch if anything goes wrong," he promised. "Now, can we sort out the bill?"

Jamal went to the computer and added up some figures. Watching over his shoulder, it looked like a long list, surgery, a dozen different medications, the after hours call out, IV fluids... "One thousand, five hundred pounds," he said when he was finished.

Baron pulled a wad of cash out of his pocket, and counted off two thousand. He handed it to Jamal, who counted it, and raised an eyebrow. "Consider it a bonus for a job well done," he said simply.

Jamal just shrugged, and pocketed the cash.

"Just one more issue before we go," Baron said, hoping he wasn't pushing too hard. They'd asked a lot of this man already, but he'd stepped up to every challenge without protest, and seemed to display a genuine concern for Skip's welfare. "There's a chance we'll need this sort of service again in the future. Our work is necessarily covert, and that limits our access to normal veterinary services and supplies. So I was wondering if you'd be interested in helping us out again? Just in case we're not able to use our regular vet for any reason. It would involve a fair bit of inconvenience," he went on, when Jamal went to reply. "Late night calls, home visits in out of the way places. But you have the sort of skills we could make good use of, and we'd make it more than worth your while."

Jamal thought about that. "I expect that, if this became a long term thing, there would be some sort of contract for me to sign. Confidentiality clauses and all that?"

"Something of that nature, yes," Baron confirmed, though he hadn't actually considered the idea until Jamal mentioned it. Once back at the Den, he would get Simon to run a more thorough background check on the man, have Silas tail him for a few days, check out a few of his more regular acquaintances. And, of course, tap his phone and his internet connection, to see if he started running any foolish searches on Britain's covert military operations. The results of all those investigations would say far more about his trustworthiness than a simple signature on a piece of paper.

"I'll have to think about it," Jamal said finally. "Helping out our nation's military is a worthy cause, but if it comes at significant personal risk, it's not a decision I can make overnight. And certainly not when I'm as sleep deprived as I am."

"Of course," Baron agreed genially. "It's unlikely to happen very often, in any event. I'll contact you again in a couple of weeks, and see what you think by then. Now, if you'll excuse me, I want to check on our patient."

CHAPTER TWENTY-TWO

Baron was exhausted by the time he pulled the van up outside the manor. As soon as Skip was awake, they'd bundled her back into the vehicle – partly due to the desire to get her home and comfortable, and partly due to the ongoing fear that the longer they stayed at the vet clinic, the greater chance there was that something could go wrong.

Halfway home, Skip had shifted back into human form, dazed and disoriented from the drugs still working their way out of her system, but calming down quickly when Heron put her arms around her and held her still, muttering soothing words into her ear... but then Skip had started giggling, a side effect of the drugs, no doubt, and had spent the better part of ten minutes repeatedly explaining that nothing at all was funny, and then breaking down into giggles again.

It was coming up to five o'clock in the morning, and no one in the van had got any sleep. But there was still plenty to do before any of them could go to bed, so Baron climbed wearily out of the driver's seat and opened the back door.

"Can you walk, or do you want me to carry you?" Silas asked Skip, and she peered up at him blearily.

"I can walk," she said confidently, then unexpectedly shifted, and promptly collapsed on the floor of the van. Silas swore as he darted forward to catch her, then lifted her gently, being careful not to tear any of her stitches.

Inside the foyer, Simon was waiting for them – a surprise to Baron, as he'd assumed that everyone else would be sleeping. He waved Baron over, casting a concerned eye over Skip as Silas carried her up the stairs, then spoke in a low voice, so as not to be overheard. "Sorry for the shitty timing," he apologised, "but we have a problem."

"What problem?"

"Tank decided to have a go at Miller." He outlined the events in the cage room, concluding with his offer to take over guard duty, and Tank's firm refusal.

Baron felt his jaw drop as Simon detailed the fight. "What the fuck did he think he was doing?" he asked, when he'd finished.

"Raniesha was there when it started. She'd know what set him off."

"Follow me," Baron ordered, marching swiftly down the hidden stairs into the basement. "Tank!" he bellowed, even before he'd got to the door of the cage room. "What the fuck has been going on?" He barged through the door and pulled up short when he saw the black eye on Tank's face, and the thick bruises around Miller's throat. "Oh, you have got to be kidding me."

"He had it coming," was the first thing Tank said, and, feeling a surge of rage at his 2IC's stupidity, Baron stepped forward and punched him in the face before he'd even thought about it. And then was instantly ashamed of his own display of temper. "I turn my back for five fucking minutes, and you *let a Noturatii operative out of his cage?* Not to mention the fact that we *do not torture our prisoners!* What the fuck were you thinking?"

Tank eyed Miller and scowled. "He was asking for it."

Baron gaped at Tank, speechless for a moment, then shook his head. "Get in the cage."

Tank looked suitably surprised at that. "What?"

"In the cage!" Baron repeated. "Until further notice, you're relieved of duty."

Tank scowled at him, but marched across the room, into the cage on the far wall.

"Not that one," Baron instructed. "This one." He pointed to the one next to Miller's. "Think of it as poetic justice," he went on, as Tank looked both baffled and disgusted by the order. "You want to be a fucking idiot about security, then fine. You can keep him company for a while. And learn to control your temper while you're at it. And give Simon your gun."

A low growl filled the room, but Tank obediently withdrew the gun from its holster, handed it over to Simon, then went to the other cage and shut himself in.

"And don't you say a fucking word," Baron snarled at Miller, who was sitting quietly on his bed, watching the entire drama. "I've been awake for nearly forty-eight hours, and I'm not dealing with either of you until I've had enough sleep for me to be able to think straight. Simon, you're on guard duty. Call Alistair and get him down here to help you. Raniesha, you come with me. I want to know exactly what happened down here, and then you're due for a rest."

Raniesha nodded silently and left the room, heading up the stairs to wait for him in the sitting room.

Baron was totally exhausted, but he couldn't resist stepping over to Tank's cage, more disappointed than angry at his failure. "You're supposed to have my back," he said. "It's a pretty dismal indication of the state of this Den if I can't trust you to keep a simple fucking door locked for a couple of hours, or if wolves that rank seven places below you have to come down here and try to put things in order."

"I'm sorry," Tank tried to say, but Baron wouldn't hear it.

"Save it," he snapped… but then suddenly, the door burst open again and Caroline and Silas marched through, a medical kit in Silas's hand. Fuck. More dramas, when all he really needed was a solid six or seven hours sleep.

Caroline saw Tank standing in the cage, and did a double take, looking from him, to Baron, and back again. And then she saw the bruises on both his and Miller's faces, and reached the obvious conclusion, rolling her eyes at them both. "Fucking teenagers," she bit out. "Well, never mind. We have a bigger crisis to deal with. Tank, Skip needs a blood transfusion, and since Dee's away, you're it."

"How did the surgery go?" Tank asked, already rolling up his sleeve and taking a seat on the bed, as Caroline unlocked the door and Silas began setting up the medical kit.

"Successful, for the most part, but she's still got a serious risk of infection, and her blood pressure's low."

"Why can't any of the rest of you give blood?" Miller asked, causing Baron to snarl at him, but Caroline didn't seem to mind the question.

"Wrong blood type," she said simply, wrapping an elastic cuff around Tank's arm and swabbing the needle site with alcohol.

"I'm O-negative," Miller announced. "You can use that in just about anyone. If you need any extra, I'd be happy to help out."

"You can keep your fucking mouth shut," Tank snarled at him, as Silas inserted the needle into his arm, and Baron opened his mouth to tell Miller that that wasn't the way it worked in shifters… but then suddenly thought better of his quick dismissal. The fact was, shifters were only able to donate blood to others of their own bloodline. Skip was of the line of Harkans, and transfusing her with blood from someone like Caroline, descended from the line of Ranor, would likely kill her. But if what Skip had said was true, and she'd somehow accidentally converted Miller out in the forest, then he would be of her bloodline. And that made him a perfect candidate for a much needed extra donor.

"Actually, that's not a bad idea," Baron said cautiously, catching Caroline's eye. She seemed to pick up on his line of thought quickly, and glanced at Silas. As far as they knew, Miller was still unaware that he was a shifter, and while they would have to break the news to him sooner or later, Baron didn't fancy doing it while Skip's health was still in jeopardy, and while Miller himself was likely still riled up over his fight with Tank.

"Let's do it," Caroline said, checking that Tank was all set up. She grabbed a second kit from the medical bag and went to Miller's cage door. "I'm sure I don't have to tell you that if you do anything stupid, this nice gentleman will kindly splatter your brains all over the wall," she said, nodding to where Simon was hovering in the background.

Miller gave her a wry smile. "I think I've got a handle on the situation."

Miller watched as the man with the scar removed the needle from his arm, then packed up the equipment and headed out of the cage. He hadn't picked up on his name yet, but he'd paid careful attention to the conversation in the room, and had learned a few of the others. Aside from Tank there were Simon and Alistair, his two new guards, Baron, the leader, Caroline, the warrior woman, and one of the women upstairs was apparently called Heron, though he couldn't yet put a face to the name.

He'd been surprised by Baron's decision to lock Tank in a cage. Apparently he'd been right in his recent assessment of the morals of these people. They fought the war with the Noturatii fiercely and without hesitation, but they also seemed to have strict standards about how to treat their prisoners, and he was relieved to find that torture was strictly off the table.

Tank was quiet now, sitting on his bed as everyone else took the blood and filed out of the room, leaving them alone with their guards. Miller wasn't expecting much in the way of conversation, and contemplated trying to get a little sleep before the dramas of the new day started up. His body was feeling strange again, his arms itching, unable to get his legs quite comfortable, and he wondered if he was coming down with something as a result of his night in the wilderness.

But just as he was about to lie down, Tank unexpectedly spoke. "Why do you care so much about Skip?" he asked, in a tone that suggested he was working hard to stay polite, and Miller floundered for an answer for a moment, not quite able to understand his own fierce protective instincts.

"She's the complete opposite of everything the Noturatii says shifters are supposed to be. From the moment I joined them, I was told you were all ruthless, violent, merciless and destructive. She's... young. Innocent. Brave. Nothing like the brutal warriors I was taught to expect."

"She's not a defenceless child," Tank snapped, and Miller had to laugh at that.

"No, she's not. She stole my gun, threatened to shoot me, and somehow, against my better judgement, managed to talk me into coming here. She's quite the force to be reckoned with."

"Well, I appreciate you giving blood to help her out," Tank said with a grudging respect. Then, lest Miller start getting too comfortable with his new neighbour, he added, "Especially since it was your fault she got shot in the first place. But get any ideas about trying to make friends with her out of your head. She doesn't owe you anything."

Miller rolled his eyes at the obvious 'older brother' routine. "Okay, Romeo, I get it. You've got the hots for her," he said, unable to resist the urge to needle the guy a little. "But I hardly think she's suddenly going to start seeing me as boyfriend material, so how about you just settle down."

"I do not have the hots for her!" Tank snapped, turning on him with a fierce glare. "And if you even suggest such a thing again, I'll gut you, you worthless maggot."

Given the circumstances, Miller found that a little funny. "I'd like to see you try, with these steel bars in the way."

Tank opened his mouth to reply… but then seemed to think better of it, and Miller hoped that Baron's earlier warning to him had sunk in. After a moment, Tank got up and went into the small ensuite bathroom that had been built into the back of each of the cages. Miller heard water running, and then Tank returned a moment later, a cup of water in his hand. He took a slow sip, then wandered over to the bars that separated their cages. "You seem to be feeling mighty comfortable, snuggled up in your safe little cage," he growled. "But don't forget – Baron's going to be down later, and after your stunt in Scotland, I doubt he's going to be taking it easy on you."

Miller got up and came to stand in front of him.

"Hey!" Simon said sharply. "I don't want to have to break anything up again, so how about you keep your distance from those bars, yeah?"

"Don't worry," Miller said, making sure there was at least a foot of space between him and the bars. "We're just having a *friendly chat*." He turned back to Tank. "Your boss seemed rather displeased when he found out you'd been giving me a hard time, so I'm thinking your threats sound a little hollow, right at the moment."

Without warning, Tank tossed the cup of water at Miller, landing a direct hit as the water smacked him in the face and drenched his clothes.

Miller calmly wiped his face. "Really?" he asked sardonically. "That's the best you've got?"

"Oh, I'm sure I could come up with a few other fluids to throw at you," Tank drawled, looking faintly amused. "But oh, wait… now I remember. Less than half an hour ago, I had you pinned up against a wall, fighting for your next breath."

"Really?" Miller asked provocatively. "You're sure there was nothing else you wanted to do to me while you had me pinned up against a wall?"

Without warning, Tank flung his arm through the bars and grabbed Miller by the shirt… or that was the intention, at least. His thick arm got stuck at the elbow, and he only managed to get a hold of his shirt by the tips of his fingers. Miller retaliated quickly, sending a fist towards his face, but Tank twisted, the blow just grazing his cheek instead. He grabbed Miller's arm, but his elbow was still stuck in the bars, and he had to fight for a moment to free himself, time which Miller used to twist free and try for that punch again, but he couldn't get a good angle, and only managed to slap him lightly on the cheek.

Tank tried to grab him by the hair, but Miller saw the hand coming, and ducked out of the way, so that Tank only managed to pat him lightly on the head.

The sound of stifled laughter got their attention, and they both pulled back. "What?" Tank demanded of Alistair, who gave up trying to smother his amusement and laughed out loud.

"Times like this I wish I could record this shit and put it on Facebook. Oh, don't let me interrupt," he said cheerfully, as they both glared at him. "Please, continue trying to bitch-slap each other like a couple of girls."

Miller snorted. "Given the way some of your women fight, that's hardly an insult."

Tank made a derisive noise. "Yeah, yeah, just go ahead and jump on the political correctness bandwagon."

"Don't mind if I do," Miller replied blithely. "You can't tell me you've never had your arse handed to you by one of your women warriors?"

"At least we have women warriors," Tank bit back. "I've never seen a single woman be employed as a soldier by the Noturatii."

"I'll mention that to my superiors when I get back," Miller said sassily. "'The shape shifters have some suggestions for how to improve our combat techniques'."

With a growl, Tank lunged for him through the bars again.

When Kwan and Aaron brought breakfast down, an hour or so later, it was to be met with a most peculiar sight. Simon and Alistair were both sitting on chairs, staring at the cages like they were watching a movie, a look on both their faces like they couldn't decide whether the show was a serious documentary, or the very best of satires.

Tank and Miller were each slouching on the ends of their beds, Miller's trouser leg rolled up, while Tank was peering at an ugly scar that ran from his ankle to his knee. "You were lucky," he was saying. "A land mine could well have blown your leg right off."

"You've got that right," Miller replied. "So anyway, the army discharged me, and I spent the next year in and out of hospital. Four operations to put everything right. I was cleared to go back to work, but couldn't figure out what I wanted to do… and then this guy shows up, talking about national security and covert intelligence work, and the next thing you know, I'm staring at a shape shifter strapped to a table, and my entire world's been flipped inside out."

Miller looked up and saw the two boys standing there. He got up, and Kwan went over to the slot in the side of his cage, pushing the breakfast tray inside, while Aaron did the same for Tank.

"So what about you?" Miller asked, once he'd thanked the boys and taken the tray back to his bed. "How did you become a shifter?"

"Pretty much the same story," Tank said, inhaling the toast and scrambled eggs. "Except the recruiting was done by the opposite team. And torturing women wasn't part of the job description."

"Touché," Miller said, digging into his own food. "I should have read the fine print a little more closely before I signed the contract."

Melissa stood at attention in the foyer of the Noturatii's main base, waiting for Professor Ivor Banks to arrive. He was the Noturatii's most senior scientist, the head of their research operations in Germany, and by all accounts, a genius. After a heartfelt plea from Melissa earlier in the year regarding the ongoing failures in the experiments the English lab was currently running on a shifter captive, he'd announced that he was coming to England to oversee and assist with their research.

Melissa took a deep breath as she heard a car pull up outside, trying to slow her racing heart. Professor Banks was one of her idols, a brilliant man who had made enormous leaps forward in the Noturatii's war with the shifters. Having him visit their labs was a tremendous honour, and she couldn't wait to get started on the experiments they would run together, already anticipating the discoveries they would make into shifter physiology.

Jacob had been planning on meeting the Professor with her, but after the disaster with the car crash yesterday morning, he was completely snowed under, wrapping up the investigation, arranging the funerals of the deceased men and trying to find a suitable replacement for Miller. He'd been the backbone of Jacob's personal security force for a long time, and finding a man even half as competent was going to be hard. In addition to that, the forensic team working on the car crash had arrived back half an hour ago, and Jacob had whisked them all off for an urgent meeting, wanting an immediate update on their preliminary findings from the crash site.

But that didn't mean Melissa was meeting the Professor all by herself. Doctor Evans, the head scientist in her team, was also there, and looking more than a little nervous as she waited beside Melissa. And she had good reason to be apprehensive. In her letter to the Professor, Melissa had been scathing in her reports on Evans' work. Their team was trying to unlock the secrets of how the shifters changed forms, and Melissa had come up with several ideas for how to improve the experiments, after early avenues of investigation had failed. But Evans had completely ignored her suggestions, and as far as Melissa was concerned, her inattention was causing unacceptable delays in their progress.

The door of the foyer opened then, two burly guards preceding Professor Banks into the room. And then Melissa caught sight of the Professor himself, and couldn't help the grin that plastered itself to her face. He was a short man, with a squarish head and greying hair, and wrinkles around his mouth that suggested he spent a lot of time frowning.

"Good morning, sir," she said warmly, stepping forward to shake his hand. "I'm Melissa Hunter. Welcome to England."

"It's a pleasure to meet you," he replied in a strong German accent. "I've been most intrigued by your ideas."

"And this is Doctor Evans, our Head of Science and Research," Melissa said, finding it surprisingly easy to be polite to the Doctor. With Professor Banks here, her patronising ways and obstructive techniques in the lab were suddenly far less of a problem than they had been of late, and the promise of real progress was making her feel generous.

"Doctor Evans," the Professor said, sounding less impressed than he'd been with Melissa. "No doubt we will have some interesting days ahead of us."

"It's a pleasure to have you here, sir," Evans said, managing not to look intimidated. "I've read some of your papers. I'm looking forward to hearing your ideas on our research."

"Let's not waste any time then," the Professor said, collecting his things from the guard. "Please, if you would show me to the labs, I will have a look around, and we can see what our first steps should be."

CHAPTER TWENTY-THREE

It was just after midday when Baron woke up. He'd finally collapsed into bed after Tank and Miller had both donated blood, Silas taking care of giving Skip the transfusion, and Caroline giving Baron sharp orders to go and get some sleep. He'd protested, wanting to see how Skip responded to the treatment, but as Caroline had pointed out, he wasn't doing anything useful at the moment, and they would call him immediately if there were any problems. So he'd relented, staggered back to his room and collapsed into bed, remembering nothing more until he woke up to daylight and John, sitting beside his bed with a cup of hot coffee in his hand.

"Here," John said, holding out the cup, once he saw Baron had opened his eyes. "Andre wants to talk to you about Miller. No rush – he said to let you wake up a bit and have a shower first – but he's having issues with his wolf."

That got Baron's attention. He sat up, rubbing his eyes, and took the coffee, slurping the hot liquid gratefully. He'd had about six hours sleep, he figured, glancing at the clock. Not enough to feel rested, but at least enough that now he might be able to think straight.

But Miller was far from his only problem, and another of the smaller, niggling ones came to mind now as he peered over at his boyfriend. "Simon said you were down in the cage room when Miller and Tank were fighting," he said, between sips of coffee. "You didn't think it was worth trying to separate them?" It came out harsh and annoyed.

John looked surprised at the reprimand. "Tank was winning," he said, deliberately misunderstanding the problem. "He didn't need my help." At the look of disbelief on Baron's face, John's own expression turned darker. "You wanted me to stop him from beating up a man who honestly deserves a slow, painful death? Shit, you're just lucky I didn't join in and help him finish the job. It would have been a pleasure. Really."

141

"And what about the fact that he has useful information that could help us fight this war? You didn't think it might be worth keeping him alive for a little longer?"

"Didn't occur to me," John said blithely. "I was more focused on the pleasure of watching his brains get splattered all over the floor."

Baron just sighed, knowing this argument wasn't going to go anywhere useful. He drained the last of his coffee, then hauled himself out of bed. "Tell Andre I'll be down in ten minutes," he told John, not knowing whether he would bother passing on the message or not. "I'm going to take a shower."

"How's Skip?" was the first thing Baron said when he strode into the library ten minutes later.

"Stable," Caroline replied, from the table where she was sitting with Andre, a cup of tea in front of each of them. "Her blood pressure's within acceptable limits, after the transfusion, and her temperature's normal. She's very tired, but she managed to eat a little this morning. Heron and Silas are still with her."

Baron nodded, knowing he'd need to go and see her himself in the near future, but he had bigger problems to deal with for the moment.

"So what's this about Miller?" he asked, turning to Andre.

"His wolf is starting to make its presence felt," Andre reported. "I went to check on him a little while ago. He's pacing, scratching his arms, complaining of a headache. Honestly, I'm surprised it took the wolf this long. Normally they're a lot quicker about it. And Miller himself still seems to be unaware he's been converted. Given that he's had no training of any kind, he's got no idea how to manage a shift, or how to handle the wolf."

"Given that he's from the Noturatii," Caroline said grimly, "the chances of him successfully merging with his wolf are slim to none. We've got a couple of days tops before he starts going rogue. So if we're going to get any useful information out of him, we're going to have to do it sooner rather than later."

"Well that would solve one problem, at least," Baron said, knowing it would sound rather macabre. "If he goes rogue, we'll have no choice but to put him down. Which sidesteps the issue of having to explain to Skip why we decided to kill him." Since her announcement that she'd been shot, they hadn't spoken of Miller with her again, much more pressing problems on all their minds. But she'd been emphatic when she'd arrived at the estate that they couldn't just shoot him, and Baron wasn't looking forward to having to make that decision.

"There's another angle we should consider with regards to using him as an informant," Andre pointed out. "We still have no idea whether we can trust him or not. So any information he tells us could be lies. In the best case, it could be a simple attempt to misdirect us, but far more likely, there would be a serious risk we could inadvertently step straight into a trap."

"On that basis, is it worth questioning him at all?" Caroline asked.

"I think it is," Baron said, after a moment's hesitation. "I certainly don't think we should act on anything he says without some careful investigation, but he should at least be able to give us the names of some high ranking operatives, for example. Once we've got the names, we can check out the people, and see what shows up. I don't want to kill innocent people by mistake, but Skip's a good enough hacker that she should be able to figure out which of them are legit, and if that gives us the chance to blow a few holes in the Noturatii's leadership structure, then it's worth doing."

When one o'clock rolled around, Miller and Tank were both sitting quietly on their beds. After breakfast, they'd both slept for a while, then Miller had woken up an hour or so ago, finding Tank already awake, and feeling restless, as well as hungry. Hopefully it wouldn't be too much longer until lunch.

Right on cue, the door to the cage room opened, but instead of those two young men returning with food, Baron marched into the room, Caroline on his heels. Baron glanced at him and Tank, and asked, with a sardonic edge to his voice, "How's it going, boys?"

Tank gave him a wry smirk. "It turns out Miller's not quite as much of an arsehole as I thought he was," he said, to which Miller let out a snort.

"It took a little while for your boy to pull his head out of his arse," he said in return, feeling more relaxed about the situation now that he was reasonably sure they weren't going to torture him. "But he got there in the end."

"Making friends, then?" Baron said. "Charming. But let's get down to business." He took a chair from the side of the room, sitting down in front of Miller's cage, Caroline standing with her arms folded beside him. "Pull up a chair," he instructed, and Miller did so, sitting down with an air of resignation.

"So this is the interrogation part?" he asked unnecessarily, and Baron nodded. But before he could start asking questions, Miller jumped in with one of his own. "How's Skip?"

"None of your business," Baron said firmly.

"Considering I gave blood for her, I thought it was a reasonable question," Miller persisted, trying to sound respectful.

Baron leaned forward, staring evenly at him. "You seem to be under the impression that you're dealing with the domesticated version of the canine," he said darkly. "Now, you might have had a friendly little pow-wow with

Tank here, and no doubt our guards have been treating you decently, but don't go getting comfortable. As far as I'm concerned, you're still public enemy number one, and if I don't find a damn good reason to keep you alive in the next fifteen minutes, then I'm more than happy to put you out of your misery. So can the attitude, you get me?"

"Yes, sir," Miller said immediately, readjusting his perspective. Sure, they might not torture him, but it seemed death was still a very real option.

"The first thing I want to know," Baron began, "is why you paid a visit to this estate a few weeks ago. You remember the nice old gentleman who met you at the gate, yes?" Miller nodded. "He called us the instant you left and told us all about it. So why were you here? How did you find us? And what does the Noturatii know about us as a result of that visit?"

It wasn't an unexpected starting point, and Miller answered quickly and honestly, hoping to put Baron's mind at ease a little. "As far as what the Noturatii knows, the answer is basically nothing. I came here to investigate whether the estate could be involved with shifter activity, and everything checked out. I did some digging into that supposed Italian company that owns the estate, and all their records were in order. So I removed this place from the list of suspect properties, and that was the end of it.

"As for why I was here in the first place, we received some information early this year that there were not one, but two shifter packs in England. Prior to that, we'd always assumed there was only one." The tip-off had, in fact, come from one of the members of the other shifter pack, the one that lived in the forests in the far north. The information had come as a huge surprise, not only because it confirmed a second pack, but because it had also made it clear that the two packs regarded each other with significant animosity. Miller refrained from mentioning exactly where the information had come from, as the last thing he wanted to do was get himself caught in the middle of an internal war between rival shifter factions. "So we started doing a sweep of the entire Lakes District," he went on. "There was nothing about this property that meant we were targeting it specifically. It was just the right sort of size, in the right sort of area."

Baron looked faintly relieved at the news. "Okay, next question. Why have the Noturatii been kidnapping people and trying to convert them into shifters?"

Another predictable question. "They've been trying to work out how the conversion process works, with the ultimate goal of finding out how to reverse it."

Baron looked alarmed at the idea. "And how far have they come towards reaching that goal?"

"I don't know," Miller replied honestly. "After the explosion in the lab, that part of the research was transferred to the head office in Germany. At that point, we had a few preliminary clues about the process, but extremely limited success in getting it to work. I haven't heard any further updates since then."

"Presumably you had to shut down the laboratory complex after the explosion. So where is the Noturatii's main base of operations now?"

Miller hesitated. That was a much more difficult question to answer, but not because of any lack of knowledge on his part. He took his time weighing up the consequences, both of answering the question, and refusing to, and finally said, "I can't tell you."

Baron shook his head. "I find it hard to believe that a man of your skills and position wouldn't know where the bases are. For someone whose life depends on his ability to give us useful information, you're being rather reticent, don't you think?"

"I can't tell you because I don't want to be responsible for a repeat of the explosion that took out the lab. Innocent people got caught in that blaze," he went on, when Baron glared at him. "Firefighters were injured. It caused a lot of damage to the neighbouring warehouses, financial losses to other people's businesses. And besides which, I know some good men who work for the Noturatii. Not all of them are thugs and murderers. There are people who were just looking for honest, paid work, and they got caught up with the wrong people. Now they keep their heads down and try to make the best of it, because ending up dead isn't high on their list of priorities. I'm here because my conscience caught up with me and I want to stop causing innocent people to die, not just switch sides and keep fighting the same fucking war."

Baron glanced at Caroline, and she nodded. "Well, I have some bad news for you then," Baron began, but Miller interrupted him.

"Look, if you want to kill me, go ahead," he said sharply, not eager to die, but also not willing to cover his hands in even more blood. "The Noturatii would do no less if they found me, and I get the impression you'd make it a lot quicker and a lot less painful than they would. So there's-"

"Shut up," Baron snapped, baring his teeth briefly. "The bad news isn't that we're going to kill you. It's that, by some bizarre twist of fate, your options for bowing out of the war have been cancelled once and for all." Miller just stared at him, not understanding what he was getting at. "There's no way to break this to you gently, so I'm just going to come out and say it. Somehow, the night you were caught in that storm with Skip, you were converted into a shape shifter. You're one of us now."

"That's impossible," Miller said immediately, not even considering the idea. "We spent months in the lab trying to work out the exact mechanics for creating a new shifter. I couldn't have become one just by wandering about in the forest with one. It can't be that easy." Besides which, wouldn't he have noticed by now?

"There are only two things needed for the conversion," Baron explained. "The exchange of blood between the sire and the convert, and the application of an electrical current."

Miller stared at him, not seeing where he was going with this. He hadn't exchanged blood with Skip, and there had been no ready source of electricity out in the… lightning storm, he realised, suddenly catching up with the implications of Baron's statement. And he had been bleeding, as had Skip, and then lightning had struck… "I don't believe you," he said simply. He couldn't be a shifter. It was an absurd idea.

"Then permit me to demonstrate," Baron replied. Caroline went to the cage door, unlocked it and stepped inside. Miller backed away from her, his mind unable to process the idea that he had become… No, he couldn't have. It was impossible…

"Stand still," Baron snapped, and Miller did so reflexively.

Caroline reached out and put a hand on his shoulder. "Brace yourself," she said, and Miller was about to ask what exactly he should be bracing himself for, when a powerful shock of electricity hit him, knocking him to the floor. He moaned in pain, feeling like he'd just been kicked by a horse… and then he realised that the moan had come out as a whine. He tried to sit up, floundered about as his limbs weren't working the way they usually did, and then he caught sight of his own front paws… and true panic set in. He leapt up, fell over, scrambled back until his body hit the wall, tried to stand and fell over again, all the while a pained whine coming from his throat.

"Sit still," Baron said eventually, when he didn't stop struggling. He crouched down at the front of the bars. "Sit still!" he said again, when Miller wasn't quite able to overcome his shock. He had paws! And black fur, and a tail! He was a wolf! The whole world seemed to have tilted sideways. "Lie still and just breathe," Baron instructed him firmly. "It's an odd sensation, I know. But it's a lot better if you go with it, instead of fighting it."

Miller finally managed to lie still, breathing quickly, eyes wide in fear. And when his body didn't do anything else unexpected, he dared to pay more attention to his new form, his legs feeling too thin and oddly short, his ears twitching at every slight sound in the room. "Now, sit up slowly," Baron said. "Your legs work differently this way, so it's going to feel a little odd." Miller sat up, fidgeting a little until he found a comfortable position for his legs, trying to breathe slowly and evenly.

"Now, if you want to turn back into a human, you need to close your eyes and imagine the change in your mind. Your legs getting longer. Your paws turning into hands. You'll feel a crackle of static electricity down your back. Don't try to resist it. It won't hurt you."

Miller closed his eyes and concentrated, and then, in a jarring shift that held none of the smooth elegance of the ones he had seen in the others, his human body was back, sprawled on the floor as he couldn't figure out how to hold himself up.

"Keep breathing," Baron said wryly, when Miller felt another fit of panic coming on. "The first time is always the worst."

Miller waited a moment until he had himself under control. "I'm a shifter," he stated, still not quite able to believe it. He peered up at Baron, fear and amazement warring in his mind. "Now what?" he asked dumbly.

"Now you take a few minutes to realise that despite your best intentions, there is no way out of the war for you," Baron said, levelling a sharp look his way. "And then you have another think about exactly whose side you're on."

CHAPTER TWENTY-FOUR

Three days later, Dee sat in the passenger seat as Silas pulled the van into the garage, waiting until he'd come to a stop and switched off the engine before unclipping her belt and reaching for the door handle-

"Not so fast," Silas said before she could go anywhere. "You need to go and see Baron. I know you've had a long trip and all, but there have been a few... developments, since you left."

"What sort of developments?" After her bold declaration that she knew the Council had been lying to her, there had been more than a few heartfelt conversations with the group, but as far as Dee knew, they'd managed to settle their differences and make some good progress on understanding the prophecy and helping her learn to communicate with Faeydir better. She was rather dismayed with the idea that they might have phoned ahead to warn Baron of some problem she was unaware of.

"The complicated sort," Silas said, which really explained nothing at all. Then he said, "And get that sappy look off your face. You're not in trouble."

Dee couldn't help but grin at that. Some things didn't change. "Good to see you, too," she said, with a wry but genuine warmth, then hopped out of the van and went to collect her bag.

Inside the manor, Baron was waiting for her, and she didn't even get the chance to put her things away before she was whisked into the library for an urgent meeting.

"Let me start by saying that Skip's fine," Caroline announced, the instant Dee sat down, "so please don't panic about anything else I'm about to tell you. We're through the worst of it, but there are a few loose ends that still need to be tied up. And I'm sorry we didn't call to tell you any of this before. We felt it more important that you focus on your training with the Council for the time being."

"Okay," Dee said, feeling baffled by the odd announcement... until Caroline explained the rest – Skip's kidnapping, her injuries and the tense exercise in getting her medical treatment, and then she was grateful that Caroline had told her that Skip was fine right up front, as she detailed the serious infection that had developed as a result of her wound, requiring high doses of antibiotics and round-the-clock care for a day or two until she was out of the woods. Now, though, Skip was doing well, eating again, after she'd stopped for a while, and able to get out of bed for the first time since she'd come home.

But that wasn't the most startling piece of news. When they told her that they had a Noturatii operative being held captive in the basement, she was surprised... but when they told her he was a shape shifter, she found herself utterly speechless. At once, she felt sick, and then triumphant. As a former captive of a Noturatii lab, she held a very specific grudge against the group, and the chance for a little payback was appealing... but after a moment's consideration, she realised that she liked the *idea* of revenge a lot better than the thought of actually carrying it out. Torturing people was abhorrent; even more so, now that she'd lived through it herself.

"What are we doing with him?" she asked, trying to keep her voice steady.

"Interrogating him. Or attempting to, at least," Baron replied. "He's given us a certain amount of information about the Noturatii, named particular staff members, detailed some operations, but there's a lot he won't tell us. He says he's trying to protect old friends, and I, for one, have no time for that kind of misplaced loyalty. He claims to have left the Noturatii, but he's far from willing to cut all ties with the group. So we have a favour to ask." The statement was said in a grim, apologetic tone, and Dee groaned.

"You want me to separate him from his wolf?"

"I'm sorry. I know you don't like doing it. But given his background, we were always expecting him to go rogue, and in the last twenty-four hours, he's become more aggressive, and the wolf is getting antsy. I think it's the best solution for everyone. And if the Council are setting up a wolf sanctuary in Romania, there's no reason to kill the wolf as well."

Dee sent a quick query to Faeydir, who replied with an easy yes, along with a wave of fury directed at Miller and the Noturatii. They had plenty to answer for, as far as Faeydir was concerned, not just Dee's capture and torture, but also Tank, and Gabrielle, and the death of Eric and Nate, who had been killed in the raid in Scotland just a few weeks ago. "Faeydir's fine with it," Dee told Baron. "When do you want to do this?"

"Now, if that's okay? We've got as much information out of him as I'm expecting to, and I'm getting sick of having to have two of my wolves guarding him twenty-four seven."

Down in the basement, Dee braced herself before stepping into the cage room. Facing up to her enemy was nerve wracking, but more than that, she was trying to fight back the odd sense of satisfaction at the idea that she was finally getting the chance for a little revenge. She shouldn't take pleasure in killing people, she reminded herself sharply, no matter how much harm they had caused her.

She stepped around the corner, seeing Tank and Andre guarding the man. She'd been told about Tank's brief stint in the cage, and apparently he'd calmed down and apologised, promising Baron there would be no repeat of his earlier mistakes, and so he'd been allowed to re-join the rotating shifts of people performing guard duty.

"Hey, good to have you back," Tank said, and he gave Dee a brief hug.

"Dee?" Miller said in surprise, when he saw her. "Good God, you're still alive."

"Sorry to disappoint you," Dee said drily, but Miller shook his head.

"I'm glad you are."

"Yeah, I'd heard you'd had a change of heart," Dee said, just as sardonically as she'd said her first comment. "You'll forgive me if I don't start celebrating right away." Miller didn't look surprised by her scepticism.

Dee took a deep breath, and looked to Caroline for her next move. As she'd explained upstairs, Miller had to be in wolf form for her to remove his human side. She wasn't sure how Caroline was going to arrange that, given that Dee had been told that they hadn't told Miller what she was going to do. First of all, it would likely make him refuse to shift, but secondly, it would create unnecessary stress for him. Il Trosa was nothing if not compassionate, and while these sorts of events were sometimes necessary, they went to great lengths to minimise the anxiety they caused to those involved.

"Dee has a few unique abilities, and we've asked her to come down and assess your wolf," Caroline explained to Miller. "There can be a few unusual side effects to the shifter magic, and it's worth checking out exactly how they're manifesting in you."

Miller shrugged. "Sure. What do you need me to do?"

"She'll need you to be in wolf form. Aside from that, you just need to stand there."

Miller cooperatively stood up and shifted, his wolf large and black, standing in the centre of the cage. Without being told, everyone else in the room backed away, more than aware of the dangers of Dee's potent magic.

Quickly, without giving herself time to think about it, Dee tuned in to Faeydir. The wolf reached out with her unique energy and felt for the two halves of Miller... and then sharply withdrew. Reached out again, in a different way, and then showed Dee an image in her mind – a pack of wolves running through a snow-covered forest... and then she added the black wolf into the pack.

No, Dee replied mentally. *He's Noturatii. He can't join us.*

Another set of images, ones that Dee had to work harder to interpret. A slobbering, rabid wolf, that faded out and disappeared. A human and a wolf superimposed on each other. A sense of grave solemnity and a firm refusal.

"Uh... could I see you outside?" Dee asked Caroline and Baron, feeling off-balance and uneasy.

"Is there a problem?" Caroline asked, and Dee nodded, and headed for the door. This was likely to be an odd conversation, and there was no way she wanted to have it in front of Miller.

The two alphas followed her out into the hall, Andre ducking out with them, and Caroline closed the door behind her so that Miller couldn't overhear. "What's going on?"

Dee floundered for an explanation for a moment. She checked in with Faeydir again, and received the same firm answer. "Faeydir is refusing to separate him," she said finally. "In the past when we've done this, it was because the wolf was going rogue, or with the one from the Grey Watch, because she was trying to kill us. But Faeydir says Miller isn't rogue. He's merged with his wolf." Dee herself currently wasn't sure of the significance of the discovery, but after her time in Italy, she was more aware than ever of the importance of listening to Faeydir's opinions, and knew that she no doubt had good reasons for her refusal now.

"I find that unlikely," Baron said. "His wolf is becoming more aggressive. He's restless, not able to control his shifts well. Those are the early signs of a wolf going rogue."

"Or the signs of a shifter frustrated with extended captivity," Dee pointed out, after receiving the same comment from Faeydir.

Caroline glanced at Baron uncertainly. "Okay, for argument's sake, let's assume you're right, and he's not going rogue. That doesn't mean he's not going to betray us to the Noturatii. If we keep him on the estate and train him as a shifter, we're just giving him the chance to gather all our carefully guarded secrets and hand them straight over to our enemies. We can't let him go and we can't trust him, so putting him down is really the only option."

Faeydir was listening carefully, and offered another wave of images and emotions to Dee at Caroline's cold, but pragmatic assessment. "I'm not entirely sure why," Dee said hesitantly, "but Faeydir's fairly convinced he's not a threat. I can't quite understand everything she's saying, but it seems to focus on the idea that if he's merged with his wolf, then he's not going to betray us." Dee gave Caroline an awkward, apologetic look. "But either way, she's refusing to separate him. You can still put him down, but it's going to have to be the old fashioned way."

"On what basis does she think he's trustworthy?" Baron asked, but before Dee could answer, Andre interrupted.

"If I could offer a suggestion," he said, "consider this. A Noturatii man wants to infiltrate Il Trosa and steal our secrets. So he comes to the Den, gets converted – accidentally or deliberately makes no difference, just for argument's sake – and he goes about charming his way into our lives, knowing all the while that he's going to go back one day and betray us all. From a human's perspective, there's nothing terribly complicated about the plan.

"But consider it from the wolf's perspective. The newly born wolf has immediate and constant access to the human's mind, is able to read his intentions, his desires, his hatred for the wolf. Now, I can well believe that a human would put up with becoming a shifter – for all that the Noturatii hate us, the human mind is nothing if not cunning, and they could well see it as a price worth paying for that kind of information. But I have a hard time believing any wolf would ever put up with that kind of deceit, and accept the human side of themselves under those circumstances." Caroline and Baron were both listening closely, perplexed looks on their faces. "If that's the case," Andre went on, "then it's an almost foolproof defence for us, because it means no Noturatii could ever successfully merge with a wolf. They'd all end up going rogue, no matter how many times they tried it.

"If what Dee says is true, and Miller can truly accept the wolf, and the wolf can accept him, then I would propose the idea that that in itself is concrete proof of his intention to leave the Noturatii."

Baron looked rather surprised at Andre's neat summary of the situation, a deep frown furrowing his forehead. "Are you seriously suggesting we keep him?"

Andre shook his head. "If I'm suggesting anything in particular, it's only that we take some time to examine the situation a little more closely. To my knowledge, we've never had a Noturatii agent successfully infiltrate a Den before to the point of being converted. We're in uncharted territory here. But you'd have to admit that Faeydir's in a unique position to understand the merging better than anyone else, so I think her opinion should carry some weight."

"Another question that's worth asking," Caroline said next, looking uneasy about the whole situation, "is even if Miller is serious about leaving the Noturatii, how did he manage to merge with the wolf? He's had no training, he knows nothing about what to expect from suddenly becoming half canine. Most normal humans couldn't manage that, never mind a man who's spent years trying to kill us."

Baron let out a heavy sigh. "Fuck. So all we really know is that we've got a shit load of questions, and probably shouldn't do anything hasty." He glanced around at each of them, looking unhappy. "Okay. Let's give it a couple more days. If nothing else, we at least need to make sure he really has merged with the wolf. And in the meantime, we can speak to the Council. See if they can offer any insights into how all this might work."

CHAPTER TWENTY-FIVE

It was late afternoon, and Miller was feeling increasingly restless. At present, he was in wolf form, pacing back and forth in front of the cage bars, unable to work off the persistent agitation he'd been feeling all day.

Since the staggering realisation that he'd been converted into a shape shifter, his mind had been working overtime. First of all he'd gone over the events that had caused his conversion; the storm, his insistence that he accompany Skip, that chance lightning strike that had altered his life so dramatically.

And then he'd contemplated the implications for his future. Even if the shifters decided not to kill him, he knew they would never let him go. His vague plans to leave the country were now impossible, as the wolves were no doubt even more strict about deserters than the Noturatii were.

But for all that he couldn't imagine ever having chosen this path for himself, he found that he wasn't too upset about it either. He'd already known his life would never be the same, once he'd decided to leave the Noturatii. Wherever he ended up, he would have spent the rest of his years looking over his shoulder, always wondering if today was the day when one of the Noturatii's assassins would finally catch up with him. At least this way he knew the score right up front, and if the shifters eventually accepted him, he'd have a reliable team of warriors behind him to help him fight for his own survival. All things considered, it could have ended up a lot worse.

Once he'd got over the shock of it all, he'd started to try to figure out his wolf side. Fitting himself into his new body was a strange experience. He hadn't been able to look at himself in a mirror, but by his own estimation, his wolf seemed fairly large. He'd spent a good half an hour just examining his own body, his thick, black fur, his legs, his tail, the odd sensation of walking on four legs, instead of two. Physically, he felt stronger than ever, the raw power of his canine body coming as a welcome surprise.

154

Now that he knew the cause of that vague discomfort, the odd feeling that parts of his body didn't work the way they should, he'd become a lot more relaxed about it. He wasn't ill. His mind wasn't playing tricks on him.

But mentally, he was also struggling to come to terms with his new dual nature. He didn't really know what to expect from being a shifter, but from the way he'd seen the others behave, he'd come to the rapid conclusion that they were not simply human minds inside wolf bodies. They behaved with a true pack mentality, a ready aggression at the slightest hint of a threat, a willing deferment to the instructions of their leaders. He knew little of real wolf behaviour, but even he knew the basics of the social structure of a wolf pack, the way the alpha led the team, the cooperative way they hunted and cared for their young.

Now, after nearly a week locked in this cage, he was feeling decidedly irritable. He'd tried tuning in to his wolf side, entirely unsure about how to do so, but willing to give it a go, nonetheless, to try and work out the cause of his agitation. There were numerous, vague cravings he was feeling, but his lack of experience meant he was unable to determine the source of most of them. The strongest was the sense of having too much energy, of needing to go for a good solid run, or have a workout session in a gym, and he'd ended up just pacing the cage for an hour, the mindless back and forth doing nothing to ease his discomfort.

His ears pricked up as he suddenly heard footsteps outside the room, and when the door opened, he was surprised, but delighted to see Skip step inside. Since he'd given blood for her, no one had been prepared to tell him anything about her condition, and all he really knew was that after being shot, she'd had surgery of some description and had had a hard time recovering, the need for a blood transfusion likely only one of a variety of complications following her injury. He shifted almost immediately when he saw her, completely unintentionally, and stumbled slightly as he found himself back on human feet.

Silas was one of his guards at the moment, a surly man who refused all attempts at conversation, and he looked up in surprise as Skip arrived. "What are you doing down here?" he asked her immediately, and Miller felt his skin tingle as he registered the vaguely threatening tone in his voice.

But Skip seemed to either not notice his hostility, or simply chose to ignore it. "Visiting Miller," she replied cheerfully. "Baron said I could."

Was it his wolf side that was making him feel so protective of her, Miller wondered, feeling the odd urge to growl at Silas. But no, he realised. He'd felt that way even before he'd been converted, just after the car crash, when she'd been injured and he'd been desperate to make sure she made it to safety.

"How are you feeling?" he asked immediately, coming to stand at the bars.

"Better, now," Skip replied. "Still pretty sore when I'm in wolf form, but over the worst of it. And thank you for the blood supply," she added with a bashful smile. "What about you? Are they treating you okay?"

"As well as could be expected," Miller replied, knowing that despite his restlessness, he had no real complaints to make about his treatment. He'd been given three meals every day, clean clothes, and even a book to read when he'd mentioned being bored. And despite Baron's harsh demeanour and his obvious frustrations with Miller, he'd kept his word and refrained from any form of torture or physical punishment for Miller's crimes.

But then he gave Skip a shrewd, knowing look. "You knew I was a shifter, didn't you? After that night in the cave. That's why you talked me into coming here." In hindsight, it seemed so obvious.

Skip shrugged unapologetically. "Yeah. From where I was standing, there weren't a whole lot of other options."

"So all that talk about your lot scratching my back if I scratched theirs?"

"A necessary deception. You're from the Noturatii," she added, when Miller looked disappointed. "You must be familiar with the art of lying by now."

"Touché," he said darkly. The girl was far cleverer than he'd given her credit for. "It seems I underestimated you."

"Twice, now," Skip pointed out, looking altogether pleased that her deception had worked.

Despite a distinct lack of appreciation for being manipulated, Miller felt a certain admiration for the girl. For all her short stature and childish mannerisms, she clearly held a significant degree of social influence among these people. Aside from Silas's initial question about why she was here, he'd said nothing more about her visit, and made no attempt to stop her from talking to Miller. Miller had also seen the way Tank had treated her in Scotland, like a younger sister, the target of good-natured teasing, but also a treasured member of the family.

And more than that, she had a disarming sort of confidence, combined with a baffling optimism, and he was certain that if she told him that everything was going to work out fine, he would believe her. She was also smart, expertly outmanoeuvring him without giving away even a hint of her intentions. There was nothing he liked more in a woman than a sharp mind, and he was somewhat surprised at himself as he realised he was entertaining the idea of developing a long friendship with this woman. And then more surprised when he realised how eager he was for that very thing.

"But not everything I said was a lie," Skip added, sounding a touch defensive. "We're still looking after you way better than the Noturatii would have." Then she seemed to rethink that statement. "We are looking after you, aren't we?" She was staring at his neck, and Miller self-consciously put a hand to where there was still a fading bruise from his fight with Tank.

"Yes," he said firmly. "This was just a small misunderstanding. It's been sorted out."

"How are you going with getting used to your wolf?" she asked next.

Miller immediately looked uncomfortable. "Patchy," he admitted, with a glance at Silas. He'd been aware of the man watching him intently as he'd paced his cage. "It's uncomfortable some of the time. And I have urges to do things that I can't do. Like running outside in the trees, or digging in the earth. It's making me jittery."

Skip winced. "Yeah, it must be rough, given that you had no training before you came here. But Baron's a great teacher, so he'll have you straightened out in no time."

Miller raised his eyebrows in surprise. "Teacher? Teaching me what?"

"How to shift. How to accept the wolf." Miller looked back at her blankly – aside from the barest instructions as to how to shift, Baron had taught him nothing at all – and then Skip's optimistic smile faded, and she suddenly looked around his cage, though Miller wasn't sure what she was looking for. She spun around and asked Silas, "Why is there no food dish in his cage? Has anyone been feeding his wolf?"

"Not that I'm aware of," Silas replied disinterestedly. "But he's been getting three meals a day as a human, so he's not going to starve to death."

"Has anyone been teaching him about being a shifter?" she asked, more sharply.

Silas glanced across at Miller darkly. "You'd have to take that up with Baron."

"I'm not asking you to run lessons with him right now," Skip snapped, and Miller was quite surprised to hear her take such a tone with the intimidating man. And even more surprised when he didn't snap back. "I'm simply asking if anyone has tried to teach him anything so far."

"No," Silas said, and from the look on his face, it was clear that he'd picked up on how upset Skip was about that.

"Fine," Skip said, firm resolve in her voice. "I'm going upstairs to talk to Baron," she said to Miller. "And I'm going to find out why no one has bothered to teach you how to shift, and then I'm going to growl at a few people until they come to their senses." With a 'so there!' look sent Silas's way, she marched out the door.

Miller felt a renewed wave of gratitude for her as he watched her leave. By Noturatii standards, this was five star accommodation, and he honestly held no grudge against the shifters for whatever their failings may have been. But Skip seemed determined to ensure that the usual standards of training, whatever they happened to be, were adhered to, regardless of who she had to snarl at to see it happen. She was turning out to be a most remarkable young woman, and Miller was more thankful than ever before that he'd taken the risks he had to save her life.

In the library, Baron was finishing telling Eleanor about Miller; how he had arrived at the Den, his conversion, and the intel they'd managed to get from him in the past few days. Caroline sat beside him, occasionally clarifying some point or adding an opinion, and Eleanor had listened patiently, but with no small amount of surprise when she learned they'd inadvertently captured a Noturatii operative.

"And... I don't mean to question your judgement, but you've actually seen him shift?" Eleanor clarified. "You're not just taking Skip's word for it?"

"I've seen him do it with my own eyes," Baron confirmed. "And Faeydir insists that, against all odds, he's merged with his wolf. We had thought he was going rogue for a little while, and asked her to separate the human out of him, but she firmly refused on that basis."

"Well, that's unexpected, yes, but remember that no one really has a foolproof understanding of the merging anyway," Eleanor pointed out. "Education and training certainly help, but there are always exceptions. Some recruits end up going rogue, no matter how much preparation they're given, while others – take Dee, or Mark, for example – manage to merge with their wolves despite extremely limited training and very difficult circumstances. That Miller has merged with his wolf is unusual, but by no means outside the realms of possibility.

"As far as getting information out of him," she went on, "it seems you've done the best you can, if there are certain things he's not willing to discuss. It's a shame he doesn't know more about the international operations. If we could get some solid information on Germany, that would do us no end of good. If you wouldn't mind, send through what you've learned to us. I'd feel happier if we got a couple of the assassins to check out some of the details, rather than letting you handle it – I have the highest respect for your abilities, but there's the risk he's lying about some, or all of it, and I prefer to have the weight of some serious mistakes on our shoulders, rather than yours."

Baron nodded, not at all offended as he saw the pragmatism of such a decision. "I wanted to talk to you about what we do with him next. Keeping him here isn't a workable solution, long term – it's wearing us all out having to guard him all the time, aside from anything else – so I was hoping we might be able to arrange to send him to Italy."

"On what basis?" Eleanor asked, surprising Baron. He'd thought it was obvious.

"On the basis that he can't stay here."

"Are either you or Caroline exercising your right of veto as alpha of the Den?"

Baron hadn't really thought about it in those terms. "A veto would imply that he was a potential viable member of this Den. I don't think that really applies in this case."

"Why not?"

"It's not like he's a normal shifter, awaiting further training and a membership vote."

"Isn't he? He's a confirmed shape shifter, he was converted from a registered bloodline, and he's merged with his wolf."

"He's from the Noturatii!" Baron insisted, exasperated by Eleanor's deliberate obfuscation of the issue.

"Then you should put him down," Eleanor said frankly. "You've had the most experience in dealing with him, and if he can't convince you that he's on our side, then it's extremely unlikely he'll be able to convince anyone in Italy. With all due respect, we have plenty of things to do here already without spending weeks assessing a man who's only going to end up being put down anyway."

Baron glanced at Caroline. "We had rather decided not to put him down for the moment," he said awkwardly. "Skip's quite convinced he's not going to betray us, as is Faeydir. She seems to think that the fact that he's merged with his wolf is proof that he's left the Noturatii for good."

"And you don't believe them?" Eleanor asked pointedly.

Baron hesitated. "Not particularly, no."

"Then put him down. I can send an assassin to do it for you, if you don't wish to do it yourself." It was a genuine offer, not a criticism of his lack of willingness to take action, but rather an acknowledgement that sometimes these things cut too close to the bone, and so required a professional hand.

"Or, if that's not a palatable option," Eleanor went on, when it was clear that Baron wasn't happy with that solution, "then put it to the vote. Ask your pack whether they'll accept him as a member of your Den. If they vote no, which, given what you've said, is the most likely outcome, then you can send him to Italy and we can attempt to find another Den for him to join. But only," she emphasised," if you have a reasonable level of confidence that he's trustworthy. I'm offering this solution as a work-around for a situation that's emotionally fraught for all of you – Miller was directly responsible for the death of at least two of your members, after all. But I'm not suggesting it as an excuse to not do your job and put Il Trosa at risk as a result."

In the privacy of his own mind, Baron had to admit it was a reasonable offer. Eleanor's frank honesty was one of the things he admired about her. She was open minded and a strategic thinker, often working outside the normal methods of doing things, but she was also a no-nonsense, straight talking woman, always willing to call a spade a spade.

But it seemed Caroline wasn't quite so on board with the idea. "You're asking us to stand up in front of our entire Den, knowing that Miller killed some of our wolves just a couple of weeks ago, and ask them to let him stay? We'd have a riot on our hands."

"You're not asking them to let him stay," Eleanor pointed out. "You're simply giving them the opportunity to voice their opinion on the matter. And given that we both expect the answer to come back with a firm no, then it shouldn't be an issue. Regardless of anyone's emotional sensitivities, that is the proper procedure. And that is the only way you're going to get the Council to take him off your hands."

Baron glanced at Caroline, who looked as peeved as he felt. Why couldn't any of this have a simple answer? "We'll discuss the best course of action," he said finally, knowing he and Caroline were going to have to have a long, hard conversation about what to do next.

CHAPTER TWENTY-SIX

Skip tapped her foot impatiently as she waited for Baron outside the library. Apparently he was on a call to the Council – not something she could interrupt unless it was an emergency – but the instant the door opened, she all but pounced on him. "Why hasn't anyone been teaching Miller how to shift?" she demanded, which pulled Baron up short.

"Excuse me?" he asked, no doubt equally surprised by the question itself, and the fact that it was being asked in such a demanding tone from such a low ranking wolf. Baron was not used to anyone questioning his authority.

"He's been stuck in that cage for five days now, and he's restless as hell, and Silas said no one has-"

"Would you like to rephrase that question in more polite terms?" Baron said sharply. And Skip took a mental step back, suddenly realising how uncharacteristic her behaviour was. She'd never been the type to make waves, and had certainly never before tried to go head to head with Baron, of all people. But oddly, since her night in the wilderness with Miller, she'd been feeling rather bold. She'd beaten the bad guys, secured her own escape from enemy hands, and successfully deceived a Noturatii operative for her own purposes. The thrill of power the realisation had given her was addictive.

But Baron was right, she reminded herself now. She was a low ranking wolf, and should have addressed him with a polite question, rather than an accusatory demand. "I went to see Miller," she explained, in a far more reasonable tone, hoping Baron wasn't going to get annoyed about it. Though she'd told Silas she had permission, she'd been fairly sure that if she'd actually asked, Baron would have said no. "And he's behaving very restlessly, because he hasn't learned how to control the wolf, or how to shift properly. I thought it might be a good idea if someone taught him

161

how."

Baron folded his arms, her guilty admission not escaping his notice, though he chose not to comment on it for the moment. "Aside from the fact that we've been flat out dealing with your medical care," he said pointedly, "we've also been spending the last few days trying to decide whether or not to put him down. Spending a lot of time and energy training him didn't seem like a good idea, when it could all end up as a waste of time."

Skip felt a wave of disappointment at the news. She'd assumed that since Miller had made it this far, he was more or less in the clear. "Are you going to kill him?" she asked softly.

Baron let out a long sigh. "We haven't decided yet," he admitted, lowering his voice and glancing around to make sure no one would overhear. "I thought it would be a lot simpler than this, but aside from the fact that you and Faeydir both seemed convinced that he's trustworthy, he's actually got the potential to be a serious asset to Il Trosa. He's military trained, he held his own in a fight against Tank – for a while, at least – and he's got the strategic planning skills to give even us a run for our money. So if he's truly cutting his ties with the past, then…" He left the sentence unfinished, but Skip could fill in the blanks easily enough. For all the Den's animosity towards him, it was entirely possible that he was too valuable to kill.

"We still haven't quite decided what to do with him, but you have a fair point, I suppose. There's no harm in helping him adjust to his wolf. I'll send Raniesha down to start teaching him how to shift."

"Or I could do it," Skip volunteered. "Raniesha's tired, cos she was on guard duty all night. And everyone else has been taking shifts, but I don't have anything else to do right now…"

Baron's eyes narrowed. "Why the sudden interest?" he asked pointedly.

Skip shrugged. "I feel like I owe him something," she admitted awkwardly. "He helped me after the car crash, and then donated blood, and I'm kind of the reason he's in this mess in the first place. I feel like I should help him out a bit."

"And your protestations that he's not going to betray us? Is that based on your genuine opinion, or are you just feeling sorry for him?"

Skip thought back to that night in the cave, the way she'd deliberately hurt Miller, and how he'd steadfastly refused to hurt her back. She was well versed in the actions of evil men, and Miller's behaviour simply didn't stack up. "I really think he's one of the good guys," she said honestly.

Baron sighed, still looking rather put out. "Fine. You can give him a couple of lessons. But only on how to shift and how to deal with his wolf. No snippets of shifter history or culture or weird manifestations of the magic. Everything else is on a need to know basis, and as far as I'm concerned, he doesn't qualify."

Skip nodded happily. "No problem," she said cheerfully. "And can I give his wolf some meat? No one's given him anything but human food."

Baron glanced at the clock. "Fine. It's nearly dinnertime, so how about you put a plate together for him as well, and take it down with you."

Feeling much more positive about the whole situation, Skip bounced off towards the kitchen.

Melissa sat in front of the computer in the Noturatii's main science lab, watching closely as Professor Banks adjusted the electrodes embedded in the experimentation table.

"Try it again," he instructed, and Melissa turned her attention back to the screen, running a check on the electrodes' readings and nodding in satisfaction as the results came up. "Discrete readings every 0.05 seconds," she reported. "All electrodes in banks one and three are working normally... but electrode number seven in bank two isn't recording anything."

"The shifter had a seizure a few days ago," Dr Evans reported, from the other side of the room. "It's possible that it caused the connection to come loose."

"No problem," the Professor said, and quickly began removing the electrode. "You have some spares, I take it?"

"Of course," Evans replied, and hurried to a cabinet on the far wall, searching through the draws for a replacement.

In the experiments to figure out how the shifters changed forms, Evans had insisted right from the start that each shift was caused by a single spark of electricity, the catalyst for the shift, and they'd run several hundred separate tests based on that premise. Melissa's own theory was that each shift required not one, but multiple charges, discrete voltage thresholds achieved in quick succession over a short period of time. But since each shift only lasted a second or two, that meant they had to push the sensitivity of their equipment to the limit. The calibrations required the utmost finesse, and making all the necessary adjustments to the machine had taken days.

"One more time?" the Professor instructed, after fixing the replacement electrode in place, and Melissa ran the test once more.

"All electrodes operating normally," she reported, then looked up with eager anticipation. "Are we ready to bring in the shifter?"

"Bring him in."

Melissa called the guards on the intercom, and minutes later, they were dragging the limp and pale shifter captive through the door. He'd been drugged, but had no other restraints, and the guards hefted him onto the table, not bothering to strap him down. They'd tried that early on, and quickly learned that the moment he shifted, he would be free of the restraints anyway, so trying to keep him tied down was a waste of time. They arranged him on his back, and Melissa checked his vital signs. The trick was to keep him drugged enough to make him compliant, but not so much that he lost consciousness. They needed his cooperation to complete the shift on demand, but had to keep him sufficiently subdued that he couldn't do them any harm, should he get any ideas about trying to escape.

With the captive arranged to their liking, the guards retreated to the side of the room, Tasers and tranquiliser darts at the ready.

"Now," Banks said, approaching the shifter and staring down at him with a firm glare. "You understand the consequences of misbehaving, I take it? After all, you've been in this lab long enough to know how things work."

The shifter nodded, then lay compliantly still. He hadn't been nearly so cooperative to begin with, and his body now bore the scars of repeated torture sessions.

"When you're ready then."

The shifter took a deep breath, closed his eyes, and then a crackle of electricity flowed smoothly over him. His body blurred, shimmered and vanished, the form of a wolf taking its place on the table.

The computer burst into life at the shift, a flood of data filling the screen from thirty different electrodes, spanning the length of the table, at split second intervals and lasting a total of five seconds.

"Excellent," Evans said enthusiastically, peering at the screen over Melissa's shoulder. "It'll take a few hours to analyse, but it's a promising start." She beamed at Banks... but the Professor wasn't nearly so quick to declare the experiment a success.

"We should run another few tests," he said, scanning his eyes over the data. "Just in case anything went wrong that we can't see right up front. It'll save time in the long run, since we've got the shifter here and everything set up."

Melissa quickly reset the program, then gave Banks a nod.

"That was very good," Banks said to the shifter, smiling down at him. "Now... let's try that again."

It was mid-morning when the door to the cage room opened, and Miller looked up to see Baron and Caroline arriving. He'd asked to see them early this morning, and he was glad they'd agreed.

In the last few days, he'd had a lot on his mind. Since discovering that he was a shifter, the battle lines of this war had been well and truly redrawn for him, and he'd spent long hours contemplating Baron's stark announcement that he needed to decide which side he was on.

Of course, it was never quite that simple, when there were men in the

Noturatii whom he considered his friends, but after yesterday, he'd found himself in a position that demanded commitment, one way or the other.

After her outburst about his lack of training yesterday, Skip had come down with dinner and spent the evening with him. As well as bringing food for his wolf, which he'd eaten while feeling very self conscious about it, she'd spent hours with him, slowly going over the process of shifting. He'd practised it dozens of times, watching Skip carefully as she demonstrated, asking questions, even sharing a few laughs along the way, and in the end, he'd become a lot better at it, the transition becoming smoother, and he'd even managed to keep his balance as he changed from wolf legs to human ones.

But it wasn't the training that had changed his mind. It was Skip herself. She was proving to be a uniquely compassionate woman, genuinely upset at the lack of training he'd received, and seeming to hold no grudge whatsoever about either his past employment with the Noturatii, or the way he'd accidentally kidnapped her, her bullet wound forgiven in an act of generosity that Miller wasn't sure he could have matched, had their positions been reversed. Up until now, he'd withheld certain pieces of information about the Noturatii, not wanting to exacerbate the war, but the lingering idea that Skip had very nearly ended up on a dissection table in a Noturatii lab was horrifying. And he'd been forced to realise that sitting on the sidelines and hoping this all went away was no longer good enough.

"What's the drama?" Baron asked, coming forward to stand in front of the cage.

"I've been thinking about what you said a few days ago, about choosing a side in this war," Miller began, without wasting any time. "And I have some more information about the Noturatii that you should probably know."

He could immediately see that he'd got Baron's attention. "And what would that be?" he asked.

"The location of each of the Noturatii's bases in England," Miller said, knowing just how important that information could be. "But before you get too excited about that one," he rushed on, before Baron could say a word, "I have to warn you that attempting to attack any of them the way you did the lab complex is an extremely bad idea."

"Why's that?" Caroline asked, disappointment in her tone.

"Various reasons, depending on which base we're talking about. There are three main bases in England, each with a different purpose. There's one near Liverpool, the weapons development facility. Now, when I say weapons, I don't mean the science experiments and high tech gadgetry they were trying to develop in the lab. I mean things that go boom. Guns, grenades, explosives… good, old fashioned weapons of war. If you make any attempt to get inside that place, there are more than a handful of headstrong lunatics who would happily blow the place to smithereens, taking you and your crew along with them. Get me a map and I can show you the location, but planning an attack on the base is pure suicide."

Baron nodded, expression grim. "Unfortunate, but I've no interest in getting my Den blown up. What about the others?"

"The second base is the headquarters in east London. It's a large building, which might seem like an easy target, but several of the floors are leased out to other companies. Any attempts to storm the castle, as it were, would lead to serious civilian casualties. The Noturatii aren't nearly as reticent about shooting civilians as you are, and if anyone got caught in the crossfire, they would neatly blame the attack on terrorists and walk away without a mark on them."

Baron looked disappointed at the news, but ultimately just shrugged. "Knowing the location of the place would at least be a step forward. What about the third base?"

"Before we get to that bit, there's something else you need to know about the second one." He braced himself, knowing that they could well react badly to his next piece of news. "Unfortunately, despite the loss of the main lab, the Noturatii are still quite eager to keep experimenting on shifters. And as we speak, the new science team has a captive shifter in the building whom they're running tests on. As far as I'm aware, he was a Russian."

Caroline gasped at the news, a look of black fury crossing her face, while Baron got a far more calculating look on his.

"What's security like there?" he asked.

"Very similar to how it was at the lab. Why? What are you thinking?"

"Given what you've said, a full scale attack is out of the question. But leaving one of our own in there to be tortured isn't an option either. But if I send that information to the Council, they might be able to do something about it."

"The Council?" Miller asked. It was the first time he'd heard the term.

"Headquarters," Caroline explained shortly. "That's all you need to know."

Miller wondered for a moment what the elusive shifter control centre might be able to do in such circumstances… and then realised he had a fairly good idea. "You'd ask them to send an assassin," he surmised. "The Noturatii is aware of the existence of your particular brand of 'special operatives'," he explained quickly, at the two alphas' astonished looks. "Which is why they've created their own. The Satva Khuli. You think that an assassin could infiltrate the base and extract your man?"

"What would be your honest opinion on the chances of success for that sort of operation?" Caroline asked.

Miller considered the question carefully. "With the right intel, and a decent amount of preparation, it has a reasonable chance of success. At the very least, an assassin should be able to get inside the complex and put the poor bastard out of his misery. Extracting him alive would be a fair bit harder, but then again, your assassins seem to be a rather talented lot, so I wouldn't presume to say what one could or couldn't do."

"It's an option worth pursuing," Baron declared firmly. "Raniesha, go grab a notebook and pen," he called over his shoulder, and the woman guarding him swiftly left the room. "I'll get you to write down everything you remember about the base, and I'll send it to the Council to assess. Now, what about the last one?"

"There's a base on the south coast, down in Cornwall. It's used as a training facility for new recruits and security staff. Theoretically, a hit against that base would be fairly simple, but there's a moral issue you might like to consider before you go in all gung-ho."

"Oh?"

"How much do you know about the internal workings of the Noturatii?" he asked.

"Not a whole lot," Baron admitted. "They're just as secretive about their organisation as we are about ours."

Miller nodded. He'd suspected as much. "There are multiple levels of operation within the Noturatii," he explained. "And the difficult thing is that a lot of the people at the bottom really have no idea what they're involved with. They're recruited from various other organisations – security firms, the police, the military – but they know nothing about the true purpose of the Noturatii. They genuinely believe they're working for the government to fight terrorism. They build guns, recruit new staff, raise funds, deal with administrative tasks, but if you confronted a lot of them with the truth about the shape shifters, they'd laugh you out of the building. It's not until you get into the higher levels that people are introduced to the secrets of what it's all really about. Which raises an interesting moral dilemma. Those people are working against you, are aiding your enemies, are supporting a dangerous institution... but they're all doing it with the most honest and honourable of intentions. They're good people, who want nothing more than to help protect their country from terror threats. Killing them all would blow a decent sized hole in the Noturatii's operations, that much is true. But it would also kill a lot of people who could, by all reasonable standards, be considered innocent bystanders to the war."

Miller waited while the truth of that sunk in... and then Baron let out a heartfelt "Fuck..."

"I'm not telling you what you should or shouldn't do," Miller said, after a moment's consideration. "But I've seen enough of your morals to know that you don't take the death of civilians lightly. So I thought you'd want to have all the information, however inconvenient some of it might be."

Baron nodded, a contemplative look on his face. "Mind if I ask why the sudden change of heart?"

"Not so sudden," Miller replied. "I've been having doubts about the Noturatii for months, so this is just the net result of weeks of hard thinking. I know I said I wouldn't give you this information before, but the more I see of who you are and how you work, the harder it gets to sit on the fence. I don't want more blood on my hands," he said earnestly. "I've told you that before. But if people here end up dead because I kept my mouth shut, it's just as hard to claim that I'm blameless as it would be if I'd kept working for the Noturatii. As a wise man once said, all that's required for evil to triumph is for good men to do nothing."

An hour later, Baron stepped out into the hall, Caroline at his heels. "Well, that was interesting," he said drily. He glanced at the bundle of notes in his hand – a dozen pages detailing the location of each base, their security measures, staffing levels, diagrams of access points to each building; a plethora of details that the Council would go over with a fine tooth comb. "This makes it rather more difficult to make a decision to put him down, don't you think?"

"Just when we thought we had a handle on the guy," Caroline muttered, looking put out. "Well, I suppose this means we're going to have to take Eleanor's advice. Put it to the Den to consider his role in Il Trosa, and take a vote."

"Damn it," Baron said, shaking his head. "I really didn't want to have to put them through that."

"Explain it to everyone at dinner tonight," Caroline said, with her usual pragmatism. "And make the point that we're only following due process. Eleanor was right – it's almost guaranteed that the Den will vote him out. And then the Council will take him off our hands, and it's not our problem any more."

Baron gave her a doubtful look. "Can you honestly say you believe he's on our side?"

Caroline scowled, running a hand over her face. "I think half the problem here is that we're letting our emotions get in the way. We both have plenty of reason to hate him. And neither of us wants him hanging around this Den." Baron nodded in agreement. "But whenever I've spoken to him face to face, I get no indication that he's lying. He came here with no weapons, no bugs, no backup. He saved Skip's life – I trust Skip enough to believe her side of the story, at least – and there is that niggling fact that he's merged with his wolf. So on the weight of available evidence, I'd have to say that yes, I believe he's trying to do the right thing."

Baron sighed, the truth inconvenient, but unavoidable, given the latest batch of information Miller had just handed over. "All right. I'll speak to the Den tonight. And we'll put it to the vote tomorrow."

CHAPTER TWENTY-SEVEN

The following evening, Skip stepped out of the shower and grabbed a towel to dry off. In just under half an hour it would be time for dinner, and then after that, the much anticipated vote on Miller's future.

When Baron had made the announcement last night, it had caused a complete uproar, shouts, curses, vehement objections to the very idea, and it had taken a good ten minutes before everyone had settled down again. As Skip understood it, the vote was a mere formality, the result an almost guaranteed no, and if she was honest about it, she was actually feeling quite sad about the prospect of Miller leaving. She'd spent a fair amount of time with him over the past few days, teaching him the basics of shifting, and he'd shown himself to be an excellent student, listening attentively, following her instructions to the letter, deeply curious about his wolf and the way the shifters normally interacted with their canine side. And there had been not even a hint of any disgust or disdain over his wolf half – quite the feat, for a former Noturatii operative.

But more than just a general admiration for the way he was handling everything, Skip found that she was actually starting to like him. He had a quick wit, a genuine empathy for the plight of the shifters, and a refreshing lack of self pity. And then there was the way his eyes sparkled when he found something funny. His hands were strong, but artistic, unexpected for one who made his career as a soldier, and she was looking forward to seeing him again tonight… Skip felt a faint blush colour her cheeks as she suddenly realised the direction her wayward thoughts were travelling.

The realisation that she was developing her first crush was both a terrifying idea, and a thrilling prospect. She'd never given the idea of a romantic partner much thought before, and for a long time, she'd been unable to imagine ever being able to find a man attractive. But Miller most certainly was. Smooth, dark skin, full lips, expressive mouth… And his wolf was a most unusual animal, Skip thought as she finished dressing, patient and watchful far beyond the normal standards for one so new to the world, and she took the time to wonder what that meant.

A knock at her bedroom door pulled her out of her musings, and she quickly opened it, finding Dee on the other side. They'd become good friends since Dee had joined the Den, and had some catching up to do, firstly about Dee's trip to Italy, but Skip also knew Dee would want to know more about her own recent adventures. Once the infection had been dealt with, Skip's wolf had begun healing properly. She still had to take antibiotic tablets twice a day, and her stitches would remain in place for a while longer, but the pain of the surgery had faded to a mild discomfort and she was feeling a lot better when in her wolf form.

But as Dee came into the room and took a seat on Skip's bed, she opened the conversation with a far different topic from the one Skip had been expecting. "I can't quite believe Baron didn't decide to kill Miller," she said without warning, and Skip was surprised enough that she found herself momentarily speechless. "After everything he did in Scotland, why are we even considering letting him stay?"

Skip shrugged, trying not to look offended. She'd been the one to bring him here, after all, the one who had decided not to kill him right back when he'd crashed the car, and it was hard not to take the vehement denouncement of him personally. "He seems fairly sincere about having a change of heart," she pointed out diplomatically. "Isn't it worth giving him a chance?"

Dee shrugged, looking mildly annoyed. "In the end, it's Baron's call. He makes enough life and death decisions for me to believe he has his reasons. But if it was left up to me? I'd have ended his life the moment he set foot on the estate."

The venom in Dee's voice was startling, and Skip had to remind herself that Dee had been held captive in a Noturatii lab and tortured. How willing would Skip be to forgive, she thought darkly, if one of her father's friends had strolled into the room and declared his sincere regret for his actions all those years ago? She would likely have as hard a time dealing with that as Dee was having dealing with Miller. But even so, it was a little surprising that Dee would opt for such a violent and deadly solution, when she was usually quite the pacifist.

Not knowing what to say, Skip picked up a comb and turned to the mirror to tidy her hair. "Well, the Den's going to end up voting him out anyway," she said, trying to sound nonchalant about the whole thing, "so then the Council will be dealing with him, and it's not our problem any more." Finishing with her hair, she picked out a set of three plastic bracelets, in vivid blue, pink and green, and slid them onto her arm without thinking... and then paused, turning her attention back to the mirror.

The reflection that stared back at her was the same one she had seen every day for years. Pink t-shirt – today's choice had a kitten on the front. Baggy shorts. Short hair. Bright, childish jewellery. And Miller's comment from the other night came back to her. 'I think you're nice to look at', he'd said, and at the time, she'd taken the comment at face value.

Skip stared critically at her reflection now, and felt her heart sink. He must have been just being nice, she realised in dismay. He was older than her, probably in his early thirties, and Skip knew well enough what men of that age found attractive. If they were like Simon, then they favoured women with a sharp fashion sense and a deft hand when it came to makeup. If they were like Tank, they were more into the down-to-earth type, women who were athletic and casual, but not sloppy. Or, if they were like Kwan, then looks weren't so important, brains far more attractive than any kind of physical appearance.

But none of the men she knew, or had ever known, would have found anything even remotely attractive about the way she looked now. She was twenty-four, rapidly heading for twenty-five, and she was still dressing like a teenager. Or maybe even a pre-teen, on some days. She looked ridiculous.

Sitting on the bed, Dee fought back the automatic anger that sprang up whenever she thought of Miller. As far as she was concerned, it was like a Nazi officer suddenly deciding, once the war was over, that he was very sorry for hurting anyone, and please would everyone just forgive him. To do so ignored the immense suffering of his victims and the lingering scars left behind, whether from physical wounds, or the more intangible gaps left in people's lives from the deaths of loved ones. As Dee saw it, some sort of justice was required beyond the simple declaration that Miller had changed his mind.

But as she sat there, mulling over the strange goings on around the Den, she noticed that Skip seemed rather distracted. She didn't seem particularly interested in talking about Miller… and now she was staring at herself in the mirror, running a nervous hand through her hair, fiddling with the hem of her t-shirt.

"Hey, what's up?" Dee asked, realising she was being insensitive. Skip had been through plenty of trauma lately, and Dee was just harping on about her own frustrations.

"Nothing," Skip said morosely.

"Seriously, are you okay?" Dee pressed. She'd never seen the usually cheerful and bouncy girl so quiet.

Skip stared at the mirror a moment longer. "I look stupid," she declared without warning.

Dee was startled by the blunt statement. "What? No, you don't."

Skip gestured to the mirror. "Yes, I do. Look at me."

Dee came to stand beside her, a frown on her face. "Why do you think that?" she asked, baffled by Skip's sudden angst.

"My hair is too short." She ran a hand self-consciously over the trimmed strands. "And I look... I just look weird."

Dee turned to face her. "What's this about? You look fine. You've never worried about how you look before." Okay, so when Dee had first met Skip, she'd thought her a little odd, with her unusual fashion sense and her fascination with teddy bears and childish jewellery. But over the months, she'd got used to the weirdness that routinely went on around the Den, and now she thought Skip's choice of clothing was no more unusual than Caroline's penchant for black leather, or Raniesha's obsession with short skirts and high heels.

But nonetheless, now that Skip had brought it to her attention, she had to admit that there was a stark contrast between Skip's baggy clothing, two sizes too big so that every piece hung on her small frame, and Dee's own clothes – currently consisting of stylish jeans and a shirt with a feminine cut, and she wondered if she had inadvertently done something to trigger this sudden discomfort. "You're allowed to wear whatever clothes you like," she said, trying to reassure her friend.

Skip didn't look convinced. She fiddled with the hem of her t-shirt again, then said, "But he..." She stopped herself. But that one slip was enough.

"He? He, who?"

"No one."

Dee's eyes narrowed. "Has someone been giving you a hard time? Because Faeydir is more than happy to go beat the shit out of whoever it is, if they have."

Skip smiled despite her doubts. Dee's wolf was earning quite the reputation as a vicious fighter, and she'd already climbed far higher in the ranks than anyone had expected. The only reason she hadn't climbed further was because she was still so new here, and there was a certain pressure to avoid letting her have too much influence until she knew their culture better.

But the smile didn't last long. "No one's been giving me a hard time."

"Then 'he' who? And what has 'he' been doing?"

Skip shrugged. "Nothing. I just..."

Another idea suddenly occurred to Dee. "Wait a minute... do you have an admirer? Is that what this is about?" Since she'd joined the Den, she'd never seen Skip show even the slightest interest in a man. Which didn't mean anything in particular. A lot of the Den's members seemed to have no real interest in a romantic relationship. But maybe...?

"No," Skip said, sounding even more morose. "Not really." There was a long moment of silence, and then… "Can I ask you a question?"

"Of course."

"I can't ask the others, because they all… They were here when I got here, so they know… but you don't know, cos you're new here, and I want… I want to know what you really think, without you knowing, because they'll all say… well, I already know what they'll say."

Dee didn't know what? It was a well known fact that everyone here had issues from their various pasts, but she'd assumed that whatever Skip's problems were, they were none of Dee's business. But the girl was clearly upset. "You can ask me anything."

"And I want an honest answer," Skip insisted. "And don't worry later that you've said something wrong, cos I'm asking you specifically because you don't know. Okay?"

That sounded bad, and Dee was suddenly cautious. "Okay," she agreed hesitantly. She was going to have to watch what she said. Which was difficult to do when she didn't know what she was watching for.

"Do you think that… maybe… a guy would… do you think he would think I was nice to look at?"

So there *was* someone she was interested in. And as Dee's mind automatically raced through the list of shifters on the estate, she came to the most obvious conclusion. "Is it Kwan?"

"What? No!" Skip said, blushing. "Kwan's just a friend."

Dee's next thought was that perhaps it was Aaron, but she dismissed the idea almost immediately. Aaron had shown even less interest in women than Skip had shown in men. "Is it someone you met in Scotland?"

"No. Sort of. Maybe… No, not really." Skip was babbling, but then she cut herself off quickly. "I just want to know if you think a guy could think that."

"I think it's perfectly possible," Dee answered, after considering the question for a moment. "There's a lot of different kinds of people in the world, and there's no reason one of them shouldn't be interested in you."

"But what if he's just being polite?"

"Well that's better than being rude, isn't it?" Dee said with wry amusement. But Skip didn't seem amused. "Look… if you're interested in someone, whether or not he's interested in you too, friendship is still a good place to start, right? So just try talking to him without putting too much pressure on either of you. Or if it's a long distance thing, call him on the phone. Or send him an email. Talk about something you have in common. Just start with something simple, and see if he seems interested in return." In all honesty, that was about the extent of Dee's relationship advice. Before meeting Mark, she'd been rather hopeless at the dating game herself, shyness and insecurities causing her to skirt around her feelings for ages before she'd ever worked up the courage to approach a man, and she wasn't sure what she was going to say if Skip asked for more advice.

But instead, she seemed to suddenly brighten. "Yeah. I can do that," she said, sounding more confident. "We have lots of things we can talk about."

Dee smiled, glad she'd been of some help, at least. "Great. Then let's get down to dinner. We've got a very interesting evening ahead of us."

CHAPTER TWENTY-EIGHT

A tense silence hovered over the entire Den as they loitered on the back patio, waiting for Baron to announce the vote on Miller's future. Dinner had been completed – a break with tradition, as the Welcoming Ceremony usually included a feast after the rituals, but on this occasion, since everyone was expecting the vote to be a no, Baron had foregone the effort of preparing one. Miller was standing in the centre of the patio, having just completed the required oath of loyalty to Il Trosa, a sacred vow in which he'd sworn to honour this Den, the Council and the whole of Il Trosa, and acknowledged that any betrayal of that vow constituted a forfeiture of his own life.

Baron had explained the vow in detail earlier that afternoon, and Miller had asked plenty of questions about it, but in the end, he'd agreed to comply. Which was just as well. If he'd refused, then Baron would have had no choice but to put him down. The Council took the ritual extremely seriously, and if Miller had refused to swear his allegiance to them, he would be seen as a traitor to their species, irrespective of his intentions to leave the Noturatii.

Silas and Andre had brought him up from the cage room half an hour ago, and the Den had reacted with trepidation and several vocal protests when they'd seen that he wasn't restrained in any way. But given the ceremony they were about to complete, there had been little other option. Despite any reservations they held about the man, this ceremony was an official invitation to join Il Trosa, and the final declaration that neither Baron nor Caroline considered Miller to be a serious threat to their safety. As such, collaring Miller would firstly have been hugely disrespectful, both to him, and to the traditions of Il Trosa, but secondly, if they were serious about accepting Miller – whether it was in this Den or another one – then they would have to start allowing him the chance to prove himself. And keeping him caged or chained twenty-four hours a day was hardly going to give him that opportunity.

However, despite the apparent display of trust in the man, all of the more senior wolves were armed – Baron wasn't so stupid as to leave himself with no plan B, should Miller actually attempt to escape. And Andre had been briefed on the potential need to track him. As a recently retired assassin, he was by far the most skilled and lethal warrior on the estate and he was now watching Miller with the focused attention of a hawk tracking a rabbit.

"You all know why we're here," Baron addressed the group, when everyone was ready. "You've been given twenty-four hours to think about this vote, and I'm sure you've all had some interesting discussions on the topic. According to usual protocol, I'd be required to ask you whether anyone knew of any reason why Miller should not be allowed to join us. But given the circumstances, let me answer that for you. He's from the Noturatii, he's been responsible for the deaths of at least two of our comrades, possibly more, he recently tried to kidnap Skip and he kidnapped Tank at the beginning of the year. But in his favour," he went on, "he helped Skip escape from that same kidnapping attempt, he donated blood to her after her surgery, he's given us valuable intel on the Noturatii, and against all odds, he's successfully merged with his wolf. Does anyone have anything of significance to add to the list? I realise there are probably a thousand minor crimes he's committed against us, but let's keep this to the big picture issues, shall we?"

"I have a question," Simon spoke up. "I'd like to hear from Miller himself where his loyalties lie. And I, along with a number of other people, would like to assess his answer while in wolf form." Wolves were far more adept at detecting lies, and Baron considered it to be a reasonable request.

"Granted," he answered easily. "Those who would like to shift, please do so."

Half a dozen people shifted, and then Baron turned to Miller. "Please tell us, in your own words, your current views on the Noturatii and the shape shifters."

Miller answered without protest. "I have cut all ties to my life with the Noturatii, and I have no intention of ever going back to work for them. I consider their activities to be morally reprehensible and I deeply regret the time I spent helping them. I never intended to join the shape shifters, but since coming here, I've seen that you're decent, honest and compassionate people, and given my accidental conversion into a shifter, I would consider it an honour to be allowed to stay with you." There was a pause, as the wolves watched him carefully, weighing up every word, his tone of voice, his body language.

"Do you have any intention of revealing any information about the shifters to the Noturatii?" Baron asked pointedly, wanting to cover all his bases.

"No," Miller replied. "You've done me a significant kindness in the way you've treated me, and I have no desire to stab you in the back for it."

"And do you have any intention of trying to leave Il Trosa, now or at any point in the future?"

"No, I do not."

"You have your answer," Baron said to the waiting shifters. "Make of it what you will. Are there any other questions?" There were no further comments, so once the last of the shifters had resumed their human form, he announced the vote. "The affirmative vote will be cast to my left, the negative vote to my right. Proceed."

Baron immediately stepped to the left, while Caroline stepped to the right. While she had decided not to exercise her right of veto, as that would have resulted in Miller's death, she'd made the point earlier that she was far from happy about him joining this particular Den.

Baron's reasons for voting in Miller's favour were a little more complicated. While he was loathe to impose his will on the Den, he also knew that if anything went wrong in the future, Baron himself would be largely to blame for it, and he was inclined to keep Miller close by, so as to be on hand to take corrective action, should he prove to be untrustworthy.

But in reality, he knew, his own sense of responsibility and desire for caution were moot points. He expected maybe one or two others to vote with him on the affirmative side, Skip, for example, or Alistair, who was known for his open mind, but the majority of the Den would be heading for the far side of the patio. He waited while the shifters moved, some quickly, others taking their time, and as the last vote was cast, he quickly counted each side... and his jaw dropped.

He counted the shifters again. And then, as the heavy silence lingered, he counted a third time.

"Fuck," he swore softly to himself. Eight shifters stood on the negative side, scowls and folded arms declaring their disgust with the man who waited patiently in the centre of the patio. And on the affirmative side... nine shifters stood nervously, glancing at each other, seeming as surprised by the final count as Baron was. Holy hell, they'd voted to keep him.

As it was, the split seemed to have happened in the worst possible way. Baron was on one side of the patio, John on the other. Andre on the affirmative side, Caroline on the negative. Tank vs Silas. Kwan vs Aaron. Mark vs Dee. Every couple, every friendship, every close alliance seemed to have been split down the middle with this one vote. And that bode extremely poorly for the continued peace and stability of the Den.

But the vote was final, nine for, eight against, and Tank stood silently by, dutifully writing down the names of each shifter, and which way they had cast their vote.

"All decisions are final?" Baron asked, trepidation in his voice. No one moved, no last minute changing of minds, and he felt his gut churn as he announced the result. "The vote is called. Nine for, eight against. Jack Miller…" He hesitated, unable to bring himself to speak the words. "Fucking hell…" He turned away, stalked to the end of the patio. This wasn't supposed to happen. Regardless of his own ambiguous feelings, he'd been fully expecting the Den to stand against Miller, particularly after the very vocal protests about this vote yesterday evening. And those on the negative side all had very solid reasons for rejecting him. Tank, Dee, John… What was this going to do to his Den?

"The vote is called," Caroline said from behind him, clearly deciding to get on with things, her voice cool and emotionless. "Jack Miller, you have been accepted into the Lakes District Den. Welcome to Il Trosa."

A moment more passed in silence… and then all hell broke loose. Those on the negative side voiced their angry denouncement of the vote. Those on the affirmative side began arguing for the validity of the result, demanding that the rest respect tradition and their democratic right to have their say. And Baron stared off into the darkness, feeling as if the earth had shifted beneath his feet. A Noturatii agent had just joined their ranks. Their world would never be the same again.

Taking a deep breath, he turned to face the arguing group. He'd done no preparation for this sort of outcome. Under normal circumstances, there should be a formal introduction of Miller and his wolf to each member of the Den, but Baron suspected that if he tried to enforce that part of the ritual now, there would be a small riot in protest.

More arguments broke out, of a more personal nature this time. Dee, on the negative side, was asking Mark how he could dare vote the way he had, when the Noturatii had imprisoned and tortured her. Where was his loyalty to his girlfriend? Raniesha was snarling at Simon, accusing him of being blind and putting them all at risk. Caroline was glaring at Andre, who had apparently taken Faeydir's claims of Miller's loyalty to heart. And John… Catching his gaze from across the patio, Baron felt cold inside as he saw the fiery rage in the young man's eyes. With more reason to hate the Noturatii than most, there was no way he was going to take this one well…

"The Chant of Forests," a voice called suddenly, breaking through the din, and Baron turned to see, to his utter shock, that it was Skip who had spoken. The Chant of Forests was a pledge of loyalty to the newly created wolf, a promise from the Den to honour and protect him for as long as he lived, and a sacred tradition within Il Trosa. It was usually performed at a shifter's conversion, but since Miller had been converted in such an unusual way, there had been no occasion to perform it before now.

"I am not swearing my allegiance to *that*," Raniesha screamed, flinging an arm towards Miller.

"The Chant of Forests!" Mark repeated, Alistair's voice joining him.

"You shit on our ancestors!" Silas yelled, and a chorus of voices joined his protests.

"The vote is called," Tank yelled back, trying to regain a measure of order. "The Den has spoken!"

"Get over here!" Baron snapped at Miller, grabbing his arm and dragging him off to the side, lest someone get any ideas about taking him out of the equation. He shoved him up against the wall, then placed himself bodily between Miller and the rest of the Den.

"What the fuck do we do now?" Caroline muttered to him, following him over to the edge of the patio. "This wasn't anywhere in the plan."

"Let them go for a minute," Baron advised. "Let them get it out of their system."

The chaos went on for a while, Baron watching carefully as even the most placid members of his Den joined in the argument, people getting in each other's faces and yelling all manner of accusations. He was waiting for the moment when someone lost their temper entirely, and a fight broke out… but as the minutes wore on, he was relieved to see that everyone was somehow managing to maintain a level of self control, despite the heated tempers.

"I call for a revote," someone yelled finally, and the chorus of support for the idea finally broke the deadlock.

Baron stepped forward, and the group fell silent. A revote went against general protocol, but given the anger rolling off the group, not to mention the most unconventional result the first time, Baron was prepared to indulge them.

"Let's have a revote, then," he said blandly. "The affirmative vote will be cast to my left, the negative vote to my right. Proceed."

The Den split once more, and Baron was actually a little surprised when the vote came out exactly the same. Given the strong loyalties within the Den, he'd expected at least one person to change their mind.

"The vote is called," he said, once everyone had moved. "Nine for, eight against. The tally stands." No one spoke, the decision much harder to challenge the second time around, and Baron looked at the grim faces all around him. "And now, as dictated by honour and tradition… The Chant of Forests."

"Well, that was a fucking disaster," Baron muttered to Caroline, much later in the evening. After his announcement that they were to perform the Chant of Forests, there had been some muttering and resentment, but in the end, most of the Den had fallen into line, though the Chant had lacked its usual enthusiasm this time around. John had been the one exception, flatly refusing to join in, and with his patience wearing thin after the arguments that had been going on all evening, Baron was in no mood to try either coaxing him or bribing him into participating, as he might have done if he were in a better mood. In the end, he'd given the boy a clear order. "You can perform the fucking chant," he'd snapped, "or you and I are going to be having serious words about this later."

John had looked him straight in the eye and replied, "You're right. We will be having words about it." And then he'd boldly gone to stand at the edge of the patio, arms folded, glaring at Miller and Baron.

After that, there had been the normal round of formal introductions. Miller had been introduced to everyone by name, asked to shift, so they could all see his wolf, and then he'd met everyone else's wolf in turn. John had managed to cooperate about that one, though his reasons had been far from peaceful. "If Miller manages to escape," he'd said, a predatory look on his face, "then I want to know his scent, so I can track him down and kill him." The statement had hardly improved the mood of the evening, but at least they'd got through the ritual without further incident.

Now, though, there were a thousand unintended repercussions from the unexpected result to the vote. "What are we going to do about security where Miller is concerned?" Baron asked Caroline. "Given that he's now an official member of this Den, we can't just keep him locked in a cage all the time."

"Well, we can hardly just let him wander about on his own, either," Caroline said. "Even Dee didn't get that kind of trust, and she had far less weighing against her than Miller does."

"Dee got Mark as a chaperone for a couple of months," Baron pointed out. "But considering Miller's skills, it would have to be someone like Tank or Andre guarding him, and fuck knows they've got enough to do already."

"If I may make a suggestion," Simon said suddenly, appearing at Baron's elbow. "I was thinking about this very problem earlier, and I might have a solution. I have a couple of ankle monitors up in the IT office, the sort the police use when they want to put people under house arrest, or they have offenders on parole. It sends a radio signal to a receiver that keeps track of the wearer's location at set intervals. We could strap one to Miller, and I could set it so that it'll sound an alarm if he goes too close to the boundary wall."

Baron felt a rush of relief at the easy solution to the problem. "Sound good enough?" he asked Caroline, and she immediately agreed. "Do it," he told Simon. "Let me know when you've got it configured, and I'll tell Miller what the deal is."

But unfortunately, that was far from the last of the problems they needed to solve. "What about his training?" Caroline said next. "Normally a new recruit gets a couple of years of education about our culture, our rituals, our history. Are we seriously going to throw that much sensitive information at Miller? If he gets loose, he could wipe the lot of us out just by snapping his fingers."

"For the time being, no," Baron said firmly. "That's too much of a risk to take. We can teach him about the magic, how to shift, how to relate to his wolf, whatever he needs to know for normal, day to day life, but the rest of it, the history, the old language, the Council… It's too soon. Let's give it a couple of months, and reassess how he's doing, then we can look at the whole thing again."

CHAPTER TWENTY-NINE

Over at the side of the patio, Miller was standing with a glass of red wine in his hand, feeling rather overwhelmed by the entire evening. It had been one shock after another – the vote on his right to stay, the very unexpected outcome, the arguments that had followed, then the chant, the introductions, the rude accusations thrown his way, and he was feeling entirely exhausted by the whole thing.

At the end of it all, Baron had announced that there was a party of sorts, and half a dozen people had rushed inside the manor, returning with beer, wine, a tray of cakes and slices and another with a selection of cheeses. Once the alcohol was flowing freely, a dozen conversations had sprung up around the patio and a young man – Alistair, if Miller remembered his name correctly – had appeared at Miller's side and offered him two glasses. "Red or white?" he'd asked cheerfully, and Miller had taken the glass of red wine with a mumbled 'thank you'. After that, he'd expected to be ignored for the rest of the evening. Even among those who had voted in his favour, none of them seemed particularly excited about having him stay.

But instead, there had been a steady stream of people wanting to talk to him. Some of the conversations had been decidedly awkward, people asking questions about the Noturatii, not out of polite curiosity about his past, but digging for information that might help them strike a blow against their enemies. Others had given him sharp warnings, words to the effect that the shifters were notoriously loyal, and anyone stepping out of line would be swiftly shown their place. Alistair had come back again, giving him a few useful words of advice. The Den operated under a strict pecking order, he'd said, with rank determined by status fights, always conducted in wolf form, always under supervision, and designed to display strength and courage, rather than do any actual damage. As the newest member of the pack, Miller would automatically be the lowest ranking member, which was important for a whole range of reasons. He would sit at the lowest end of the table during dinner. He would be given one of the least comfortable bedrooms. He could easily be kicked out of a dog bed or off a couch by one of the more senior wolves. There was nothing personal about the treatment, Alistair had emphasised, no intended bullying or intimidation. It was just the way things were. As the lowest in line, Miller was going to get pecked the most.

Once Alistair wandered off again, another man approached, with an odd symbol on his face. This was the man who was Melissa's brother, Miller recalled, having run into him during the Den's invasion of the Noturatii lab. The symbol hadn't been there at that time, and he wondered what the significance of it was. It wasn't quite a tattoo, Miller thought, trying to get a better look without being too obvious about it. It looked more like a… burn?

"It's a brand," the man said, though Miller couldn't remember his name just at the moment. "I betrayed the Den last year, and this was part of my punishment. It's the mark of a traitor, to remind everyone I'm not to be trusted."

"You don't sound all that unhappy about it," Miller observed with curiosity. The man's name was Mark, he suddenly remembered, grateful that he'd been spared the awkward need to ask again, given that they'd been introduced not even half an hour ago.

Mark laughed and shook his head. "It's rather complicated, but the short version is that I came out of the whole thing rather well. Certainly far better than I had expected. The Council could have had me killed for what I did." A sly smile crept over his face. "And there's no shortage of irony in that, given that you're standing here now."

"What did you do?"

"You remember when Dee was converted and escaped the lab? The entire team of scientists was killed. Someone made a mess of your IT office, killed a bunch of guards."

"I remember."

"That was me."

Miller's jaw dropped. "You were the one who broke into our labs? Fucking hell… and your Council declared you a traitor for it? That's ridiculous."

"Like I said, it's more complicated than that," Mark said again. "But if you notice people generally giving me a hard time, then that's why."

"Dee doesn't look particularly happy with you at the moment," Miller said, noticing the woman across the patio, glaring daggers at Mark.

"Yup," Mark said, looking slightly miffed. "I'd noticed." He took a sip of his wine, and Miller wasn't sure whether he was going to explain that one, though he didn't want to pry…

"We're dating," Mark said finally. "And she's not thrilled about me voting in your favour. Which is understandable, given what your mob did to her back in the lab, but then again, it would be fairly hypocritical of me to deny you a second chance, when I was given one of my own only a few short months ago. You know the story: no good deed goes unpunished."

Miller laughed, the first time he'd felt like doing so in a long while. "True enough." But then he hesitated, choosing his next words carefully. "After what happened back in the lab, it... well... I'm aware that Melissa is your sister. I was wondering if you'd..."

"No," Mark said firmly, shadows appearing in his eyes. "For a whole pile of complicated reasons, I have no interest in hearing anything about her."

"But she's your sister. Even though she's working for the other side, I thought you might-"

"I will say this only once," Mark said, turning to Miller with a cold glare. "I have no sister. The woman you worked with chose a path of cruelty and destruction, and I want nothing more to do with her, save to put a bullet in her, should we ever meet again."

It was said with such cold finality that Miller couldn't think of a single thing to say in response. He let his gaze wander over the patio, trying to come up with a different topic of conversation, and noticed another man glaring at him, John, the one who had refused to perform the Chant of Forests.

"What's John's story?" he asked cautiously. Mark was one of the few people who had neither tried to interrogate him about the Noturatii, nor threatened him in any way, and he seemed more sympathetic to Miller's situation than most people, so he was hoping the man might be willing to share some information with him.

"I would stop staring at him if I was you," Mark said sharply, and Miller wondered what he'd inadvertently done wrong now. The social rules of this place seemed complicated beyond all understanding. "You'll figure out soon enough that everyone here has had something of a rough past, and joining the shifters has often been a form of salvation for a lot of people. We don't talk about other people's pasts, and asking the person directly is generally frowned upon. It's one of the most personal things you can ask. So I can't tell you much about John. But I can say that he had a difficult time before he came here, even by shifter standards. And he has more than enough reason to hate you. So if you want my advice? Stay away from him. The kid's insane." It was said so bluntly that Miller had to assume that Mark meant the description literally. "Don't talk to him, don't antagonise him, and if you ever find yourself in a room alone with him, leave as quickly as you possibly can. Given the opportunity, he'll kill you, with absolutely no regard for any laws that forbid it."

The grim news was rather startling. "Is there anyone else I should particularly watch out for?" Miller asked.

Mark shook his head. "Given your position, it's generally a good idea not to go out of your way to piss people off. But no, there's no one else likely to do you any serious damage. Now, I'm going to go get another glass of wine," he said suddenly, draining the last of the liquid from his glass, "but don't think I'm abandoning you. I've just noticed there's someone else who's been eyeing you up for the last five minutes, and the moment I'm gone, she'll be over here like a shot."

Skip noticed Mark leave Miller's side and made a beeline over to the space he'd just vacated. There had been a steady stream of people talking to him, but Skip was rather hoping for a quiet chat, so she'd lingered in the background, hoping for a moment when he would be alone.

"Hey. How's it going?" she asked awkwardly. After the ruckus that had happened during the ceremony, Miller was hardly going to be feeling on top of the world, but she wasn't sure how else to start a conversation with him.

"Feeling a little off balance, quite honestly," Miller said. "This place certainly takes some getting used to. But this officially means they're not going to kill me, right? So I'm not going to complain."

Skip smiled at his droll comment. "Yeah," she agreed. "I always try to find the positive side, no matter how messy things are getting. Um, hey, I was wondering," she said awkwardly, not sure how her next question would be received. For all the time she'd spent teaching Miller to shift, they had yet to discuss anything of a more personal nature. "If you don't mind me asking... do you have any family? I mean, are people in the Noturatii allowed to get married and have kids, and stuff, or is all that considered a threat to secrecy?"

Miller looked vaguely surprised at the question, but answered it easily enough. "People are allowed to get married. But they're always given a solid cover story about what their work entails, and anyone who starts leaking secrets tends to... suddenly disappear. As for me, no. I'm not married. I was single when I was recruited, and trying to have that kind of relationship when I can never tell the other person who I really am or what I really do just seemed hollow. I don't think I could do that for long without the need for honesty starting to drive me crazy."

Skip laughed, then realised it might be inappropriate, but Miller didn't seem to take offence. "I know, I know," he admitted wryly. "No shortage of irony right there. I'm too honest to lie to a woman, but I'm happy to lie to everyone else? I guess the truth finally caught up with me. And delivered a rather firm kick up the arse, in the process."

"Well, I'm rather glad you had your change of heart when you did," Skip said, giving him a sideways glance.

"Actually, on that note, I've been meaning to ask; how are your wounds healing? No one would tell me anything while I was in the cage, and I've been worried."

"Healing well," Skip reported. "I had surgery to remove the bullet, and then had an infection for a few days, but it looks like it's all on the mend now."

Miller went to say something, changed his mind, and then had another go. "Would it be okay if I had a look at your wolf?" he asked. "I hope that's not an inappropriate question. It's just... no one here has really given me much in the way of straight answers, and I'd feel a lot happier about it if I could see for myself. If I'd been paying more attention to the fact that Steve was still alive, I could have stopped you being shot in the first place."

Skip was about to agree when Baron, Caroline and Simon suddenly came marching across the patio, straight towards Miller.

"Okay, so here's the deal," Baron announced, sounding tired and irritable. "We're willing to give you a chance, but letting you roam freely about the estate is basically suicidal, so we're going to compromise. This is a radio monitor," he said, holding up a small, black device. "You will wear it, strapped to your ankle, at all times. It sends a radio signal back to a receiver every thirty seconds, and if you either attempt to take it off, or get within twenty metres of the boundary fence, every fucking alarm in this place will sound, and you'll have a dozen wolves suddenly on your tail, all willing and eager to chew your legs off. Are we clear?"

"No problem," Miller agreed, looking rather overwhelmed, and then Simon bent down, tugged Miller's trouser leg up and secured the device to his ankle. Then he asked Miller to shift. He did so, and Simon secured another device around his neck, making sure it was a snug fit that couldn't slip off over all the loose fur.

When he was finished, he told Miller he could shift back, then he pulled a small receiver out of his pocket and fiddled with the settings.

"All good," he reported to Baron. "It's waterproof, so don't worry about getting it wet in the shower. The receiver is set up to respond to either transmitter, and it'll only sound the alarm if it doesn't get a signal from either one. Any questions?" Miller shook his head. "Good. Then we're done." He glanced at Baron, who nodded, and then all three of them marched away, leaving Miller looking miffed, and more than a little confused.

"Are they always like that?" he asked, and Skip shrugged.

"Yes, and no. They take security very, *very* seriously. But so long as you follow the rules and don't do anything to get on their bad side, they're usually very reasonable. You wanted to have a look at my wounds," she reminded him, bringing them back to their previous conversation.

"If that's okay with you?"

Skip nodded, then shifted, presenting her back leg for Miller to examine. The fur had yet to start growing back to any real degree, and she winced as she felt the cold air against her skin. Miller bent down and examined the puckered sutures, the bruising where the bullet had gone in, and then the long, straight line the surgeon had cut along her abdomen.

"It's looking good," he said, probing the wound with the gentlest of fingers. His hands against her skin felt odd. Though she'd been touched as a wolf before, it had always been through her thick coat of fur, and the warm brush of his fingers was both unsettling, and oddly tantalising. It was far from unpleasant, she realised with a jolt, astonished that a man from such a violent past could have such a gentle touch.

And her heart started racing all of a sudden, as she realised that no man had ever touched her like this before. Her father and his friends had been brutal, firm grips, quick to slap her if she resisted too much. The men in the Den had generally refrained from touching her at all, or, on the odd occasion when they had needed to, it had been brief, a firm but cursory touch in order to pull her out of danger, for example, or to carry her, as Silas had done when they'd got home from the vet, the contact swiftly ended once the required task was complete.

But Miller's fingers lingered, a touch full of concern, and then he gave her a relieved smile when he finally pulled back and stood up.

Skip shifted back, managing a wobbly smile, taking a sip of her wine to hide her discomfort. But the soft sensation of his hand upon her skin lingered for a long time afterwards.

Up in the bedroom he shared with Baron, John grabbed an armful of clothes out of the wardrobe. Hangers clattered to the floor, but he ignored them. He stomped out the door, down the hall, up the stairs and into one of the empty bedrooms on the manor's third floor. He dumped the clothes onto the neatly made bed, then stomped back downstairs, to repeat the exercise again, and then again. As well as the clothes, there were also shoes, toiletries, his video games and the console Baron let him keep in their bedroom, and three books that he was currently reading; John was quite startled at the amount of stuff he'd managed to accumulate during his stay in Baron's room. It was going on six years since he'd joined the Den, but the time had flown; it still seemed like just yesterday that Baron had pointed a gun at his head as he sat beside the bloodied corpse of a farmer and asked what the fuck he thought he was doing. After that, he'd dragged him back here, into the secret home of the shifters that John had been searching for ever since he'd escaped from the Noturatii weeks before.

Life here had been good, he would have admitted easily enough. Food, sex, plenty of violence in battles with the Noturatii to pass the time, and other shifters who were strong, ruthless, and far easier to respect than the weak, pitiful creatures he'd known early in his life.

But all that had changed tonight. That Baron had kept Miller alive for this long was lamentable, but understandable; he had information Il Trosa needed, and the Council were likely inclined to suck everything useful out of him before they finally disposed of him.

But the announcement that they might allow him to join the Den had left John shocked, speechless, his mind reeling as his entire world seemed to have tilted sideways. The Noturatii were the enemy. *His* enemy. The reason why his wolf was scarred from head to toe and why he still woke up screaming at night.

Baron should have kicked Miller out. Should have killed him. Should have prioritised his Den and his home and his pack far above the supposed rights of one worthless man.

Well, there wasn't much John could do about Miller now. The Den had voted, not once, but twice, which meant that in all practical terms, the decision was now set in stone.

But as far as his own situation went, it was not to be tolerated. By allowing Miller to stay, Baron had betrayed everything John had believed him to be.

So he was moving out.

He was on his fourth trip, arms full of shampoo and razor blades, and his own personal dog bed that sat on the floor in the corner, when heavy footsteps came echoing down the hall. John recognised the person approaching from the sound alone; Baron had arrived.

He took one step into their bedroom, saw the mess John had created, and stopped in his tracks. "What the fuck are you doing?" he asked, more baffled than angry.

"Moving out," John replied, fighting to control his emotions, which seemed to be swinging wildly between rage and fear. Not that he was afraid of Baron. For all the man's physical size, John had learned long ago that he was an even match for the huge black wolf in a fight. Rather, he feared disappointing the man, his own mental equilibrium very much dependent on keeping Baron happy. It was the motivation behind a large number of his daily actions, whether it was biting his tongue when someone pissed him off, or fulfilling his duties in keeping the manor clean, or warming his alpha's bed at night. If Baron was happy, then John got to continue living his relatively peaceful life, safe within the walls of the manor, protected against his own paranoia and the rages that sometimes swept through him, out of control.

But this time, bowing to Baron's natural authority and the emotional hold he had over John wasn't an option. He'd stood by and allowed a

Noturatii man to infiltrate the Den, had accepted his oath of allegiance, and sworn one in return. The betrayal of trust inherent in those actions was unforgivable.

"What do you mean, you're moving out?" Baron asked, as John headed for the door.

"You like your Noturatii man so much better than me?" John said, working hard to sound flippant. "Fine. You can have him. Just don't expect me to stick around and lick your arse while you stab me in the back." He ducked around Baron, who was still too startled to stop him, and dashed off down the hall.

"You get back here!" Baron snarled a moment later, rushing after him. He darted forward and grabbed John's arm, yanking him around so that he dropped most of what he was carrying. "You can't just fucking up and leave like that! You damn well explain yourself. I followed proper protocol, and let the Den vote on Miller-"

"You should have put a bullet in him the moment he walked through that fucking gate," John yelled back at him, his anger outweighing his fear for the moment. "You know what they fucking did to me! To Tank! To Dee! They killed Nate and Eric. They killed Luke. They fuck up every single one of our lives! You want to let him stay? Well, screw that. I'm not going to keep bending over for a guy who thinks the fucking *Noturatii* are more important than his own boyfriend!"

Their argument had attracted some attention, and he was vaguely aware of Caroline appearing at the end of the hall, with Andre close behind her, of Tank sticking his head out of his bedroom, and Dee appearing at the top of the stairs.

"You put your fucking shit back in that bedroom, and-"

He didn't get any further, as John swiftly kicked him in the balls and wrenched his arm free. But Baron wasn't giving up so easily, and he made a grab for John's shirt, hunched over in pain though he was.

"Baron!" Caroline moved quicker than John would have believed, inserting herself between him and Baron. "What the fuck is going on?"

"I'm moving out," John declared defiantly. If Caroline wanted to stop him, she'd have a fight on her hands. He'd fought her before, and won, and he'd damn near ripped her throat out before Baron had managed to drag him off her. He was more than willing to have another go at it now.

"You get back in that fucking room," Baron said, face red, trying to see around Caroline to glare at him.

"No," John replied, desperately wanting to pick up the things on the floor. He hoped none of it was broken. "I'm moving into a bedroom upstairs. *Alone.*"

"You're not going anywhere-"

"Yes, he is," Caroline replied, which made John look up in surprise.

"What?" Baron asked, as if she'd just grown a second head.

"If he wants to leave, then he's allowed to leave," Caroline stated firmly.

"Living with me was the only way we ever kept him under control," Baron spat. "You know that!"

"If John wants to leave," Caroline repeated, emphasising the words, "then I will not allow you to stop him."

Baron managed to stand up straight, though he was clearly suffering for the effort, and stepped up close to Caroline. "You get out of my way."

A low growl filled the hall, and it took John a moment to realise that it was coming not just from Caroline, but from Andre as well. The man stepped up beside Caroline, and looked Baron in the eye. "You threaten my woman again, and you and I are going to have words," he promised coldly.

Watching on, Tank was looking tense and apprehensive. For all the common arguments between Baron and Caroline, physical fights were rare, and Tank was no doubt wondering if he'd have to step in and break things up – a daunting prospect, when Andre was involved as well.

John stood very still, keeping his breathing slow and even, trying to blend into the background. He'd lived through far too much trauma to take the current standoff for anything other than what it was – a leadership challenge between the ranking wolves in the Den – and the almost tangible anger flooding the room was terrifying.

After a long pause, Tank finally stepped forward. "How about we all take a breather," he suggested mildly. "Go get a stiff drink, have a little time out, and come back to this when we're all thinking more clearly."

"Fine," Baron conceded gruffly, then stalked back into his bedroom and slammed the door. Andre gave Tank a tight nod of thanks, gave Caroline's shoulder a brief squeeze, then headed off to his own room. And John avoided looking at either of them, still unable to make sense of Caroline's unexpected support, and set about collecting his things from the floor. There was more of his stuff in Baron's room, but there was little chance of collecting the rest tonight. He headed quickly back up the stairs, closed the door to his newly claimed bedroom, and set about arranging his things to his liking.

CHAPTER THIRTY

Melissa stood in the Noturatii's shooting range, watching her instructor prepare the equipment for her practice. When she'd written to Noturatii headquarters earlier in the year, detailing her research ideas, her letter had also included suggestions about improving the firearm skills of the science and administration staff. The attack on their lab last winter had caused the death of dozens of people, and it was Melissa's firm opinion that many of those lives could have been saved had the staff been armed with handguns.

Headquarters hadn't got back to her with an official response, so far merely stating that they were considering the idea, but Melissa was nothing if not determined, and with Jacob's approval, she'd been having lessons with one of the security guards in her free time.

Today was one such day, with the experiments on the shifter captive at a temporary halt. They'd successfully recorded the shift a dozen or more times, and spent long hours analysing the data, building up a solid picture of the shift from an electrical perspective, but then Doctor Evans, of all people, had suggested that perhaps they should run the same tests from the opposite side of the coin; beginning with the shifter in wolf form, and recording the readings as he became human.

It was an excellent idea, as the next stage of the experiments – attempting to feed the electrical charge back into the shifter to force a shift – would require a complete reconfiguration of the electrodes – but the downside was that the current setup wasn't capable of taking readings through the wolf's fur. The solution was conceptually simple, yet difficult in practice; they would need to shave the wolf.

When it had become apparent that the shifter was going to put up a fight over his new haircut, a whole squad of guards had been called in to subdue him, leaving the science team with a break in their work. Never one to be idle, Melissa had brought herself down here, ready for her next lesson in self defence.

"Okay, we're going to try a more powerful gun today," her instructor told her, handing her a gun that was noticeably heavier than the one she had been using up until now. "This is a 9mm semi-automatic. You'll find it a little more difficult to handle. The basic rule is, the more powerful the gun, the more recoil you're going to get, which makes it harder to shoot straight. The upside, of course, is that this gun will do more damage, and it has a better range. With practice, you should be able to hit a live target up to fifty metres away."

Melissa listened to his instructions patiently, paying close attention to every detail, then she put on her earmuffs and took the gun, lining up her shot carefully. When she pulled the trigger, she found that he was right – the gun had a significant kick to it. The bullet went wide of the target, and she felt a stab of disappointment at the result.

But if at first you don't succeed…

Melissa had another go, and then another, sometimes managing to hit quite close to the centre of the target, sometimes going quite wide. But she liked the weight of the gun in her hand, the cool metal, the feeling of power it gave her, and after a time, she started getting used to the recoil, anticipating it, enjoying it, even. And instead of the blue silhouette of a human torso, she imagined she was shooting at a shifter's heart instead, bullet after bullet sent hurtling down the range, each one a step closer to her dream of eradicating the shifters once and for all.

Jacob was on his way to the shooting range for a practice session when Abdul, the head of their small forensics department, stopped him in the hallway.

"I have the report on the car crash, sir. You said you wanted to know the moment it was complete."

"Excellent." Jacob took the report from the scientist, waving at him to walk with him as he continued towards the shooting range.

He skimmed through the information, planning on having a more thorough look later on, but he could at least get an overview now. "The vehicle was traveling at high speed. Skidded on the corner and hit the wall. Cause of the crash unknown, but it may have had to swerve to avoid an obstruction. The crash could be consistent with trying to avoid an oncoming car. Interesting…" He paused to open the door to the shooting range reception area, then turned the page. "No sign of the other vehicle, no tyre tracks on the road, no debris that didn't come from our car." He looked up at Abdul. "I'm sorry, I'm not quite following this. The report says the crash was consistent with avoiding another vehicle, yet there's no evidence of any other vehicle being present."

"Something must have caused the car to skid," Abdul pointed out. "There was no mechanical fault that we could find. The basic cause of the crash was sudden braking, causing the tyres to lose traction, but why would they suddenly hit the brakes like that? There had to be a reason, and given the circumstances, the most likely cause-"

"Could equally have been a stray sheep in the middle of the road?" Jacob finished his sentence for him, and the scientist looked vaguely embarrassed.

"I suppose that's a possibility, yes."

They paused at the security desk, where Jacob picked up a pair of earmuffs and safety glasses. The door to the range opened, and Melissa came out, a gun and a pair of earmuffs in her hand. "Another practice session?" he asked, as she saw him.

"Yes, sir," she replied crisply. "We're waiting for the shifter to be prepped for the next round of tests in the lab, so I thought I'd make use of the time."

"An excellent idea," Jacob said, beaming at her. "You see, Abdul, this here is the sort of member we need. She thinks outside the square, she goes above and beyond the call of duty, and she's always looking for methods to improve the way we do things. This young lady is going places, I guarantee it." Dismissing Melissa with a smile and a nod, he turned back to his report. "The two bullet casings found inside the car were from a Glock 22. Which, coincidentally, is the same gun used by the majority of our security staff," he said drily. "And also the type of bullet that killed Steve. There was no gun found on Steve's body... so according to this report, it's entirely within the realm of possibility that someone took Steve's own gun from him and shot him with it?"

"Yes, sir."

Standing at the security desk, Melissa handed her gun back to the security officer at the window. Once she gained her full licence, she'd be allowed to carry one with her full time, but until then, she had to check it in and out each time she came for practice. As she initialled the sign-out form, her ears pricked up at the conversation happening behind her. The whole building had heard about the crash, and the rumours that Miller was now in the hands of the shifters. Jacob had made the firm point that until the official report came in, everything else was nothing more than gossip and hearsay, but from the sounds of it, that report had finally arrived. Melissa took her time with signing off. Any excuse to stay a few moments longer, and hear the results of the report.

"Daniel was killed in the crash," Jacob was saying, "but what about any sign of Miller? Are you certain he was the one driving?"

"Yes sir," the other man replied. "His fingerprints were on the steering wheel. He'd been injured – his blood was on the front seat and the door handle. There might have been more evidence, but unfortunately, the rain could have washed a lot of it away. But I can confirm that Miller was driving the car, he was bleeding when he left it, and his phone was left at the scene. There's no other trace of him at all."

Listening carefully, Melissa got her security pass out deliberately slowly to show it to the guard, fumbled with it and dropped it on the floor as she went to put it away. News of Miller was a topic of great interest to her. He had helped save her life after the attack on the lab, though disappointingly it had been at the expense of letting their prisoners escape, but even so, she held a certain professional respect for him as a result. Most of the guards weren't the sharpest knives in the drawer, heavy-weight grunts who fought well, but didn't do so well on the thinking side of things. Miller had seemed to straddle both sides of the coin, and Melissa was curious to know what had become of him.

Jacob was still peering at the report, and he flipped the page... then the next, then hurriedly turned back to the start. "Abdul," he said suddenly, a warning tone in his voice. "There's nothing in this report about any other bullet casings recovered from the scene. Is there more evidence still being processed?"

"No sir. That's all of it. There were only the two casings found – both of them inside the car."

"Okay, then for argument's sake, let's go out on a limb and assume that the captive herself managed to take Steve's gun from him and shoot him with it. No sign of the second bullet, but that doesn't mean anything in particular. Perhaps they were fighting over the gun, and a bullet was fired off into the fields. If it went any significant distance, we'd never find it. But according to the evidence, a grand total of two shots were fired. The prevailing theory on this case was that the shifters came after their captive, ran the car off the road and kidnapped Miller in the process. So could you explain to me how that could all have happened, with no confirmed evidence of a second vehicle, and without anyone else firing a single shot?"

Melissa had wasted all the time she could without drawing unwanted attention to herself – getting pulled up for eavesdropping when Jacob had just given her a shining appraisal in front of her colleague would only make her look silly – so she gathered her things and headed out the door.

But as she climbed the stairs and walked back to her office, her mind was chewing over the information she had gleaned from Jacob's conversation.

She didn't have all the details, she knew, and besides which, solving the mystery of Miller's disappearance wasn't her job. But out of pure curiosity, she couldn't help trying to fit the pieces of the puzzle together. What were the possible scenarios that could have led to the available evidence?

Well, option one was the most obvious. Miller had indeed been kidnapped by the shifters, and his fate was beyond their control. If the other car hadn't skidded or hit anything, then there wouldn't be any evidence of it left behind, and perhaps that second bullet had hit Miller, and he'd been injured and unable to defend himself as a result.

Option two was similar: the shifters had come after their captive, but in this version, Miller had survived the crash and hidden somewhere nearby, escaping before the shifters got a hold of him. If he'd been hurt, then he could be either trying to make his way back to the Noturatii somehow, or lying dead in a ditch somewhere, overcome by his injuries.

Option three: there had been no second car, in which case something else had caused Miller to crash the car. It had been a wet and stormy night, after all. Hazardous driving conditions. A stray sheep, or a dog running in the road? But that ultimately brought her back to option two – Miller was either injured or dead, somewhere lost in the countryside, the captive shifter having presumably run off sometime after the crash.

Option four... what was option four? What if the captive hadn't run off, Melissa wondered idly. What if, by some freakish twist of fate, she'd managed to take Steve's gun, shoot him, then she'd taken Miller captive? If he'd been injured, he might not have been able to fight back. So she'd captured him, taken him away – on foot, if there was no second car involved – and then either handed him over to the shifters, or killed him at a later time, somewhere in the middle of the countryside. That seemed less likely, as Miller was a seasoned fighter, and should have been able to take on one shifter relatively easily, whether they were armed or not. But it was a possibility.

And then a fifth idea occurred to her, one that she dismissed without even considering it... but then a moment later, she brought the idea back around in her mind. This one was even less likely than the last, going against everything she knew about Miller. But that was how real investigators had to think, she reminded herself, how the Noturatii had to think, when they were dealing with a species as malicious and devious as the shifters, and Melissa let her mind linger on the strange and unsettling idea.

Perhaps no one had kidnapped Miller at all. Perhaps, after the car had crashed, he'd... released the captive? she thought, running with the most outlandish scenario she could imagine. Perhaps the captive had bribed him, offered him a ridiculous amount of money for her own freedom... and then Miller had... decided to help her? Allowed her to go free? And disappeared off the radar, to begin a new life elsewhere? Traitors within the Noturatii were few and far between, but certainly not unheard of. They were all swiftly hunted down and killed, and Melissa would have found it easier to believe that aliens had finally landed on earth, than to believe that

Miller had betrayed the Noturatii. But nonetheless, the idea was there, filling out her list of possibilities as to what could have become of the man.

The mystery would be solved one way or another, she knew, as she reached her office and put the idle thoughts aside. The Noturatii were nothing if not thorough, and one way or another, they'd track him down – either the man himself, or his remains. But until they did, the mystery remained a tantalising puzzle to be solved, and she was rather proud of her own deductive skills in coming up with a range of possible scenarios. She would wait eagerly to discover the truth, once the investigation was complete, and then she'd see how close to the target she'd managed to get.

Three days after his acceptance into the Den, Miller walked into the dining room, feeling a little more spirited than he had been lately. After he'd been released from his cage, he'd been told that he was to have formal lessons on shifter life; the rules around the estate, the mechanics of shifting, and the war with the Noturatii – from the shifters' perspective this time, rather than the Noturatii's. At first, he'd been looking forward to the lessons. Days of sitting in the cage with little entertainment and no purposeful work had left him feeling bored and restless, and though Skip had made the effort to teach him the basics, there was much more he still wanted to know.

But then had come another piece of news that had been rather startling: Tank was to be his tutor. Apparently it was a punishment of sorts, for the fight he'd started with Miller in the cages. But the idea made Miller a little nervous. Though they'd found some common ground while they were both locked up, and though Tank had voted for him to be allowed to stay, it was also clear that the man hadn't got over everything about Miller's past. Which was understandable, Miller reminded himself. Tank had suffered tremendous pain and lost numerous close friends as a direct result of Miller's actions, and working through all the residual anger and grief was going to take time.

The other thing that was taking a significant amount of getting used to was the mannerisms of the shape shifters. The basics of the 'merge' had been explained to him, the need to accept the wolf's desires and thoughts as his own, but seeing the result up close and personal in his tutor was more than a little unsettling. Tank had a tendency to watch Miller with a predatory stare, like a wolf stalking a deer. He possessed an almost preternatural stillness, a lithe gracefulness when he moved, an uncanny alertness to the things going on around him.

But it wasn't just Tank. Everyone around the estate displayed the same unsettling blend of human and wolf traits, civilised people seamlessly merged with wild animals. And Miller was starting to wonder how long it would be before he began to develop the same traits.

Tensions had been running high over the past few days, and it had taken Miller a little while to discover that it wasn't all due to the decision to let him out of the cage. Apparently, the vote had also caused a rift in the relationship between John and Baron. The news that they were in a relationship in the first place had been unexpected – not because they were both men, but because they seemed like such vastly different people. He wasn't sure at this stage whether the split was a serious one, and would have liked to apologise for his part in it... but given Mark's warning about staying away from John, he hadn't dared.

Thankfully, though, other parts of his daily life seemed to be going a little better. One of the first things Tank had explained to him, once his lessons began, was the rules governing status within the Den. Status fights were largely ritualised, he'd explained, particularly at the lower end of the ranks. Once you got up near the top, the fights tended to be tougher, but there were still rules against doing anyone serious or permanent damage. Intrigued by the idea, and with Tank's assurances that it was within acceptable behaviour standards, Miller had challenged George to a fight this afternoon. The elderly man was ranked one place above him, and by all reports, he held that low position through choice, rather than lack of fighting ability.

The fight had been short and simple, with Miller declared the winner, much to his own surprise, as he'd attempted the fight more from curiosity than from any expectation of winning, and he'd come down to dinner feeling pleased with himself. It was a small step up the pecking order, but a good start, given that he'd only been here a few days. He didn't intend to try to rise too quickly through the ranks – firstly, he needed time to learn to fight as a wolf, which was a huge change from fighting as a human, but secondly, he didn't want to antagonise anyone by being too pushy about things.

But when he stepped into the dining room, he stopped and looked at the seating arrangement in surprise. George was in his usual place, Mark at the bottom of the table and an empty seat between the two.

"Excuse me," he said to George, while the man tried to avoid his gaze. "But I believe I won the fight this afternoon. My understanding was that I have your seat now." It was said as politely as possible – perhaps Miller had misunderstood the rules?

But George meekly shook his head. "You'll have to take it up with them," he murmured, nodding to the far end of the table... and Miller was a little alarmed to see Tank and Silas standing up, both of them staring at him levelly.

"You won the fight," Silas said calmly. "But the thing about that is, rank in a wolf pack isn't just decided by who's the stronger fighter. There's also a whole pile of social wheeling and dealing to be done. And the long and the short of it is that if the pack doesn't support your rank, you don't get to keep it. No matter how good a fighter you are."

Miller glanced around the room, wondering if what Silas had said was true. But no one else moved or said a word to contradict him.

"But you let me stay," Miller protested, not quite understanding the sudden swing of opinion against him. "You voted to allow me to be a member of your pack."

"The two things have nothing to do with each other," Simon spoke up, from further down the table. "It's like saying you deserve a promotion just because you work for the company. Doesn't work that way. You have to earn it."

The news was disappointing, but it also made an odd sort of sense. He'd only been here a few days, and it likely took a lot longer than that for newcomers to start earning a measure of social standing. Not wanting to make a fuss, Miller shrugged, and took his seat next to Mark. That in itself was an awkward situation, he'd been told. Under normal circumstances, as the newest member of the Den, Miller would hold the lowest rank. But due to the conditions of Mark's punishment, he was relegated to the rank of omega until a full year had passed since his sentence was handed down, which wouldn't be until the end of March next year.

Mark gave him a tight smile as the last of the Den drifted in the door and took their seats, a silent acknowledgement that life at the bottom of the pecking order could be trying. Then Baron stood up to announce the evening's news, and the meal began.

CHAPTER THIRTY-ONE

Tucked under a fallen tree in the heart of the forest, a safe distance from the Grey Watch's camp, Genna concentrated on the collection of rocks in front of her. Over the past weeks, she'd continued experimenting with her unusual talent, going on regular 'hunting' excursions, and once she'd made sure she'd caught something to take back to camp, a rabbit, perhaps, or a pheasant, she would spend fifteen or twenty minutes testing the limits of her abilities. She had to be careful, of course, conducting rigorous checks to see who else was around, as she didn't want to risk getting caught. And if she took too long to catch something, her practice session would have to wait for another day. But all in all, she'd managed to practise at least twice a week, and was making slow but steady progress.

Today, she was testing out how far away an object could be before she couldn't affect it any more. She'd already conducted tests on the size of object she could magic away, with the answer surprising her. She'd somehow assumed that the magic would be dependent on weight, but from her experiments so far, it seemed that size was a far more reliable indicator. She could manage anything up to about a foot long, but beyond that the strain was too much. She'd also discovered that once she'd made an object disappear, the very next time she shifted, the object would reappear. There seemed no way around that, and she'd been very careful since then not to leave anything 'hidden' for long periods of time, in case she suddenly needed to shift and the reappearing object gave her secret away.

For this experiment, she'd lined up five rocks, each an inch or so further away than the last. The first was just an inch from her hand, and she concentrated, making that one disappear quite easily. She brought it back, set it to the side, and moved on to the next one. That one went too, but the third was more difficult. She felt a build up of charge against her skin, but then suddenly her hand cramped up, forcing her to relax and shake her fingers out before trying again. It was a common side effect of pushing her powers too far, she was learning, but not necessarily an indication that she couldn't go any further. Like any new skill, it was just a matter of practice, trying new techniques, approaching the problem from different angles.

This time, instead of using one hand, she held up both, and was pleased when the rock disappeared. She brought it back and tried again with one hand, getting accustomed to the feel of reaching through empty space to focus on the object, and though it was an effort, the rock obediently disappeared. Okay, so three inches was possible. She brought the rock back, set it aside and concentrated on the fourth-

"That's an interesting trick you've got there."

Genna leapt a foot in the air, cracking her head on the branch she was sheltered under as she heard Sempre's harsh voice cut through the silence. Fuck! She'd been so focused on her experiments that she hadn't been paying enough attention to her surroundings, hadn't heard the woman approach until it was far too late.

"I discovered it yesterday," Genna said, rubbing her head and making an effort to look embarrassed and fawning. "I thought I should try it out a little more before I told you about it. I didn't want to disappoint you if I couldn't do it properly." It was a speech she'd rehearsed repeatedly, aware that if Sempre ever discovered not just what she could do, but how long she'd been keeping it a secret, she'd be in deep trouble. She was royally screwed as it was, the greedy look in Sempre's eyes confirmation enough of her selfish desires, but there was no point making it any worse than it needed to be.

"Really," Sempre said, her glee at the discovery meaning she wasn't paying too much attention to the details, and Genna held her breath as she wondered if she'd got away with her lie. "Come out then, and show me what you can do," Sempre commanded, standing back so Genna could crawl out from beneath the branch.

"It's not much, really," Genna said nervously. "I can make small things disappear. Like this rock…" She set one on the tree branch and placed her hand over it, making it vanish. And then brought it back a moment later. "They don't stay away for long, though. It's like I drop them, if I try for too long, and they slip back into reality. And I was just trying to see how far away things could be for it still to work."

"And how far away is that?" Sempre asked, a look of cold calculation in her eyes. Genna dreaded what was going to happen when they got back to camp.

"About three inches," Genna admitted, trying to look defeated at the admission. "I just can't reach any further than that. It's not very impressive," she added, hoping to dissuade Sempre from some of her enthusiasm.

"Well, no," Sempre agreed, and Genna felt a moment of relief. "But you're still young. As a human, and as a shifter. This is a remarkable talent," Sempre said, putting an arm around her shoulder and leading her back towards the camp. "And with the right help, it can be turned into the most amazing of gifts. We must discuss this with Lita," she crooned, making Genna's gut churn. Lita, if it was possible, was even worse than Sempre. Sempre might be strict and angry and aggressive, but Lita was manipulative, devious, with all manner of tricks up her sleeve to twist people in knots. "You'll have to be trained," Sempre decided. "Give it some time, but don't worry. We'll help you develop this talent to its full potential."

Genna felt cold as she trod the overgrown path back to the camp. Training? 'Help' with her talent? Not likely, she thought, a heavy weight settling in her chest. They were going to enslave her, force her to perform ever greater feats of magic, punish her for every failure and ask for more and more with every success. And then, when she reached the limits of the magic's natural reach, they would delve into the spirit world, steal power that was not rightfully theirs, and set Genna on a path that would suck the life right out of her, just as it had done to Lita.

Baron stalked out onto the manor's back lawn, feeling uncharacteristically irritable. Tensions were still running high around the Den, with ongoing arguments continuing to break out about Miller's acceptance into Il Trosa, despite the fact that more than three weeks had passed since the decision had been made. When Baron had told the Council the result of the vote, Eleanor had seemed more amused than surprised, and her apparent lack of concern for how seriously things could go wrong if Miller betrayed them was aggravating.

In addition to that, John had firmly refused to move back into Baron's bedroom, despite repeated attempts to reason with the boy. He'd collected the last of his things, with Caroline acting as his chaperone – something Baron had seen as completely unnecessary and almost as infuriating as his boyfriend's unwillingness to see reason – and then spent the past few weeks being belligerent and insulting whenever Baron asked him to do anything.

Baron's own moods had suffered as a result, and he'd had to work extra hard on keeping his temper, when Miller's presence was already causing more than enough strife as it was. Suddenly turning celibate after years of a regular sexual relationship was putting him on edge, and while he didn't hesitate to take matters into his own hands, so to speak, he was still finding the lack of intimacy frustrating. Going back to his room at night, to be met with a cold, empty bed, was just as jarring now as it had been that first night when John had made his dramatic exit. Sitting watching the television, he still expected a small, warm body to suddenly appear and curl up next to him. Coffee no longer arrived in his bedroom in the morning, a trudge down to the kitchen required to acquire a cup of the hot, black wake-me-up. A thousand minor adjustments had had to be made, and it was startling to realise how closely his and John's lives had become entwined, in a relationship that was ostensibly only to keep the boy stable and stop him from wreaking havoc on the rest of the Den.

But the problem wasn't just an emotional one. He'd quietly pulled Andre aside one evening, needing to have a serious chat with him about John's behaviour. "Every now and then, he gets out of control," he'd explained to Andre grimly. "He's got a sharp temper and enough trauma behind him that he can't always see reason. You've been here long enough to see how that sometimes plays out. In the past, it was my job to talk him down, or physically restrain him, if that didn't work. Given the way things are between us now... I'm afraid that responsibility is going to have to fall on you."

Andre had looked suitably surprised by that. "What about Caroline? Or Tank? They've known him for a lot longer, and-"

"They'll have a go at trying to reason with him, I've no doubt about that," Baron had agreed. "But if the shit hits the fan... the truth is, you and I are the only two people on this estate physically capable of beating him in a fight. Silas can take him in human form, but as a wolf, he's unstoppable. He's beaten Tank in a fight before. Damn near killed Caroline once. I hope it never comes to that, but you need to be aware that if things get out of hand... I'm going to need you to take him down. By whatever means necessary." His voice shook as he said it, the combined emotion of having to acknowledge his own failure in managing a member of his pack, and the dread of seeing the boy hurt.

Andre had nodded, accepting the grim duty with resignation, and neither of them had spoken of the matter again.

The other thing that had been trying Baron's patience lately was the ongoing status fights that had been plaguing the Den. Since Andre's arrival, things had been a little tense as he'd worked to find his place in the pecking order. Now, with Miller here, a new round of fights had started up, only this time, it wasn't a case of friendly bouts to test each other's strength. The more recent fights were a result of very real grudges being held, as various people objected to the result of the vote and sought to trump those who had sided with Miller. And they were met head on in return by those who saw the resentment as a lack of respect for due protocol, and were more determined than ever to hold their own ranks.

The latest development on that front was that Skip, of all people, had decided to challenge Cohen. It was years since Skip had fought anyone, aside from brief, half-hearted scuffles as a newer but stronger wolf slowly climbed the ranks. Her strategy had been simple and obvious, right from the time she'd been converted. Skip hated fighting, hated conflict of any kind, so she'd fought her way up the ranks just far enough to avoid the regular squabbling that went on at the bottom of the pecking order, but no further than absolutely necessary. She wanted a quiet, peaceful life, and seemed to have found the perfect spot to achieve that. Her sudden determination to rise in the ranks was uncharacteristic, and all the more unsettling because of it.

Out on the lawn, Baron sighed as a crowd of spectators gathered in the light drizzle. Skip had made no secret of the fact that she supported Miller, and Cohen, her opponent, had voted against him. As far as Baron was aware, there had never been any animosity between Skip and Cohen, but as they eyed each other across the lawn now, there seemed to be a very real anger in Cohen's eyes, and an equally fierce determination in Skip's.

"Begin," Baron called, when they were both in wolf form and ready to fight, and they both threw themselves into the battle, fur flying, snarls echoing around the lawn. Far from the ritualised posturing and feinting blows that were common in fights of low rank, this fight was as real as they came. Baron shifted into wolf form, keeping a close eye on the battle, lest he be required to step in and cool things off, if anyone got too serious about making their point.

Miller stood beside Mark, watching the fight with an odd mix of interest and trepidation. Getting to know Skip over the past few weeks had been hard work, not because she was particularly evasive or laconic about her views, but because at every turn, she seemed a complete mess of contradictions. Meek and yet fierce. Polite, but not willing to let her opinions be pushed aside. Compassionate, but also realistic, sympathising with Miller's position in the Den, while telling him in the same breath that life as a wolf was tough, and if he wanted to make anything of himself, he was going to have to be tougher.

So far, Miller had been having difficulty figuring out how to relate to the members of the Den. He didn't particularly want to let people walk all over him, but getting in people's faces and standing up for himself just tended to cause them to become even more belligerent. He had yet to find a happy medium that allowed him to stand his ground, but didn't piss everyone off.

But in the process, he was also developing a strong affection for Skip. Along with Mark, she was one of the very few people who seemed genuinely interested in getting to know him, and more and more, he found himself looking forward to the regular runs they took around the estate, the long chats in the evenings after dinner, her girlish enthusiasm every time she discovered a new program or managed to hack a new database. She was, in a word, captivating, and he was now being forced to admit that he felt something more than simple friendship for her. And yet, for all the time she spent with him, she seemed to have a natural hesitancy about developing a deeper relationship, so he'd held back, not making any obvious overtures about his feelings for her. She was warm, genuine, compassionate, and yet oddly shy, after their fiery first meeting.

As he stood watching her fight, he was confident that she could handle herself. She gave no ground, didn't whine or whimper when Cohen succeeded in injuring her, and refused to relent when she scored blows of her own. But even so, he was concerned at the idea of her being hurt. She had a fragile exterior, with an inner core of solid steel, and it was never a given which way she would respond to any particular situation.

The yells of encouragement and jeers of derision were loud around them as the two wolves continued to fight. Miller was a long way from understanding all the social complexities of shifter life, but some of the insults seemed to go well beyond good-natured heckling.

"I've seen dogs fight better than you!" someone yelled, as Skip was knocked off her feet, and Miller had learned enough in the past few weeks to know that calling someone a dog was one of the worst insults a shifter could throw at another.

But Skip wasn't without her own supporters. "One little bite, and you start whimpering like a puppy!" someone else yelled at Cohen, who put his head down and bared his teeth in response. Miller was a little startled to realise that he'd started to growl himself, a strong, protective instinct rising up as Cohen bit Skip on the back leg – the same one where she'd received her bullet wound. Though still quiet, and far more reticent than other people's wolves seemed to be, his own animal side had slowly begun making its presence felt more often, refusing to back down from a challenge, or, like now, assailing Miller with a fierce need to protect and defend when someone or something he cared about was threatened.

But true to form, Skip succeeded in surprising him yet again. She spun around, leaping on top of Cohen as her leg started bleeding, and for a moment, it was impossible to tell which wolf was which, legs everywhere, the two furry bodies tumbling over each other again and again... until Skip came up with a mouthful of Cohen's scruff in her teeth, shaking her opponent viciously as he tried to regain his feet and failed. A moment more of panicked flailing, and the fight was over.

"Skip now outranks Cohen," Baron announced, resuming his human form. "Somebody help these two get cleaned up. I'm sick of seeing blood tracked across the carpet." He turned and stalked away without another word, leaving the gathered spectators to grumble about the result. Heron led Skip back towards the house, volunteering to treat her wounds, while Kwan and Aaron did the same for Cohen. The rest of the group slowly began to drift away.

"It's not as bad as it looks," Mark said softly from beside Miller, as he watched Skip head for the house. "Baron would never have let her fight if her wounds weren't healed well enough."

"She's bleeding," Miller contradicted him, though even he could see that the wounds weren't serious.

There was no reply, and he glanced at Mark to see him watching him carefully. "You've been spending a fair amount of time with Skip lately," he observed. "Sounds like you're developing a soft spot for her."

"Is that a problem?" Miller asked automatically. Some days it seemed no matter what he did, there was someone ready and eager to complain about it, and though Mark was more willing to befriend him than most, Miller was still cautious about doing anything that would antagonise people.

"It's not a problem per se," Mark replied. "But it does come with some potential complications. Just to get things clear… what exactly are your intentions towards her?"

Miller snorted in disbelief. "That's a little formal, isn't it? What do you want me to say? That I'm going to propose marriage and make an honest woman out of her?"

Mark let out a laugh at that, causing Miller to scowl all the more. "Relax. Shit, you're really on the defensive, you know that? I wasn't trying to do the intimidating older brother routine. I just meant, are you interested in her romantically, or is it just a friendship thing?"

Miller blushed at his own tendency to meet opposition head on. "I'm not really sure at the moment. I mean, I'm interested. But I'm having a hard time working out whether she is."

Mark nodded. "Skip's a little more complicated than most people. Like I've said before, other people's stories aren't mine to tell. But I would strongly suggest that in her case, you take things slow. She has good reason to be nervous about intimate relationships."

The implications of Mark's words were obvious. "Somebody's hurt her," Miller concluded easily.

"Not my place to say," Mark replied enigmatically, but the dark look in his eyes confirmed Miller's suspicions, and he immediately resolved not to do anything that might make Skip uncomfortable or that might cause her to question her trust in him.

"How are things going with you and Dee?" he asked, aware of an awkward silence developing between them, as he and Mark turned and headed for the house.

"Making progress," Mark said. "We've had arguments before, and while we don't always end up agreeing with each other, we usually manage to see the other person's point of view. Don't worry." He gave Miller a wry smile. "We'll work it out in the end."

In the ensuite bathroom adjoining Skip's bedroom, Skip waited patiently while Heron rubbed antiseptic cream into the bite wound on her back leg. Her fur hadn't grown back yet, so without the usual thick layer in the way, the bite had hurt more than it normally would, but Skip bore the pain bravely. She'd been itching to fight Cohen ever since she'd got back from her adventure in the wilderness with Miller, feeling bold and daring after holding her own against a Noturatii soldier. She'd had to wait patiently for four long weeks while her wounds healed – Heron had already checked the surgery scars, and confirmed that none of them had reopened during the fight – but the urge to get out there and kick some arse had been relentless, a far cry from her usually placid personality, and Skip had been both baffled and excited by the changes in herself.

Once Heron had finished with the wounds, Skip shifted, helping her clean up the first aid supplies, then wandered into the bedroom. "Could I ask you something?" she said hesitantly, stopping in front of the mirror and staring at her reflection critically.

"Of course, sweetie," Heron said. She stopped beside Skip and ran a gentle hand over her hair. "What's up?"

"I wanted to… Do you think I could…" She stopped, unsure how to put her thoughts into words. "I want to change the way I look," she said finally.

"What do you mean?"

Skip bit down on the surge of distaste she felt at her reflection. Heron had always been unwaveringly supportive of her, short haircut and odd fashion choices included, and if she just came out and said that she looked stupid, Heron would just deny it and tell her she looked fine. If she wanted to make any progress here, she would have to express herself in far more empowered terms.

"I want to…" She fumbled for a way to explain it. "I want to buy some new clothes. Older clothes." She plucked at the hem of her t-shirt awkwardly.

"What sort of clothes would you like to wear?" Heron asked, looking a little confused.

A thread of fear shivered down her spine. "I don't know. Maybe something more like Dee wears." Of all the women in the Den, Dee was probably the most down to earth in her clothing choices. Raniesha favoured short skirts and blouses at the height of fashion. Caroline had her skin-tight black leather, of course, and Skip couldn't imagine herself ever wearing anything like that. But Dee favoured a casual look, jeans, for the most part, tops that found an easy compromise between comfortable and trendy, or the occasional t-shirt. "And maybe I should grow my hair…"

Heron looked a touch concerned at that. "Why do you want to grow your hair?"

"Because that's what women do? People like long hair, right?"

"There are plenty of women who have short hair," Heron said gently. "Look at Caroline. Hers is even shorter than yours. You don't have to have long hair just because you're a woman. And for that matter, men don't have to have short hair, either."

Skip looked back into the mirror again, and sighed.

Heron took her hands gently and led her to the bed, sitting down on the edge of it and beckoning Skip to do the same. "Sweetie... what's this about?"

Skip sighed, knowing she wasn't hiding anything from Heron. The woman was just too observant, and knew Skip far too well to have the wool pulled over her eyes. "I dress like a child," Skip explained morosely. "I'm twenty-four. It's time I started dressing like an adult."

"There is nothing wrong with the way you dress," Heron said, the predicted denial, and Skip bit back her irritated reply. Why couldn't people accept what she wanted to do and help her with it, rather than telling her it was all fine and she didn't need to do it?

"Yeah, so one day I'm going to be seventy years old, and still wandering around in bright pink t-shirts with unicorns on the front? That's stupid. I'm not saying I want to turn into Paris Hilton overnight. I'm just saying I want to... start dressing more like an adult." She could see the denial gathering in Heron's eyes, so she pressed her point home again. "I'm not stupid. When I came here, I was a mess, and I'd never really had a childhood, and you and Caroline and everyone here let me have one – a bit late, compared to most people, but even so, I got to be a child for a good couple of years. And I needed that, and I'm more grateful to you all than I can ever express. But... I can't keep hiding from myself forever. So I need some help to figure out how to change, in a good way, in the right direction." She looked imploringly up at Heron. "Can you help me with that?"

Heron was silent for a long moment. "I can. But on condition that you assure me that you're doing this for yourself, not because you think anyone else expects you to."

Skip sighed. "That's not practical," she said, her inherent realism showing up again. "Everyone does things because other people expect them to. The way we dress, the things we eat, the jobs we do. People expect me to train in self defence every week. They expect Baron to solve all the problems that no one else wants to solve. They expect John to learn to control his temper. And some of the things they expect of me are actually quite fun, like learning new computer programs, and some things are just necessary for everyone to live together, like John's moods, but we all have to make adjustments for other people. So yes, it's for myself, because no one's bullying me into it, or telling me I'm dressing the wrong way, but it's also for other people, because sometimes, we just need to blend in a bit. Wolves and humans are both very social creatures. Why is it such a bad thing for me to want to be a bit more like other people?"

Heron sighed, then smiled at her, a pensive expression as she gently stroked a hand over Skip's hair. "You are a remarkably insightful young woman," she said, pride strong in her voice. "And while I don't think there's any *need* for you to change the way you dress, if it's really what you want, then I'm happy to help."

Skip smiled back, glad she'd made her point, but apprehensive about what the result might be. Miller had been a perfect gentleman over the past few weeks, warm and friendly, but making no attempt to take their relationship any further, and Skip was feeling a growing frustration at the knowledge that her fumbling attempts to get his attention were failing. In all honesty, she had no idea what he really thought of her, or what he would find attractive in a woman, but it was a fairly good guess that sparkly unicorns and pink flowers wasn't it. So if she was ever going to pique his interest, she was going to have to go out on a limb, and try a daring new approach to the way she saw herself.

CHAPTER THIRTY-TWO

Three days after Skip's successful fight against Cohen, Miller walked into the dining room, feeling frustrated and annoyed. He'd challenged George again that afternoon, the fourth time the pair of them had fought for status, and he could tell that George was as tired of the battles as Miller was. The older man had chosen to remain at the bottom of the ranking ladder quite deliberately, in order to avoid the need for regular fights. Most people only ever fought him once, a token battle which George politely lost, and then the newcomer went on climbing the ranks, leaving George to get on with his duties in peace.

But each time Miller had bested him, he'd been swiftly kicked back to the curb by a vocal protest from the rest of the Den, and after weeks of living on the estate, learning their rules and customs and doing his best to fit in and convince everyone that he was well and truly on their side, he was reaching the end of his patience.

This evening, as he looked over the seating arrangement, he saw that George was once again back in his old seat. He glanced up at Miller with a dismayed, apologetic look, but since he was of such low rank and had little social influence in the Den, there was little he could do about the decree from the more senior wolves that Miller not be allowed to climb the ranks.

But Miller was done with rolling over and playing the proverbial doormat. The room was only half full, but there were a couple of people here who he was fairly sure would support him, so he deliberately went to stand behind George's seat. "I won the status fight today," he announced, just loud enough to get the attention of the rest of the room. "You're in my seat." Up until now, he'd gone out of his way to be polite and respectful to everyone, regardless of rank, but he was slowly learning that that was not the way of it with wolves. Their society was not built like that of humans, and the wild predators were quick to challenge anyone seen to be taking liberties that they were not entitled to.

"Sit down, you mangy pup," Silas snarled from the far end of the room.

"No," Miller replied firmly. "I earned my status. For the fourth time, I might add. I want my seat."

"I say let him claim his rank," Kwan spoke up from further up the table.

"He hasn't earned his rank yet," Raniesha argued. "Sit at the bottom of the table."

"You're being petty," Mark joined in. "It's stupid to go on holding a grudge forever." While those on Miller's side were by no means winning the argument, it was heartening to hear people speaking up in his favour, and Miller felt a faint hope that things might end differently today.

"I don't want to hear a fucking word out of you," Silas snarled at Mark, getting to his feet. "You shouldn't even be sitting at this table, so you certainly don't have the right to speak at it." Miller's heart sank. Mark had been firmly supporting him, but given his own low rank, and the grudges several people held against him, Miller wasn't actually sure whether Mark was doing more harm than good by taking his side.

More people were filing into the room now. Alistair and Simon merely glanced at the standoff and found their own seats, ignoring the ongoing tension, but Heron paused when she saw that the regular argument about Miller had started up again.

"This is doing the Den no good," she declared firmly. "Miller is a strong fighter, and this pointless bullying is just creating tension for everyone. Let him climb a place or two, and then everyone can settle down a bit."

"If you want Miller to stop causing arguments, we could just shoot him," John offered, slouching into the room. He'd been in a strange mood ever since moving out of Baron's room, as if he was proud of himself for taking a stand, but also depressed about the inevitable result of it, and Miller found himself wondering about the boy once again. His understanding of it was that his relationship with Baron had been going on for about five years, and that was long enough that a breakup would be causing them both significant upheaval. And he couldn't help but wonder what John had been through that made Miller's presence a more important factor in his life than his long-term boyfriend. The Noturatii's reach was long and insidious, but Miller himself had had nothing to do with whatever had been done to John…

"You're not helping," Heron admonished John sternly, a statement that, coming from anyone else, would have resulted in a swift yelling match, or even a fist fight. But with Heron, John merely snarled, a sullen show of teeth before slinking off to his seat.

Tank was the next to arrive, and he sighed as he saw Miller standing there, Silas on his feet, everyone's attention focused on them. "Fuck, not again," he swore, sounding tired. "Just sit the fuck down and shut up," he snarled at Miller.

"I would like my seat," Miller repeated, speaking to George, and the meek man started to get up.

Silas was down the end of the table like a shot, a firm hand on George's shoulder. "You stay where you are," he ordered.

"Get out of my way," Miller said, drawing himself up to his full height. He was bigger than Silas, both in height and weight, and though he knew the man was a seasoned fighter, holding his place at the high end of the pecking order, he was fairly certain he could take him in a fight.

"Make me," Silas replied, eyes never leaving Miller's.

Miller raised his hands to push Silas back – in general, fist fights were not allowed in the Den, but Miller was done with playing nice, since it was clearly never going to get him anywhere, and he was prepared to push the rules a little to see where it got him.

But he'd barely touched the man when Silas shoved him back forcefully, far stronger than his wiry frame suggested he would be, and Miller stumbled, catching his leg on the chair and crashing into the wall.

He picked himself up and faced off against Silas again. Raised his fists, ready for a fight, and threw out the first punch towards Silas's face-

In a split second, Silas was gone, ducking out of the way of his fist, spinning around behind him and twisting his arm up behind his back in a move so quick, Miller couldn't quite figure out how he'd done it. His face was mashed into the engraved wooden panelling of the wall, his shoulder protesting as Silas kept his arm pinned firmly. And once again, Miller realised, he'd badly underestimated one of these wolves.

Silas sighed into his ear. "Listen, sweetheart," he said, sounding resigned, and almost bored. "I'm one of the people in this Den that you really don't want to start a fight with. John and Andre would be the other two, just for future reference. So how about you stop flouncing about, sit down, and shut up."

Silas released him, stepping back quickly in case Miller decided to try something else. But Miller had had enough. Not just of the stupid battles for rank, but of the entire Den, the constant bullying, the incomprehensible rules, the feeling that he was always taking one step forward and two steps back. He looked around the room, seeing the solemn faces staring back at him, no one of rank willing to stand up for him in any significant way... and then he turned and marched out the door.

Or that was the intention, at least. But Baron was coming in, just as Miller tried to leave, and the huge alpha pulled up short. "Where do you think you're going?" he asked, his voice a low rumble that rolled menacingly across the room.

"I'm not hungry," Miller said flatly.

"That's not what I asked," Baron said. "You know the rules about dinnertimes."

Miller sighed. Yet more pointless orders that he was supposed to follow. The rules were simple – whether they wanted to eat or not, everyone was required to show up for dinner, listen to the day's news and recite the prayer to Sirius. And after that, he would be free to leave, but even that small concession required him to sit in that damned seat and accept having his rank stripped from him again, something Miller was in no mood to do.

"Sit the fuck down," Baron growled, likely far more interested in the fact that one of his wolves was trying to leave, than because of any concern about which particular seat Miller sat in.

But Miller wasn't ready to simply roll over yet, regardless of the fact that it was the alpha of the Den telling him what to do. He met Baron's glare with one just as fierce. "I won that fight. I earned my rank. And I've no interest in playing your games when you keep changing the rules."

Baron laughed, a cold, cruel sound. "You feel hard done by, do you?"

"I feel like you asked me to join your pack, only to turn around and stab me in the back at every opportunity. This is it, is it? Sit down, shut up and let myself get trodden on like a doormat for the rest of my life? I never chose to become a shape shifter, and given the rampant narcissism going on around here, I'm rather beginning to regret that I did. Just because we're part wolf doesn't mean we have to behave like fucking animals!"

If he'd thought Baron was angry before, it was nothing compared to the look of cold hatred that settled on his face now. His hand twitched, a long, low growl rising from his throat, and Miller took it as a sign of just how badly he'd pissed the man off that Tank quickly stepped forward, placing a restraining hand on Baron's shoulder. Miller felt a trickle of fear as he got the impression that Baron was working hard to hold himself back, struggling not to just grab Miller and slam his head into the wall.

"You don't seem to realise how great a mercy it was that we allowed you to stay," Baron said, his voice a low growl that Miller could feel almost to his bones. "But if you're so unhappy with the arrangement, you have a couple of choices. You can appeal to the Council for a transfer. At which point you would have to find another Den who would accept you. Do you really think anyone else is going to take in a murderer who's spent years trying to exterminate us? Do you think they're going to welcome you with open arms and hand you life on a silver platter? Do you?" he demanded, when Miller said nothing.

"No," he admitted, not liking the fact that he was backed into a corner, metaphorically, as well as physically.

"Or, if you really dislike our way of doing things so much, the offer to put a bullet in your head still stands." Miller said nothing. "You see that seat?" Baron growled, pointing to the empty one beside Mark. "Nate should be sitting in that seat. Except he's not, because he was shot by one of your *esteemed colleagues*. Or Eric could be sitting there. Or Luke. Or Kendrick. Raven. Marianne. Bohdan. Sabine. Amedea. Do you want me to continue? Because I can recite the names of *dozens* of shifters who have died at the hands of the Noturatii in the past ten years alone. You have no rights here, no grounds for protest, and a hell of a long way to go before you understand that we *are* animals. We are half wolf, and we *proudly* embrace our animal sides, their instincts, their social structures, their innate sense of justice. And you should damn well be grateful for the fact that wolves are far more forgiving than humans, or your corpse would be rotting in a shallow grave in the forest by now. So are you going to sit down and do as you're told, or am I going to remind you just how seriously we view any form of disloyalty?" He pulled aside the edge of his jacket, revealing a handgun sitting snugly in its holster under his left arm.

Miller stared at the gun without speaking. And then he sat down, a cold, heavy weight in his chest. He'd badly misjudged the situation here, the realisation coming far later than it should have done. He'd been so caught up in his own story – an attack of conscience, a bold and brave decision to turn away from the side of evil, a few token efforts to make things right, and he'd felt like he was some kind of hero, worthy of the second chance he had demanded for himself.

But Baron's short lecture had finally hit home, had finally made him really see things from the shifters' perspective. He was the enemy. He would always be the enemy, no matter how long he lived here, no matter how well he fought their war. Because in their eyes, he wasn't Jack Miller, misguided soldier turned accidental wolf. No, to them, he *was* the Noturatii. He was the scientist who ran gruesome experiments on their kin. He was the soldier who shot their comrades in cold blood. He was the police officer who accepted bribes in exchange for looking the other way, and the hacker who searched for records of people who had strangely 'disappeared' and the weapons expert who invented new and better ways of blowing things up.

He was the Noturatii. And it would be a cold day in hell before these people saw him as anything else.

Miller had left the table as soon as the meal began, and Skip ate in silence, not inclined to join in any of the conversations around her. A part of her felt sorry for Miller. His intentions to change seemed genuine, and he was working hard to learn the rules of the Den – a difficult task when most people had two years of training before they were actually converted and had to face the sorts of challenges he was having to deal with.

But at the same time, she could well understand the perspective of the rest of the Den. People had died, often in horrific ways, and such wounds, both old and new, did not heal quickly. She'd said nothing during the standoff between Miller and the other men. It wasn't because she didn't support Miller or want to help him adjust to this life, but rather because she empathised equally strongly with both sides of the argument.

Once dinner was over, Skip slipped away quickly and shifted in the hall, using her sensitive nose to follow Miller's trail up the stairs and into the second floor sitting room. He was standing at the window, staring out across the estate, the room slowly growing dimmer as the evening closed in. Skip shifted, then stepped forward, deliberately letting her feet make some noise, so as not to startle him.

"Hey," she said softly, as he glanced over his shoulder.

"Hey," he replied, sounding as gloomy as she had expected.

An awkward silence followed, and Skip wondered why she'd followed him up here. Notionally, it had been to offer some sort of comfort, but what could she say? Empty platitudes weren't going to make a difference, and nothing more truthful would be of any help. *Sorry everyone hates you, but that's the way it is, so you'd best get used to it.* It was hardly going to make him feel any better.

"I don't belong here," Miller said finally, still staring out the window. "Maybe Baron's right. Maybe I should bow out of this war gracefully, rather than sticking around just to piss everyone off."

The stark announcement was alarming. He was contemplating suicide? After having come so far already? "No one belongs here," she said softly. "Not really. Everyone has something wrong with them. They're too shy, or too extroverted; too violent, or too angry. By all rights, Baron shouldn't even be alpha. That only came about because of a bizarre twist of fate. Caroline, too. No one thought she was really suitable for the role when she took it, but she stuck it out, made it work. But it took a long time. We're the strangest bunch of people you're ever going to meet. But when you're going through hell, the only thing you can really do is keep going." The early years of her life had taught Skip that lesson well enough.

"What's the point?" Miller asked sharply, turning to face her. "People don't want me here. I don't want to sound like I'm whinging about it all the time, but at some point, you have to realise there's no point in flogging a dead horse."

"Would you be surprised if I said that no one really wants John here, either? He causes far too much trouble, and half the Den are scared of him. But on the other hand, he's an excellent tracker, and a brutal fighter, and back in Scotland, when we were attacked by those dogs, he was our first line of defence. People put up with him because he's got enough useful skills that he's worth putting up with. Certain people would say the same about me," she added, with no hint of shame at the admission. "I'm not a strong fighter. I've never killed anyone. I'm terrified by violence. But I can hack almost any database in the world. So people are happy enough for me to live here, but every time we go into battle, they still have to work around the fact that I'm a liability in combat."

Miller sighed. "So what have I got that people are going to want badly enough to put up with me?"

It was a good question, and Skip shrugged helplessly. "I don't know. You're a decent fighter – as a human, at least – but we're not short of those. You need to work out some particular skill you have, some knowledge or talent that sets you apart. And then leverage the hell out of it. But in the meantime," she added, having caught Miller's comment at dinner about them all 'not being animals', "I'd recommend you get one of the books in the library on wolf behaviour, and start doing some serious reading. I don't mean to be rude, but you don't seem to know much about wolf psychology. Denying your animal side is one of the quickest ways to piss people off. And wolves behave nothing like domestic dogs. Their minds work entirely differently, and there are actually very few comparisons that can be made. Socially, our Dens work a lot more like wolf packs than human communes."

Miller gave her a look of chagrin. "Yeah, I'd noticed that people took exception to that part."

Skip's face fell suddenly. "Sorry," she apologised quickly. "I didn't mean to give you a hard time about it. You've really been thrown in the deep end here, being converted before you knew anything about us, and people should be cutting you some slack because of that. And here I am, just telling you that you're doing it wrong all over again."

Miller laughed, surprising her. "At least you're telling me what I can do to fix some of it. That's a huge step up from what most people have been saying to me."

Skip managed a smile, but also felt a wave of disappointment. Over the past few weeks, she'd been trying to get to know Miller better, her curiosity piqued by his inexplicably gentle ways while they'd been in the cave together, and kept inflamed since then by his unique mix of polite forbearance and hard hitting stubbornness. Strangely enough, he reminded her a lot of Andre, the former assassin a consummate gentleman, whilst also being the most lethal warrior on the estate.

But every time she tried to have a friendly chat and probe what was going on beneath the surface, they ended up just talking business, with Skip explaining some rule or custom about the Den, or the conversation turning to some conflict between Il Trosa and the Noturatii. But with the stakes so high, it seemed rather ridiculous to try talking about his favourite radio station or whether he liked winter better than summer. And on the flip side, leaping into a deeper conversation about his history in the military or how he felt about the friends he'd left behind in the Noturatii seemed far too personal and abrupt.

She was hopeless at flirting, Skip acknowledged sadly to herself, and as strange and unsettling as her feelings towards Miller were, she was annoyed at herself for not finding a way to investigate them further.

"You look different," Miller said suddenly, and Skip looked up to see him casting an eye over her clothes. It was true – after their discussion on Skip's fashion preferences, Heron had helped her choose some new things to wear, placing an order online that had arrived just this morning.

The shopping had been nerve wracking and frustrating, not going as far as Skip would have liked with her new experiments in fashion, but at the same time, going far further than she was comfortable with. As it was, her new clothing wasn't all that different from her old style – plenty of pink and yellow, flowers or butterflies decorating each piece. But this time, the clothes had been chosen in a size that actually fit, rather than hanging on her small frame. Nothing was tight, no plunging necklines or singlet tops, no *short* shorts, and the designs retained a faintly childish quality, far from the more elegant womanly styles that Skip had started out looking at, until Heron had gently dissuaded her from making too big a change too quickly.

And now, Skip was grateful for Heron's insight. She wore a pair of jeans that seemed indecently tight, though they were a straight-leg design that allowed some room to move, and a normal, standard t-shirt that somehow made her feel half naked. But she had been determined to wear the new clothes, and for the last half an hour, she'd actually managed to forget how uncomfortable she felt in them. She could feel herself blushing fiercely, grateful that the room was quite dim by now, and struggled to find something to say.

"Do you like it?" The words slipped out before Skip could stop them, her mouth somehow bypassing her brain, and she cursed herself for the absolute lack of subtlety. She may as well have just begged him to tell her he fancied her.

Miller looked baffled for a moment, while Skip tried to act natural. "I think it looks good," he said finally, and Skip dared to glance up at him.

In the fading light, she wasn't quite sure how to read the expression on his face. It was a look that contained a wealth of tenderness, an odd hopefulness, lingering doubts… and yet it was strangely familiar.

And then she felt a wave of surprise when she realised where she'd seen that expression before. Way back when Dee had joined the Den, before she and Mark had got together, she'd caught her looking at Mark with that same expression of hopefulness and doubt… and seen Mark look at her the same way, when he'd thought no one was watching.

The realisation sent a rush of nervousness through her. Miller… liked her? As in, really liked her? Gosh, she sounded like a twelve year old, she admonished herself, even though the running monologue was only within her own mind.

"How old are you?" Miller asked suddenly, and Skip couldn't quite work out why he was suddenly interested in her age.

"Twenty-four," she replied. "Why? How old are you?"

"Thirty-one. I just..." He shook his head. "Never mind." He paused, seeming to choose his next words carefully. "I've been meaning to tell you that I... well, I really appreciate you taking the time to get to know me. And not judging too quickly, based on where I've come from."

Skip looked at him slyly, a wry smile on her face. "You've done enough to prove that you're not a typical Noturatii soldier. I just figured I should give you a chance."

"And now that you've given me a chance? What do you think?"

Skip smiled, unable to help herself, and blushed again. Miller had leaned closer during the conversation, his eyes holding her gaze, his expression shy and hopeful. And it was so different from the way any man had looked at her before that she completely forgot to be afraid of him, of such a large, strong man standing so close to her. She could tell him to back off, she realised with a strange jolt, and he would do so. She was absolutely certain of it. But what if... what if she didn't tell him to back off? What if she leaned a little closer to him?

She felt a light brush of skin against her fingers, and realised that Miller was gently taking her hand. Her fingers twitched in response, the touch so light that it was almost ticklish, and she felt her heart rate speed up a little, at this strange and new and inexplicably exciting moment.

"Would it be okay if I kissed you?" Miller asked, his voice low, a deep rumble that reminded Skip of the sound of thunder in winter.

She nodded, unable to quite find her voice, and waited, not sure if she was supposed to close her eyes, not sure how to kiss him back, suddenly fearful that he would be disappointed by her ineptitude, and yet also suddenly craving the feel of his lips against hers in a way she'd never imagined she would. She'd had dreams about kissing men. Kissing them voluntarily, that was. She had other dreams as well, of course. And she'd occasionally wondered what it would be like kissing Kwan. He was her own age, handsome enough, in an understated sort of way, confident but never imposing...

Oh wow... Miller's lips were soft, firm, the faint scent of wolf emanating from his clothes, his thumb tracing lines across the back of her hand in an almost hypnotic rhythm. Skip tried to stay still, so as not to dissuade him from his task, though she had little idea as to how to return the affection. Then he opened his mouth just a fraction, catching her lower lip between his, moist warmth a surprising sensation against her skin, and she pulled back, feeling rather breathless. But the grin on her face was sign enough that she had liked the kiss, should Miller have any doubts about it, and the grin widened when she saw him smile in return.

He didn't speak, but lifted a hand to stroke the back of his fingers gently down her cheek, and Skip felt an unwelcome shiver of fear at the gesture. "Um… I should go," she excused herself, easing around him, fighting to keep the smile on her face. "I have to check the computers before I go to bed. But… this was nice," she added, meaning it, her wayward emotions aside. Way back when she'd been having therapy with Nia, they'd discussed the possibility of Skip having a romantic relationship in the future, in purely hypothetical terms, and Nia had mentioned that it was likely that Skip would feel very conflicted about it, should she ever venture down that path. She'd given her a few pertinent pieces of advice, and told Skip that she could call, if she ever needed to discuss anything in the future. Skip had dismissed the idea at the time, unable to imagine ever feeling any kind of affection for a man, but she'd taken note of the conversation nonetheless. And while she didn't feel the need to call her old therapist just at the moment, she also remembered that Nia had said she should give herself plenty of time and space to process the situation, should it ever arise.

"Sleep well," Miller murmured, making no move to stop her as she backed away. "I'll see you tomorrow."

Skip waved, a small, timid gesture, and slipped away out the door. Her lips were tingling from the sensation of his own against hers, a feeling that was both tantalisingly pleasant and startlingly unfamiliar… but she was utterly pleased with herself, both for being able to go through with the kiss, and for finding a measure of enjoyment in it. Small steps, she counselled herself, a mantra that Nia had repeated dozens of times in the year they'd spent together. She'd just had her first kiss, successfully flirted with a man for the first time in her life… and she was feeling a heady excitement at all the possibilities that seemed to have suddenly opened up before her.

CHAPTER THIRTY-THREE

Miller watched Skip walk away, feeling pleased and surprised and scared all at the same time. Mark had been right, he acknowledged to himself. One kiss and Skip had turned tail and run like a frightened rabbit. But at the same time, she'd expressed no dislike of the kiss, said nothing to imply that he'd done anything wrong in asking for it. All indications were that she returned his cautious affection, and his regard for her went up another notch. If his guess was correct, and she'd been hurt by a man in the past, then she was bold beyond measure for daring to express her affection for someone such as himself, a man who had kidnapped her, caused her to get shot, and created a rift among the people she called family. Her courage seemed limitless, and his admiration for her was just as strong.

But aside from the warm emotions he was feeling about Skip, he was also rather surprised at himself. Romance had been nowhere on his agenda, his life far too complicated at the moment to be spending time trying to woo an apprehensive young woman. But she had a way of breaking through the barriers he tried to erect around himself, of making him relax in a way that he wasn't entirely sure was wise.

He headed for the door, feeling a little better about his situation, and intending to go to the library to look for the recommended book on wolf behaviour... but before he got halfway across the room, a dark shape stepped out of the shadows, and Miller tensed as he recognised Silas's wiry form.

"What the fuck do you think you're doing?" Silas asked, his voice a menacing growl.

"Not sure what specifically you're referring to," Miller replied. He wasn't intending to antagonise the man, but he'd done rather a lot of things lately that Silas might have taken exception to.

Silas stepped up close to him, Miller not backing up a single inch. "Let me make this perfectly clear. If you want to keep breathing, you will never, ever touch Skip again."

"Well, I think that should be Skip's decision, rather than yours." Fuck, he was getting really tired of this shit. Why couldn't these people have a normal conversation, insult each other a few times, yell a bit, maybe? Why did they have to resort to knives and guns and threats to kill each other on the slightest whim?

"Skip doesn't know what she wants," Silas hissed. "She's naïve and innocent, and probably doesn't even realise the implications of what she was doing. But you most certainly do. So you're going to stay away from her. Understood?"

"Give me one good reason why."

"Because I'm not going to stand by and watch while yet another man takes advantage of her. You might be trying to play the hero for the moment, but we both know what sort of man you really are."

The insult was no surprise. Silas had made it abundantly clear what he thought of Miller, his defection from the Noturatii an irrelevant detail in what Silas considered to be a vile and amoral life.

"I have no intention of hurting her in any way," he told him, not sure if the words would make any difference. Silas didn't seem the most reasonable sort of man, after all. "I'd never do anything she didn't want me to."

But despite his protests, Silas's words were having the desired effect. Miller had been in the military before joining the Noturatii, a lifetime of violence and fighting and war under his belt. He was a soldier, a murderer, even, a long way from the gentlemanly type that Skip deserved, and his own bleak self-assessment made him suddenly doubt his own good intentions.

"Then stay away from her," Silas growled. "Seems the easiest way to make sure you don't hurt her, doesn't it?"

While Miller had little inclination to bow to Silas's aggressive demands, he had no desire to cause Skip any more harm. And Silas's fleeting admission that another man had already taken advantage of her did nothing to reassure him of his own ability to see to her happiness and wellbeing. Old wounds didn't always heal well, and if he inadvertently did something to reopen them, he'd never forgive himself.

"Understood," he agreed finally, looking Silas in the eye. "I didn't mean any harm, and if I was out of line, then I apologise. It won't happen again."

"You see that it doesn't," Silas said coldly, and then he was gone, ghosting out the door as silently as he'd arrived.

It was quiet in the Noturatii's science lab, the building empty but for a few security staff rostered on for the night shift, and Melissa fought back a yawn as she helped Professor Banks set up the next phase of their experiment. They'd finally finished analysing the data they'd collected from all the shifts, and were now just finishing up with configuring the equipment for the second stage – forcing the shifter to change forms.

By all rights, they could have called it a day several hours ago and carried on in the morning, but now that they were so close to a result, neither of them had wanted to quit without at least running a preliminary test. If they knew they could force the shift, then the analysis and fine tuning could wait until tomorrow, but Melissa knew she would never be able to sleep if she left now, with so many questions still unanswered, when victory was so close at hand.

All indications so far were that her theories on shifter physiology had been correct; the shift consisted of four distinct voltages, each lasting a fraction of a second, and flowing over the shifter's body in a coordinated wave that began at his head and spread down his body like water flowing down a hill.

They'd made further adjustments to the equipment, setting the table up so that rather than recording the voltages, it would deliver them to the shifter's body, a tightly controlled wave of electricity that should, all going according to plan, force the shifter to change forms.

Heading back to the computer, Melissa glanced up at the Professor, and saw a look of gleeful expectation on his face that matched her own. "Ready?" he asked, making a few last minute adjustments to the controls, and Melissa nodded.

"Ready and waiting."

"All right," the Professor said, fingers poised over the keys. "Let's make some history. In three... two... one." He hit the controls, initiating the wave of electricity. They watched as the shifter twitched, the electrodes shocking him a hundred times in rapid succession, and they waited for the moment when he would change forms...

Nothing happened.

"What the hell?" Melissa demanded, going immediately to the computer to check the readings. According to the screen, it had worked perfectly, every voltage discharged on time, every shock carrying the exact amount of current their experiments had recorded.

"Try it again," Banks instructed her, a frown appearing on his face, making his wrinkles look deeper than usual. Melissa did, activating the controls, watching as the computer spat out a flurry of information... and once again, absolutely nothing happened.

"Perhaps he's resisting," Evans suggested, watching meekly from the side of the room. She hadn't wanted to do this tonight, stating that they would do better to try it in the morning when they were all fresh and wouldn't make mistakes, but when Melissa and Banks had out-voted her, she'd insisted on staying to see their results. In response to her suggestion now, Banks went immediately to one of the guards waiting at the side of the room and snatched the Taser out of his hand.

"You mess with us again, and I'll Taser you," he told the shifter sharply. The man's eyes opened wide in fear, but he shook his head.

"I'm not doing anything," he said, his voice rough and husky. "You said to just lie here, and I am. I swear."

"One more time," Banks insisted, and Melissa hit the controls again. The same wave of electric shocks once more flowed down the table, with the same result: absolutely nothing.

Melissa sank into a chair, feeling almost dizzy at the wave of disappointment she felt at the failure. "What did we do wrong?"

Banks looked as lost as she was. "I have no idea..."

Miller saw Skip the next morning in the kitchen at breakfast. By the time she arrived, Miller was already sitting at the table, toast and coffee in front of him, and she waved happily, before weaving around the other people in the kitchen to fetch herself some food.

As he watched her, Miller was feeling every bit as awkward as he'd expected to. This morning would have been uncomfortable even under the best of circumstances, as he didn't know whether Skip would want the rest of the Den to know they'd kissed, and while in public, he didn't know how to walk the line between affectionate love-interest and platonic friend.

But after what Silas had said last night, he was even more conflicted. What was he supposed to do now? Should he just end the budding relationship? With no explanation, that would come across as rather heartless. Should he ask Skip for more details on her past? If he knew in what way she'd been hurt or betrayed, he might be able to form a more realistic assessment of his own ability to be a decent boyfriend for her. Except that that option sounded like an imposingly personal question, and he wasn't sure it was his place to ask.

Or should he tell Skip what had gone down after she'd left the sitting room yesterday? The latter seemed the most logical way forward, the least likely to inadvertently offend her by blowing hot and cold without any apparent reason.

But Skip was a strong woman in her own right, he acknowledged to himself, as she took a seat next to him with a bowl piled high with cornflakes, a mischievous grin on her face, and he couldn't help but smile back, muttering a greeting through a mouthful of toast. For all that Silas said she was naïve, he didn't think it fair to simply dismiss her opinions without at least discussing them with her.

But then again, it was early days between them yet. One kiss didn't imply any kind of long term commitment, and if he'd been out in the real world, meeting a normal woman who'd sparked his interest, he would hardly think it appropriate to start having conversations about the long term implications of their relationship after only one date.

But in all his internal musings, he had failed to take into account how perceptive shifters were, and he was finishing his coffee, having exchanged a few mild remarks on the weather when Skip turned to him with a quizzical look.

"Is something wrong?" she asked bluntly, and Miller was surprised enough that he fumbled for a reply, rather than delivering the quick denial that might have been less awkward.

"It's complicated," he hedged, not wanting to open that sort of discussion right in front of the other people in the kitchen.

Skip sighed. "Who was it, and what did they do?"

Miller glanced around the kitchen. Silas was nowhere to be seen at the moment. "Maybe we should talk outside," he suggested, the decision largely made for him that he was going to have to explain to Skip what Silas had said last night.

He led the way out the back door, Skip at his heels. "Silas saw us kissing last night," he said bluntly. "And he was fairly upset about it. He warned me to stay away from you-"

"He what?" Skip shrieked, startling Miller. "What did he say?" she demanded angrily. "Word for word, what did he say?"

"I really don't think hearing it is going to help," Miller said hesitantly.

"What did he say?" Skip demanded once again.

Miller sighed, unable to see another way out without sounding rude. "He said that you'd had some difficult times in your past – he didn't go into any details – and he didn't think starting a relationship with me right now would be appropriate."

Skip's jaw dropped... and then her astonishment turned swiftly to anger. She marched over to the kitchen door, yanked it open, and glanced around, then yelled, "Silas! Get out here!"

Miller was taken aback. Silas would certainly not respond well to being given orders by this slip of a girl, and Miller didn't know whether to be shocked that Skip would dare to speak to him that way, or fearful of what he was going to do in response.

But to his surprise, Silas obediently came striding out of the back door, coffee cup in hand and a scowl fixed to his face – evidence of his displeasure, though any more overt protest was markedly absent. But when he saw Miller standing there, the scowl deepened. "What's he done now?" he asked impatiently.

But Skip was having none of it. "What the hell did you say to Jack yesterday?"

Miller was a little surprised to hear her call him by his first name. He'd been called 'Miller' for so long that 'Jack' just seemed out of place. But if Skip had taken the kiss at face value and assumed it meant a deepening of their relationship, then she'd clearly decided that they were now on a first name basis.

Silas raised a sardonic eyebrow at Miller. "Aww, the big, tough Noturatii can't take the heat? So you run off to hide behind your little woman?"

Skip's eyes opened wide. She turned to Silas, mouth hanging open in outrage, and swiftly punched him in the balls. "You use 'woman' as an insult again, and you'll find out exactly why 'hell hath no fury like that of a *woman* scorned'."

"My mistake," Silas groaned, bent over in pain. "Fuck, you know how to throw a decent punch, I'll give you that."

"And don't you forget it," Skip said, standing up tall and proud. "You have no right to be discussing me behind my back. So what did you say to Jack?"

Silas took a moment to catch his breath, struggling to stand up straight. He looked at Skip, an odd expression of tenderness on his face. "You've got no business getting involved with the likes of him," he said softly. "I was watching out for your best interests."

"Why do I have no business with it? Because he was with the Noturatii, or because he's a man?"

"Either," Silas said firmly. "You shouldn't have been kissing him, and I won't have him pawing at you. He needs to learn to stay away from you."

"Even when I told him it was perfectly okay for him to kiss me?"

"Even then."

"Fuck you!" Skip snarled at him. "You have no right to tell him what he can or can't do, because it's *my choice*!"

"Exactly!" Silas hissed back. "I'm trying to make sure you have a fucking choice, not just get dragged into something against your will."

But Skip shook her head, her anger not appeased in the slightest. "Before I came here, I didn't have a choice. And finally being able to say no was the most outstandingly awesome thing in the whole world, but if I don't have the freedom to say yes, then saying no doesn't mean anything. It's not my choice, it's just another set of rules and restrictions imposed upon me by someone else who wants to control me. And I've been through enough bullshit that no one is going to do that to me again! So if I want to spend time with Jack, or kiss him, or do anything else with him, then it's not your decision, and it's none of your damn business!"

With that, she swung around and grabbed Miller, pulling his head down and planting a firm kiss right on his lips. Then she shot a final glare Silas's way and stalked off, back into the kitchen, anger radiating from every inch of her.

Miller simply stood there, frozen in shock. He'd known Skip had a backbone of steel, but to see her stand up to Silas like that, a man who had regularly threatened to gut him or slit his throat, was shocking.

And even more shocking was Silas's reaction. As he watched Skip walk away, there was no hint of anger or violence in him at all – rather, his face held all the guilt of a man who'd just accidently kicked a puppy.

"She's quite the little firecracker, isn't she?" Miller observed drily.

Silas turned to him with a look of disbelief. "Uh… I seem to have overstepped my bounds," he said finally.

But that was only a part of the conversation they'd just had. Skip's words replayed in his mind, and Miller felt a wave of nausea at the implications of what she'd said. "What did she mean about not having the choice to say no?"

Silas growled, though Miller got the impression his anger wasn't directed at him for once. "You know well enough what it's called when a woman says no and a man doesn't listen," he replied, and Miller gritted his teeth at the cold confirmation of the situation.

"But she was right," Silas admitted, looking unhappy about it. "It should be her choice. If she wants a relationship with you, I won't stand in her way."

"But let me guess," Miller said. "If I hurt her in any way, I'll be hearing about it from you?"

"Right," Silas confirmed, a gleeful look of malice back on his face.

Miller nodded, and Silas walked away, disappearing back inside the manor, leaving him with the odd thought that he was finally starting to get the hang of this place.

CHAPTER THIRTY-FOUR

Several days later, Miller was feeling rather nervous as he stepped into the library. Baron and Caroline were already seated at the table, Tank and Silas following him through the door, and he took a seat, hoping he hadn't sorely misjudged these people's perspectives.

Since his conversation with Skip about providing something useful for the Den, he'd been wracking his brain for anything he could do that would hold meaning for them. He'd already told Baron everything useful he could about the Noturatii, and been told in reply that the information had been sent to headquarters for further analysis. Given that he was still under firm restrictions about his activities around the estate and the depth of knowledge that he was privy to, it had been hard to come up with anything that wouldn't breach one or more of the rules imposed upon him.

But then, in the cold dark of 3am when he'd been lying awake, contemplating his new life, the answer had suddenly come to him. He'd taken another two days to think the whole thing through, not wanting to make any hasty decisions that he would regret later, and also wanting to make a real contribution to the Den, rather than just flail around trying to bolster his own pride.

Skip had been an incredible help, providing a map of east London for him and printing off a few pertinent details from the Noturatii database she'd hacked earlier in the year. She'd also taken every opportunity to flirt with him, patting his shoulder, sitting closer than was strictly necessary, and she'd managed to manufacture at least one opportunity to kiss him again each day. Given what Miller now knew about her past, he was prepared to take things slowly, but Skip seemed quite determined to give their budding relationship frequent nudges in the right direction. They'd gone for a walk in the gardens one evening, and Miller had dared to take her hand, receiving shy glances and bashful smiles as a reward. And then the routine nightly kiss had turned into something more, small fingers wandering down to brush against his buttocks, eager hands tugging his body against hers. Miller had felt like he was fifteen again, making out with his girlfriend in the bushes beside his parents' porch, eager to go further, and yet always holding back, not wanting to push too hard.

But their frequent private interludes had not gone unnoticed. The following morning, Heron had pulled him aside, after glancing furtively around to check that Skip wasn't about, and had told him that if he valued his relationship with Skip, he was never, *ever* to tell her she was pretty. He'd been taken aback by the odd warning, but had thought better of asking for details as to why. Heron no doubt adhered to the shifters' honour code that said other people's stories weren't open for discussion, and he was only likely to offend yet another tentative ally by pushing for too much information.

"You said you wanted to see us?" Baron said, once everyone was seated around the long table in the library. "So what's the problem?"

Miller didn't waste any time in getting started. "There have been lingering doubts around the Den about how genuine I've been about leaving the Noturatii," he said bluntly. "And while I've explained that attacking one of their British bases would be a bad idea, it's now occurred to me that there is something else I can offer you, that would make a huge dent in the Noturatii's operations in this country, but without impinging on anyone's moral sensibilities." He pulled a couple of rumpled sheets of paper out of his pocket, and spread them out on the table. "This is a profile of Jacob Green. He's the British Chief of Operations, the most high ranking member of staff in the entire country. He was my direct supervisor, when I was working for them." He turned to the map next, a small area of a couple of blocks highlighted in yellow, with several pertinent landmarks outlined in red. "A lot of the Noturatii's staff live in their own houses or apartments. But there are also a number of small compounds, gated communities, where some of the more senior staff live. Each complex has several apartment blocks, a few small offices, security buildings and guards posted at every entrance. No one gets in or out without the right security clearance, and everyone living or working there is employed by the Noturatii. No civilians, no low level employees who are just going through the motions in what they believe is a legitimate job. Everyone in these complexes is aware of what the shifters are, and the true nature of the Noturatii's operations." He paused a moment to let the news sink in.

"Jacob Green," he went on, when he was sure he had everyone's attention, "lives in this complex." He pointed to the area he'd highlighted on the map. "His apartment is on the third floor, on the east side. Security is tight, but I know the system well enough to work around it. And if you've got a small team capable of carrying out a discreet assassination, then I can get you in, point out Jacob, and you can take him out. And throw the entire British division of the Noturatii into chaos in the process."

Silas snorted. "Okay, does anyone else see the word 'trap' written all over this?"

"It's waving a few red flags for me," Tank said drily.

But Baron was silent. He stared at the map, then glanced at Caroline, and an unspoken communication seemed to pass between them. He turned back to the map, regarding it silently for a long moment.

"Why would you want to do this?" he asked Miller finally. "The guy was your boss. You must have worked with him on a daily basis. Got to know him. You've already said you don't want to hand over the people you were friends with. Or did he do something in particular to piss you off?"

"Nothing in particular, no," Miller replied, not at all offended by the pointed question. "And I wouldn't say I was ever friends with him. Jacob is brilliant. Organised. Arrogant, and yet strategic. And absolutely ruthless. There is nothing he wouldn't do in order to destroy the shifters. He takes risks, but they're calculated risks, with the highest possible payout, which makes him not just intelligent, but dangerous. He became Chief of Operations ten years ago, and he's grown the Noturatii's operations in England significantly since then. He was promoted after the last man in that position was killed."

"Really?" Baron seemed unusually intrigued by that.

"What of it?"

"Based on that information, then I daresay I'm the man who killed his predecessor," Baron said, a hint of satisfaction in his voice.

"How do you know that?" Miller asked. "That was a long time ago. There were a series of raids, back about ten years ago-"

"Five raids, carried out over a period of eight weeks," Baron interrupted. "June through to August. The hits were purposely coordinated to take out some of your highest ranking officers, and instigated by a highly successful attack against us. It was originally believed that you had wiped out the entire shifter pack in England. Until we started showing up in unexpected places and blowing up your men."

Miller rubbed his face, amazed at how the pieces of history fit together in such unexpected ways. "*You* did that?"

"I did that," Baron confirmed smugly. "And while I can hardly claim it was a solo effort, I'm also sure – with no misplaced pride – that without my organisational skills, the attacks would never have been successful. Now, what were you saying about Jacob?"

"Uh... I was saying I'm offering him to you because Jacob is the most significant strategic target I can give you, without risking all your lives in the process. It should be possible to get to him with a small team, two, maybe three people, a minimal risk while doing maximum damage."

"An interesting idea," Baron mused. "Why can't you just show us a picture of him, and we do the rest?"

"There are no pictures of him," Miller stated flatly. "Skip went through all the information she got off the Noturatii's database at the start of the year, and there's not one single photo of him. And I'm damn sure you won't find anything in any public files. At an official level, the man doesn't exist."

"Well, that's all very interesting," Baron said drily. "But that happy little coincidence means that this operation would be neatly placing you squarely back on Noturatii turf. A little convenient for you, don't you think?"

Miller had anticipated this objection to the plan. He was learning how Baron thought, picking up on his priorities and concerns about safety... and being wholly impressed along the way. "It does," he admitted easily. "And I realise you still have your doubts about my intentions. But one way or the other, you're eventually going to have to decide to either trust me... or put me out of my misery. So we can keep skirting around the issue for the next month, or year, or ten years, but sooner or later, some situation is going to come up where I have the opportunity to betray you and you're going to find out which side of the fence I'm really on. This plan weighs the risks in your favour more than most would. You'd only be risking one or two of your team, you'd be fully prepared for me to do something stupid, and if it all goes south, then at least I'm out of your way before I learn anything about Il Trosa that could really make the shit hit the fan."

"You know the location of our Den," Baron pointed out darkly.

"And given the skills and discipline of your team, you could have the entire place locked down and prepared to evacuate in less than half an hour. Losing this estate would be bad. But if I understand the structure of Il Trosa correctly, then there are dozens, maybe hundreds of other Dens across Europe who would happily take you in. I'm not saying the plan is without risk. I'm just saying that at this point in time, those risks are quantifiable and controllable."

"Miller has a point," Caroline spoke up finally, not having yet said anything throughout the meeting. "We accepted him into this Den on the basic assumption that he had turned his back on the Noturatii. And if we don't really believe that, we've got no business keeping him here."

Baron's mouth twisted into a hard line... but then he nodded. "Fair point. Go on."

"This assassination would need some careful planning," Caroline continued, "and I'd certainly not want to go ahead with it without assessing all the risks and creating a few contingency plans. But if we can take out the leader of the British arm, we'd be buying ourselves significant time to implement other strategies in the plan to end this war. So call me crazy... but I think it's worth a shot."

Genna stood in the tent in the Grey Watch camp, concentrating on the metal bucket in front of her. It was bigger than anything she had successfully made disappear before, well beyond the limit of her powers, but Sempre refused to take no for an answer. And so Genna had been standing here for well over an hour, her muscles cramping with every new effort, her head aching, her skin tingling as her body protested the overuse of magic.

It had been like this every day since Sempre had discovered her abilities, test after test to probe the limits of her powers. At first, Genna had deliberately fumbled the experiments, returning the objects earlier than Sempre had wanted, protesting that certain items were too large or too far away, and the ruse had worked to a certain extent. She'd rationed her successes, making Sempre wait a few days for each new improvement in her abilities, becoming devious as she spent the time honing her skills in private, while feigning ineptitude in public. But in reality, she knew that all she was doing was buying time. Sooner or later, Sempre would tire of her claims that she had reached the limits of her powers, and start delving into darker methods to enhance the magic.

Pleading exhaustion had also become one of her staple forms of self-preservation, but now the exhaustion was no longer a ruse. Lita had joined Sempre in the sessions, creating more and more challenging tests. Could she target an object that was hidden from view? Could she perform the feats in wolf form as well as human form? Did it matter what the object was made of; wood, versus stone, versus metal? The tests had been endless, each question answered creating a wave of new ones.

Fed up with the ongoing bullying and torment, Genna resolved to end the session, for all that it would annoy Sempre and lead to a vigorous scolding. Reaching out with the magic, she focused on the edge of the bucket and sent out a wave of static. A chunk of the bucket vanished, a section perhaps six inches wide, leaving a gaping hole in the metal and rendering the bucket useless.

"I'm sorry," she gasped out, swiftly returning the chunk of metal to the table, her hands cramping up again as the magic took its toll. "I can't do it. It's just too big." She was swaying on her feet, desperate for a break, and for once, her protest was genuine. The bucket was simply too large for her to grasp it with the magic.

Sempre looked outraged at her failure. She picked up the bucket, examined the hole, then tossed it to the ground. "Foolish girl," she snapped, then slapped Genna hard across the face. "You think we have enough resources lying around that you can just go around breaking things? I've done everything I can to help you learn to control this gift, and you throw it back in my face like this? Get out!"

Genna didn't waste any time, just darted out of the tent and away across the clearing. She was desperately hungry, but too tired to hunt or fight for a coveted piece of bread, so she simply shifted, then stopped to take a drink out of the water bucket before collapsing in a sheltered spot at the edge of the camp.

After about fifteen minutes, she heard footsteps approaching, and opened her eyes. Luna was standing beside her, and the woman lowered herself to the ground, running a gentle hand through Genna's fur.

"Here," she said, reaching into her cloak and pulling out a fist-sized hunk of meat. "It's the end of last night's roast. I know you haven't eaten all day."

Genna sat up and took the meat, licking Luna's hand by way of a thank you, before swiftly devouring the meal.

Luna was an unusual one, and Genna wasn't quite sure what to make of her. She was kind and generous in private, offering words of encouragement to the lower ranking wolves and handing out favours like the piece of meat with no thought of getting anything in return. She was strong, confident, and had risen three or four places in the pecking order in the last few months. But she was also cunning, agreeing with Sempre and the senior wolves when it suited her, criticising the younger wolves when it would earn her favour in the ranks, and keeping her acts of charity strictly under the radar. Genna could never quite decide which side of her personality was the real one; the side that cared for those more vulnerable than herself, or the side that was slowly manipulating her way up the ranks.

Several days later, the library was once again buzzing with activity. All of the Den's best fighters were seated around the long table, notebooks, laptops and maps spread about, grim faces all around. Miller was also there, a key component in the developing plans to assassinate Jacob Green, along with Skip, who was providing advice on the technological aspects of the plan.

"So my first question," Andre was saying, "is do you want this to be a clean hit, or a messy one?" Having worked as a professional assassin for years, his input would be invaluable. "For example, if you have a politician who wants to make a journalist disappear, that's a clean hit. No witnesses, no links to the guy who ordered the kill, no collateral damage. On the other hand, if you have a crime lord taking out a rival drug dealer, that's a messy hit. Audible gun fire, bystanders caught in the crossfire and bodies showing up five miles down the river in two weeks time. Everyone knows that the guy was taken out by a rival criminal, but at the end of the day, no one really cares, so they don't bother covering their tracks any further than is necessary to keep them out of jail."

"Messy," Caroline spoke up immediately. "Given who Jacob is, the Noturatii are going to assume we were responsible, no matter how well we cover it up. And we already know they're not going to get the police involved. And given that Miller said everyone else on the property is fully in the know about what the Noturatii is doing, I don't have any particular reservations about taking out a few extra security guards along the way."

Andre smirked. "Messy it is. Should be an interesting change of pace from what I'm used to. Okay, Miller. What have you got in mind?"

"The nuts and bolts of it is simple," Miller began. "Jacob's apartment building is on the east side of the complex. There's an underground parking lot beneath his building where he parks his car at night. Security on the premises is concentrated at the entrance gates and the perimeter fence, so there should be minimal interference inside the building. So we need to get a small team into the carpark late one afternoon, lie low while we wait for Jacob to arrive, shoot him, then get the hell out of there."

"Simple enough," Baron conceded. "But what about this security force? How are we going to get inside without getting noticed?"

"The main entrance to the complex is a boom gate with security guards," Miller explained. "Getting in will be the hardest part. I'm hoping that Skip can create a fake work order for some sort of maintenance work – an electrical fault, maybe – and we can pretend to be tradespeople."

"That means the driver will have to be someone the Noturatii won't recognise," Caroline pointed out. "They know some of our faces."

"Simon could do it," Skip suggested. "He's not on the database. He's got decent driving skills, and can join in a fire fight if anything goes wrong. Assuming he's okay with it," she added. "I'm guessing this is going to be a volunteers-only sort of mission?"

"Right," Baron confirmed. "I'm not dragging anyone into this one without their agreement."

"Getting out of that gate will be messier, but easier," Miller went on. "If everything goes flawlessly, we might be able to just show our security passes to the guards and they let us go. But if anyone sounds the alarm or they hear gunfire nearby, then the plan is basically to ram the boom gate, mow down anyone who gets in the way and hightail it out of there."

Andre laughed at that one. "Well, we did say it was going to be a messy hit," he pointed out, at Baron's pained look.

"But one serious downside to that part of the plan is that it would trash your van," Miller pointed out.

"Don't worry about the van," Baron said. "We go through at least one of those each year, so buying a new one is no drama."

"Okay. So after we get in, we head down into the underground car park. There's an electronic gate that needs an access code to open it, but if we get the appropriate security clearance from the main gate, they should give us a code. After that, we just hang out in a quiet spot for a while. There are security cameras down there, so Skip would need to hack them and feed a false loop through. Then we wait for Jacob. He always travels between home and the office with a security detail tailing him, but once he's inside the complex, they should head off, so if we're lucky, it'll just be him. If not, we might have a small fight on our hands."

"Body armour," Andre said to Tank, who was taking notes about the whole plan. He nodded, and jotted down the detail.

"And then, after Jacob's dead, we get the hell out of there as quickly as possible," Miller concluded. "Simple, quick, effective."

"So who goes in?" Silas asked next.

"Me," Baron replied. "And Miller, because I need him to point out Jacob. And a driver. That's it."

"This is an extremely high risk operation," Tank pointed out. "Strategically, putting the alpha of this Den at risk is a bad call."

Baron shook his head. "That's not up for debate. I chose to let Miller stay, and if the shit hits the fan, first of all I need to be onsite to make sure he's dead." He levelled a cold glare Miller's way. "But secondly, I can't in good conscience risk someone else's life for my mistakes."

"*Our* mistakes," Caroline jumped in, looking pissed. "You can't take all the blame for Miller. I jumped on that bandwagon right alongside you."

"And if you fall, there's no one in the Den who could replace you as alpha right now," Baron said grimly. "But Tank is right. This is a high risk operation with a good chance of going south. So if I get taken out, then Tank, you step into my place as alpha." He could see Tank grinding his teeth, clearly unhappy with the cold assessment. But he nodded, grim and resolute. "Andre, you're out as well. I know you're the best fighter we've got, but..." He paused.

"But what?" Andre prompted him. Baron's gaze flickered unintentionally across to Caroline... and she rolled her eyes as she no doubt picked up on his line of thought.

"You and Caroline... Well, you're still pretty much on your fucking honeymoon, aren't you?" Baron griped, feeling awkward at his own uncharacteristic moment of tenderness. "I'd feel like a right shit if I went and got you killed when you've only just got here. Besides which," he added, wishing he'd thought of this first, "if I'm not here, I need you to look after John."

"I'm coming with you," Silas said softly.

"No, you're not-"

"If the shit really does hit the fan, you and Simon are going to be sitting ducks. Particularly if muggins here decides to jump ship," he said, jerking a thumb Miller's way, who, to his credit, took the repeated doubts about his integrity with remarkable calm. "You'll need another strong fighter on your team if you're going to have a hope in hell of getting out of there alive."

Baron sighed, weighing up the options in his mind. "Fine. Silas comes. Which doesn't mean I think you're expendable in any way," he added, levelling a serious look at the man who had been the backbone of the Den for longer than Baron had been alpha.

"I'm touched," Silas said drily.

"Okay, so we have a reasonable primary strategy," Tank said, keeping the conversation moving. "Some of the details need to be hammered out, but it's a good start. But we need to talk contingencies. One of the big ones would be what to do if the van is somehow disabled or the exit is blocked. How are you going to escape if that happens?"

"We could have four of us waiting outside the gates with motorbikes, as a backup getaway plan," Caroline spoke up. "Even if the van does make it out, you could be tailed, and the bikes would make us far more manoeuvrable, if we're trying to take out enemy vehicles."

"I like it," Baron agreed. "Assuming we can make it out the gate, we could catch up with you as wolves, and then ride pillion on the bikes."

"We could always provide a diversion if you need help getting past the fence," Caroline suggested. "Nothing like a nice exploding grenade to get people's attention."

"How close is the complex to civilian premises?" Andre asked Miller.

"Across the street. The Noturatii owns the entire block, so you'd have a road's width of a margin on any given side."

"That's enough to make it work," Andre said. "But if it comes to that, there's a high possibility of civilian witnesses, so you're all going to have to be careful when and where you shift."

"Noted," Baron said. "All right Miller... let's talk about alternative exit points. Out of the basement, as well as off the property."

CHAPTER THIRTY-FIVE

Miller sat nervously in the back of the van, listening to the silence coming through his earpiece.

"I have control of the security cameras," Skip informed them suddenly, her voice tinny over the radio link. "You're good to go." She was stationed in a small car around the back of the Noturatii's complex, discreetly parked and far enough away that there shouldn't be anything to link her to the main operation. Tank was with her, a bodyguard in case of emergencies, but all going well, she should be well clear of any real danger. Much to Miller's relief.

Before they'd left, she'd given him a long hug and told him sharply that she expected him to come back alive. He'd looked her in the eye and told her to be careful, and then said, "Thank you. For everything. For not shooting me, and for converting me, and believing in me. For everything. And no matter how this turns out, I'm grateful that I got the chance to put a few things right."

Stationed a few blocks away, Caroline, Andre, Raniesha and Kwan were waiting with the motorbikes, armed with guns and grenades, and ready to unleash hell on the complex, should anything go wrong.

"We're up," Baron announced, then shifted into wolf form and crawled inside a large cardboard box. Miller did likewise, waiting while Silas closed the box and taped it shut.

Miller listened to the dim noises that followed, the shuffling of equipment, the slam of the car doors, and then he felt the van lurch as Simon started the engine and headed off. A minute or two later, they came to a stop, and Miller held his breath, knowing they had reached the security gate at the entrance to the Noturatii's compound.

Silas was in the passenger seat, his tattoos covered with long sleeves and the scar on his face disguised with an expert makeup job. The Noturatii didn't know his face, but showing up to repair an electrical fault with a man in the car who looked like a killer for hire was bound to make things go badly.

Skip had proven her worth once again, creating a fake work order and scheduling a visit within the complex's security files, and then ordering two new fake driver's licences from whatever shady connection the shifters used to manufacture such things. The van had a brand new logo plastered down the side, with the name of some minor electrical company or other displayed in bold blue letters, and with a small pile of guns and ammunition stored discreetly under a panel in the van's floor, their setup was complete.

As expected, the guards asked to inspect inside the van before letting it pass, and Miller crouched lower inside his box. It had a false top on it filled with a variety of electrical components, fuses, switches and the like, just in case anyone got curious and decided to open the box. But luck seemed to be on their side for the moment, and after a tense silence, the van door was slammed shut again.

"You're good to go," one of the guards said. "Here's your security code to get into the basement, and two badges. Keep them displayed at all times, and we'll collect them when you leave."

The van moved forward again, and Miller's heart rate kicked up a notch. They were past the first barrier, but there were plenty more to go before they could call this mission a success.

A few slow turns later and they stopped again, then started forward down a slope, and he had to assume that they'd made it past the gate into the basement. The van rolled to a stop, then the back door opened.

"We're clear," Silas said, reopening the boxes, and Miller and Baron climbed out, shifting back into human form. "No one in the vicinity. Let's get set up." They all donned bulletproof vests, in wolf form as well as human. Though Miller had seen the wolves' Kevlar vests before, he was intrigued by the design, not having had the chance to examine them up close before.

Baron and Silas armed themselves with guns, ammunition and grenades. Simon took a single handgun, though if the plan went well, he shouldn't even need that. And then Baron turned to Miller, handing him a pistol with a wary expression on his face. "I don't have to tell you what happens if you make any bad decisions here today," he said gruffly, and Miller nodded, not bothering to protest his innocence. They weren't going to believe he was on their side until this was all over, and he was content to let his actions speak louder than his words.

"All right, time to lie low. Places, everyone."

The van was parked in the corner of the basement, facing the exit so as to make for a quick getaway. Simon returned to his place in the driver's seat, while Miller found a comfortable spot around the back of the van, where he had a clear view of the entrance, but was hidden from sight. Baron and Silas got back in the van, but left the door slightly open, so they could keep an eye on Miller, as well as the entrance.

"You know," Simon said after a time, "it was never explained to me how we know Miller's telling the truth about this Jacob guy. There are no photos of him, so how do we know he's not just going to point out some random Joe and claim that he's killed the bigwig chief?"

"Look for some ID on the body, if we get the chance," Baron said. "Or if that fails, we'll have to wait and see what the fallout is. If it really is Jacob, there should be some significant waves created within the Noturatii's ranks in the next few weeks. If not, then we know we got the wrong guy."

Simon made a speculative noise, and then fell silent again, and the wait continued.

Melissa packed up her laptop, feeling drained and discouraged at the end of another unsuccessful day. Repeated attempts at forcing the shifter to change forms had failed, and the lab team had gone back to their original data, re-examining it to see if there was something they'd missed. A technician had been called in to run a thorough screening of the lab equipment, but no faults had been found, and with Professor Banks due to leave for Germany in the next few days, they were running out of time to make any significant breakthroughs.

Further questioning of the test subject had also yielded no useful information, as, despite increasingly intense torture sessions, the man had continued to insist that he didn't know how a shift might be triggered.

"Melissa," Banks said, as she picked up her bag, ready to head home. "I was wondering if you might be able to come over to my apartment this evening. I've been looking through some of my old research, and I think I might have found some things that could help us solve this mystery." Banks had been remarkably patient throughout the experiments, unperturbed by the lack of progress. 'Rome wasn't built in a day' was one of his favourite sayings, and Melissa had tried to learn from his Zen-like attitude, taking comfort in his insistence that they would reach their breakthrough sooner or later. 'Fortune favours the persistent', he would say calmly, while Melissa was struggling not to throw things across the room at their repeated failures.

"I'd love to," she said, in reply to his invitation. "Anything that can give us some new ideas is worth looking at."

"Excellent. Just give me a few minutes to get my things together, and we'll be off."

Ten minutes later, Melissa was seated in one of the most luxurious cars she'd ever been in. Banks had been given the use of a Mercedes for his visit, and he handled the powerful car like an expert. The corners were smooth, the gear changes almost undetectable, the engine a soft purr that sounded more like a cat than a car. The seats were leather, and Melissa tried not to stare at the decadent interior.

Banks was staying in an apartment complex about half an hour from the base. The Noturatii owned several such complexes, designed to provide secure housing for the more senior members of the organisation and temporary accommodation for any visiting dignitaries, and Banks had been given a small flat in the same building as the one Jacob lived in. Melissa had never been there before, but had heard reports that it was a five star setup, complete with a gym and an indoor swimming pool. It would be interesting to see it in person. And to imagine where she might be living, once she got a few solid scientific discoveries under her belt and started getting the promotions she firmly believed she deserved.

"I've been meaning to talk to you about your experimentation technique," Banks said after a few minutes. "Not so much about the details, but about the way you look at the bigger picture. You're a very intelligent woman," he said, glancing sideways at her, and Melissa couldn't help but glow under the praise. Banks was one of her heroes, and his acknowledgement of her hard work was vastly encouraging. "And you have an eye for detail," he went on. "A thoroughness that anticipates every problem we might encounter. But there is one thing you are missing, which could perhaps be holding you back."

"What's that?" Melissa asked, both eager to hear how to improve herself, and dreading the criticism.

"Imagination," Banks said. "You approach every task as if the only purpose of it is to reach the stated goal. Now, don't get me wrong, pursuing the goal is important. But if that's all you're doing, you're missing out on the other possibilities of your work. Sometimes you need to step back and think 'what else could I learn from this experiment?' Something completely unrelated to the task at hand."

He glanced over at her, and must have registered the baffled look on her face, so he explained himself a little better.

"Let me tell you something: in my laboratory in Germany, I have a wall of shelves. And these shelves are full of jars. From each shifter that has died in my lab, I have taken specimens. A wolf paw in one jar. A human heart in another. A jaw bone, or a knee joint... Why, you might ask? No reason but curiosity. After each shifter died, I took the time to dissect them. I was not looking for anything in particular. I thought I might find anatomical differences between shifters and natural wolves. Or indications of disease processes on their internal organs, perhaps. But in real terms, I did not have a specific goal for that part of my work. I was simply curious, like a child who tips baking soda into a bottle of coke, just to see what will happen.

"You've been feeling discouraged from our failure to achieve our goal," he said, giving her a sharp look, which made her feel like a child being scolded. "But stop to consider what else we have learned in the process. We have a wealth of data on the process of shifting. We have a better understanding of the drug doses needed to sedate shifters. We have learned which restraints are useful on them, and which are not. Keep all of these things in mind, as you go about your work. And you never know when something will pop up that answers a question you weren't going to ask for another three years."

"I'd love to see your office," she mused wistfully. "I hadn't thought of dissecting them. I'd assumed they'd just be like normal wolves, once they were dead. Or normal humans."

"And this is why you must learn to be more curious about the world," Banks said, apparently pleased with her enthusiasm.

"I will be," she promised. "Anything, if it gets us closer to winning this war."

From his hiding place behind the van, Miller watched as a silver BMW pulled up at the security gate. "That's Jacob's car," he hissed, drawing his gun. Baron had made it clear that taking out Jacob would be Baron's job, but Miller wanted to be prepared.

Baron was on his feet in an instant, Silas a silent shadow behind him.

"His parking spot is halfway down the row," Miller told them, "so we should get a clean shot when he walks to the elevator."

Baron didn't reply, but raised his gun, staying hidden in the shadows of the van, and aimed for the car. There was no sign of any security guards, and they were hoping that the combination of the silencer on the gun, and the dulling effects of the concrete walls would stop any sound from being heard above ground.

Jacob parked the car exactly where Miller had said he would. He took his time getting out, opening the door, then fishing around for his briefcase and a bag of groceries. Miller watched the whole time, feeling strangely numb about the whole thing. This was the man who had recruited him into the Noturatii, the man he'd worked under for years, the man who had masterminded a great many hideous and vengeful strategies against the shifters. And the man who had also treated Miller with the utmost professional respect and consideration. He'd been uncertain what he would be feeling when this moment came, whether it would be a deep regret for ever having met the man, or a wistful sadness and guilt that he was betraying someone who had done so much for him. But now that it had come to it, he found that all he felt was relief, like a bad nightmare was about to end, and he would finally be free to wake up and get on with his life.

Jacob closed the car door and locked it, the bright flash of the indicator lights threatening to reveal their position for a moment… if Jacob had been looking this way. But, confident in the complex's security measures, he was paying little attention to his surroundings, and he strode towards the elevator, oblivious to the presence of four would-be assassins, stationed only metres from him.

Baron lined up the shot, his attention sharply focused. He waited until Jacob cleared the line of cars, held his breath, and pulled the trigger. Jacob went down immediately, a bullet lodged firmly in his skull as the sound of the gun echoed around the concrete walls. The bag of shopping hit the ground, a bottle of milk spurting open and sloshing all over the floor. The briefcase fell with a clatter.

Not wasting any time, Baron dashed over to the body, searching through his pockets for his ID. "Jacob Green," he muttered, finding a security pass with Jacob's photo on it. "Looks like you're in the clear," he said to Miller, hurrying back to the van. Miller and Silas were already inside, Simon starting the engine to get them all the hell out of there-

"Car coming!" Silas hissed urgently, and Miller felt a rush of dread as he turned to see that Silas was right. Another car had pulled up at the entrance, and the heavy security gate was already swinging open.

"Fuck!" Baron swore. Jacob's body was lying in plain sight, and there was no opportunity to even attempt to hide it. Even if they could manage to drag it out of the way without being spotted by the occupants of the car, there was no way they could clean up the blood stains in time.

"As soon as they're clear of the entrance, get us out of here," Baron told Simon, jumping into the car and sliding the door shut. The newly arrived car was a black Mercedes, expensive, and no doubt carrying someone of significant importance. It eased through the gate and headed towards them. Miller held his breath, praying it would turn into a space before it reached-

The car jerked to a sudden stop, the brakes having been applied with startling force, and Miller knew they'd spotted the body. The passenger door opened, and… oh fuck, it was Melissa. She jumped out of the car, dashing over to the body with a cry of alarm, even while the driver yelled at her to get back inside the car.

"Go!" Baron urged Simon, and he started the engine, swinging out of their parking spot, tyres squealing. The roadway was partially blocked by the Mercedes, but there might just be space for them to squeeze past.

But not without doing some damage to the other car in the process.

The driver of the car must have realised their intention, and seen it for the threat to his life that it was. He dived out of the still open passenger door, while Melissa screamed for help. As predicted, the van scraped along the side of the Mercedes, ripping off the wing mirror and leaving deep gouges in the car. The noise was bound to draw some attention, if Melissa's screaming didn't, and guards wouldn't be far away.

As they swerved towards the exit, Miller craned his neck back, and caught sight of the man who had leapt from the car. Holy hell, it was Professor Ivor Banks. He'd seen the man's picture before on several reports, had heard the rumours that he was the most talented scientist the Noturatii had ever employed. The experiments he had performed on the shifters were enough to turn the stomach of even the most hardened soldiers, and Miller knew that taking him out would carve a greater hole in the Noturatii's operations than even Jacob's death would.

Simon stopped at the gate, frantically plugging in the code to open it, and the heavy gate began to swing open.

But they couldn't leave yet. Not without taking care of that one last piece of business. Miller lunged for the door, grabbing the handle and shoving the thing open, even as Baron yelled at him to stay put.

"It's Professor Banks," Miller snapped, knowing the name would mean nothing to Baron, but he didn't have time to explain himself any further. Two guards had heard the commotion, and were running down the ramp towards them. Miller dived for the cover of a nearby car, and pulled out his gun.

Baron was right behind him, gun aimed at Miller himself, so he rolled, slid in between two cars, and fired a shot. It missed, Banks having taken cover behind his own car, but then Miller's gaze fell on Melissa. She was young. Had been something of a friend of his, though they worked in separate departments and only crossed paths on occasion. But since he'd saved her life, back in the lab explosion, she'd seemed to have taken a liking to him. And that faint thread of friendship made him hesitate.

Melissa raised a gun she had somehow produced out of nowhere, and fired a shot at him. He swore and ducked, just in the nick of time, as the bullet caught the edge of the bonnet, where his head had been mere moments ago.

Return fire from Miller's left; Baron seemed to have caught onto his intentions, the bullets causing Melissa to duck for cover.

"Take out the man," Miller hissed at him.

"What the fuck are you doing, Miller?" Melissa yelled. Guards had arrived at the entrance now, with Silas and Simon working quickly to take them out. But more were on their way. "You're on our side!" The girl didn't seem too quick on the uptake, and Miller knew he'd have to kill her. As it stood, the Noturatii thought he was dead, and he wasn't keen on letting them find out he wasn't.

Another bullet came his way, the gunshot deafening, and an urgent voice came through Miller's earpiece. "What the fuck is going on down there?" Caroline demanded. "I can hear gunshots."

"Complication," Silas replied, as both Miller and Baron were occupied at the moment. "We'll let you know…"

Banks was still sheltering behind his car. No misguided heroism from him. He seemed content to take cover and wait for backup. But Miller wasn't going to let him get away that easily. He was too important, held too much influence over the success or failure of the Noturatii's ongoing experiments to let him walk away. And for the first time, he felt a real anger at the things that were going on inside that dark and mysterious organisation.

Or perhaps it wasn't his own anger, he realised a moment later, but that of his wolf. The quiet, reticent animal rarely made itself known, but the cold rage at the thought of the shifters who had suffered at the Professor's hands seemed more intense than Miller would have expected from himself.

"Cover me," he snapped at Baron, then fired two shots at the Mercedes and dashed across the roadway, sliding into cover behind another of the parked cars. And for a split second, he had a perfect line of sight to where Banks was cowering beside the car. He raised his gun and pulled the trigger, a perfect headshot that sent the man sprawling to the ground, blood spraying over the side of the car.

But an instant later, he felt the hot bite of a bullet in his own shoulder. Baron was beside him in an instant, a volley of bullets sending Melissa into cover, retreating deeper between the cars, out of sight for the moment. "Guards!" she screamed, though Silas hadn't let any of the men get any further than the gateway.

But Miller was having trouble focusing on anything other than his own pain. He put a dazed hand to his shoulder, feeling dizzy as it came away coated in blood. Fucking hell, where had Melissa learned to shoot like that?

"Shift!" Baron ordered him. "We need to get out of here."

"What?" Miller asked, not understanding. He was bleeding heavily, his shoulder feeling like a hot poker had been stabbed straight through him, and Baron wanted him to pour energy and effort into shifting?

"I said shift! Right now!" Baron said again, firing another shot at the car as Melissa tried to peer over the top.

Miller struggled to concentrate, but finally managed the shift… and was entirely startled when the searing pain immediately vanished.

"Into the van," Baron ordered, retreating after him, and the two of them made it back to the vehicle in record time, Baron taking out one more guard on his way.

"Silas! We're out of here," he yelled. Silas was crouched beside the security bollard, exchanging fire with the guards attempting to gain entrance to the basement.

With Baron covering him, Silas bolted for the van, leapt inside and slammed the door. Simon was still at the wheel, shooting through the window, and he slammed his foot to the floor, the van lurching forward with a squeal of tyres.

"We're on our way out," Baron informed Caroline and the others, waiting with the bikes. "We're going to need covering fire."

"Copy that," Caroline replied calmly, and Miller smiled at the thought of the four of them, racing towards the complex, the bikes sleek and fast, but also light and manoeuvrable. He suspected that the fierce woman would get a kick out of this, for all the seriousness of the situation.

There were more guards up the ramp, Miller straining to see out the front windscreen from his lower position, but Simon didn't even hesitate. Just ploughed straight through them, hitting one who was either not quick enough, or not smart enough to get out of the way, and sending him to the ground with a wet thud. Then the main security gate loomed ahead of them.

"Get down," Simon ordered, sliding lower in his seat. The windscreen, like the rest of the van, was bulletproof, but if enough shots were fired at it, it would still break. There didn't seem to be many guards left – most of them had probably been killed in the basement. But there was still the boom gate to get through.

Two men at the gate were firing at the van, the thuds of the bullets hitting the side loud and terrifying. "Hold on!" Simon yelled, then put his foot down, barrelling towards the boom gate with no intention of slowing down.

The collision made the van shudder and swerve, Miller being thrown about as Baron and Silas both held on. The revving of engines could be heard from nearby, and Miller jumped up on his back legs, peering out the window and seeing two motorbikes racing towards them. More shots were fired, a car that tried to pursue the van put out of action as Andre expertly shot its tyres out, the last of the guards taken out as Kwan and Raniesha appeared out of the darkness, controlling their bikes effortlessly with one hand while the other held a submachine gun.

"We're going to have to ditch the van," Simon said, after a minute or two had passed, and they were sure there were no more pursuers. "It's riddled with bullet holes, and we'll never get back to the estate without attracting some unwanted attention."

"Can't," Baron contradicted him. "Miller's been shot. You stay in wolf form!" he snapped at Miller, when he stepped forward, ready to shift. "You shift now, and you'll bleed out before we get you back to the estate."

So that was how it worked. He'd wondered why Skip hadn't been more concerned about her injury, back when she was shot after her kidnapping, and he longed to ask for details now. But that would have to wait. The simple answer seemed to be that staying in wolf form prevented him from bleeding, and that was all he really needed to know for the moment.

"Miller can't ride a bike as a wolf, so we'll have to hope for the best."

"Skip and Tank have a car," Simon pointed out. "If we can rendezvous with them, they can take Miller, and the rest of us can go on the bikes."

Baron considered that for a moment, then pulled out his phone. Skip would be too far away by now for the radio link to work. "What's your position?" he asked, when she answered.

"Clean and clear. Heading for the motorway," came the reply. "No sign of pursuit."

"Find a quiet backstreet and pull over, then text me your position. We have a delivery for you." Baron hung up, then glanced at Miller. "Once we get back to the estate, you're going to have some serious explaining to do," he said grimly. "There had better be a damn good reason for you fucking up our escape plan to kill whoever the fuck that was."

"What he means to say," Silas said, from where he was watching the road behind them, in case of being tailed, "is that you need to stay in wolf form until we get back, and then I'll remove that bullet from your arm for you."

If he had been in human form, Miller might have laughed. As it was, he gave Silas a grateful whine, a tentative wag of his tail, and then settled in for the ride home.

"So who was this guy you needed to kill so much?" Baron asked Miller. It was three o'clock in the morning; another sleepless night after the long drive home and Silas's careful efforts to remove the bullet from Miller's shoulder. He was placing the last few stitches in the wound now, an IV line in Miller's arm delivering a blood transfusion, compliments of Skip. When she'd heard he'd been shot, she'd volunteered to give blood immediately, as well as repeatedly reassuring him on the way home that Silas was an excellent surgeon, and they had plenty of medical supplies on hand for the job. Now, the local anaesthetic was making his arm feel strange, not quite numb, but heavy and uncooperative, and he thanked Silas for the expert job as he snipped off the last piece of suture material.

"Professor Ivor Banks," Miller told Baron, as both Caroline and Andre appeared in the doorway. "He's the head scientist from-"

"No fucking way!" Andre interrupted him, staring at him in amazement, the curse word an unusual thing to hear from the usually genteel man. "Ivor Banks? From Germany? He was here?"

"So it seems," Miller said, not sure why Andre was so interested in him. "I'm not sure when he arrived, or why he was here, but it was definitely him."

"Excuse me?" Baron interrupted, trying to regain control of the conversation. "Who the fuck is this guy?"

"He's the Noturatii's most senior scientist," Andre filled him in. "Runs the lab in Germany. The Council has had dozens of reports about his work. The things he does to shifters makes Freddy Kruger look like a charity worker. Where is he now?" he asked, turning back to Miller.

"Dead," Miller said. "Single shot to the head."

"Nice work," Andre said, genuine admiration in his voice.

Baron looked momentarily nonplussed. "So he was a big deal, yeah?" he clarified.

"Absolutely," Andre confirmed. "Taking him out should set the Noturatii back at least five years in their research."

"Fine. Then… good job," he said to Miller, looking pained by the concession.

Miller laughed, holding the end of a bandage for Silas as he finished dressing the wound. "Oh, come on. Does it really hurt that much to admit that I got something right?"

Baron tried to glare at him, but couldn't quite manage to look angry. "Yeah, okay. I'll give you credit for this one. But don't let it go to your head."

"Does that mean I can get this damned tag off my ankle now?" Miller asked, holding out his leg. The tracking device had been temporarily disabled while he was off the property, but Simon had activated it again the moment they got back, and if he was honest about it, Miller was feeling rather resentful about the continuing sign of their distrust.

Baron glanced at Caroline, who nodded. "Yeah, okay," Baron agreed. "That little excursion didn't exactly go according to plan, but from what Andre says, the mess was worth it. So I think you've earned your freedom. I'll get Simon onto it first thing in the morning."

"Thanks," Miller said, then stood up, eager to get to bed now that his wound had been seen to. Silas removed the IV from his arm and covered the spot with an adhesive dressing. But then he noticed Andre watching him strangely, and Miller felt a little unnerved by the expression on his face. "What?" he asked, trying not to sound confrontational with the question.

"Just thinking," Andre said. "Baron's given me a review of the mission. And it seems you had a run in with Melissa while you were there."

"We did," Miller confirmed. "This was her doing," he added, pointing to the wound on his shoulder.

"And she's still alive?"

"She is." Miller was far from happy with the situation. He'd done a rather good job of playing dead, as far as the Noturatii were concerned, and now that they knew he was alive…

"Then we have a rather serious security issue," Andre said, glancing at Baron. "Deserters from the Noturatii are treated just as seriously as we treat ours. Which means they're going to be sending a Khuli after you," he told Miller. The Satva Khuli, or the Blood Tigers, were the Noturatii's own brand of professional killer, a perfect counterpart to the Council's assassins. Andre himself had fought one back during the raid on the lab, and had won the battle only by the narrowest of margins.

"I'm aware of it," Miller acknowledged with a heavy heart. "So what now?" he asked Baron. With a Khuli on his tail, it wouldn't be safe for him to remain in England, and he waited to be told that he would be sent elsewhere. To this mysterious Council, perhaps, or to another Den, far away from here-

"So now we batten down the hatches and wait," Baron said, sounding strangely calm about the whole thing.

"You're not sending me away?" Miller asked, surprised by the answer.

"There would be no point," Baron replied. "National borders pose no barrier to the Khuli. We could send you anywhere in the world, and they'd still manage to find you, one way or another. And if we send you to another Den, we're just making them a target." He shook his head. "Much as I don't like it, we're the ones who chose to accept you, so we're the ones who will have to deal with the fallout."

"I don't want to put you all at risk," Miller protested, but Baron wouldn't hear it.

"You're familiar with the phrase 'all for one, and one for all'?" he asked, a wry amusement in his voice, despite the serious issue at hand. "We tend to take that rather to extremes here. Like it or not, Miller, you're one of us now. Looks like you're damn well stuck with us."

CHAPTER THIRTY-SIX

Miller stepped into the dining room, feeling a tense apprehension about what was about to happen. It was two weeks since they'd assassinated Jacob, and as predicted, the Noturatii had been thrown into chaos. Skip had access to a small number of communication routes used by the organisation, a few phones she'd tapped, email accounts she'd managed to hack, and the news had been encouraging. The staff were disorganised, no new scientific endeavours to speak of, no planned investigations or raids for the security staff, and the Noturatii's head office had made the unfortunate error of describing Jacob's death as a suicide. While it was a neat sidestep that avoided the need to explain a fire fight in a Noturatii complex to any official stakeholders, it had also spread a wave of doubt through the Noturatii's various financiers, with members of parliament and the heads of several large banks all rapidly re-evaluating the benefits of pouring funds into an organisation that had apparently been headed by someone of questionable mental stability. It would take them weeks, if not months to regroup, and the shifters were enjoying a small respite from the constant worries of being attacked by their enemies.

The electronic tag had indeed been removed from Miller's ankle, but Baron had taken the time to explain his new place in the Den to him. He had earned a measure of trust, he had acknowledged, but Il Trosa had strict rules in place as to the expected conduct of its members. If he were ever to betray them, Baron had told him, reminding him of his oath during his welcoming ceremony, then every member of Il Trosa was charged with his execution. He'd also been warned that he would be required to remain on estate grounds for the foreseeable future. With a Khuli trying to pick up his trail, keeping him out of sight was their best defensive tactic for the moment.

In the spirit of his renewed acceptance and the slightly less severe restrictions on his movements, Miller had once again challenged George to a status fight. The older man had rolled his eyes, and surrendered almost the moment the fight started. Miller had already proven himself the stronger fighter, and the challenge was entirely for show.

So now, he was to see the result of this latest challenge. Would Silas, Tank and the other senior wolves finally allow him to begin climbing the ranks, or would they once again kick him to the curb?

Miller glanced around the seats. Mark was in his usual place at the bottom of the table, and half of the other seats were filled, while the rest of the Den straggled in for the evening meal. George hadn't taken his seat yet, still ferrying dishes in from the kitchen, so there were no clues there as to where Miller was expected to sit. He glanced at Tank, who was engaged in a heated discussion with Caroline, and hadn't noticed him arrive, and then at Silas, who raised a sardonic eyebrow at him, and then pointedly ignored him. Hoping for the best, he headed for George's usual seat, one place up from Miller's old spot, and sat down, holding his breath as he waited for a reaction from the others.

Nothing.

The rest of the Den filed in, taking their seats, and George sat down beside him, looking vaguely relieved about the new seating arrangement. Baron tapped his glass, getting the attention of everyone in the room, and Miller waited, expecting some last minute objection to his new rank...

"Any news?" Baron asked, and a moment's silence followed as everyone shook their heads. Baron lifted his glass. "To those who still run," he recited, pride and admiration in his voice for the members of this eclectic family.

"And to those who have fallen," the Den replied in unison. "May they be welcome at the table of Sirius at the setting of the sun."

With that, conversations sprung up all over the room, and everyone dug into the food.

Baron opened the door to his bedroom, not bothering to turn on the light. The room would be empty, as it always was these days, and having to stare at the unoccupied bed, the vacant desk by the window where John had kept his gaming console, the neat floor devoid of randomly scattered clothing was too disheartening to draw attention to it all by illuminating the room.

He stripped off his clothes, automatically tossing them into the laundry hamper, and headed for the shower.

He'd contacted Dr Nagi, their vet friend, a few days ago, reiterating his request that the man assist them with the occasional veterinary crisis. Skip had done a more thorough background check on him since her surgery, and

Simon had been monitoring his phone and internet accounts. He'd done nothing suspicious or unexpected since that night, making no mention of his encounter with strange military types to anyone. When Baron spoke to him, Nagi had thanked him for giving him the time to think his offer through, and had agreed to help them, on a number of conditions; none of his staff were ever to be put at risk, Baron was to pay him double the usual fee for any required procedures and the moment any nefarious types started asking questions, the deal was off. Baron had agreed to his conditions, and gone out one evening to meet the man, presenting him with an official-looking contract. He'd also informed the Council of their new alliance, and been praised by both Eleanor and Feng for his quick thinking and his success in saving one of his Den mates under such pressing circumstances.

Miller was shaping up well. After their assassination of Jacob and Professor Banks, the majority of the Den had lost some of their antagonism towards him, and he'd started combat training again, several sessions with both Silas and Tank testing out his abilities and highlighting any areas that might need more work. All things considered, the decision to keep him was turning out rather well.

But the one sore spot in Baron's life remained his relationship with John. The boy had stubbornly refused to reconsider his position on Miller, despite the success of the assassination, and was still going out of his way to be uncooperative where Baron was concerned. On the bright side, if it could be called that, John seemed to be making more of an effort lately to control his temper, spending regular sessions in the gym to work off his inevitable frustrations, asking Tank and Silas for sparring sessions, and while he was still vocal about his opinions, he had managed to go a full two weeks without breaking anything around the manor. Heron had quietly reported that she'd even seen him down in the laundry the other day, washing his own clothes for the first time in years, and despite knowing that he should be proud of the boy for finally taking responsibility for his own life, Baron couldn't help his disappointment that John seemed to be proving himself capable of living comfortably without him.

He shut off the water and dried himself off, avoiding looking in the mirror. Since John's departure, he hadn't been sleeping well, and he knew that the face in the mirror would show evidence of that, bags under his eyes, a grim frown etching creases into his skin, a hollow expression staring back at him.

Not bothering to put any clothes on, Baron headed for the bed and lay down, the curtains still open, letting in the faint light of the moon. It was still early, but he was in sore need of catching up on some sleep, and he deliberately closed his eyes and slowed his breathing, determined to ignore the ache in his chest and get a decent night's rest.

It was heading for ten o'clock at night as Miller followed Skip up the grand staircase to the first floor landing, his heart thumping in his chest. They'd just spent the past hour wandering the rose gardens, fingers entwined, talking about everything and nothing, and sharing kisses that had become progressively more intense, until Skip had finally pulled back, looked up at Miller with a mischievous smile on her face, and asked if he'd like to come up to her room. He'd nodded and said "I'd love to."

Over the past two weeks, their interludes had become longer and more heated, and a few nights ago, Miller had dared to slide his hand beneath Skip's shirt, stroking her skin with tentative fingers. She'd squirmed and giggled nervously, stating that she was ticklish, but then slid her own fingers beneath Miller's shirt to return the favour. The feel of her small hands against his skin had made his muscles tighten and twitch, along with a corresponding tingle in another part of his body.

And then, that same evening, Skip had suddenly and without prompting launched into a brief explanation of her childhood; her father, his friends, and the evil they had inflicted upon her. The revelations had been shocking, far worse than anything Miller had imagined based on the few scant details he knew of her past, and hearing it had made him feel sick, overwhelmed by his outrage at the men who had harmed her. He'd tried to stop her, told her that she didn't need to tell him anything if she didn't want to.

"He's not in control of my life any more," she'd replied defiantly. "I'm not ashamed of who I am, or what I had to live through to get here. And it still hurts, but... not everyone is like him. He got to go to jail, and I got to become a magic wolf. This time around, I'd say karma did its job perfectly."

Her resilience and the positive outlook she maintained on life had awed him yet again, though the news had cooled his romantic interests for the evening, and the following night, he'd held back, deliberately letting her make the next move.

But Skip had proved that she knew what she wanted, and truth be told, he was finding himself increasingly eager for their relationship to move to the next level. She was a beautiful woman, small and compact, yet strong, defined muscles on her arms, with dazzling hazel eyes that never failed to captivate him.

Now, he followed her into her bedroom, reminding himself to take things slowly.

But Skip had other ideas. After closing the door, she tugged him close and kissed him again, picking up right where they'd left off outside. Their bodies were pressed tightly together, the heat of her radiating through both their sets of clothing to leave him feeling flushed. A faint mew of pleasure escaped Skip's throat, and he couldn't help but smile against her lips. He'd slept with women before, but not for a long while, and none of them quite like the woman in his arms now, and it reassured him to realise that she was enjoying this as much as he was.

When Skip finally pulled back, her cheeks were pink, and she was breathing fast.

"Is it me, or is it hot in here?" Miller asked. His skin was glowing warmly, his own face flushed in a way that had little to do with the temperature.

"If it's too warm, then you should take your shirt off," Skip said, with such nonchalance that Miller didn't quite know how to respond. Not sure if she was joking or not, he reached for the hem of his t-shirt, lifting it slowly while keeping an eye on Skip, in case she changed her mind.

But she was watching him intently, a shy but eager smile quirking at the edge of her lips, so he pulled the shirt up and over his head, dropping it carelessly to the floor.

Her eyes were fixed on his chest, and he stood still, waiting for her verdict. "You're beautiful," she breathed softly. "Wild and strong, like a wolf." She touched him tentatively, a soft brush of her fingertips over his abs, up his chest, around his waist, and he couldn't help reaching for her in return, his hands stroking her hair, her neck and shoulders.

"Do you want me to take my shirt off?" she asked, and Miller nodded, not really thinking the question through. She was captivating, beautiful, wild and courageous, and he was suddenly eager to see more of her.

Skip stepped back and stripped off her t-shirt quickly, dropping it to the floor, and then she stood in the middle of the room with nothing but her bra covering her upper body... and suddenly seemed to freeze, her expression going blank, her body motionless, and Miller felt a rush of dread. This was clearly too much, too soon, and he turned away quickly, offering her a measure of privacy while trying to give her time to recover.

"Sorry," he apologised, not knowing what else to say. "Do you want me to get dressed?"

No response, and he waited, holding his breath.

"No," came the whispered reply. "I just... I'm sorry..."

"You don't need to apologise," he told her. "If you want to stop, that's perfectly fine."

The sound of Skip suddenly bursting into tears had him spinning around in alarm. But rather than looking horrified, or running for the bathroom, Skip instead unexpectedly launched herself into his arms, and he caught her in an awkward hug, acutely aware of their naked torsos pressed against each other.

"You would, wouldn't you?" she asked, her voice shaky. "If I said stop, you would."

"Absolutely," he murmured into her hair. "This is your choice. Every step of the way."

She pulled back and peered up at him, the tears already drying. "You're a very strange man," she told him frankly, and Miller had to smile at that.

"Then it looks like I fit right in here," he said wryly, which made Skip laugh. She glanced down at herself, to where her bra was still covering her chest. She was stroking his arms, seemingly unaware of her own actions for the moment.

"I'm not..." she began, doubt filling her eyes.

"You're perfect," he told her firmly. "Strong and fierce and powerful. Like a wolf should be."

She smiled at that, a blush turning her cheeks pink, and he couldn't help but lean down to kiss her. She tilted her face up and kissed him back, and the embrace lasted for several long minutes, desire overcoming fear as her hands became bolder. He allowed himself to touch her more firmly, exploring the curve of her shoulders, the dip in her waist, the tantalising curve of her buttocks. And then her knee was suddenly insinuating itself between his thighs, and Miller felt himself swell inside his trousers.

"You're beautiful," she told him, tracing the contours of his muscles with a fingertip. "I like your skin."

"I like every part of you," he said, a mischievous finger tracing her breast along the edge of her bra.

She grinned, half embarrassed, half pleased, and began coaxing him towards the bed. The backs of his knees hit the edge and he sat down, then wriggled back at her urging, until they were both sprawled on the bed.

They continued for a while in the same manner, plenty of kisses, gentle touches that became heated strokes, and then there was a moment of awkward fumbling as Miller draped a leg over her thigh, and she immediately pushed it off again, avoiding his eyes and trying to look nonchalant about it.

"Sorry," he apologised again. He had to wait a moment for Skip to pull herself together.

"Maybe..."

"Do you want to stop?"

"You're kind of heavy," she said, her voice sounding stilted, and Miller immediately shuffled back, giving her more room. Let her stay on top, he counselled himself sharply, aware that there must have been plenty of times in the past when she felt overwhelmed by the force of a male body on top of hers. When she didn't say anything more, he moved to get off the bed, but was stopped by Skip suddenly taking his hand.

"I don't want to stop. I just..." Her free hand fiddled with the blanket.

"Take your time," he said, perfectly willing to let her take the lead. She made an effort to smile, though it came out slightly wobbly.

"My wolf is playing up," she admitted awkwardly. "She's very protective of me, and I think she just wants to assert her dominance a bit." It wasn't often that any of the shifters referred to their wolf side in third person, but Miller himself had felt the occasional surge of emotion from his animal half that seemed at odds with his instincts as a human, though he was aware of the importance of accepting the wolf's demands as his own. In response, he lay down on the bed, much as a wolf might lie down to show its submission to a more dominant member of the pack, and then he watched as Skip's head went up a fraction, her shoulders straightening, her expression altering so subtly that he couldn't have described the change, but knew at an instinctive level that Skip had accepted his surrender and now felt more at ease with her own more dominant position. In the past week or two he'd been putting a fair amount of time into studying wolf behaviour, and was gratified to see the research paying off now.

Her hand reached out again, tracing a line from his knee up to his hip, lingering at the waistband of his trousers, and he slowly edged his own hand over to explore her waist, her ribs... Her eyes met his, and he slowly, deliberately eased his hand higher to lightly cup one breast.

Skip leaned into his touch, biting her lip. Her breathing quickened a fraction, her fingers digging into his skin, though he wasn't sure she was aware of what she was doing. But then her hand slid downwards, brushing lightly over his groin... and then, when she saw him twitch, she did it again, firmer this time.

He rolled over onto his back, tugging her with him, and she leaned down to kiss him, pressing her chest harder against his hand in the process. Their strokes became bolder, faint moans drifting out of the comfortable silence between them, until, long minutes later, Skip finally pulled back.

"I like this," she told him, with such sincerity that he had to laugh.

"I'm glad. So do I." His groin was throbbing, his heart beating fast, but he got the impression that Skip had had enough for the evening.

"It's getting late," he said, sitting up and kissing her gently. "I should let you get some sleep."

Skip nodded, smiling shyly at him as she shimmied off the bed and reached for her t-shirt. She waited while he did the same, then stopped him at the door to kiss him again. "Sleep well," she murmured, then opened the door, watching him go with eyes full of mischief and delight.

Skip closed the door after Miller left, turning around to lean against the smooth wood with a sigh. A small, satisfied smile settled on her face. Miller's body was beautiful; smooth, dark skin, defined muscles, the natural grace and litheness of his wolf side beginning to show up in his human form, and she blushed as she realised that she was already eagerly anticipating the next time they would try something like this. There had been a few moments when she'd become nervous, dark memories threatening to ruin the happy evening, but Miller had been so different from the other men. Patient, where they had been demanding. Gentle, where they had been harsh. And yet he had also been passionate and excited, but in a way that had made her feel important and valuable, rather than cheap and worthless.

In the morning, she was going to have to call Nia and ask for some advice, a few questions in her mind that were creating a mild apprehension about some of the details of this new development in her life. Small steps, she reminded herself, knowing that this evening had been a huge leap forward for her, though it had probably been rather mundane for Miller. But next time, she might find the courage to go further, to take off her bra, perhaps, or maybe even her shorts. It would be a while before she felt comfortable taking off her underpants in front of him, but she was prepared to wait. Six months ago, she'd never even entertained the idea of sleeping with a man, and here she was, having let him see her in only her bra, and having explored his body in a way that had been tantalisingly exciting, seeing his pleasure and enjoying the power of knowing that he was holding back for her, waiting for her, because her opinion mattered to him.

Small steps, she repeated, reaching for her pyjamas to get ready for bed. But she was looking forward to taking the next one.

CHAPTER THIRTY-SEVEN

Genna stepped into the tent in the Grey Watch's camp, responding to Sempre's shrill demand that she come at once. But when she saw what was on the table in the centre of the tent, she stopped dead in her tracks.

It was a small bird cage, a tiny robin fluttering about inside, wild and terrified at its inexplicable captivity.

"We have a new task for you to try," Sempre said gleefully, moving to stand beside Lita, who was hovering near the bird. "So far you've only tried your magic on inanimate objects. Today we'd like you to try it on the bird."

Genna stepped forward, her heart beating fast as she stared at the tiny creature. "That's crazy," she stated flatly, knowing it would get her in serious trouble. "We have no idea what could happen. We've never tried this sort of thing on a living creature before. What if it dies?"

"It's just a bird," Lita snapped impatiently. "It hardly matters if it dies or not. But that information will be invaluable to us. More secrets of the shifter magic laid bare before our eyes."

"I... But what... No!" Genna protested. "That's just cruel."

The slap across her face was not unexpected, but it stung nonetheless. "You dare to defy me, you weak pup?" Sempre accused, her voice cold and cruel. "You think yourself so important that I would tolerate such a thing? Or do you honestly think you're stronger than me?"

"No, I don't," Genna said, backing up a step and searching for a way out of the corner she had been backed into. "I don't mean any disrespect, it's just... I was taught that we should live at peace with the natural world. To harm one of its creatures just seems wrong."

Sempre stepped forward, an expression of dark anger on her face. "You listen to me, girl," she hissed, lowering her face until she was eye level with Genna. "You test the magic on that bird, or I will demote you to the rank of omega and lock you in a cage for a week."

Genna felt herself go cold at the threat. After all the time and effort she'd spent climbing the ranks, fighting for food, for the small privileges that came with status, such a huge step backwards would be agonising. And she knew from seeing it happen to others what life in the cage was like. No food, little water, no shelter from the rain. A life of misery for herself, or the life of one small bird. As much as she wanted to take the moral high ground, to protest against Sempre's ever increasing cruelty and selfishness, she was barely holding her own in this camp as it was.

Feeling sick, Genna walked over to the cage. Get it over and done with quickly, she told herself. If she was lucky, that would be it for the day. And if things went really well... who knows? Maybe the bird would survive. She reached out her hand and pressed it against the cage, focusing on the bird. A quick burst of electricity and the bird vanished.

Heart in her throat, Genna turn to the side and brought the bird back, setting it down gently on the table...

And closed her eyes, tears immediately springing up behind her eyelids. The bird was dead.

"Disappointing," Lita said coldly, and Genna forced herself to open her eyes, holding back her tears.

"Is that all?" she asked, praying they were done with her.

"Not quite," Sempre said. She removed the bird cage, then set a large tray on the table. It was once again larger than anything Genna could make disappear... but then her heart sank when she saw that Lita had a second cage in hand. Another bird, larger than the first.

"You're aware that our magic can be enhanced with blood rituals?" Sempre said, as Lita took the bird out of the cage. "Lita is going to help you perform your first one. And then we'll see if you have the power to move something that's actually a useful size."

Genna felt numb as she watched Lita prepare for the ritual. She wanted to say no, wanted to protest any number of things that were wrong with this situation, but the terror of her long-awaited fears made real left her speechless. Incense was set up around the room and lit, fragrant smoke filling the small space. Muttered chanting grew gradually louder, as Lita wafted the smoke over the bird in her hand. And then she waved Genna closer, Sempre physically dragging her over to the tray when she didn't move, and she pressed the bird to Genna's forehead, reciting an incantation that Genna had heard her repeat on these sorts of occasions before, but the meaning of it was beyond her.

Lita picked up a small knife. She slit the bird's throat and held it over the tray, head thrown back, one arm held high.

The first drop of blood hit the tray. A great swirl of static electricity filled the room, making Genna's hair stand on end.

And then Lita let out a loud cry, dropped the dying bird on the table, and collapsed to the ground, her skin a deathly grey, her body lifeless.

Genna stood in the circle of shifters, watching the clouds creep over the moon, blocking out the faint light. Lita was dead. The funeral ceremony was nearly over, the required chants having been performed, Sempre giving a rousing speech about the woman's devotion to her pack and encouraging, or rather demanding, that every other shifter present follow her example. Their individual needs and desires came second place to the welfare of the pack, she insisted, seemingly unmoved by the fact that her selfish demands for power and prestige had been the cause of Lita's death, the blood rituals having slowly sucked the life out of her over the past decade.

But Genna was finding it hard to feel much sorrow for Lita's passing. Perhaps at first, she'd been coerced into her role by Sempre's manipulations, but in her later years, she'd embraced the blood rituals wholeheartedly, lending her own powers of coercion and manipulation to Sempre's quest for power.

The pack as a whole seemed more stunned than saddened by her death, a thick silence having descended on the pack when the announcement was made. The funeral pyre had been set up quickly, the prayers to Sirius commencing the instant the sun had set, and now it was fully dark, the night warm and humid, as summer was not quite over for the year.

"With Lita's passing, I nominate Feriur as my new second in command," Sempre said, as the funeral pyre continued to burn before them. "I expect you to show her the same respect and obedience that you showed Lita." With that final announcement, she turned and walked away, leaving the rest of the pack to tend the fire and scatter the ashes, once it had burned out.

Closeted away in the library of their Italian villa, the Council members were seated around a long table, locked in a debate that had lasted for three days so far. Now that the Russian Den had successfully been relocated and that small section of the war wrapped up, the Council had finally turned their attention to the other important matter weighing on all of their minds: the proposed plan to take the shifter nation public.

Over the past three days, they'd discussed the idea from every possible angle, and so far the only thing everyone could agree on was that the situation was unbearably complicated. Expanding their numbers to meet the Noturatii's opposition would require significant time and resources, both in terms of manpower for recruiting and training the new members, and the financial weight of their upkeep. Exposing the shifters to the public breached the Treaty of Erim Kai Bahn, or rather nullified it, as the whole purpose of the Treaty had been to keep the wolves safe and hidden in the face of overwhelmingly negative public sentiment about their existence. And if the Treaty was nullified, there was a very real risk of war with the Grey Watch. There was also the risk of retaliation from the Noturatii, once they figured out what the shifters were planning, and even dissent from within their own Dens, as not every wolf in Il Trosa would agree with a plan to go public, despite the growing unrest about their current course in the Endless War.

"The Grey Watch should have a say in this plan, I agree," Paula was saying, "but they don't have any form of centralised governance that we can appeal to. It would be a case of asking each and every pack individually, which would take an enormous amount of time, and the chances of them actually reaching a consensus on the issue seem slim at best."

"It's not just the Grey Watch," Feng added. "There are the other shifter species to consider. If we expose the wolves, it only takes one person to ask the rather obvious question of whether there are any other species of shifter on the planet, and then the cats could be exposed. We could end up at war with Asia."

"Or with North America," Elise reminded them. "And if that happened, we would most definitely lose."

A tense silence descended on the room, nobody liking the latest assessment of the overwhelming risks they were facing. The quiet was broken only by the faint rustle of paper being shuffled and the restless fidgeting of tired bodies. Someone cleared their throat.

"Okay, let's ask a slightly different question," Rafael spoke up finally. "What we need to think about is what's going to happen to the wolf shifters if we do nothing. We've spent the past ten years debating this issue, in various forms, and we've considered numerous strategies in that time. The idea of going public has come up repeatedly, and we've always found a reason to reject it, but we've never found a viable alternative. We lost an entire Den, just a few weeks ago in Russia. We lost the estate for the Scottish Densmeet over the summer. We lost a member of this Council last spring. Leaving aside for the moment the question of exactly what we do next, can any of you honestly tell me that you think we can afford to continue keeping our heads down and hoping for the best?"

The already grim atmosphere became even more severe, as everyone slowly shook their heads.

"Rafael is right," Feng agreed. "The time has come to make some hard decisions. We must choose a decisive course of action if we are to survive."

"Philosophically speaking," Paula spoke up, "being open with humanity about our abilities isn't a new thing. For thousands of years, the shifters lived alongside humanity, in peace, and with a deep mutual respect for each other. It's only in the past six hundred years that that's changed, which, if you look at the whole of human history, is not all that long."

"In principle, North America should have no objection to us going public," Elise mused. "They run their own affairs, as we do ours. There have never been any contracts or treaties between the different shifter species. And the same applies to Asia. We hold no grudge against the cats, but we owe them nothing, either. And we need to remember there's a big difference between a random member of the public asking the question 'Are there any others?', and us pointing a neon sign at Asia and saying 'Hey, look here, there are cat shifters everywhere!' I think first and foremost, we need to agree that there should be no deliberate attempts to expose any other species, but beyond that, we cannot take responsibility for every other shifter on the planet."

"May I point out another issue?" The diffident question came from Yegor, a Russian man and the newest member of the Council, who had been chosen to replace Amedea, the Councillor who had died in the spring. He was still finding his feet in his new role, hesitant to speak up, but Eleanor was glad to see him getting involved in the discussion now, and she nodded for him to continue. "Something we must consider," Yegor said, "which is going to force our hand one way or another, is that technology is advancing faster than we can keep up with. Sooner or later, there's going to be a public leak that we can't control. All it takes is someone with an iPhone and thirty seconds of decent footage, and six hundred years of hard work is down the drain. Now, we can prepare for that day, create contingency plans, work to gain public support behind the scenes so that when it does happen we have a solid base to work from, or we can pretend this is not an issue and then stand around laying blame on each other while our entire history burns around us."

It was unpleasant to hear their situation summed up in such neatly catastrophic terms, but Eleanor also had to admire Yegor for having the courage to say it out loud. Perhaps, over the past few years, the Council had been rather inclined to bury their heads in the sand, and a new voice, a fresh perspective on the world was what was needed to make them all sit up and pay attention.

"I believe Rafael and Yegor are both right," Eleanor spoke up finally. "We've reached the point where we can no longer bide our time and do nothing. Some day soon, the rest of the world is going to take that decision out of our hands. And I, for one, believe that Andre's plan for a slow, careful 'coming out' is the best chance we have for survival."

"A plan of slow steps over several years has many benefits," Feng agreed. "At each step of the way, we can re-examine the success or failure of each strategy and make the necessary adjustments. I believe it is time we put this idea to a vote. We've spent three days talking about this, and we all understand both the risks and the benefits by now."

A murmur of agreement met the suggestion, so Eleanor called the vote. "Those in favour of beginning a controlled plan to go public?" She counted the raised hands. "Those against? The vote is called. Nine for, three against. All right then, ladies and gentlemen. Let's talk about how we're going to break this to the Grey Watch..."

Melissa sat in her office in the Noturatii's lab, the room silent around her. After Jacob's death, there had been little going on, with the staff waiting for official orders as to who would be Jacob's replacement, and which of their projects should continue or be shut down. Melissa herself had been fighting off a strong feeling of desolation since Professor Banks' death, though she had been far less upset about Jacob. Their former Chief of Operations had been a brilliant man, there was no doubt about that. But he'd also been domineering, petty and, in Melissa's opinion, short sighted about some of their goals. As far as she was concerned, the worst part about his death was having to acknowledge that the shifters had once again outwitted them. Aside from that, it was just another bump in the road, their path to be smoothed over again as soon as headquarters got around to assigning someone as his replacement.

But the loss of Professor Banks was a far more concerning issue. Despite his last pep talk in his car, encouraging her to open her mind to the possibilities of her research, his death had put a serious dent in her enthusiasm. Doctor Evans had been absolutely speechless when she'd been told, unable to form a sentence for a full five minutes. The other scientists had taken the news with calm resolve. Such losses were always difficult, but were not a wholly unexpected part of their lives. The Noturatii were at war, after all.

Checking the time, Melissa opened her laptop and set up a secure link through to headquarters. She'd filed a report on the assassination the same day as it had occurred, as she was the only real witness to the events in the apartment block carpark, though even her account of the battle was sketchy. She'd been too busy trying to stay alive to pay attention to the finer details. But the important facts had all been in her report, including one pertinent and startling discovery: Jack Miller, once presumed dead, was well and truly alive, not only having joined the shifters, but actually having become one of them. Melissa had all but fainted in shock when she'd seen him shift, helped into the van by that huge brute of a man who'd led the raid on their laboratory complex all those months ago.

Now, she had been asked to attend a video call with some of the senior staff from Germany. No doubt they would want to question her more thoroughly about the assassination.

"Good afternoon," she said politely, when the call came through. "Mr

Bosch. Mr Winter. Mr Gerber." The three men were among the officials who ran the German head office, highly experienced and intelligent men, and she braced herself for a thorough debriefing.

"Good afternoon, Ms Hunter," Mr Winter addressed her first. "Let me say first of all that we greatly appreciate your report about Jacob Green's death. It was disappointing to realise how easily the shifters breached our security, and we've ordered a full review of procedures."

Melissa nodded, feeling a small satisfaction at the news. That the shifters had managed to get all the way inside their complex without raising the slightest suspicion was unsettling, to say the least.

"But aside from that," Mr Bosch took over, "we wanted to inform you that we've chosen a replacement for Jacob." He gave her a look of smug satisfaction, and Melissa waited with curiosity to find out who her new boss was going to be. She hoped it would be someone with a sense of vision and urgency. "We'd like you to take his place."

Melissa's jaw dropped. She looked from one grey, wrinkled face to the next. "Me?" She was too stunned by the announcement to even pretend to be pleased. "Why me? I'm too young. I haven't made any real advances in the lab. I'm not even the head of my department. Why would you choose me?"

Bosch looked put out by her questions, and his bushy eyebrows bunched together in a tight frown. "Are you saying you don't want the position?" he asked, a hint of disdain in his voice now.

"No, not at all. I'd be honoured to be Chief of Operations," Melissa assured him hastily, getting over the shock of it a little. "I'm very sorry, sir, I didn't mean to sound rude. I just wasn't expecting this."

"It's true, you are rather less experienced than the majority of people who hold this sort of position," Mr Gerber told her. "But after some careful consideration, we're confident that you're the right person for the job. You've proven yourself to be resourceful in the lab – both with your work on the conversion project, and with your ideas on your latest experiments. We read your suggestions on weapons training for non-security staff with great interest. Your ideas show a firm dedication to our cause and a capacity for long range planning. And you've managed to survive not one, but two attacks on the Noturatii's facilities in the recent past. All of that points to a most resourceful and insightful employee. As I've often said, skills can be taught, but the right attitude is the mark of a real winner."

"I'm honoured, sir," Melissa said, feeling a flush of pleasure at their open praise for her efforts over the last few months.

"We'll make an official announcement in the next day or two," Mr Bosch said, "but we wanted to let you know first. I'll be forwarding you your new contract, and I'll expect a signed copy to be returned to me by the end of the afternoon."

"Of course, sir. I'll get right on it. And thank you." She smiled, her mind already running over all the plans she would make, all the projects that would advance their cause. All the shifters who would die as a result of her efforts. "I promise I won't let you down."

CHAPTER THIRTY-EIGHT

Andre sat at his computer in his and Caroline's bedroom, gazing at the twelve miniaturised faces of the Council members on the screen.

"What news?" Eleanor asked Andre, after he'd formally greeted the Council.

"A rather unexpected development," Andre told them. "And one that perhaps I should have picked up on sooner, though there have been plenty of dramas to keep me distracted. I apologise." He took a breath, and then told them his news, not bothering to sugar coat the situation. "The Black Wolf has risen," he said flatly. "Jack Miller. We don't have a copy of the prophecy in the old language in this Den, but I had a brief look at the text over the summer, while we were in Scotland, and I checked the English translation this morning. He fits the bill perfectly. His wolf is jet black, barely a grey hair on him anywhere. He was our enemy, as stated by the prophecy, and he betrayed the Noturatii to become our ally. And he was converted in a lightning storm – 'forged of lightning', as the text puts it."

"Excuse me a moment," Eleanor said quickly. "I'll need a copy of the prophecy before we continue." She got up quickly and disappeared from the screen, then was back two minutes later with a thick book in her hands. She flicked through it until she found the appropriate passage. "Negur Ulis, the Black Wolf," she said, when she found the page. "Forged of lightning, betrays our enemies... What of this next part?" she asked, showing her fellow Councillors the passage. "He will 'cast down the Man of Jars'."

"Professor Ivor Banks," Andre replied, feeling a shiver run down his spine just at the mention of the man's name. "There was an assassin who broke into his lab twenty years ago, before he was promoted to become the head of science for the whole of the Noturatii. Even back then, he had a penchant for dissecting shifters, and keeping body parts in jars. Maybe we should have picked up on that years ago, but the prophecy of *Negur Ulis* is an obscure one. No one looks at it much. But it's obvious, when you can see the whole picture."

"We received Baron's report on the assassination," Eleanor confirmed. "And it's a relief to know that Banks is dead. We would have liked to send an assassin to take him out years ago, but security around the German office is just too tight." She let out a long sigh. "Can I assume you've also read the rest of the prophecy?"

"I have," Andre said, his tone confirming that he knew the particular passage Eleanor was referring to. "The prophecy has been notoriously difficult to translate, and the accepted version states that the Black Wolf will arise between two performances of the Eil-Mei-Kyntrosi." The 'Chant of Gathering Shifters' was the most sacred of shifter ceremonies, calling all the shifters of a single species together in one place, via an electromagnetic beacon visible only to those who possessed the shifter magic. The last time it had been performed had been in the middle ages, a reaction to the imminent extinction of the wolves, and an open declaration that the shifters were facing the most dire of emergencies. "But what is less well known – and still debated by some of our scholars – is that the second occurrence of the Kyntrosi will occur within the Black Wolf's lifetime."

Twelve stern, worried faces stared back at him from beyond the computer screen, a heavy silence weighing on them all. "So Fenrae-Ul has returned," Eleanor summarised. "The Council has set in motion a plan to take the shifters public, over a period of years; a desperate move by anyone's standards, but our only chance to win this war, and now we find that, sometime in the next few decades, we shall have cause to bring the entire shifter nation together in one place." She glanced at the Councillors around her, fear and trepidation on all their faces. "There are three thousand wolves in Il Trosa, and nearly as many in the Grey Watch. I can think of very few purposes for that sort of event. Most likely is that we lose significant numbers, and have to band together once again, as we did in the middle ages. Or, if our numbers hold, then the only reason for six thousand wolves to come together is to fight the mother of all battles." She took a shaky breath, fighting for control. "Every single move we make seems only to damn ourselves further."

Andre rubbed his eyes. He refused to believe that the end of the wolf shifters was imminent. But even he had to admit that the recent convergence of events was difficult to ignore. "If the wolves truly have an expiration date, then all the plans and weapons and contingencies in the world will not change our fate," he conceded finally. "But I, for one, intend to go down fighting."

"It's a noble sentiment," Eleanor said, sounding tired and irritated at the same time. "But as we all know, the road to hell is paved with good intentions."

In the expansive library in the Council's Italian villa, Caleb sat hunched over a thick text. The book was ancient, the pages discoloured with time, and yet even this volume wasn't the original copy of the book. That one had long since crumbled to dust, painstaking efforts being made to replicate the volumes every few hundred years, with a team of scholars permanently assigned to the delicate task of copying out each book by hand.

Now, of course, with the advent of modern technology, efforts were being made to preserve the information in digital form, as well as physical copies. In one of the offices that the historians used, each page of each book was being scanned, catalogued, digitally enhanced and archived for future reference.

Since arriving in Italy and beginning his training as a historian, Caleb's education into the old language had been progressing well. He was fascinated by the structures of the language, as well as the information that the old texts contained, and he was more grateful than ever for the opportunity to come here and be trained for service to the Council. It was the chance to make a real difference in preserving and understanding the history of their species, not to mention the sheer pleasure of studying the language.

And today, he was re-examining the prophecy of Fenrae-Ul and the destruction of the shifters. After Dee's visit, the Council had spoken of little else, and he'd heard a dozen different theories from the historians about what the words in the old language might actually mean. Translating them was hard work, with nuances in the language that were at odds with modern language structures, and some words remained unknown, their meaning being gleaned from their use in only half a dozen contexts in as many different books.

Earlier in the year, Caleb had been in Scotland, where he had met Nikolai, the alpha of the Ukrainian Den, who had helped him re-examine another prophecy – that of *Negur Ulis*, the Black Wolf, and through that conversation, it had become apparent that some of the ancient prophecies had been mistranslated over the years, as the various modern languages used by the shifters had evolved.

And so Caleb had taken it upon himself to have another look at Fenrae's prophecy, hoping to see if he could make any sense of it before his tutors caused him to form biases that would forever colour his understanding of the passage. He took out a copy he had made of the prophecy in English, the most recent translation having been done around the year 1550. And then he placed a notebook beside the English copy, ready to make his own notes as he worked to translate the original text.

Hours later, Caleb finally sat back, exhausted, but pleased at having completed his work. He reread the old translation of the prophecy, knowing he'd found several errors in the language.

'Thus be the truth of the wolfe Fenrae-Ul. The daughter twice removed from Faeydir-Ul. The cause of the death of her mother's unhappy tale. By magicks deep and ancient, she shalle return henceforth to life anew. Ye shalle know her by the separation of wolf from man. And under her reign, the shyfters shalle be restor'd to the natural order. No more divided, but united as one being. And peace shalle reign as the old discord is laid to rest.'

He flipped over to his new translation, the pages of his notebook full of scribble and random notes as he'd gone in circles at times, looking for a proper definition of some of the words. He read it through now, pleased to discover that the first half of the prophecy had been translated fairly well. Right up to 'the separation of wolf from man'. But after that... Caleb frowned as his notes took a decidedly different turn.

'And under the duration of her reign,' he had written, *'the shifters shall be reunited. No more divided, but aligned in purpose. They shall be one collective, one pack. And peace shall reign as the ancient conflict is laid to rest.'*

He sat back in his chair and rubbed his face. His tutors were not going to be happy with this. According to his own translation, the prophecy didn't state that the shifters were going to be returned to one being, one form, but rather that they were going to be reunited as *one pack*. As things stood, they were divided now, the Grey Watch constantly at odds with Il Trosa. It wasn't certain, but it was possible that the prophecy spoke of a reunion between the two factions, an end to the six hundred year old split in their ranks.

But the far more interesting part was the final line. The original translation had spoken of the 'old discord'. It wasn't inaccurate, though Caleb had translated it as 'ancient conflict'. No great difference in meaning there. But he'd also listed half a dozen words that the old language phrase could also mean. The word for 'ancient' didn't necessarily mean something that had happened a long time ago. It could also refer to something that was ongoing, beginning in ages past, but continuing to this day. And there were plenty of options for 'conflict'. Argument. War. Disagreement. Discord.

Beneath his gaze, two words seemed to line up on the page, and Caleb felt his heart lurch as he stared at the completely unintentional translation that had just appeared in front of him. Was he imagining things, or had he just stumbled upon one of the greatest secrets in the history of their species?

'Ancient' could also be translated as 'endless', and 'conflict' could just as well read 'war'.

And peace shall reign as the Endless War is laid to rest...

ABOUT THE AUTHOR

Laura Taylor has been writing since she was a teenager, spending long hours lost in imaginary adventures as new worlds and characters spring to life. The House of Sirius is her first published work, a series of seven novels following the wolf shape shifters and their war with the Noturatii.

Laura lives on the Central Coast of NSW, Australia and has a passion for nature, animals, hiking, and of course, reading.

https://www.facebook.com/LauraTaylorBooks
laurataylorauthor@hotmail.com
http://laurataylorbooks.weebly.com/
https://www.smashwords.com/profile/view/LauraTaylorAuthor

Made in the USA
San Bernardino, CA
28 April 2017